THE BEGOTTEN SOME

REALMS' ANCHOR III

REALMS' ANCHOR III

THE BEGOTTEN SOME

WILLIAM H. NUGENT

Publisher Name: Wiesbaden Press
Legal Names: Tom Kuhar and William H. Nugent
Location: Forest, Virginia USA

ISBN: 978-1-7327950-8-2 (hc)
ISBN: 978-1-7327950-3-7 (sc)
ISBN: 978-1-7327950-9-9 (e)

Library of Congress Control Number: 2023912494

CONTENTS

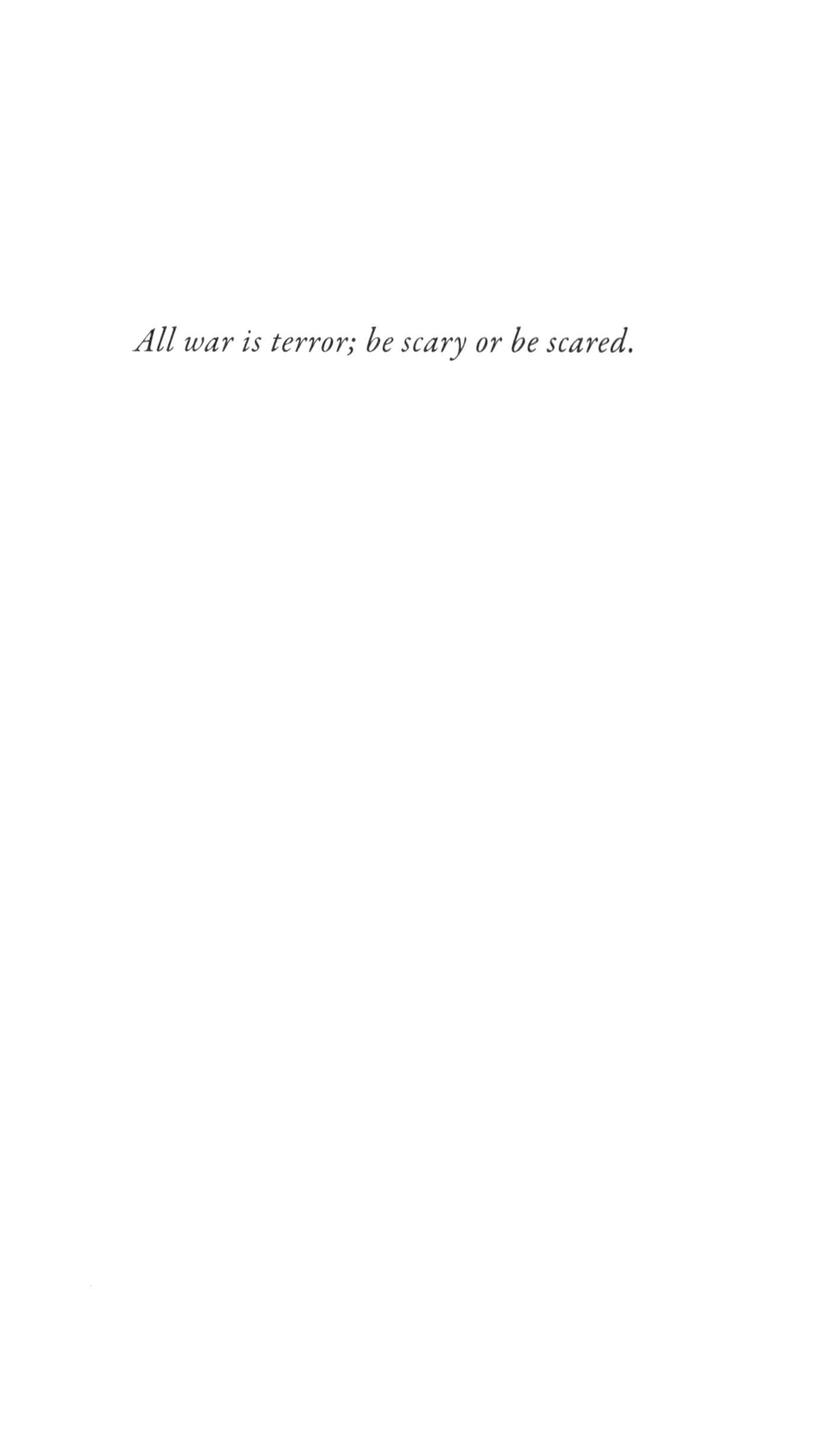

All war is terror; be scary or be scared.

PROLOGUE

The halls were bright, their oft dark sconces and torches lighted to ward against the shadows. His footsteps fell without echo as the loneliness of this place was given a reprieve. Sharp eyes followed beneath the long row of crimson helms. He bade the silent soldiers of the Ruby Branch no mention as he passed. There was naught of questions to ask nor answers to give. That he walked here meant he belonged.

That they stood watch meant his appointer was also here.

Two broad-shouldered guards, draped in the heaviest plate forged for men, waited at the hall's end. Their faces were hidden, but he knew them to be Sirs Lydus and Nothon: two of ten charged with protecting the greatest man alive. They parted at his approach but naught from familiarity. Powerful words commanded them this night, a script struck tight to burst at a single stumble.

Stepping with care, he entered the inner reliquary—a private place few alive knew of, less had seen. Within, it was dark. Dark because it was safe.

"So, ye hath come," spoke the voice that cowered millions and held-aloft the last bastion of freedom in the world.

I must be firm; he cannot deny what hath transpired. "Dare I resist a summons to the Hubo Reliquary, my lord?"

"Shall we speak in titles? Or as whence first we marveled upon these ageless treasures?" Dark lips curled. "These secrets."

It was a fond memory for them both, the culmination of plans forged in strife and quenched in blood. The end of ends. *The beginning.* "Aye, Father. The world was smaller after that day."

The darkness thickened betwixt them. The talk of remembrance was finished, giving way to words that would bind all the remaining free lands to their course. *Pray ye, at last, see the truth of this enemy.*

"It grows ever smaller," rasped his lord father. Aged hands that retained the strength of youth cracked the lid on one of the stone repositories, and he peered into its depths. "Ye are returned from Portcullis ahead of ye's host."

Be swift; seize the discussion! "Aye, I bear grave—"

"Graves," Father said with the voice that had commanded silence since the dawn of his memory. "Wounded. Desertion. Aye, ye bear them and more."

"The battle—"

"Is known to me. Tell of the Obantum Carre usurping Portcullis' defenses falls from the lips of mine advisors and street gossipers and Criers here in Durador to no end. What I know naught of is ye's mind, mine son." The Reliquary's silence poured in, suffocating. Suddenly, that aged fist pounded the stone. "He yet lives, Artur!"

Lord Commander Artur Bayliss of the Sapphire Branch and many a governance swallowed. Few were the men he found intimidating, but his lord father on the speak of *him*—Benton Feo'bathan—could turn the unnatural might of a Southron Storm. "I am a beneficiary of his life, it seems."

A flick of the wrist inspired a thrill that Father might summon Sirs Lydus and Nothon to disastrous ends, but words came in their stead. "So honied now is his sick syrup that mine own son doth seek me wroth in his name?"

"Our time grows desperate and needs common, Father. United, we turned the treachery of our Commander Mendo—a false-faced, dark servant known as Isllor Mortund."

"Can a son's vision never meet or surpass his father's? Mine enemies battle to their mutual deaths on the realm's edge, and all ye see is happenstance. Naught a finger, I commanded. Yet ye meddled and were lured by stories sold to peasants. Heroes who would save us. The few who can do what the many cannot. Are ye mad?"

"Is victory so distasteful?"

"Victory." The word fell to the stone floor as shit from a horse's ass. "Indeed, a powerful enemy lies defeated, but already the strong fury of another rises to take his place. This was our chance to claim the enemy's tools and tricks. Instead, they hath fallen into Benton's fumbling hands. Benton, who styles himself a lord once more, rallies Portcullis to his buried banner. Hath ye come to beg I join Benton in the fight?"

"Nay," Artur said, stepping forward. His father had not yet regarded him through the darkness. *Dismiss me not!* "I come not as Benton's puppet, but his better. These tools, hides of Vissl and Isllor's master rendercrafts that nigh tore a chasm in our defenses, rest with us now."

"An act of theft makes us mighty?"

"There is more. The Sapphire Branch hath withdrawn to Lord Ross' castellum at Tollshire. Portcullis withers, starves, and strives under Benton's leadership whilst I seek to raise banners. Upon mine return, they shall beg me to take the lord governorship. Benton shall tithe to me and—"

"As the pebble parasite tithes to the mighty dockfish?"

The memory was old but fresh. When the Bayliss family's meager foundations were still set in far Estmaw, Father was a council lord. It was a simpler time when the pleasure of each other's company still outweighed the pleasure of each other's power. On a crisp day warmed by the Lamp, they sat by the Seafill River. As casts went unrewarded by the clever fish who swam the cold waters, the unhappy child who was Artur—son of who was then Teth to those dear—pointed to the many wriggling green bodies beneath the chop. *Why can we not cast for them?*

Because they are bad, mine son, Father had said. When young Artur insisted, a bargain was made. *Catch one and eat it ye must, no matter how vile.*

Dockfish, poisoned by pebble parasites, remained one of Artur's most potent lessons. Still, the wisdom of age put it in a new light.

"Aye, so are many of the court," Artur Bayliss said. "But did ye know the Uplanders hath earned a harder stomach for sick Dockfish? So too hath ye's tutelage hardened me against the treachery of the retinue."

"Ah, how the sweet song of Benton pours from mine son's lips. He would hath ye believe we are in common cause, letting his schemes issue from ye's hands. The terror of the Genisans, the unstoppable force that threatens us all. Aye?"

Artur shifted, his illease rising as Father's truths pierced deep. He had come to this meet armed with purpose and direction. At last, the pettiness of the Varigan Court—tucked safe behind stone, swords, and wards—was small against a true threat. They would stand united! Alas, always when Artur thought his picture of the world complete, Father drew back an even greater tapestry. "Is the Pandonis Immortalis not a grave threat?" he asked.

A nod. "It heartens me ye can still pause ye's fury to seek wisdom. They are one of many dangers but minor against what lies ahead. Indeed, the Genisan force that hath swept Nuada is what the common fool can grasp.

Thus, it is what Benton peddles to justify his existence. Be not blinded, mine son. It is a distraction."

"Is the destruction of our Fifth Army a distraction?" Thousands upon thousands of Coal Cloaks were sent to retake Portcullis' sister city Val'Narden. The Fifth was to be Galimay's resurgence against an ever-victorious enemy, its first offensive since the Fourth Army was sundered in the Haquatian Wetwood.

And we hath naught to show for it!

"A terrible tale," Teth said with a cackle. "Since ye insist I wipe ye's chin, so be it. Naught of Bayliss nor our allies filled the ranks of the Fifth. It pains me that ye might think I would put a fool such as Morhock at the head of our greatest armies. Nay, the Fifth was a crop of loathsome villains who sickened our lands. Their defeat upon the slopes of Val'Narden was our leechdom."

A flush of anger as more of the tapestry was revealed. *Another test I hath failed. He never tells me false but always plants doubts to crush underfoot. And always do I let them sprout.* "Forgive me."

"Bah, the world is rife with pettiness. Spend too long in the weeds, and ye shall find a fondness for muck and pearl-pocketed mushrooms too. We, as stewards to millions and the future of all, must rise above and see what shakes the trees, moves the clouds, and sails Bergreth's Lamp through the skies." Sharp eyes tucked into the creases of age regarded him now. "Hold the Sapphire Branch at Tollshire and let Portcullis be a tomb for Benton and his ilk."

"But the Genisans!"

"They will learn the truth of their prize as they find themselves bare to Ajid's Winter and all of Galimay's strength."

The strategy was devious but sound. Portcullis' might faced north, making it difficult for the enemy to capture and trivial for Galimay to retake. If Benton remained a threat to rule, his death at the enemy's hands would solidify the Bayliss line and rally the countryside to battle. Still, something had happened in Portcullis that could not be ignored. "And what of the strangers?" As Teth's eyes darkened, Artur knew he needed not explain which.

"It was but a matter of time before the cursed *Corsan Carre* revealed themselves. An inevitability as with the rising of the Lamp, or the aching chill that creeps upon the land."

"Now, which of us speaks the words of Benton? For only he and that odd wife of his hath named them so," Artur said. The Corsan Carre were curious folk with strange customs and unfathomable weapons. So too did they bear little semblance to prophecy.

"Enemy doest not mean daft," said Father. "Galimay is rife with Benton's Procult, legions waiting to herald these cursed harbingers. He would not name them by mistake."

Cursed? Harbingers? Dangerous words to the wrong ears. "Hath we decided to embrace the teachings of the Anticult?"

"Does His Reverence of Galimay kneel before the scripture of man?"

"Nay, but—"

"The Corsan Carre are a sign. One not beholden to the cults, and, as ye will see, not above the law."

"They are more than mere signs," Artur said. "The Powers are a true force in this world but pale beside the might of men. Power cannot tame the wilds, drive back the Gra'nuul, feed millions or create the like of the vintage that awaits me when this meet is ended. These strangers embody that spirit in the like of none I hath seen. With fire and thunder, they drove back Mendo's . . . ah, Isllor's minions. Plate armor shattered beneath an invisible hail, naught a touch of the Power to be had. And then, unseen, one of them slew Isllor from a far place. But only after these feats did Benton name them Corsan Carre. Else of the prophecy was forgotten. Indeed, Benton hisself was half daft in the days preceding, his wife a simpleton. What proof beyond prowess is—"

Artur's words froze in his throat as Lord Tethredon Bayliss, His Reverence of Galimay, pushed the repository's lid back and revealed its contents. *Impossible.*

"Their arrival hath but one meaning." Teth's voice creaked with wisdom beyond age. "The world shall end. Again."

CHAPTER 1

THE SOME

Ten-HUH!"

Beneath a grid of white LED floodlights, neat rows of overburdened men stiffened. Grays, beige, and muted colors of painted metal, not stone or wood, dominated the expansive compartment. Motor oil and pesticides floated on stale air instead of manure and mildew. The solid deck below was another modern comfort as power thrummed up through firm boot soles.

A beige military officer—Marines, not Navy—stood before the troops. He was young, familiar in an adjacent sort of way. In another life, he might've fit right in with a bunch of happy hour stockbrokers, drinking by night, climbing the corporate ranks by day. But here, his eyes could cut steel, and the diffuse contracture scaring on the right side of his face told of a jagged and jaded existence.

"It's quiet," he said. A pause let it sink in. "This time, there's no rock 'n' roll. No jams blowing up enemy comms. No strike group, bomber runs, or forward positions. No backup. The C-monster's shed its skin to become the night's silent death."

C-monster, *she recognized. The—her—Marines' unit back on Earth. She'd heard so much but knew so little. They were her saviors, maybe the only ones back home who had any clue about the threat facing Earth.*

Murmurs of agreement followed. Tension. Whatever they were headed into did not look like a prepackaged win.

"I can't replace them," said the officer. Captain, by the two dark bars pinned to his collar. The name Lyons came from a foreign memory. "But I don't need to. Captain Saunders and Master Sergeant Brines never claimed to be the best, only that they worked with the best." A few nods and shoulders squared. "If we were any other company, leadership would've diced us and all those medals up to man recruiting depots. It'd be the Army Rangers, SEAL, or

any number of teams with a special forces patch waiting for that ramp to drop. Instead, they reinforced us, gave the C-monster a chance at revenge."

"Oorah," shouted a deep voice from what seemed to be her vocal cords. Did I say that? *The Marine lines returned the shout.*

"It won't be easy. I don't need to remind you about Mina Bazar and the aftermath." Nods all around. "Gunnery Sergeant Carneal"—eyes shifted to her. That must be me?—*"and I were not exempt from whatever psyche job shit they hit us with. Expect more of the same. Expect our objective to be blackout conditions pissing hell's fury in our faces. Expect also that we will adapt, overcome, and destroy those fuckers where they live." The lights dimmed, and hydraulics whined from behind. Then, a chilly wind filled the compartment with crashing waves and sea spray. "May fortune favor the ballsy. Carneal!"*

"Fall in!" boomed Gunnery Sergeant Carneal's voice from her—really his—mouth. These dreams were always disorienting, reliving someone's experiences, feeling what they feel, without having any control.

The deck became organized chaos as the rows shifted into columns, squads, and fireteams. "We know they can beat us in the air," Carneal barked, turning toward three lanes of parked vehicles like one might see on a ferry crossing. In the place of minivans were the tracked, gun-covered behemoths Carneal knew to be AAVP-7A1 "AMTRAK" amphibious assault vehicles. One by one, their engines sputtered to life, and the adrenaline began to flow. "Let's see if they can beat back the sea."

Dr. Patricia Bowman snapped awake. The foaming ocean, salty air, exhaust, and motor oil became ash from a spent fireplace, warm blankets, and morning breath. A few months ago, she might've wondered which one was the dream, pinching herself until either drawing blood or returning to the sterility of the digital age. But she was long since sold that Portcullis—the medieval city on another planet—was real. Maybe more real than anything she'd ever known.

Ironically, it wasn't the terror and need or starvation and slaughter of this world that had snared her. No, it was something else. A stupid, ridiculous, absurd, and positively artificial thing that always ended in a smile, no matter how hard she tried to dismiss it.

Even now, in the absurd luxury of having her own room with its hardwood walls, plank floors, and a white carpet as thousands suffered in the cold streets outside, she found the corners of her mouth tugging. Her thoughts turned playful as she realized the second set of lungs beside her had adopted a standard tidal pattern. He was awake.

"How long have you been staring at me?" she asked without looking.

"Long as you been starin' at me," answered Mike Brines.

She turned. He was smiling that smile, the one he must've practiced in the mirror for weeks because it hid that awful scar on his left cheek. "I just had the strangest dream."

"Yeah?"

"I was in a man's body. Like physically merged, feeling what he felt."

"It's nice, right Pat?" he said, holding that smile.

One-track mind. "Do you know a Gunnery Sergeant Carneal?"

The smile cracked. "Shit, one of *those* dreams." Mike rolled onto his back, bed creaking. "He was a staff sergeant last I saw him. Didn't happen to be spotting you on the bench press, was he?"

"Is that a thing?"

"Fer me, I guess. Had a dream 'bout it when I passed out on the ruck up Twin Tithes. Wasn't nothin' real unless I'm the new world champion powerlifter."

"I bet no one here has ever done or seen a bench press." She ran her fingertips across his broad chest. "De facto champion."

He scrunched up his face as if trying to rank himself on some sports-driven ladder of testosterone. Finally, he said, "Sergeant Smith can throw some iron around, but I'll take it till he does." He stared at the crisscrossing beams on the ceiling, maybe imagining some epic strongman competition. Right as she was about to click her tongue and roll back to her side of the bed, he laughed. "You know you ain't gotta sweet talk me, right?" Suddenly they were a tangle of legs, two puzzle pieces fitting, refitting, and finally connecting seamlessly.

Later, when the room was a little brighter and her smile a little bigger, Mike asked, "Anything happen in that dream I gotta report?"

She gave him the salient points, wishing she could remember *Captain* Lyons' entire speech. Mike was more fixated on the fact that everyone had gotten a promotion. She did remember the last line, though, the one about the Air Force having difficulties."

"More Black Robes," he said.

"Yeah." Mike liked to call them wizards—something semi-normal here on Scianas but completely unexpected and dangerous back on Earth. He and his Marines killed one rescuing her from Mina Bazar, Pakistan, but there were allegedly two more. No one fully understood how their Powers worked, even here with the supposed experts. Whether they needed special rings, jewelry, or just the right words, it was magic plain and simple. And its danger seemed only limited by the wielder's creativity.

"Heard some weird ones lately," he said, changing the subject. "Captain Saunders was tellin' me he saw some chick makin' shoes. Like an all-night dream puttin' those shittin' leather socks together."

"Seems random, but they can't be. You know?"

"Yeah. The ones showin' us what's happenin' back home make sense: world's fucked."

"Any more for you?"

"Nah, just the bench press thing. Thinkin' it was a special situation. Mix of delirium and . . . ah, that's when Ann reached out. So maybe I'm exempt."

Mike tried to hide it, but the leather always softened when he mentioned Ann. "She adores you," Pat said, tracing a finger through his meticulously maintained crewcut.

"Don't start that shit again. Kids will latch onto anything."

"Not every little girl's dream can come to life and tear the heart out of her worst nightmare. You gave her something special."

"Fuck all that. Still ain't convinced any of this is real."

"Which part?" She slipped a hand between the sheets. They weren't 100% hand-brushed Egyptian Cotton, but the innkeeper, Uumhrat, got pretty darn close. Smooth and cool.

"Heh, yeah, the part where I'm in bed with a gorgeous doc. I hate doctors." He pulled her close, warmer than any blanket.

She slid her chin past his cheek and whispered in his ear, "Say that part about hating doctors again."

"C'mon, yer ruinin' my candlelight routine," he breathed before their lips locked and her heart raced.

Sometime later, the clang of a bell in the distance brought Dr. Pat back to the room. Mike was already up, muscular form bathing in daylight from the windows. "That the Dawn Guard changing out?" she murmured.

"Think so," he said, pulling on his beige trousers. It was comforting to know that if you only had one outfit to wear for the rest of your life, the

Marine Corps Combat Utility Uniform (MCCUU) was long-lasting and durable.

Time was hard to track here because the calendar was divided into "tendays" and seasons, of which there were eight. But by Dr. Pat's reckoning, Mike and the other Marines were going on two months in the same uniforms—desert-style fatigues designed for mid-summer combat.

It was becoming an issue as the weather changed from pleasant smells of falling leaves and morning dew to crisp and snowy. The mountains above the stone city were all white now, and most days started with a frost. The big snow, according to the locals, was yet to come.

"So, same time tomorrow?" she asked.

Mike cocked his bruised and scarred meathead head. "Don't you mean tonight?"

She offered a coy shrug. "Well, we did say this was all just for fun . . ." It was the truth, but also a tease.

The Marine sat on the bed and began lacing up his boots. "Yeah, don't mean nothin' at all. Two adults, y'know? A Porsche ridin' down a street full of potholes and landmines 'cause there ain't no other road."

"Am I the Porsche or the road?"

"Don't know, but I'm callin' pothole."

She scoffed if only to mask the ridiculous smile that perpetually wanted to be plastered to her face lately. "Careful, self-deprecation might make some of those cobblestone paths up on Eastside Rise look pretty smooth."

"Yeah, been thinkin' about rotatin' the tires and takin' a chance on that uh, other doc they got 'round here," Mike said without missing a beat. "The wisewoman. What's her name? Don't care what I ate fer breakfast or how many cigars are keepin' the ship level. Keeps quiet about shit like blood pressure and toxic testosterone. My kinda gal."

Dr. Pat hurled a feather-stuffed pillow at him. *They learn how to push your buttons so fast!* She searched for a comeback, not wanting to escalate the playful banter, but bringing up Wisewoman Alena was war. Suddenly, a different bell struck in the distance. The bigger one.

They waited. It rang again.

"Shit," said Mike moving fast. More clanging erupted from the North and South Walls as the city went on full alert.

Dr. Path threw back the covers and found a fresh white rough-spun dress. It was a lady-like apron, a decent approximation of a lab coat that served as her uniform in the clinic she'd established with Wisewoman Alena.

Commotion outside joined the tolling. Mike didn't bother, but she couldn't help peering through the single-paned window. It was a mix of white tabards and glinting plate armor, all with swords pointing and shouting.

"They sendin' 'em north?" Mike asked.

"I can't tell. They're looking up at something."

"At the slopes?"

"Just . . . up."

"Shit. Probably ain't no flock of geese." He pulled on his bullet-proof combat vest, a silly thing in a place of swords, arrows, and magic, but she figured it was his security blanket. The large rifle with the grenade launcher did most of the talking anyway.

Bells ringing louder and boots thudding through the hall outside ratcheted the urgency. She needed to get the clinic ready; no doubt there'd be wounded. Mike made for the door but stopped halfway and turned. "Babe, sounds like tonight ain't happenin'. But I'll see yer ass in the morning."

Is that an order? "Stay safe, Brines," she said. Then the reprieve was over; they were back at war.

Captain Ronald Saunders, commanding officer of Charlie Company 1/2 United States Marines, watched as the courtyard below filled with Watchmen. Half were in their white tabards, and the rest were still hiking up their britches beneath tarnished mail coats. Meanwhile, the Blue Cloak leftovers from when Lord Bayliss pulled out of the city were assembled in neat rows of plated mail. It was the difference between the daily grind of a city-wide police force and time served drilling with a professional army.

"Ten-minute response time," Saunders said. Not great, but twenty *fucks*—a valid unit of measurement in this medieval society—better than it had been. He glanced at the sky, still clear.

"They gather thus, turning the yard to a great feed bowl for the beast," said Chief Dalmore from behind. The former Blue Cloak lieutenant had distinguished himself during the Black Robe attack on the Assembly Hall almost two months ago. Since then, the Watch and about 500 Blue Cloak defectors—Deadlies as Dalmore labeled them—had profited under his command. Despite initial appearances, he turned out to be all parts level, reasonable, and not a psychotic, self-feeding introvert.

The man also had a point. The Watch Keep was a stone fort within the city of Portcullis that resembled a mini castle. The back courtyard was enclosed by a curtain wall. Perfect for defending on a two-dimensional battlefield, but from up in the keep, it was hard to unsee it as a feed bowl.

However, the near anarchy in the aftermath of the Assembly Hall battle demonstrated what decentralization did to combat effectiveness here. Lack of real-time, distributed communication had turned a cohesive force into confused, functionally rival gangs. Likewise, the ongoing presence of an insurgent organization known as the Anticult made it necessary to keep battle plans close to the chest.

So: rally, receive, then position.

"Nay, the wards are risen and strengthened," said Lord Governor Benton dismissing an aid and joining them. "Else, we too would be cinder." Somehow, the people's hero in his gallant white plate and flowing cape had arrived at the Watch Keep seconds after hearing that first bell. It probably didn't hurt to have an enchanting wizard witch wife around for punctuality. Plus, as far as anyone knew, Benton didn't have kids. That would fuck up even an instant teleporter.

"With this grave threat, I must ask once more," said Dalmore, polished armor creaking as he folded his arms. "If a city ye's lady can protect, Lord Benton, can she not dispose of this winged menace? Indeed, I hear she hath defeated his kind before." Murmurs of agreement rose from the crowded hall behind them. The ranks of city personnel ranged from representatives from the Merchant District and the mysterious Town Crier media organization, to the *Korigi Carre* fire brigades. It was nice to see everyone in agreement for a change.

"Aye, so the talk of taverns would hath ye believe," said Benton. "The northron folk hath long steeped in fear of this ancient terror and look to the Power for comfort. But 'twas not Lady Ceal who slew the beast's mate upon the Dawn Mists slopes. We did. The Company and a host of Lord Dain's fine archers were near as it found purchase upon the ground. Then chance guided our steel through ancient scales."

"Ho, I had heard Ceal the hero of that tale," said Dalmore. "Still, today is a fine day to chance the Power."

"Nay, I shall not risk her."

"Guys, we've been over this," Saunders huffed, turning back to the courtyard. "Plan A."

"Mayhap we should convene upon it once more," said Benton.

Another meeting? It never ceased to amaze Saunders. A fucking feudal, medieval society where master lord's word was law, yet every decision or friction point STILL needed debating.

Lord Benton's Portcullis was straight out of a fantasy novel: a city of stone wedged high into the mountains protected front and back by massive walls. They packed a lot between those walls, too. Slate roofs to rival a solar panel farm, soaring keeps, cobblestone streets filled with horse-drawn carriages and manure, and over ten thousand residents. With a dozen commercial, industrial, residential, and government districts, it was a significant administrative job.

Also, since reconnecting with command, fleet, or even Earth was presently beyond anyone's means, it was the default home for Saunders' dozen Marines. There were other options, other localities within the larger nation of Galimay, but Portcullis came with some hard-earned assets.

An alliance.

Proximity to their point of arrival.

And most critical, Benton's wife, Ceal.

Call her a wizard or witch—Dr. Pat Bowman preferred *bitch*—she was the world's expert on magic. Everyone agreed that she was their best chance of figuring out how to open a portal, wormhole, or whatever back to Earth.

Portcullis' liabilities were the usual: a mysterious enemy waiting in the winds to slam down and obliterate them, organizational dysfunction after a massive decapitation strike on their government, evil shit lurking in the surrounding mountains, and because the city relied almost entirely on outside support, they were almost out of provisions.

Like any good American, Saunders was all-in with the underdog.

City leadership—Benton and Dalmore—had helped by branding the Marines with a sort of savior label. What *Corsan Carre* represented was incompletely clear, but it got them in good with the commoners. Also, a seat in the recently reorganized city council.

Which meant meetings.

They fucking met about everything, too. Indecision over pest control, food allocation—*food acquisition for that matter*—guard routes for their crippled security forces and . . .

Justice.

Christ was their justice system broken. Under Lord Bayliss and his 2,000 Blue Cloaks, it was biased, belligerent, and little more than a form of entertainment. But it worked. Since taking over as Lord Governor, Benton decided to institute a primitive version of due process and totally botched it. Turned out that if people didn't believe in it, justice—no matter how legitimate—wasn't served. So, the result was Benton having to personally hear every case.

Not just him, but the ranking representative of the free world, democracy, the Bill of Rights, and herald of the all-mighty lawyer: Ron Saunders.

"No," Saunders told the lord governor. "Questions are directed to the oversimplified flow chart titled Plan A."

"Hear, hear. Our time grows short," said Dalmore handing a parchment to Sergeant Batoth, who handled security on the South Wall. After hitting the Assembly Hall, the enemy tried to secure both city gates instead of focusing on the more important one to the north. A costly mistake. Still, it was confirmation that the South Wall was a security priority.

"But what of—"

"Benton, we're at critical mass," Saunders said, heading out to the wooden balcony.

The mountain crosswind immediately cut through Saunders' battle dress uniform, which was designed for the intense heat of the Arabian summer, not a bone-chilling, alpine city. But he still wasn't ready to wrap himself in fur. So long as he was here, he was on duty. And an on-duty Marine was cut, clean, and sharp. No beard, still bathing despite severe limitations in hygienic approaches, and the uniform.

The clamor below died as eyes rose to meet his. *Not in command, let Dalmore and Benton do the talking.* Saunders took his place on the righthand flank and beamed back what approval he could. Some of these men had seen combat with his Marines, and most had drilled with them over the past few weeks. Mutual respect. There was also that air of bullshit reverence because of the contrived Corsan Carre prophetic stuff. Still, while the Marine Corps preferred to forge its own legends—which it had—it would take the assist if it got results.

Dalmore stomped out, heavy-footed in his gleaming plate armor—leftovers from his service to the Sapphire Branch—and panned the crowd. It wasn't that robotic feedback loop—the ridiculous act that somehow endeared him to the higher-ups at the Sapphire branch—he'd performed when Saunders first met him. It was a fighter inspecting his crew. From the moment he spectacularly resigned from Lord Bayliss, Dalmore became a man of action—hands-on and willing to wade deep into the blood and guts. He was dangerous with a sword and adaptive enough to grasp elements of 21st-century tactics. Most of his subordinates could not say the same.

"So, it has come," Dalmore began, his voice settling the antsy garrison. "This winged terror, long dismissed by Lord Bayliss and the Sapphire Branch, smells the blood upon our battered city. The like of a great bird called to the worms after a rain. But it shall find our taste bitter, meat stout, and squirms swinging steel. Our plans are given to ye's sergeants. Find ye's places and courage. Resist death!"

Short and sweet. Dalmore was great at projecting that confidence even when he didn't fully grasp the situation. The various elements that would hopefully combine to score a win were lost to him, but he had some degree of trust. Also, Plan A wasn't the only plan. So, he just needed to wait for his turn if 21st-century hardware wasn't up to the task.

Benton, on the other hand . . .

"Defenders of Portcullis," said the lord governor, stepping up in his pearl-white plate armor and snowy cape. He looked good, formidable, but it was usually downhill once he opened his mouth. "We hath faced the Tel'racs before. The mate we did defeat with the aid of mine friend Lord Dain upon the slopes of the Dawn Mists." *Decent, keep the energy positive.* "But it was by luck and happenstance!" *Dammit, no!* "So, I must implore eac—"

Saunders reacted before it happened. A flicker in the corner of his eye shortcut active thought to reflexes hardened by years of combat experience, or maybe he heard something. Maybe his brain just didn't log the sequence of events. Regardless, he was on the plank deck a split second before the western section of the courtyard's wall exploded.

Dalmore and Benton stood fast as the blast buffeted the balcony. "To ye's posts! Resist death!" Dalmore shouted into the erupting chaos below. Saunders could only hope the swarms of Watchmen and Deadlies had read their orders and retained a cursory understanding of their rally and trigger points.

"The Bark is paramount!" cried Benton over the clamor, capping his speech. Nothing like a little pressure to press out excellence.

The Bark—a dome-like shield encompassing the city—was the only thing keeping the enemy wizards—Black Robes—from wiping them out and sweeping south into the last free nation of Galimay. The device, a glowing gem, was encased in a reinforced vault with eight-foot stone walls. It should've been fine, but there was no acceptable level of risk given its importance.

A screech ripped across the sky, and Saunders unslung his MP5 close-quarters combat gun. He didn't expect that this fucking Tel'racs—a dragon for all intents and purposes—would get close enough to enjoy a 9 mm bullet shower, but stranger things had happened.

"How dost it strike us here? Hath Lady Ceal's wards failed?" cried Dalmore, ducking as another wall section burst. The city taking direct fire was not part of Plan A.

"Nay, by some nefarious means, she is countered," Benton growled, staring south toward City Square. He didn't even flinch when something the size of a cinder block slammed him in the chest.

"Pray tell?" Dalmore waved a group of Deadlies still in formation toward the balcony.

Saunders sort of understood. The Bark was supposed to stop one type of Power—magic to anyone with a tag on their underwear—from being used in and against Portcullis. Locals called it the Quotidian, and it was the primary weapon of the enemy magic corps—the Obantum Carre. But there was another frequency called Stochal, which Ceal and that scumbag Isllor Mortund could use despite the Bark. So . . .

"The Obantum Carre aids the Tel'racs with their Stochists," Benton said, ushering them back inside the stone keep. That pairing was identified as a worst-case scenario during the weeks of brainstorming about possible enemy moves and countermoves. Sir Krue, a survivor of the doomed Fifth Army's recent assault on Portcullis' sister city, Val'Narden, mentioned the Tel'racs was back in the area after years of dormancy. A wild "what if" combined the enemy wizards and the dragon into a force capable of penetrating Portcullis' defenses. It was nuts, farfetched. Man and nature were two distinctly dangerous and immiscible forces.

Just another Tuesday on a medieval alien magic world.

Saunders caught eyes with Private First Class Licht and the radio strapped to his back. The Marine captain wanted to be shouting orders and grabbing reports from his men, but Plan A was postured for this curveball. Coordinating the city's response through Dalmore and Benton took priority because it meant saving lives.

"Aye, but where?" asked Dalmore, giving a fist-to-chest salute to his squad of Deadlies coming up the stairwell. "Answer swift, and mine men shall run these fools down." Another flash with report engulfed the hall. When Saunders ran to the window, he determined it was a mid-air detonation. Ceal's wards were still partially effective.

"Nay, our skill in the Sense is restored," said Benton. "Any of the Obantum within our walls would be known to us. Mayhap an assassin could slink through our midst, but Ceal is within the Vault with the Bark. Well-guarded by Watchmen and a four-team of the Corsan Carre."

"Fireteam," Saunders corrected. Sergeant Smith, Lance Corporals Light, Gladstone, and Garcia were the assurance. After Isllor—the Black Robe posing as a Blue Cloak commander named Mendo—had teleported an entire army into the Assembly Hall, troop movements and approaches were impossible to anticipate.

But bullets were faster than swords and arrows.

A flash mob expecting an easy strike on the Vault would be in for a big surprise. And that, Saunders was repeatedly assured, was the only way the enemy was taking out Ceal. This Stochal interference from the Obantum Carre was a separate angle of attack. Like radio jamming, except the enemy probably wasn't pounding a 5.1 Dolby version of "Stiff Parrot" into Ceal's head.

"Then our enemy lurks beyond our walls," said Dalmore. "In the Del where our scouts hath seen theirs. By horse, mine Deadlies might find our quarry before the city is ash, but they are no Corund Corps. They cannot counter the Power in the broad of day,".

"It's under contro—" began Saunders.

A tremor shook the Watch Keep—a structure designed to hold back a world of meteoric magic—and the hall went pin-drop quiet. Reams of dust fell from the ceiling planks, and a deep rumble registered. This was more than just an explosion or another fireball; something with mass had smashed into the city.

Dalmore stayed calm, but Benton's face matched his formidable winter armor as he stared toward the city's smokey core, seeing something no one else could. Grabbing his longsword, he cried, "The Tel'racs hath taken to the ground. Come, mine lady is in danger!"

The command element leaping into the fray was also not part of Plan A.

Sergeant Jason Smith went down on record as the first United States Marine to not shit himself when a dragon landed on his position. That didn't stop him from diving for the sandbags and hollering for everyone to take cover, though.

"Loose!" shouted Watch Sergeant Teague. The broke-tongue dude held his ground as his Watchmen engaged. Stood stoic as the house-sized dinosaur with wings turned to look him right in the weird under-chin low and tight beard. The guy who feared fire like he got born burned lasted almost ten badass seconds before bolting for the Vault.

"Light it up?" asked LCpl Garcia, sighting his M4 combat rifle over the sandbags as Sergeant Teague ran by.

Smith wanted to drop a definitive *hells yeah, only a goddamned crackhead wouldn't shoot that fucking monster,* but that wasn't Plan A.

"Fall back," he said as crossbow bolts pinged off black scales. The Watch's low-tech ammo had about the same punch as Marine 5.56 mm NATO at this range and wasn't even scratching the surface.

Cap'n was right.

Smith hefted his powerlifting ass into gear and followed Garcia to the Vault's blast door. A roar and shouts to *loose-at-will* came from all over City Square, but he didn't dare look back.

The entrance to the stone chamber housing the Bark was sandbagged and, more importantly, stocked with the aluminized-fiberglass fire blanket someone grabbed from their crashed helicopter a few months ago. Instead of just keeping a few folks warm in camp, it meant they could take a hit if dragons actually breathed fire. None of it would stop a swipe from one of those three-foot talons, though.

"Sergeant, should we—"

"Git back inside!" Smith yelled at LCpl Light's fucking head poking through the doorway. "Seal it up!" That wasn't exactly what he wanted to say, no sane person wanted to be out here in the shadow of that monster, but something went wrong with the captain's plan, and Teague's Watchmen needed cover fire. Armor-piercing or not.

"Thought it was supposed to stay in the air . . ."

"I said git!" Heat baked into his back, and Light's pale face blazed orange.

Guess breathing fire is real.

Smith dove back behind the sandbags and let the flames blow over top. Then he was up on a knee with the fire blanket in one hand and his M240B machine gun—the Pig—in the other.

No target.

City Square was all smoke and black wings whipping about. A wall of fire rushed through the flanking formation of Watchmen. Two went down, thrashing in agony. The rest held, stomping on their crossbows to reload.

The smoke suddenly sucked toward the center, and the dragon's black-horned face, jaws agape as it filled with breath, became visible.

Opportunity.

Smith tagged Garcia and dropped the blanket. "Aim for the head."

The Marine's rifle cracked twice.

It did little more than get the dragon's attention, and Smith found himself staring into the sun a split second from incineration.

CHAPTER 2

ONE SHOT, ONE KILL

"Where?"

"728 meters along the far shore. Put your dot on the hooked root of that tree with mushroom plates at its base," Peter Francisco said. Those probably weren't mushrooms, but the description was sufficient to guide his former apprentice's crosshairs.

"Got it," said Lance Corporal Fischer.

"Track vertical. Slowly. See it?"

"No. Wait . . . yeah. They layin' stiller than snail shit."

"That's them. Wind's at three knots, moving with the river. We're set."

"Reckon we should move closer?"

"Closer?" Francisco asked, sliding his eyes from his M151 Spotting Scope to the bells and whistles Nightforce SHV 5-20x56mm scope on his .50 caliber 'Bullpup' sniper rifle. "You worried about hitting your mark, Fish?"

"Hell no, hoss," said the born and raised Virginia native resting cool and comfortable behind his M40 rifle. "Just worried 'cause we got tossed outta bed and flashed into these woods real quick on a hunch. Just when that hunch finally starts pannin' out, there ain't no high-priority pretty boy in a black robe."

"Did you just assume gender?"

"Only thing I'm assumin' is that we might have ourselves a wizard slink up and piss acid on our backs."

"Five bucks says we can do four of 'em before that acid eats through our vests," Francisco said. Dark humor usually kept a sniper warm on a long, cold stalk. Today it spoke to the tactical possibility that those Black Robes had Superman hearing and X-ray vision, which would negate the marksman's advantage. But he and Fish had approached quietly, and that river was a natural sound barrier. Plus, they were downwind.

"Ain't takin' no more bets till we're back home where they got pumpkins, corn, and places that turn white when it snows."

The greenery of this forest—locals called it the Lower Del—and the Dowdale Valley to the north didn't jive with the whole dead of winter thing. They stayed lush year-round, maybe protected by the encircling mountain systems. Down here in the woods, the air was crisp as back in the city, but water still flowed, and the cricket-like things still chirped. "Yeah, it's evil as fuck here. That's why I don't think this is just another scouting party."

"Does it make a lick o' sense them only sending one team?"

"No, but I'll take it," Francisco said. "We'll wait a few minutes, see if they relocate or get comfortable enough to pop that top button. If a Black Robe appears, don't hesitate. Pulp the head."

"800 meters ain't no joke for a headshot, hoss."

An understatement but unavoidable. "Element of surprise is critical. You guys unloaded buckets of ammo at the Black Robe in the Assembly Hall, close range, and didn't hit a thing. Because even if he didn't understand bullets, he saw you coming." Francisco scanned the party again. It was a bunch of what Cpl Nickels called "Snouthelms"—infantry in heavy, crimson-dusted plate mail with pig-like helms. Hundreds of them had flashed into the city during the Assembly Hall fight. Francisco, positioned in overwatch, had held fire, stomaching the slaughter in the streets to get a clear shot. It wasn't easy, but patience was rewarded. The purple-glowing wizard—Isllor Mortund, or Mendo as he was known incognito—eventually slipped into the crosshairs, and the magic show was over.

Then and only then did Francisco's reticle turn to the rampaging Snouthelms. No mercy.

Peter Francisco had never considered himself a sensitive sort, even before becoming an instrument for the military. What usually bothered others came across as background noise. But those jagged swords slicing through men, women, and children amid the screams of terror and pleas for help had hurt. Not many people could have held fire.

"Distance is . . ." he began, an old sniper's mantra he'd drilled into Fischer. It was a reminder that most folks never knew they were being watched.

"Them gettin' careless. Got it. Well, whatever they waitin' on, we gonna—"

A screech pierced the quiet forest, and the canopy above whipped like it was buzzed by a fighter jet.

Fischer swore but held his target. "Guess I'm a gen-u-ine believer in the dragon thing now."

Francisco chuckled. "Dealing with people here is like talking to a pathological liar. No amount of credibility gets you past the feeling they're making it all up."

"Well, them Snouthelms ain't impressed. Do you think—"

"Guys," hissed a voice from behind. LCpl Buontempo. "Captain just radioed in. They're in a panic up there. Need a SITREP on Black Robe activity."

Damn. "Contact, no PID."

"Wait one," muttered Buontempo pressing the headset to his ear.

Francisco panned the scene again, letting the connections form in his brain. When that dragon ripped over their position, the Snouthelms all but cheered it on. It confirmed suspicions that the Genisans had acquired aerial capability. Was this the major enemy advance everyone was expecting, or a diversion? Too early to tell, but everything hinged on one missing puzzle piece.

That damned Black Robe.

"Shit," said Buontempo. "They're out of options. Light it up."

"Hoss?" asked Fischer, uncertain. The captain was looking for a distraction, but their cover was blown the second they took that shot. If there was a Black Robe nearby, it might buy time for the city. But only so long as it took the powerful being to decide their fate.

In Francisco's limited experience, magic was a sadist's wet dream.

Smith closed his eyes. Not because he didn't want to see it coming—the thought never occurred—but because the dragon's breath was *that* bright.

The blistering flash promised to eat him down to the bone, but then everything was cool again. Not numb, but like someone closed the oven. He always thought burning alive would hurt more.

Mailed hands grabbed his vest, dragging him backward.

He forced himself to look. The world was still what a moth sees from the inside of a blow torch. But somehow, he was safe while the sandbags were ash just feet ahead.

Ceal.

"Git off me," he said, twisting free of the Watchmen. He kicked himself into a back roll and got to his feet smoothly. *Fuckin' guy can move, right?* Wishing he had his shades, he found Garcia a meter forward watching the flames like hiding behind an invisible forcefield was normal. He grabbed the Marine and herded the group into the Vault.

The gate slammed down, and the steel blast door closed behind it. Wood smoke billowed after them, and everyone was sucking wind. Smith hoped the Watchmen out in the square had the sense to get the fuck out while the dragon was distracted.

"Are you guys okay?" asked LCpl Light, rifle trained on the door.

Smith let his eyes adjust from the solar inferno outside to the dim chamber. The Vault was a single room, the underside of a turtle's shell. The ovular footprint was cupped by arching walls of stacked stone and mortar. It was also much smaller than it looked outside because the walls were thick, like a cargo container was wide, and reinforced by an iron skeleton. The only other exit was a grate in the floor where subterranean air was fed in from some other place. "Yeah. 'Preciate it, Ceal."

Benton's lady was standing behind the huge gem—a lava lamp of swirling reds and blues that was supposed to protect the city from magic—in a blue robe. Not a Black Robe, but something light and comfortable like what a chick might watch TV in right before bed. The only difference was this had some silver lace that wasn't silver at all. It was shit that could take a hit from a hammer like Superman's Kryptonian skinsuit.

"The last of mine aid is spent," she gasped through deep concentration. "A box they hath built, and against closing sides I must push."

Smith took stock. His three Marines and what they called a half-ten of Watchmen and Sergeant Teague were staring back, rifles and swords ready. "What you need us to do?" he asked Ceal.

"Naught," she breathed.

"She said it's a Black Robe, Sergeant," said Light.

"Here? Fuck it, we go kill 'em."

"This battle wages over great . . . great distance." Her face was scrunched like she had a pounding headache.

"The Obantum wishes t' lure us from the Bark," spat Sgt Teague. His death grip on that sword said he wanted back out there, no matter the risk.

Getting cut off from the team like that hurt. Smith understood, but Teague was seasoned enough to know when to stand down.

"Who cares? We forget there's a dragon outside?" said Garcia watching the door like all that steel mounted into solid stone wasn't enough. *Maybe it isn't.*

"I cannot protect . . . protect the city," Ceal stammered.

Smith wished he could help her, but while it looked like a bad panic attack on the surface, she was probably deep in some battle of the minds. Breaking her concentration might fuck everyone. If those Robes were outside the city wall, then Pete's team was on it. Right now, he had to concentrate on—

"The dragon is the real problem," said LCpl Gladstone. "It wasn't supposed to land."

Stone had been quiet up to this point, standing there beside Ceal like a Swiss Guard. Now his tactical shotgun was at the ready, and his eyes were moving, assessing. But he was also giving that weird vibe from when they had first arrived in Portcullis: lost in his head, staring at everything, and fucking flinching at invisible shit.

At the start of it all, Lance Corporal Gregory 'Stone' Gladstone was a green-as-fuck combat engineer who'd come over from Bravo Company. Operation *Sea Monster* was his first taste of war, and that drop into Mina Bazar left some marks. Whatever he saw in that Pakistani hell sunk deep into those once clear and smooth eye sockets. Waking up on an alien planet wasn't the best after-action recovery plan, either. Still, he was right.

Plan A needed that dragon in the air.

"Fuck it," Smith said. "We go back out there and light this bitch up. Garcia, I want—"

The stone walls thundered, rattling Smith's bones and sapping the strength from his legs. Then it happened again. And again, drowning his voice when he tried to shout over it. After the dozenth time, the faintest sound of glass cracking stabbed his ears.

"It will not hold!" Ceal shrieked in a voice way more terrifying than the mind-numbing pounding. Before Smith could get a look at the Bark, the Vault's eight-foot walls began to shake like flimsy movie props.

Suddenly, their sturdy bulwark against the entire world was nothing more than tons of rock about to drop on their heads.

The fire burning in Gunnery Sergeant Mike Brines' trunked legs pushed back the numbing cold and biting wind as his lungs grasped for every particle of oxygen in the thin air. It was at least a half-hour since Ceal transported them to the glacial heavens above the city. Almon's Peak. According to Captain Saunders, the mountain was bigger than Everest with sheer on three sides.

The drop put them on the Shoulder, a relatively flat spot often lost in the clouds where few men, and certainly no Americans, had trod before. Problem was they were nowhere near where they needed to be, and time was a racehorse pissing in their faces.

Brines was not a runner. The red meat in his legs wasn't designed to scissor back and forth for hours on end; it was made to back-squat a small building. Explosive strength with the mass to back it up. Chuck him in a cage with five guys, and he'd battle to the top. Even the younger bulls like Sergeant Smith had to bring their A-game to keep pace in the weight room. But forget running, especially at altitude. That was a sport for gangly jockeys rocking 5% body fat.

Brines' boots slipped on a windswept patch of glacier, and his weight went down on his ankle. The iron-forged strength in his calves stopped the ligaments from shredding, but it still hurt. It was better than falling, though. The walls of the blown-out pass were a frozen mix of rock and wind-pulled icicle spikes promising a gory end.

Instead of stopping and inspecting the injury, the pain got weaponized and poured into the drive forward. The agony was better than three cans of that energy pop Smith drank. It allowed Brines to focus on something real, meaningful, and familiar. Pain and victory were the only ways to stay grounded in this insane world.

A sharp incline hammered his endurance again, but he refused to give in, even if it meant being gassed when they got to the objective. One fucking second too late was an absolute possibility when fighting the supernatural. So, the fatigue, mortal desire to rest, and the bitching of his aging body got shoved aside by an iron will to stay on target.

A paranoid thought stole the opportunity to surface. In his fatigued state, any of these wizards or magicians could slip out of thin air and catch him off guard.

His fists tightened.

That's what they wanted him to think, no matter how true it might be. They wanted him on edge and worried, stressed about something he couldn't control. He refused. Pain and pounding snow were his life until he was in position. If someone else showed up to kick his ass, the green machine would respond.

Brines finally crested the ridge and took the full force of the morning sun to the face. More than just a fucking alien star that the locals called Bergreth's Lamp, its rays were amplified off the field of bright snow drifts ahead. Light sensitivity had always been a thing for him. Whether it was due to the faded blue pigment of his eyes or the wiring into his brain, he didn't know. It came with excellent night vision, and that's what mattered. A bright day could be handled by a pair of black, polarized sunglasses well enough.

Unless, of course, they happened to be sitting in a locker on another planet.

Operation *Sea Monster* had been nocturnal, which meant their combat loadout included night vision equipment out the ass, but no shades. He brought a gloved hand up as a shield and kept his eyes on the trail.

The crunch of boots from behind drove a new urgency into conquering the climb.

"Comin' up, Gunny," panted Captain Rath. Brines felt the cold squeeze of his adrenal glands. Every bit of fatigue vanished, and he broke into a sprint. There was no way in hell he was letting the goddamned pilot take lead.

It could've been worse. Captain Saunders had considered pairing him with Corporal Nickels.

The name shot a ripple of irritation through the agony.

Brines grabbed it, compressed it, and tossed it on the fire. The kid from Jersey was from the wrong side of I-95. He was a good Marine, amazing to have in a firefight, but his redeeming qualities ended there. The uniform was a paycheck to him, maybe bragging rights for a future career selling life insurance.

Pathologically disrespectful.

The infuriating thing was that Nickels had his moments, glimpses of potential. Like that fight against the Black Robe in the cave. He'd gone dark, about to shut down after the team took a beating. But seconds before it came to fists, he let Brines' words through that thick skull. Then the two of them led the fight to victory. Hadn't batted an eye later at stepping through a magical portal to help bail the captain out of the Assemble Hall shitshow, either. Now all that was done, and Nickels was back to his old ways.

Captain Rath's huffing and puffing faded into the distance as Brines put the last of himself into his legs. The finish line was dead ahead, an icy outcropping overlooking the vibrant Dowdale Valley where they'd first crashed. The valley was immune to winter frosting all around, kinda like the Superdome with perpetually green astroturf to accommodate any rivalry, any season. The comparison made even more sense because it was the flashpoint between Benton's people and the supposedly unstoppable Genisans.

The way the locals described it, the Genisans were a dark, enveloping force wiping out everyone on the planet due to some alternative interpretation of scripture. Well, not really scripture. They didn't have official religions here, but still had camps of people believing in shit.

Like the internet.

Same old goddamned story, and the Genisans surely had their version. But those fucks with their Black Robes and wholesale slaughter of unarmed civvies had earned the privilege of being downrange of the US Marines.

Then again, you got slimeballs like Lord Bayliss selling their own people out.

Brines focused back on the pain. Drowning in bullshit was easy as getting blindsided by a goddamned fact of life in this crazy place. Everyone's hands were dirty. The only question is whether that dirt meant a million people got fed or a million got buried.

The final climb was steep, but it was his hill to die on. And he would if it meant showing Captain Rath he could compete on every level. Rath wasn't fit like Saunders—a mountain goat born and raised in the Rockies—but he was still hiding out in his twenties with the joints of a man in his teens. Meanwhile, Brines' knees cracked if he stood too long taking a piss.

The field of snow and rock opened into soaring heights, a paratrooper's view from the ramp.

Relief.

If this were Earth, we'd be dead up this high, Brines thought as his lungs beat against the air. But Francisco had mentioned the air pressure was different here. Just enough to breathe and survive.

"Whew! Normally a sight like this comes with a cockpit," huffed Captain Rath skidding to a stop and dropping his overloaded pack. Brines ignored the fact that the officer was hauling a heavier load. Gear weight, body weight, it all evened out in the end. Brines was pissed that he couldn't catch his breath long enough to talk, though.

"Shit," muttered Rath.

Brines knew that tone. The words changed but held the same meaning as the first grunt from the beginning of time: danger.

He dropped his pack, forgetting about his lungs, and swung his M4 carbine with attached M320 40 mm grenade launcher into 'low ready.' It wouldn't do shit against that dragon, but it was more than his fists. "Report! Where is it?" he shouted as Rath stood there, not getting his ass in gear.

"Smoke," the pilot said, pointing down to the gap between mountains where Portcullis was wedged. "City's on fire."

For the first time since arriving on Almon's Peak, Brines felt a chill. But it wasn't his soaked uniform, cutting wind, the ice, snow, or even the realization they were too late.

Christ, Pat's down there.

"Orrugant!" Saunders shouted through the crowds, smoke, and cinder. The senior Watch sergeant was stationed outside the Watch Keep's gatehouse. With one arm pointed toward the courtyard, the other moved the influx of civvies along with a smooth, rotating wave. Like a traffic cop, minus the belted white tabard painted with a crude, orange eye—the emblem of disgrace that the Watch had taken to embrace. "Sergeant Orrugant!"

The stout man looked over and nodded. He handed off his signposting duties to a subordinate and waded through the throngs. When he reached conversational range, he said, "We fill the lower keep with those on these near streets, as commanded."

"Copy, but that was before the dragon landed. This logjam is impeding tactical response. Get these people indoors. Any doors. Shelter in place."

Orrugant's eyebrow reached up to his chainmail coif. "Shelter in their place? What good be doors against the Tel'racs' breath of fire? I cannot offer false hope."

"If we don't kill it quick, they'll get smoked out same as burned out. We need to get through!"

Orrugant glanced at the twenty chrome Deadlies in two perfect columns behind Saunders. The plates in their armor were apparently enchanted or mixed with a special alloy. Point was it had a degree of heat resistance that might give them a chance against that dragon. Dalmore and a larger group were taking the long way down Middleton Avenue. Eggs in one basket and all that. *Fuck, we need to be there ten minutes ago.*

The logic connected for the Watch sergeant as he took in the enormity of hundreds, maybe thousands, pouring out of the Market District. "Aye," was all he said, waving over a trio of white tabards.

Behind Saunders came a cough that probably was unrelated to smoke inhalation.

"Sir," said PFC Licht. It was hard to tell if the lowest-ranking Marine on the planet was edgier since being put on trial by Lord Bayliss and ridiculed in front of thousands. The near-death experience that wasn't quite resolved yet didn't help much either. But he was here and mostly himself. Coughing or any preamble usually meant a bad report.

"Go ahead," Saunders said as Orrugant's people took their time opening a lane. The Deadlies could probably push through, but one thoughtless shove might turn the procession into a stampede. The fire brigade—yellow-cloaked personnel in thick, boiled leather called *Korigi Carre*—up street were brute-force parting rivers left and right, but they were also a familiar sight. A bunch of former Blue Cloaks in mean mail, swords, and led by an alien from another planet during a dragon attack? Not so much.

"Del team reports no PID, sir."

Fuck. Should've sent two teams. His fault for not predicting where the Black Robes would appear, but also a limitation of four-dimensional thinking where objects had to transit space and time. These fuckers could show up anywhere. Except—allegedly—for places they'd never been before. But Del Team not reporting positive identification meant they were covering a decoy, and the Black Robes screwing with Ceal were somewhere else. Impossible to find.

Engaging the dragon was the only option.

"Tell them seconds count," he said, ordering the ranks of Deadlies forward. *Screw orderly.* "Move! Move! Make a hole!" Lord Bayliss' former troops, accustomed to pushing through crowds, stormed ahead. As expected, the situation turned chaotic, but they were moving again. Saunders broke into a run with a trio of armored soldiers plowing his road.

They cut through Song Street, which was lined with smithies and always smokey and hot anyway. With few people around, boots pounded cobblestones in a desperate race. At the end of Song was Gates Street and a row of government buildings holding back the billowing black clouds, orange glow, and screeching horrors of City Square.

Despite the obvious danger, Gates Street was insane—foot-mobile I-95 on Memorial Day weekend. Saunders' column slowed to a crawl and almost got swept away by the sheer mass of human flesh headed for South Gate. Luck snagged them on an empty alley leading to the square. It was nice and clear because a decent summary of all human nightmares was at the other end.

The medieval people plow on point stopped short of entering the normally open space of festivals and formal gatherings. Saunders had them duck down and find cover—because that was effective combat positioning versus puffing out that chest and shouting challenges—and panned City Square's volcanic landscape.

Visibility was decent; an updraft was pulling the smoke off the fires. There were bodies, mainly charred remains, scattered across the formerly white stone. Neither the Watchmen security forces nor his Marines were anywhere to be seen.

The Vault was a mess but intact, resembling a giant stone egg lying on its side and half-sunk into the ground. Cpl Nickels once called it a *fuckgloo,* an immature approximation of igloo. Its surface was now more like the inversion of a blast crater, blackened and pocketed by car-sized holes. The surrounding area was filled with rubble, corpses, and . . .

A house-sized dragon guarding its egg.

"Milord," whispered one of the Deadlies over his shoulder. Sergeant Forest, the Blue Cloak who'd been shackled and locked away so he couldn't testify at PFC Licht's trial. It didn't take much convincing for Dalmore to bring him into the rebel fold. "A puff of his breath will take us quick."

Yup, this alley's a wind tunnel.

Options were limited, and timing was everything. To the right was a door through stone walls capped by a slate roof. One of Lord Ross' offices, according to the Four Thorns sigil painted above. But the Vault was a shining example of how well bunkering against this dragon worked. Plus, cover only helped an attack plan when engaging at range.

Mobility.

It was usually the correct answer, but then there was the timing issue. Until Dalmore's forces arrived, they were rats before a motion-sensing tyrannosaur. Plus, the best plan of attack was unclear. Grenades? Licht had a launcher on his M4, but shot placement was critical, and they didn't have enough ammo to guess and check. Bullets weren't going to make a dent. At least Saunders didn't think so.

Just as he was about to order everyone inside the building, a glint of metal caught his eye from across the hellish square. Dalmore's people.

"Make ready," Saunders shouted as the silhouettes of Dalmore's forces spread through the stone wreckage of a structure the dragon had *walked* through. *Unbelievable.*

"We going hot, sir?" asked PFC Licht.

The PFC's proactivity was appreciated, but this was a reactive situation. They had two angles of attack on a single target, which was good. But there was also a near 100% chance that all these medieval troops would melt like gray plastic army men out there.

"SITREP from Peak Team?" he asked the radioman instead of answering.

Licht sent the request into his SINCGARS, one of three working radios they'd salvaged from the crash. Despite initial concerns—namely lack of communication with command on faraway Earth—they worked fine here on Scianas for intercommunication. Right now, Saunders wished he'd given Captain Rath's radio—the DCS-10B device—to Sgt Smith so he had intel on what was happening inside that Vault. To know if his Marines were alive at all. "Peak Team in position, sir. Reporting a lot of smoke and say they can't—"

"Understood." Saunders didn't need to hear why Plan A specifically and forcefully called for keeping this fucking dragon in the air. Letting it land was suicide, which was the inverse of what he knew about fighting against aircraft. Typically, helicopters and planes were most dangerous in the air and vulnerable on the ground. But they weren't mythical monsters on another planet, either.

The square flashed as the dragon blew more fire at the Vault's steel door. The damage to the exterior stone was impressive, but why spend time digging in the dirt when you've got a blow torch and tin foil in your way? Sure enough, when the dragon paused for a breath, the metal was glowing yellow and falling apart in molten chunks.

"It's not gonna hold," Saunders said.

Across the square, Dalmore was waving a red flag—the prearranged signal that meant *Plan A is fucked, time for Plan B.* Plan B was basically a war of human sacrifice to overwhelm the dragon's appetite for carnage. Insane, but that's how medieval battle commanders reasoned.

Problem was there didn't seem to be a better option.

"Licht, grab the red flag," Saunders said. "Plan B is a go. And get that grenade ready. If we can get the dragon's attention and fuck up its face, it might buy time for Dalmore's guys."

The Deadlies behind him drew their swords, tense and quiet. Conflicting military terminology and approaches aside, the impending green light, go, or order to charge was universal. Anticipation mixed with fear and the understanding that, however impossible it seemed, they were seconds away from running toward the worst danger imaginable.

PFC Licht waved the red flag.

Horns blew, and Dalmore's forces formed into columns.

The PFC set his radio aside and planted his M4 rifle's stock against the cobblestones to steady his aim. The chambered grenade was an M406 high explosive round designed to be specifically effective against soft tissue with a lethal radius of five meters. It wasn't ideal, but the fragmentation might sting the dragon. Maybe.

God, I'd kill for a couple of FGM-148s, thought Saunders imagining the Javelin antitank missile punching right through those scales. He readied the order to fire.

Commotion from three o'clock stopped him.

"Holy shit, what's that?" asked PFC Licht over the rising roar.

Saunders could only smile. "That is fucking Plan Alpha!"

"Ain't gonna be pretty, hoss," Fischer said, dreading the pop of his M40 sniper rifle. Range was good, but bullshit if that Black Robe came by. Then there was the fact that the Snouthelm patrol had multiplied. A dozen of 'em were now milling about, acting safe and careless like Francisco always said, but maybe they had more than those jagged swords up their sleeves.

"Remember, the one with the horns stays alive," said Francisco. "Got it?"

"Yeah, that there's another detail I ain't lovin'." *Horns* was who they figured was in charge for no other reason than his helmet having horns. Francisco's theory was that even magic wizards in black robes had superiors, maybe officers. Made sense to a Marine. At least one from Earth. Once the officer called for backup, Francisco hoped to get his shot at the Black Robe.

If we don't die instantly.

"You wanna relocate?" Francisco asked. "Take your shot after they liquify my corpse?"

Fischer held fast.

"Suit yourself. Ready?"

Fischer released a cool breath and watched the last few seconds of his target's life. Under that dark, red-speckled armor and the pig-faced helmet was a human being. At least as human as anyone was around here. They were aliens but physically no different from people back home. Fischer didn't know, just that this should have felt like a damned video game and didn't. "Ready."

A heartbeat away from a back full o' acid piss.

The crack of his rifle was lost in the thunder of Francisco's .50 cal. The two Snouthelms at the river's edge pitched backward into a cloud of fine pink mist. The drab figures nearby approached to investigate.

"Another round?" asked Francisco. The firing solution was the same, just needed to hop to another target. "I've got Tourist," he said, referring to the one looking up into the forest's thick canopy to see what might've fallen on his dead friend.

"I want Shorty," Fischer said.

"Save Shorty for when they're on the move. Do Ass Scratcher. He doesn't look like he'll be instrumental in developing their counterattack."

The rifles boomed again, and two more bodies fell. The survivors got wise and circled up, cowering like the trees were raining death. One pointed towards the Marine's concealed position. It was Horns.

"Definitely the leader," said Francisco.

"They don't look like they wantin' to come over this way." *Please don't signal the Black Robe.* Fischer wasn't ready to be booted from life.

"Let's drop the two on his flank. You go left; I'll go right. That'll be a nice sixer for us."

Blood sprayed, and the group bolted from where their buddies were dying. At 50% strength, the patrol was starting to look manageable, something they could finish off at range and relocate. But then, the thick brush along the riverbank came to life. "Shit, another team?" Fischer said.

"More like a platoon," breathed Francisco.

Dozens crawled out from concealed positions that must've been set up to ambush anyone attacking the patrol. Horns and crew fell right in, forming a battle square with full shield coverage. Fischer could probably find an opening to sink a bullet if they stood still, but the metal melee brick was on the move, splashing through the river that Cpl Nickels had correctly named Balls Deep.

"Shit, they're comin'," said Fischer. "At will?"

"Negative, waste of ammo. Hold your mark on Horns and do him when they're 100 out. Then we book."

"Cutting it a little close, ain't we?"

Francisco answered by sending two shots downrange. The larger caliber rounds of his Bullpup had no trouble penetrating those shields, the armor, and the guy behind.

Sweat rolled down Fischer's cheeks as he followed the stumbling leader onto the shore and through the brambles. They were headed toward a clearing that gave them space to line up a charge. Something bullets couldn't stop once it got going.

"Want I should take a practice swing? Slow Horns down a bit?"

"100 meters," was all Francisco said.

It made sense to wait, but why was this supposed Black Robe also waiting? The Bullpup thundered again, knocking out a straggler who wasn't keeping up with the block.

"You just bein' sadistic there, hoss?"

"He woulda done worse to you. And made me watch."

The enemy hit the clearing and planted their shields just outside of 100 meters. "Pretty sure they're making eye contact with us," whispered Buontempo from behind. Francisco offered a thumbs up; no question their position was blown.

Horns moved to the front of the line, sword high.

"Come on, gotta be close enough," Fischer whispered.

"You're like a kid."

The Snouthelms roared, an intimidating ruckus of screams and metal.

Raw manpower at its finest. Then they charged, turning that field into a lane of oncoming traffic.

100 meters.

Fischer didn't bother timing his breath as the M40 cracked. It was like hitting the broad side of a barn with the ass side of a Clydesdale. The bullet slammed into Horns' chestplate, stopping him cold. Then he dropped as his body caught up with the reality that his heart was splattered against his armor's backplate. The rest of the block gave zero shits and stormed right over him.

Fischer slung his rifle fast and got on his haunches. But Francisco stayed, training his eyepiece downrange.

"That there is some fucking dedication," Fischer said, dropping back down. *Two shooters are better than one if that Black Robe shows up.*

Suddenly, the brush on the far side of the field exploded. Not in red or purple fireworks as an evil wizard joined the fray, but in beautiful, ratcheting gunfire from an M249 squad automatic weapon (SAW).

The torrent of hot steel core tore into the charging mass from behind, collapsing the rear ranks like dominoes. It was a hard-learned lesson from the Assembly Hall fight that Snouthelm armor was thinner in the back. But even 800 cyclic rounds per minute wasn't enough.

Setting his rifle on the log he was using for stabilization, Fischer drew down a line and fired. A 7.62 mm NATO planted itself squarely in the snout part of their fastest guy, killing him instantly. Fischer slammed the bolt back and fed in another round.

"Cease fire," said Francisco. "Eye on the prize." Then louder, he added while cutting a finger across his throat, "Christ, Nickels, stop wasting ammo. Let the locals have a go at it!"

Crazy. Fischer drew his service pistol. "Boss, they're right on top of—" The block of sharp shit stopped ten meters out and pivoted left.

Corporal Nickels' SAW fell silent.

And a flood of white-hot Watchmen with long, metal spears crashed into the fray.

The Snouthelms, with their comparatively shorter swords, didn't stand a chance. The Watchmen hit them from three angles turning the offensive charge into desperate defense. The shields that did manage to block those deadly tips only deflected them into the man behind.

"Reach advantage," said Francisco. "It's why tall boxers kick ass and why they invented guns."

The Bullpup thundered.

"Thought we were *eye on the prize,* hoss?" said Fischer studying the melee. The Watchmen in their white tabards had enveloped the enemy and were hanging back, prodding with their spears. The Snouthelms were bunched up behind their shields, but it was only a matter of time.

"I reserve the right."

"You like that?" came a shout. The brush concealing the ambush position fell aside, and a beige Marine stormed into the killing field. "Count 'em up, Francis!" said Corporal Nickels panning his SAW over the trail of bodies. "All me. Ain't no denying it this time. Everyone saw. Toblerone, motherfuckers!"

"Did he say *Toblerone?*" Fischer asked, moving to the spotting scope to prevent myopia. So far, still no Black Robe.

Francisco sighed. "Lately, he's been using words that don't translate across this . . . magical translator thing that lets us all communicate. Said the idea is to make them hear his real voice instead of some dubbed approximation. It's a sickness, man. They'll ask him what a Toblerone is, and he'll go into a diatribe about his white-chocolate shaft."

"Who wants to keep resisting?" Nickels shouted, aiming his SAW at the shrinking mass of Snouthelms.

A reasonable group would've laid down their arms at this point, but the crimson powder-coated soldiers went left at the fork and attacked. Against the Watch's spear wall, it was like bringing their faces to a knife fight. Nickels didn't have to lift a finger, just stood there heckling the blood bath.

"We done here, hoss?" Fischer asked.

"We'll get on the move once they've secured the area. Stay—" Francisco's rifle boomed. Once, then again. "Shit."

Nickels dropped prone, swinging his automatic weapon in a full 360° rotation, searching for Francisco's target.

"Where?" Fischer asked, getting behind his sights. Despite the intensive Marine Corps SSC training, his heart raced as he panned the loud but otherwise still forest. He'd fought these Black Robes before, and knew what he was here to do, but nothing could prepare him for it. His breath caught as his crosshairs settled on a distant, dark figure who seemed to stare right back through his scope. "Ah, fuck. Takin—"

"Hold fire. You won't hit it," Francisco muttered.

"So? So, what? The fuck do we do?"

His answer came in the form of the sun fading from the forest like a cloud was passing overhead. Instead of becoming overcast, though, the daylight bled fast, leaving them in total darkness.

"Door ain't gonna hold, yo!" Garcia said, backing his South Texas ass away from the glowing metal.

It's melting, Smith realized, pulling his shirt over his face. Everyone was coughing from the bitter, metallic fumes filling the room. Steel-plated, secondhand smoke: a burn pit on steroids.

He pulled his Marines away from the blistering heat, taking up firing positions behind Ceal. The Watchmen were huddled around the ventilation grate, making zero progress pulling it up.

"We could blow the grate open," suggested Gladstone, eerily detached from the fact that they were in a pizza oven.

"Blow our fuckin' ears at the same time," said Garcia. He was right. The tight, domed ceiling would focus that sound like a lens, slamming it back down on them. Not a pleasant thought, but better than melted Marine pizza. *Hold the pepperoni.*

"Maybe we blow the door?" Light said. "Scare the pants off the dragon and charge out. If we scatter—" Light never finished as the steel flared again under another burst of heat.

"Christ, yo, it's boiling!" said Garcia. Solid steel was bubbling like an over-done Stouffer's Mac&Cheese.

"Teague," Smith said in the no-bullshit voice. Burning alive wasn't happening. Neither was stuffing themselves into that tiny crawl space with the dragon stomping around above. "Set those shields up and get everyone behind them. Plant one in front of Ceal."

"I am . . . am warded," she panted. Ceal didn't look protected unless being drenched in sweat counted. But fuck it, they needed every scrap of shielding they could get.

"At it, lads," said Teague dragging his men off the grate.

"Stone, the C4."

"Little late to go near that door, Sergeant," said Garcia.

"The C4 will just burn," said Gladstone reaching into his pack like he was grabbing his phone or something.

"Ain't no one goin' near that door," Smith said. "Plug one of them blasting caps into the clay and throw it. If it don't blow, we shoot it till it does. Copy?"

"That's stupid!" said Garcia.

"Caps are the only way this C4 blows. Gotta trigger it with the detonator," said Gladstone. Dude was pale and somehow dry. Maybe he already cooked off all his water, but it was weird as him being calm right now.

"Fire blankets over the shields," Smith said, ignoring the lecture. The Watchmen started laying their iron-reinforced round shields on the stone floor and covering them with blankets. "No!" Smith ran over. "Make like a wall. Big shield to stop the lava spray."

"There's still time to blow the grate," said Gladstone at an almost inaudible conversational level.

"Fuck the grate! We blow the door and bring the war," said Smith shouldering the Pig for effect. That fucking dragon was gonna find out what happened when it poked the hornet's nest. "Teague, tuck 'em in." Smith ducked behind Ceal. That put the podium and her magic shield—at least that's what he hoped she meant by "wards"—between him at that door. Getting splashed with molten steel did not sound like fun, and there was not enough room for him with the others. "Good to go?"

"Devil fuck this. Oorah, Sergeant!" shouted Garcia. Normally, his Spanish cussing coming across translated was hilarious. Right now, it was a reminder that a lot of stuff didn't work as intended here.

"Bohu!" cheered Teague. The guy had that ramp-drop pump. Might be a second from burning through and through, but he was in the fucking zone.

"Stone, throw!"

"Wait, I'm not—" began Light, but then that little clay brick was hurling across the smokey chamber.

Smith clamped his teeth and braced for the shockwave. Blast was the worst, every bone in the body getting hit with an electric jolt at once. And then all that shot up into the head, leaving that right-cross-to-the-chin mark on the brain.

Nothing happened.

"Fuck!" Smith shouted.

"Hold on," said Stone fumbling with the detonator.

"Someone shoot it!" Smith yelled, hoping Stone hadn't fucked them. Rivers of molten steel were pouring out of that door, with flames starting to shoot through. The room was heating way too fast, and the air was too hot to breathe. It was now or ne—

His skull exploded.

Stars, darkness, the feeling of a discombobulated body trying to catch pieces of itself before they floated away. Ringing.

". . . arms, protect the . . ."

"I am . . . to the . . . unbearable . . ."

"Get in front of her. Sergeant! Sergeant!"

Smith's brain managed to clamp down and vent the fog. A dark hole had opened in that molten maw. The C4 worked as intended. But instead of clearing an exit, it widened the entrance. And just beyond was a fucking dragon's face rearing back to fire the oven.

Smith made a promise to himself as the Pig began to jackhammer against his shoulder: he would hold that trigger down until the ammo box ran dry.

No matter how much it hurt having his skin burned away.

War horns.

A savage thrill overtook Captain Saunders as trumpets and battle cries blared into the square with all the accouterments of a cavalry charge.

Because that's what was happening.

Sergeant Leod's Watchmen—the primary defense force around the Bark when the dragon landed and smoked the place—were gone when Saunders arrived. Presumed KIA or routed. But now they were back: mounted, couched, and fucking glorious. Between Dalmore's horns and the Vault door suddenly blowing up in the dragon's face, they had the initiative.

"GO! GO! GO!" Saunders screamed.

The wave of horses rushed across the cobble-paved grounds. On the opposite side, Dalmore's chrome columns snaked toward the Vault. Saunders' boots were already pounding stone, more Deadlies on his six. It was the ultimate gamble. One twitch of that dragon's head and they were all ash.

Contact.

Saunders didn't see the lances strike but heard the dragon roar. Horns blew louder, and he caught the mass of men and beasts droving into the dragon's side, knocking it away from the entrance.

A few meters.

With their momentum spent, horses neighing and rearing up as they registered proximity to the king of all alpha predators, the dragon reacted fast. Like, a cat with a mouse, fast. It curled around the mass of kicking horse legs and white tabards and yawned, tonsils floating in magma.

Lungs burning from smoldering particulate, the heat of the molten Vault, and the full sprint across City Square, Saunders realized rescuing his Marines would mean sacrificing all those Watchmen. His mind raced, gears spraying sparks in search of a better solution.

Fuck it, Monkey in the Middle.

If he could keep the dragon's head moving, hungering after new and tastier targets, then maybe it wouldn't have time to stop and torch the roses. He waved the Deadlies forward and dropped to a prone firing position. The MP5 shuddered against his shoulder, 9 mm rounds popping off black scales. The dragon could not have cared less.

So much for . . .

An M4 cracked beside him. *PFC Licht!* The Marine had a knack for just . . . being there. Run through hell, never looking back; somehow, Licht always kept pace.

This time the dragon reacted, jerking its head as if annoyed by a fly.

"Keep firing," Saunders ordered. Dropping out the MP5's empty magazine and slapping in another, he wondered why Licht's rifle had so much more punch. The difference between 5.56X45 mm NATO and 9 mm at this range shouldn't have been that drastic.

He's firing the black tips.

Standard Marine ammunition for the M4 carbine was a green-tipped, 5.56 mm cartridge. Affordable and environmentally friendly, it made sense against soft-tissue targets. The black-tipped shit was the same caliber but effectively armor-piercing. And the dragon was feeling them.

Licht demonstrated his marksmanship by snapping off five more rounds; all but one were headshots. Saunders reached down to a side pouch hanging off his warbelt and got a grip on an M67 fragmentation grenade.

Wait.

"Rifle grenade!" he shouted. Half of Leod's cavalry had already escaped as the dragon struggled to prioritize its next meal. The rest could follow if Licht could keep it distracted, maybe even a little hurt.

Saunders stole a glance at the Vault. The Deadlies had the entrance encircled with their shields raised. They were covering a team of three trying to make entry through the smoldering doorway. It was happening too slowly, though, and all they were doing was calling attention back to the prize of the fight.

Before he could wave them off, the dragon whipped his head around. The MP5 came up as he shouted for Licht to fire, but none of it was fast enough. The dragon had made its decision.

The Deadlies scattered.

Saunders' submachine gun crackled, sending 9 mm bullets whizzing around the creature while Licht fumbled to aim his launcher.

But all they could do was watch in horror as a liquid inferno poured into the stone Vault containing four US Marines, Benton's wife, and the Bark—the city's last line of defense.

———

"Yo . . ."

"Dawg, you said it."

"I'm gonna be sick."

To Lance Corporal Gregory Gladstone, the voices of his fellow Marines were distant and disembodied as he stared into the wreathed luminous zone of a million BTUs. Once again, the dragon's breath was kept at bay. Through the flames, he could see the Tel'racs' face, black eyes locked on his. Knowing.

"Ceal, that you?" asked Sergeant Smith, probably beginning to understand he was not on fire.

"It . . . it . . . I do not . . ." the witch stammered as her dark bindings fell away. For some reason, the Black Robe had released its hold on her. A shame but secondary to the true prize of this battle.

The Genisan plan was . . . elegant, not unlike how they conducted operations back home. Misdirection through shock and awe. Make the world believe the hardon was for that patch of desert in Iraq and not rights to the base in Turkey that would sinch the noose tighter on Russia. Ceal surviving was a surprise given her history with the Tel'racs, but strategy was all about the ends.

Gladstone brought his Benelli tactical twelve-gauge to bear. The next moves were as predictable as they were unavoidable.

The flames went out, plunging the Vault into darkness.

"It is ye's time," announced Ceal, her shrill voice strong.

"Wind's at our backs," said Sgt Smith. "On me, MOVE!"

The fireteam stacked up with Gladstone as caboose and launched into the fight. They snaked through gobs of molten metal and exited into a visage reminiscent of the endgame at Mina Bazar. The sky was dark and raging, a low ceiling held up by fires and screams.

Lord Tel'racs was swimming in mailed and mounted soldiers. Crossbow bolts were twanging, clanging against jet scales. The dragon tried to draw back a breath, but Gladstone knew something would deny it the necessary oxygen.

Ratchetting gunfire erupted as Sgt Smith unleashed his M240. The machine gun jackhammered a spread of 7.62 mm bullets into Tel'racs' side. Gladstone's ribs ached, but he tried not to show it. Then, a charge of a dozen men on horseback whipped around to line up an angle. They were cavalry, not quite knights but like the lightly equipped scout units Gladstone had used in another life for recon in medieval battle simulators.

Wind.

Those beautiful, midnight wings stretched out into the turbulent, black sky and brought the air down on top of them. Hurricane force, much worse than a chopper taking off. When Gladstone could stand to look again, the creature was gone to his eyes, but he knew in his heart it was soaring for the heavens. Free.

The place of stollen stone and murdered trees burned. Its soft flesh, pricklier than ever before, scurried in fear. But so too did it squeak for joy, mistaking reprieve for victory. He, the ancient one who witnessed their rise from the food of this world to its greatest hunger, would not long be denied his revenge.

He lifted himself into the wind, higher and higher away from those who believed him beaten by the workings of tiny hands and heads. Loathing rage filled his gut, hissing the tiny bones and flesh within. His love, Heb'azile, flashed before him as if once more alive in winged flight, the two mightiest birds covering all the lands.

He longed.

Heb'azile's killer, the witch, remained encased in the stone wrought by those tiny hands below. With craft and deceit, she had hidden from his view but not Master's. Power—the true Power of the wise and learned—undid her veil, and once more, she was known to the alar Lord Tel'racs.

Master's offering.

With sudden fury, Tel'racs had blasted through her wards to the level of the low. Defenders cowered; her shell melted away. At last, she was his!

But no such succulence hung from his teeth now. Master had stolen his breath.

Tel'racs wanted to howl, to breathe a world of wind upon the lands until it showed black as his scales.

Master's words in the way of their speech came fast to soothe. ***The raw cooks better after wriggling.*** They spoke of suffering so sweet his breath hissed steam. And so Tel'racs would circle and wait as the witch writhed. Broken Powers from tiny hands could not reach him upon the wind.

As he spiraled higher, thin tendrils of ice slipped into the folds of his great mind. Master was delicate, looking through his impeccable memories. Were it any other, Tel'racs would reach back through the link and shatter the invader's skull from within. But he knew the Master had a purpose, and each step brought him closer to that which was too long in coming.

Tel'racs' great belly rumbled as his thoughts returned to the last meal Master had prepared. It was prettier, arranged in neat rows and scented of flowers and hope. As the storms that oft set upon the lands, pummeling with flash and flood, so did Tel'racs turn that order of tiny hands into a blackened tapestry. Such a mark he did leave on the slopes of what the Master's tongue named Val'Narden, that the others of his kind would long know the vastness of his territory. In his love's memory, Lord Tel'racs would rule these lands evermore with fire and eternity as his vengeance. Then—

A spec in the snow, a glint the like of a gem, caught his eye. It was upon the high rock, indeed much higher than tiny hands could climb or dare draw breath. The ancient beast decided to have a look while he waited for Master's plan to unfold.

———

"There!" said Captain Rath pointing at something rising out of the gray smoke below.

"Finally spooked 'em," Brines said. He stomped his heels into the compacted snow to secure his footing on the icy ledge.

"Now the hard part, Gunny." Captain Rath hefted the FIM-92F Stinger Missile launcher onto Brines' shoulder. It'd been years since Brines fired one of these surface-to-air systems, and there was no guarantee it would even operate. "He's coming up fast."

"Hang on." Brines pulled the BCU canister from his side pouch and locked it under the weapon. The electronics came online, and a hiss told him the argon coolant had survived their long ordeal.

"Shit, he's coming this way. Don't let him get above us."

Brines turned out the commentary. Telling someone to drive faster never shortened the trip. The dragon was still small against the white of the mountain slopes. Problem was that it kept passing over the dark cloud below. Two issues: First, the missile might not get a good contrast of black on a dark background, so he needed to line it up against a slope. Second, if he waited too long and the dragon got above them, the missile's heat-seeking capability might lock onto the sun instead of the dragon. *Only got one shot.*

He waited until it took a long arc over the opposing slope before popping the actuator switch. The tracking tone rang out over the frozen quiet. Before he could get a lock, the bird cut back over the cloud. "Fuck."

"Now . . . shit!" said Captain Rath. It looked like the dragon was making a run for the valley, but then it banked vertically, wings pumping hard. Somehow it managed to keep using the background smoke like camouflage.

Brines wondered how smart these things were. To him, it was a fucking dinosaur, but hearing the reverent way the locals described it, he was facing a god.

Excitement rippled. *A god.*

"Just fire. Fire! That BCU isn't gonna last!" shouted Captain Rath.

Brines ignored the order, and in the blink of an eye, the prehistoric monster was all rippling, jet scales in his sights. Then, it was above them.

"We're fucked!"

Brines cracked the bones in his neck. *A god.*

The tone changed, and the bone transducer vibrated against his cheek.

A lock.

The missile popped out of its tube into the endless volume of airspace below. Then, with a roar and a blast of hot exhaust, it zipped out over the mountains. For a moment, it flew straight and dumb, and Brines' nuts tightened. Then, it swerved, arcing around toward—

"Fuck, the sun!" shouted Rath.

Yes, the sun. But more importantly, the black dragon in front of it. The 70 mm missile intercepted its target, engulfing the beast in a little ball of grey smoke. The report crashed against the mountainside a moment later.

"Jesus," said Rath, dropping to his knees in the snow.

"Rah," Brines muttered, studying that cloud. The smoke swirled, and the dragon emerged, beating its wings.

Well, wing.

A shriek slashed across the icy heights, and like someone who couldn't swim, beating became thrashing became falling. As it picked up speed, Brines noted the creature had gone ragdoll. Then, it was lost in a puff of white snow as it slammed into the peak above.

They waited a full minute for it to emerge, but it didn't. It was just Brines, Captain Rath, the snow, and the wind. "Guess we can call that in as a kill, sir," Brines said. He set the spent launcher tube down, wondering if he should bring it back. It wasn't like they could reload it, but—

A crack echoed off the world, and then came the thunder.

Brines' heart kicked into full alert. He didn't need Saunders' high-altitude experience to know what it was.

"Avalanche!" screamed Captain Rath as the great white of the mountain slipped off like the silken robe from a lady's shoulders.

CHAPTER 3

PLAN A COST SHARE

Eyes," Captain Saunders yelled. "We need a vis—, uh . . . the sky. We need to see the sky!" He spotted Ceal in her tougher-than-nails cocktail dress stumbling out of the charbroiled igloo. "Can you clear the smoke?"

He knew he should give her a minute to get her bearings but had zero fucks left. Right now, they were blind against an enemy with air superiority. And Brines was up there.

"I shall," she panted, muttering something under her breath. Probably Portcullisian profanity. But it got the job done, and the air above started to swirl as if being sucked into a gigantic HEPA filter.

"There," said Sergeant Smith, pointing.

Saunders spotted the black spec fluttering around Almon's Peak like a moth drawn to a flame. Unfortunately, that flame was likely his gunnery sergeant stationed on the Shoulder. Thoughts raced, drowning in a sea of helplessness. Ceal was the only option, but Benton was adamant about keeping her away from the dragon.

Screw it; we've got the guns. She's going—

Suddenly, the black moth exploded.

Oh shit.

A hush fell over City Square as everyone stared. When Saunders' Marines had first arrived, Sergeant Teague joked that newcomers—tourists—always looked the same way. "Up." At the time, it was a cute way of saying Portcullis' crown of frozen peaks was unique, but now, it took on a whole new meaning.

Unity.

Everyone—townies and interplanetary guests alike—were looking up in awe at something individually and collectively unique.

Ingenuity, adaptation, the impossible. Plan fucking A.

"We killed a goddamned dragon. OORAH!" boomed Smith, breaking the silence. A cluster of *oorahs* joined the Watchmen's *bohus* and Deadlies' *resist deaths,* and the square went from ground zero to Independence Day.

It was a big win. A powerful enemy slain and freedom from an ancient terror. The locals would be talking about this till their end days. But for Saunders, there were bigger fights on the horizon. Right now, he needed a headcount on his people.

Smith's fireteam, all accounted for, was drenched in sweat and not feeling the fact that it was balls cold not five meters from the smoldering Vault. But they were on their feet, cheering.

PFC Licht was still online and receiving an update from Del Team. Peak Team would be next. The tension eased.

Blue and elegance floated through the charcoal tapestry of medieval soldiers, horses, and stone. Ceal. "You okay?" Saunders asked.

She wasn't smiling nor soaked in sweat and soot like his men. Somehow, the girl—woman of unknown age—had freshened up while everyone else was celebrating. "We must talk," she said in a no-bullshit voice. "A great—"

"Leod! You motherfucker! I saw that shit! I saw it!" Sergeant Smith shouted at the one-armed Watchman dismounting from a white mare. At least it looked like a mare from this angle. "Epic, motherfucker. I said epic!"

Watch Sergeant Leod, who had lost his arm during the battle against Mendo/Isllor the Black Robe, tucked his chainmail coif between his legs and slicked back his black hair. He sprouted the stupid grin that just about every young PFC or lance corporal wore after a hold-my-beer moment. "Aye, takes a beast to best a beast."

The testosterone-driven warrior in Saunders wanted to belt an *oorah*, but the analytical side—the commanding officer waging war with limited forces and strung-out provisions—sighed. Cavalry against a dragon? Yes, it worked. Yes, it was fucking awesome.

But it was far from clean.

Many of those horses were banged up and limping; riders were down. It was hard to get an exact count, but the city would not be fielding another cavalry force at that strength for a while.

"Does everyone here know how to ride a horse?" asked LCpl Light from outside the ring of beige Marines and white-tabarded Watchmen. A few heads cocked at the absurdly disconnected question, but no one answered. Instead, Smith and Garcia hoisted Leod onto their shoulders as an ovation spread throughout the square. Saunders gave in and cheered along with everyone else. *Fuck it, no pain in the winner's circle.*

When things calmed down, he remembered Ceal. "What was it you—"

The heavens rumbled, and heads craned up again.

Saunders' blood pressure spiked. He knew that sound from one of the most terrifying moments of his childhood. The skies were still hazy, and he didn't have time to zero it, but his men were up there. Ceal gave a knowing frown.

"Can you?" he managed.

She nodded, moving into an open space. A high-pitched whine rose, and the air folded, plucking her from existence. It didn't help Saunders' anxiety—an ingrained phobia of that much snow on the move—but it was their best chance.

"We need to move!" shouted Captain Rath, head snapping around, desperate for an exit. Brines understood but also made a point of always knowing the way out. Up here, with that pass about to vanish under 50 feet of snow, the cliff was their only option.

Ain't no one gonna feel good with that much air between him and the ground, he thought, staring at a length of 550 cord.

Goddamn.

Ron had packed some metal anchors forged by the fucking medieval, zero-quality-control-standards, coal-fired blacksmiths. They were meant for climbing *up* with plenty of time and redundancy to chance them holding weight. All parts bad, but the only option. He began hammering one into a patch of windswept rock.

"There's no time," Rath said, maybe wondering if he had better chances against the avalanche.

"Tie the other end tight around yer belt. Then hook up the carabiners so you can rappel. Know how to do that?" Brines asked. A lesson was out of the question at this point. Worst case, he'd just shorten the rope.

Rath worked fast and hooked himself in. As he set up the descender, he looked up at the incoming tidal wave and asked, "Can it hold both of us?"

There were no good answers. 550 wasn't just a stupid government way of indexing a product; it was named that because it was rated for 550 pounds. Together, Brines' 250 and Rath's 2-210 or so plus gear were pushing it. And these were less-than-ideal conditions.

"Go, I'll be right behind you," Brines shouted over the roar.

"No, I'll stay till you get—"

The ice behind them came alive.

Not shifted or bucked under tectonic stresses but stalked out of the snow on legs of blue-green shards. Insect-like at first, it stood erect before them, a humanoid icicle about the size of a child with black eyes. God-damned evil.

"What the fuck is that?" cried Rath, rifle tangled in the rope.

Brines knew. From Ann, of all people.

The Gra'nuul.

Soulless killing machines that lived in the rock and ice. Like ants to sugar, they were drawn to warmth. It was the original reason for Portcullis' huge walls and aggressive military presence. The creatures were supposed to be dormant, trapped in their tunnels after some shit that went down with Ceal several years ago. But the way Ceal's eyes went dark when the topic came up meant no one ever let their guard down.

To Brines, history didn't matter. This was just something trying to squeeze in one last fight before nature finished him off. A lesser man might've thought it was karma.

"My last meal," Brines growled, launching a boot into Rath's chest and sending him over the edge. It was just Gunny and the creature now, seconds away from obliteration. He wished he'd brought his knife.

Movement snagged the corner of his eye. Expecting more ice monsters or who knew what else, he stole a look. What he got was a glimpse of a woman in an elegant blue robe, and then it was gone. *Just a figment of my desire to survive,* he guessed as the Gra'nuul lunged for his throat.

Sorry, Pat.

Captain Case "Padilla" Rath was an experienced combat pilot used to living without a net. But something about hanging by a thin rope at the top of forever on, as far as his paygrade was concerned, an extraterrestrial planet without aircraft, search and rescue, or even the ability to make a decent after-action martini had him scared shitless.

The roar was deafening now; the sheer ice lining the cliffside inches away was cracking and shaking free. Still, he wasn't budging until Gunny Brines hopped over the edge after him. He gave it what felt like a lot of time (but probably wasn't) before deciding something was wrong.

What the hell was that walking ice sculpture?

Rath yanked his pistol free. Moving up was an easy sell because down was infinite. Fingers freezing, half numb in his gloves, he grabbed the rope and hoisted. He didn't have the arms to pull himself up, but he had the legs and knew enough to use them. He pushed, gaining a foot and then another. He could make it in time to . . .

Screams: one human and the other piercing like a dentist's drill.

Then the sky was a raging white river.

The rush of snow overhead vacuumed the air from his lungs. He dropped fast, trying to escape. Then, realizing the anchor to his thin rope was getting power blasted, he lunged for the mountainside, hands and feet scratching the rock and ice for holds. If he could just find something to grab, he'd have a—

A block of snow the size of a minivan smashed him in the face. It broke apart and fell away, but that only paved the way for another. And another. Pretty soon, he was drowning and forgot all about rappelling, the rope, or even how far he had to fall.

Burn.

It was the worst form of traumatic injury. Maybe not from a surgeon's perspective, but on the *floor,* it was hell. The problem was the skin. It was the first and most significant line of defense against a world of microorganisms waiting to chew into the vulnerable tissues beneath. Searing off large swaths left the immune system overwhelmed and in need of considerable outside support.

Treatment went beyond antimicrobial films and surgical repair. Patients needed fluids, antibiotics, and constant, in-life monitoring. The care was staff intensive and demoralizing as a beautiful person sloughed and blistered in howling pain. It put the best medical burn teams and units to task, trying to save not only a life but a human being from awful disfigurement.

And medieval society, from Dr. Patricia Bowman's every conceivable perspective, was not prepared.

"The Apperis Sap can . . ." began the local medical director, Wisewoman Alena. Apperis Sap was a true miracle: a liquor made from the secretions of an Apperis tree that could mend tissues within days, maybe hours. It also had some anti-inflammatory properties but teasing them apart from the impact of rapid wound healing was difficult. Unfortunately, it could not supplant the need for antibiotics.

"Keep boiling the rags and save the Sap for the bleeders," Dr. Pat said, finishing a wrap of sanitized cloth around Watchman Niall's neck. The skin below was retracted, totally cooked. Another problem with Apperis Sap was that it could not regenerate tissue if the vasculature was collapsed and cauterized. The Sap didn't work topically and wasn't miscible with anything they could infuse intravascularly; it had to be oral. Four patients had already vomited in the attempt.

A tongue click reminded her who she was speaking to.

"Can we not spare the boiling of these cloths? It slows us, a waste of good firewood. Look here; they are clean, white as snow."

White as snow and smell like mildew. Despite Dr. Pat's best efforts to turn the remains of the Blue Cloak's Provincial Post—a formerly solid keep that fell during the fight against the Black Robe Mendo—into a modern medical treatment facility, progress was slow. No level of cleaning, sanitizing, or barriering could erase the fact that it was still a damp, stone structure reliant on a stiff breeze for ventilation. *Stagnation* was the word that came to mind, like those puddles of standing water that bred mosquitos.

"No," Dr. Pat said.

She moved on to the next patient before Alena could pop another tongue click. The man's plated armor marked him as one of Dalmore's Deadlies—a group of Blue Cloaks who'd chosen to stay and fight over giving into corruption. The Wethands had already removed the sleeves, helmet, and trim around the charred chest piece. A careful peek beneath showed the thick cotton underlayment unscathed. The issue here was his breathing—rapid and shallow. Smoke inhalation with possibly thermal injury to the lung tissue, which meant he could not exchange enough oxygen and carbon dioxide. With lips that blue, she didn't need a Pulse Ox to know he was already hypoxemic. "Alena, this one needs to sleep."

"Sleep? His breath comes difficult even awake. He needs Shalestem Incense to clear the sputum and restore depth to his chest."

Like taking a drag before giving CPR.

"No, we need to lower his metabolism and ventilate him with the bellows." The bellows was sent over by a blacksmith from Song Street. Hooked to a wax mold of the human face and caked in grease to make a seal, it was *the* medieval ventilator.

Shalestem Incense had zero therapeutic benefits, and even Alena acknowledged that. All it did was make a room of death smell better.

"But burn the incense anyway," Dr. Pat added.

Alena's face, a ledger of arrogance accounted by the creases of age and experience, was stone. "Cild, fetch the bellows of Doctor Pat and fire the Shalestem to lighten the air."

Suddenly, Dr. Pat's sixth sense—clerk of a fine china and crystal store—triggered. Something precious was about to get broken.

"No!" she yelled, bringing the floor to a dead stop. There, beside a mother of two with burns over 35% of her total body surface area, was one of the newer Wethands. He was using a pitcher to top off the glass reservoir feeding her IV line like a fish tank.

That intravenous setup was a monument to ingenuity and determination. No one grasped the need to push fluids into a vein when the patient had a perfectly good mouth, so Dr. Pat had been on her own to get it done. Finding a glassblower who could make a bulb with a hole at the bottom compatible with her saline bag spikes was the easy part. Creating saline in a world of strange ingredients and stranger names for things like salt was a hair-pulling nightmare. Still, after all that, keeping it sterile was the real war.

"She does not like to mix the waters," Alena semi-scolded. They would all laugh about it later. "Bring a fresh bottle, and we shall link the, ah . . . tube."

"I'll do it," Dr. Pat sighed. Only herself, Micky—singularly qualified because she had literally stayed in a Holiday Inn before—and LCpl Buontempo were allowed to touch, let alone run, the precious polyethylene lines salvaged from the Marine medical supplies. Alena's people had no concept of what introducing air bubbles to the circulation could do to a patient. Even small ones.

A tongue click, and probably an eye roll, followed her to the wash station—a sink over a dug pit with a leather water bladder above. "Dr. Pat," said Alena. "I hath indulged your methods and needs. Now I must see to the whole of this mess and not just its pieces."

"What?"

"More come now." She pointed out the high window at the flatbed carts filled with writhing casualties. "Our work is too slowed to help so many."

"We need more nur—Wethands from the Guild Hospice," Dr. Pat said. The Wethands had no formal medical training, the equivalent of orderlies or CNAs willing to get their hands dirty. Some were better than others, but still a far cry from even the nursing staff of that chop shop in Mina Bazar. The Marines were off fighting, so Micky was the only one trustworthy to oversee the resuscitation patients. Then there was—

"See now? Watchman Daire cries not in pain," Alena continued. "He is calm. Should we not tend him later?"

Hard stop.

She thinks we're focusing on the wrong people. It made sense on a superficial level. Shock could look like someone watching late-night TV if the glassy eyes, pale skin, and cognitive deficits were ignored. In Alena's world, the howlers with broken arms and stable vitals took priority.

"We need to open the reserve wards," Dr. Pat said. "If they're coming through that door, they need immediate assessment. Pale and withering beats crying and thrashing. Understood?"

Wisewoman Alena rolled her eyes.

Unbelievable.

Dr. Pat grabbed the older woman's arm, not with a vice grip, but handshake firm. It was enough to force eye contact. "Look. Daire isn't calm because he's feeling no pain; it's because he's fading. A lot of people are going to be like that. They deserve a first look before we decide whether to move on."

Rigidity.

Okay, different approach. "You told me you served in a battlefield setting before, right?"

"Aye."

"Then try to remember the faces, the injuries. Past the blood and yelling to the eyes staring back at you. Which ones made it, and which ones didn't? Who could wait . . . and who couldn't?"

Alena's jaw tightened, but her eyes also widened. It was game recognizing game, her finally seeing past the younger upstart to the real-life experience within. The technologies and treatment modalities between them were medical bookends, but the patients were still the same. "Watchman Daire's needs are great," she said, "but he will die."

"Yes," Dr. Pat admitted. The reality was less important than the attitude that Daire was fine because he *looked* fine.

"Watchman Beagan, however," Alena said, walking over to another pale form, "can benefit. But our time is short." She eyed a pair of Wethands setting a broken leg. It looked bad, but the bleeding was staunched with a tourniquet, and the young man's color was good. "Over here, quick."

Encouraging, but all too often, thawed ice in one spot meant the oceans rising in another.

"Do we have any ointments, uh, salves?" Dr. Pat asked amid the icy waters of cooperativity. "You must've treated people in house fires before. Something you spread on the flesh to help it mend."

"Nay," she said, helping the Wethands to roll Beagan onto his stomach. The prone position would help his lungs work, but his legs needed attention. Heavy third-degree burns. The char was so bad it was hard to tell where the leather britches ended, and flesh began. "Only the Sap and Shalestem to ward against Flame Sickness."

Flame Sickness. Sepsis from having no functional integument. *Great, so she's at least aware of what's next.* "How do you normally treat Flame Sickness once it presents?" Dr. Pat asked, hoping against hope these people might pull an effective antimicrobial out of their asses. But Alena's attention was lost in the rush of new patients.

"On the tables, not the floor!" shouted Micky Toms heading off the influx. She looked like one of the clinic's staff in her white dress, but in no way would Dr. Pat ever see her as a medical practitioner. Micky was a minimally functional kindergarten teacher, the bubbly girl at the bar who would never grow up but one day get old.

"Micky, send them to the other wards."

"Yes sir, Dr. Pat, sir," she chirped, redirecting the breathless stretcher teams into the hallway. Another *perk* was that Micky happened to be the president and sole member of the Dr. Pat fan club. Annoying on a good day but agonizing on the job. Problem was that everyone else who spoke 21st century was on perpetual combat duty. Mickey would never be a nurse, but she was a fast learner and skilled at making herself indispensable.

"Milady, we 'ave more'a comin'," said one of Dalmore's people. His shiny armor was a smear of blood and soot. None of it was his, though. "What d' ye need?"

"Get them on the tables," Dr. Pat repeated. "Don't touch the burns. If they're bleeding from legs or arms, belt it. If it's from the head, neck, or chest, come get me."

"Lots o' bleedin', milady. 'Ow much is a worry?"

Ugh, how do I explain flow rate to these people?

"If it spurts or fills a cup in half a *width*, it is a worry," said Wisewoman Alena. Widths were their unit of time, about fifteen to twenty minutes. A cup—which was closer to a pint—or more every ten would put a bleed rate of . . . *Yeah, that works.*

"Wisewoman. Milady," farewelled the Deadlie before heading back to the street.

Another moaning train of stretchers—bedsheets hammocked between two carriers—funneled in. Dr. Pat dipped her hands in the alcohol bowl. It was their strongest proof, something Sergeant Smith—a hobbyist beer brewer—had certified at 53% alcohol by volume. It wasn't hand sanitizer, which was optimally effective at 70%, but it was guaranteed sterile and would seriously fuck up any pathogens on her hands.

Without contacting any of the non-sterile surfaces of the biofilm-laden, medieval dungeon, she grabbed a boiled cloth and sanitized the elbow vein on a pale woman's good arm. The other arm was edemic, deformed. Likely a childhood break that was never treated or a congenital defect. Either way . . .

Dr. Pat's thoughts trailed off as the influx of wounded died down. *Just leather and mail, no beige Marine uniforms.*

Yet.

She blew out a breath. *You'd better not show up burnt to a crisp, Mike Brines.*

A palm struck her ass.

She didn't flinch. The emotional availability to do anything but grind was nonexistent in triage mode. However, some small uncommitted resource in her mind considered the small list of possible offenders. Mike rang loudest due to wishful thinking, but as he said, tonight wasn't happening. Hell, given the caseload, tomorrow morning was a stretch too.

A giggle in her ear.

The second, of course, was Micky. Also, nothing alarming. Micky's playful lesbian stuff was confusing, at first, because it seemed to be entirely for shock value. Turned out it was her way of assessing mental status. *Like poking a wild animal to see if it will bite you.*

"What?" Dr. Pat asked without taking her eyes off the IV needle feeding into her patient's cephalic vein.

"Okay, so some good news: the newbies are hurt, but the real bad ones got here first. The bad news is we're running out of saline."

"Micky!" Dr. Pat snapped.

"Hey, I did like you asked: rationed that shit like titties in a kiddie movie. But this is a mass casualty event."

Micky had a weird way with words, sometimes childish, but then she'd drop the lingo like a pro. "We need a count of need and our reserve."

"Got twenty liters and a rising count standing at thirty-one who will need it."

"That's a stretch. Average person is taking a full liter. Can we red tag any of them?" In a triage setting, resources needed to be prioritized for those who could be saved.

Micky's smile faded. "I can do that, Pat."

Something was off about that answer. "What? No, I mean, how many meet the crit—"

"Make a hole!" boomed authority—Marine authority—and in rushed beige. Two Marines, Smith and Gladstone, had someone on a stretcher—a real stretcher, the orange-webbed fold-up they'd carried Micky on from the crash—and grabbed a table.

Through the jumble of bodies and shouting as Wethands, Alena, and patients all competed to be the loudest, Dr. Pat's heart skipped a beat.

It was Captain Rath.

He was blue, *fucking blue,* and quiet—the opposite of everyone else in the room.

"Doc, we need him thawed out and awake," said Captain Saunders on the heels of his men.

Micky grabbed his wrist. "Gosh, he's cold, but we've got a pulse. He's . . ."

The rest was lost against the roaring blood in Dr. Pat's ears. Past Saunders was another Marine posted by the clinic door. Garcia, not Mike. It didn't mean anything, yet Brines and Rath went up that mountain together.

To battle a fire-breathing dragon.

And one came back half-frozen.

Dr. Pat forced her breathing to stay even, fighting down the primitive fight response that some people dressed up as woman's intuition. She was calm, in control, running a trauma center in the middle of a battle.

"No, we need him awake. Now!" insisted Saunders, dissatisfied by something Micky said. "Warm him the fuck up. Use that fucking Sap, whatever it takes." Alena approached with her hands raised in a disarming fashion. The captain blew past, sticking his head out into the hallway. "Ceal, I need you back up there. We can't wait on Rath. Find him!"

Him? Dr. Pat's stomach dropped. In a place of horrors, Saunders' tone was the lead gut bomb she'd been dreading. He wouldn't dare order Lady Ceal around unless the situation was desperate.

The Wisewoman followed Saunders, repeating Dr. Pat's words from minutes ago about patient prioritization. Right now, Rath was hypothermic, but aside from some superficial contusions, not critically injured. Low body temperature was usually protective, sometimes even employed during risky surgeries to preserve tissues and organs.

But none of that mattered if he knew something about Mike.

"Captain Rath is the priority," Dr. Pat growled.

Benton Feo'bathan—Procult Chair, restored Lord of Oxhold, and risen Lord Governor of Galimay's last defensive frontier, Portcullis—paced in his manor home. Beyond the warmed stone walls lay the frozen night. At last, the embers of the fired city had cooled by mountain frosts and the quick work of the Korigi Carre. In the spite of their losses, Portcullis had endured the ancient Nuadian nemesis written about by the likes of Lords Taichleach and Haimroth.

The Tel'racs.

In another age, the skies would wince from the light of celebration. Alas, the cold city sat shuttered and guarded.

Against what is to come, the great winged lord is a pittance.

The grand worries of the larger world were an armor this night as more pointed concerns sought to strike Benton's core. He glanced again out the window. Two Watchmen stood shivering at the property's gate, the brazier beside them unlit to save wood. Naught else stirred within the darkness. He returned to the dining room, clinking and clanking from the Everwinter Steel that still clung to his agile body.

"M'lord," began his housemaster, Comack. The man, whose fealty ran thicker than blood, gestured at the paltry spread upon the table. A banquet in this time of shortage.

Benton sighed. "I find no comfort in meals or soft chairs while mine house is incomplete."

"The lady's health and spirits are restored, m'lord. So too, the demands upon her. A starving man ye shall be if this table calls for a complete house."

He allowed a short laugh. Comack spoke to reason: Lt. Maon of the Watch had sent word that Ceal joined the Corsan Carre—*Marines* in their way of sounding—in a search for missing men. Still, Benton's heart did not lighten, knowing their efforts had lasted so long after dusk.

Mayhap my lady now returns to her evening duties?

Before her sickness—born of Isllor Mortund's evil—she oft burned low the candles at court. Even here in Galimay's now farthest outpost, her unique mastery over the Stochal Power drew attention from influential lords and their retinues. Many saw it instructible as the Quotidian Power was fashionable. Thus, days were filled with frivolities, and her true work forced to the quiet of evening and night.

The work of the Procult.

For countless years since the Retethering, they had prepared for the coming of the Corsan Carre. It was not the work of sharpening swords, raising stone fortifications, or filling storehouses for the famines to come. It was the war of whispers. Teaching the many high and low that the Corsan Carre were salvation. The tool to prevent the Second Stochasm.

It was a war they were losing to those who took a more dire interpretation of the Corsan Carre. The Anticult.

If the Procult filled the skies with birds singing songs of hope, the Anticult covered the lands with serpents whose hisses bore venom. In the spite of vigilance and high walls, the Anticult's hisses had spread throughout Galimay, carried on the fearful lips of refugees. Where despair drew breath, doom rang loud in all ears. Corsan Carre was a name more cursed than ever before.

But here in Portcullis, where the deeds of the Corsan Carre thundered, the Procult was strong. Dalmore and the council lords were men planted in the rock of these Paling Mountains, unconcerned with the schemes of far-away lands. It was the same with the Corsan Carre. Their desires rested in returning to their home, which meant ensuring Portcullis and mayhap all Galimay stood long enough to see it done.

With no Procult business in the city and a world quiet to our Long Voice beyond, what is left to keep her?

A gust of chill air brought flowing blue and Benton's answer into the dining room. Ceal.

Alas, his love's face did not melt upon seeing him. It strained, her breath fast through thin lips. He thought her cold, but for the warmth he knew surrounded her despite the illusion of thin dress. She stopped long enough to rest a hand upon his shoulder plate. The respite was their connection, that which she always made time for. Still, much was amiss.

"Are ye wounded?" he asked as she joined Comack at the table. The man was quick to pour her a cup of wine, which she drank with a shaking hand. "I hear no bells. Doth the city rest this night?"

She gave no answer, emerald orbs fixed through the arched windows to the backyard. There was naught to see; few lights burned in this time of need and tightened provisions. Still, if she so wanted, her eyes could be keen in the deepest cave that knew nothing of light and warmth. His Sense of the Stochal, a gift from long ago, said she was unaided.

Benton sat in the hard-backed chair beside her, caring not for the scratches his armor would leave behind. Comack started but held his place. Apologies were for later. "Mine love, I wish ye would speak," Benton said. "The horrors I hath seen ye endure, always poised and strong, would melt most men's bones."

Silence.

"The losses to the city were terrible, but not in the like of Bedinch so long ago," he said. "Seventeen homes and shops could not be saved from flame, and the Vault still stands. The wounded are many, but so will many rise again. I hath visited the old Provincial Post. Hath ye been? Wisewoman Alena and the *Doctor* Pat work wonders."

She swallowed the last of her wine.

"Comack, a finer vintage must appear if we are to coax words."

"Wouldst a Fallsvest, first pressing, suffice?"

A taste of their lands within Dryreach. "A light in these dark days," Benton said, and Comack hurried to the cellar. He would not be long now that the many shelves sat empty.

Benton fast took his wife's free hand; she did not resist. "My love, I hath failed ye." She regarded him but with pressed lips. "I was not by ye's side in the Vault, defending the Bark. Never should I hath let ye stand alone against the Tel'racs. Before, whence we faced his mate, Heb'azile, we were bolstered by our Companions and a bright world filled with life, trade, and hope. To face such here, in the cold and muck that sinks our hearts low, was folly."

Those warming lips parted, but her eyes stayed dull from the burnt aftermath of inferno. Her body and mind were surely weary from the battle, but this silence—he dared not call it fright—could be naught from effort and strife.

"What sight vexes ye so?" he asked, not wishing to name more demons of her past. A shiver rolled through the heat of his body. *Could Isllor Mortund hath returned once more?* It was impossible, but so too was it impossible for the Betrayer to assume the guise of a commander in Galimay's Sapphire Branch and usurp Ceal's mind beneath the greatest wards woven in the name of defense.

"Them," she seethed.

Comack returned and uncorked the bottle. Notes of water spilling over the dry, cracked soil of Fellsvest filled the air. Benton took both cups, handing one to Ceal. The wine was the wet and warmth a throat raw from shouting, smoke, and cold most desired.

"Who?" Benton asked, the drink restoring strength to his voice.

As she summoned the answer, the strain upon her face brought a rush of memory.

Horses at full gallop.

The long climb to Elzdeth Academy ever too slow.

Smoke in the distance, flashes and thunders cracking their might upon what should have been impregnable stone guarded by the world's Power. The battle was cooling by the time Benton arrived, but late in coming, he was not.

Them.

His company dismounted, driving into the swarm of living ice with steel and renderstone. 'Twas a clash without like with naught to win, only endure. Galimay's nemesis eventually retreated to their hidden caves and hides, a mountain of corpses in their wake.

He found Ceal, aghast, the last of her students torn and bloodied outside her barred door. They had given their last in her defense as she could do naught. The creatures, long held at bay with steel and stone, had struck hard and with impunity against the Powers.

It was the moment of Isllor's first betrayal. The first time the great plague of the Palings had served the bidding of men.

"The Gra'nuul," she whispered.

Benton's heart tightened at the thought of two formidable enemies returning within a day. Still, her face never seemed so pale, even as old wounds were rent and salted. That day's losses went beyond her students, a mortal blow that doomed Galimay. But, naught of it was so fresh as her pain now.

"What else?" he asked.

"Del Team's five minutes out, sir," said LCpl Garcia from the doorway. Captain Saunders let the dark rooftop of the inn and the frozen breeze between them serve as acknowledgment. Garcia understood and headed back down below.

Saunders wondered if the word *fuck* translated across the magical *whatever* that allowed people to hear different languages as their own. Would the parents in all those darkened homes cover their children's ears if he shouted it so loud it caused another avalanche? If not, what would they hear? The literal translation might be a command to start intercourse, but he knew there was person-to-person variation in what was heard. It was some combination of personal vocabulary and the speaker's true intent. So maybe they'd hear him scream *why*. Or *what the hell*. Or—

"Party time, motherfuckers!" came a shout from down in the yard. Del Team returning.

Francisco and LCpls Buontempo and Fischer looked spent, muscling forward with that legs-on-autopilot, straight-to-a-hot-meal-and-bunk stagger. They'd been out in the brush for over 30 hours since Lt. Maon's scout rangers first spotted enemy movement hugging the valley's rim. Cpl Nickels, however, was ready to run his victory lap.

"Yeah, bitches. Yeah! Fuck were all yous doin' up here while we were in the trenches?" he shouted, arms wide.

A group of Watchmen, white tabards glowing against the oil lanterns they carried, met them in the center of the yard. After a quick exchange, laughter floated up and knocked on a cold shell that wouldn't answer. Saunders was glad his men were accounted for but dead to the high-fives and promises of buying each other beers. This winner's circle was made of thorns.

Francisco glanced up, but the others paid no attention to the shadow that might be watching from an elevated position. Saunders offered a nod, expecting those keen eyes could probably catch the gesture. Part of him was interested in what happened. Last action report indicated a Black Robe had Del Team dead to rights and the city doomed to fighting an invincible dragon. Then poof, it was over. The rest . . . he searched the silhouettes looming above the blacked-out city . . . was all noise since the avalanche.

"No fucking way!" echoed Nickels' voice through the quiet night. "Leod, you animal. You hear that, Fish? That's why he's my boy. Fuckin', that is the correct use of horses. Not fuckin' trying to shoot them all hangry and shit. Suck my 40-inch stallion, dragon!"

"The Tel'racs nigh feared the neigh, but with such force we struck that it did move," said Leod, fending off a playful Nickels with his one good arm. What remained of the left was strapped with a special silver buckler. Benton had awarded it when he learned of Leod's sacrifices to free the White Wolf, Palefang, from Mendo's lair. It was made of a Renderstone alloy that could take a pounding. Saunders wanted to care but couldn't. He was empty, pissed out, and retched dry.

"It moved!" Nickels shouted. "Beat that, Francis. I saw your whole game this time. You didn't hit shit; that bitch just winked out 'cause he knew the Toblerone was waiting for him."

"What is the *Toblerone*?" asked Leod, stumbling over the alien word.

Nickels put his arm around the Watchman, who had since been promoted to sergeant for his valor and injuries. "Glad you asked, son. Let's find Bone, grab some brewskies, and I'll tell you."

Warm light and laughter poured into the yard as they entered the inn below, and then it was dark again. *Good.* Part of Saunders didn't want to bring down the celebratory mood. His men had earned the night, waging war against the impossible on another world while managing a patchwork of regional security forces whose capabilities ranged from mundane to extraordinary. They protected a city on his orders alone, completely cut off from the 25th Expeditionary Unit, Fleet, the United States, and every human being on Earth.

If anyone's left back home.

He banished the thought by kicking one of the stone columns that held up the First Inn of Portcullis. They were spaced about two meters apart, providing an exterior scaffolding for the inn's wooden superstructure. The door to the stairs opened again, and near-silent footfalls brought another Marine out onto the roof. It could only be one: the third of an elite little band once called heroes for doing the unspeakable to survive in a faraway land called Iraq.

"You heard?" he asked Francisco.

"Request permission to keep searching, sir."

Saunders didn't answer, couldn't answer. They'd been here more times than he cared to count, and the drive to find each other never let them down. But now, no amount of *oorah*, sweeps for IR beacons, or scouring with wizards could make them whole again.

He studied the stone support. Death on the battlefield could happen in the unceremonious blink of an eye. To anyone. But while most men were the wood, providing strength, structure, and character, a few were the stone into which the team was mortared.

Saunders cast his eyes out over the darkened city and again wondered what the Portcullisians might hear if his lungs threw the summation of his frustrations against the night. A mighty vow of vengeance from a Marine infantry commander or a whimper from a guy who just lost one of his best friends.

CHAPTER 4

DAWN OF MOURN

It was snowing.

Little flakes floated down from heavy clouds. They gathered into floating rivers and waves, wafting across the windswept walkways and headstones. The grass between, wilted and dormant in its wintry state, was wiry enough to catch them, and that is what first faded to white.

Voices droned as puffs of hot breath floated off the still crowd—a parking lot of humans idling in the cold. Their eyes were on her, awaiting a lecture she couldn't give. Instead, ears tuned to the lords and ladies of this time-lost alien city as they accounted for their dead. And tried to convey appreciation for *his* sacrifice.

I'll see yer ass in the morning.

Dr. Pat shuddered. The words were haunting, spoken by a man who saw a future for himself. Agonizing as a child on their death bed, asking what they were going to do tomorrow with their last breaths. Too innocent and hopeful for a final farewell.

For him, for Mike Brines, it didn't matter. He probably spent his end annoyed that something got the best of him. She could hope there was some thought to who he was leaving behind, but even that would probably get batted back with some excuse about duty and sacrifice. Oddly, she understood. Gone was gone, and that was fine for the man, them, and her.

But something about his last words.

They kept playing in her head ever since she left the clinic. It must've been . . . close to what was 3:00 AM back home. Here in Portcullis, the day was about 25 hours long. Everyone had adapted to having an extra hour in the day, which was nice. But keeping time was a bizarre hybrid of relation back to what they knew and the Portcullis concept of intervals—widths—between pliable times of the day such as evening, night, dawn . . .

I'll see yer ass in the morning.

She shook again and wanted to slap herself. *It was a fling in a fucking combat zone. Fuck is wrong with me?* Yes, it was sad, even heartbreaking. That personal connection with a patient who didn't make it. There were regrets, a desire to understand how Captain Rath survived when Mike didn't. How . . . how the Lady Ceal, with all her magical powers to fight dragons, teleport, and make the heavens shake, couldn't even fucking find a body. But it was all on the level of sympathy for loss, *not* the brutality of losing someone close. Dr. Pat could even picture Mike's face, remember his warmth, and laugh at his less elegant moments without her throat tightening.

Nope, the singular issue was those words for some reason. The farewell that didn't even leave her with the dignity of a sappy love note. It was him ordering a piece of ass off the next day's breakfast menu.

A procession of knights in gleaming armor and flowing cloaks that blended with the falling snow approached. They were the retainers of Lords Colm and Ross, who could not make the trip. Dignitaries who would pay their respects to Mike's empty casket and the crop of fresh-planted corpses beyond. Then they would retreat to their lands, dress whites untarnished.

Meanwhile, Mike's memory would go down into their crypts beside Williamson—the Marine killed in his bedroom by an eight-foot doppelganger wolf.

What's the point?

Without a body, the coffin wasted space in an otherwise hygienic place to store cadavers. Dr. Pat appreciated the ceremony, of course, but Mike would've been fine if someone dropped his knife in any old hole.

That stupid knife.

Mike made that pint-sized machete himself, practically slept with it, and somehow forgot it on the last day of his life. Now it was the only thing left of him.

She glanced to her right, where it was hanging off Captain Saunders' left hip, nasty bone handle and all. Ron had held it together while delivering that sterile analysis of the avalanche and rescue attempts. But now, he was stiff at attention as if straining would keep Mike's ghost from coming over and tapping him on the shoulder.

All the Marines were hurting, even Corporal Nickels. He was Dr. Pat's least favorite and certainly a thorn in Mike's side. But for all those nights

Mike came back swearing up a storm about something the corporal did, there was always that level of... not respect. Connection. Easy to pass off as that macho *all Marines are bros, brah,* nonsense, but Nickels looked like a kicked dog right now, so maybe there was something to it.

The swish of steel against leather filled a silence she hadn't noticed. Dalmore's speech was over, it seemed. The knights each touched the tip of their bluish swords to Mike Brines' empty rock box and headed out into the field, performing the same ritual at each marker.

The city cemetery was nice: stone vaults and headstones among gridded walkways and grass plots. Much more elegant than the muddy field they kept beyond the mammoth North Wall. They called that one the Doormat—a shitstorm of shallow graves and stick markers reserved for Portcullis' enemies.

Benton ordering that disgrace decommissioned is one of the few things he's done right.

Behind the knights came a group of city officials—most new to the job—and local merchants. Master Walram made eyes at her, but she shut it down hard. Mike called him a scumbag once, and so it was written. *Fuck off.*

She did smile at their innkeeper, Uumhrat, who Mike loved antagonizing. It was a size thing. Mike was a strong guy, wide, the sort people got out of the way for. But Uumhrat was taller and a few shirt sizes up. Uumhrat was also the gentlest person she'd met since coming here. He took everything in stride, letting despair and strife wash off him as he served what joy he could to those in need. He lingered a moment longer than the rest to pay Mike his respects. It was touching.

It was also damned cold.

The speeches were done, and the over-capacity clinic needed her. The burn patients who survived the night were on the critical second day when sepsis became a concern. In a world lacking antibiotics or competent medical staff, she had to—

Another joined the precession.

Dr. Pat swallowed hard. Beyond the ceremony and the platitudes, this bereaved was different. The Marines were strong; theirs was a world of death and destruction. They'd hit the bottle, get into fights, or just break shit to deal with their pain. But the half-sized little girl in the plain white dress—the prettiest outfit she had—wasn't ready to lose her hero.

Ann.

Heads turned as she made her way to the casket, back straight and arms still. She was determined to see it through, but her usual smile was missing. Brave was the word for it, a little girl meeting the cold, brutal world for the first time. The revelation that forever wasn't.

It reminded Dr. Pat of the five-year-old version of herself she kept locked away in her head. It was a metaphor, protected by a soft bedroom with pink walls, for the goodness she refused to spoil in cynicism. Innocence, naivety, immaturity. Things unbefitting adults that most adults could benefit from.

Ann waited her turn, russet eyes welling but not breaking. Somehow, when they'd first arrived, Ann saw straight through Mike Brines' rough leather to the man inside—a nightlight against the terrors of her dark bedroom. For his time and comforting words that he called a *half-assed, get-away-from-me* pep talk, she had offered a warning about a monster that hunted her.

And then Mike made her problem his. He stood up to her boogeyman as only he could and showed her there were people out there who gave a shit. Ann drew from that strength, becoming more than anyone in any world might've imagined. When that boogeyman, unveiled as the Black Robe Isllor, came for her and thousands more again, he found fierce in the place of fear. She'd shone with that light, a hero's light that Mike had given her.

No one breathed as Ann touched the cold stone of the empty coffin. Her face held as she turned and approached Saunders. He looked down and offered a nod, a sympathetic smile. A blood transfusion from one anemic patient to another. Tears were about to flow.

Dr. Pat searched the crowd for support and found it standing in the front row beside the Marines at rest.

Micky.

If anyone gave zero fucks about ceremony or presentation, it was her. She had the emotional Rolodex of a news anchor, calling on and dismissing the perfect disposition with no attachment. Right now, she was glacial. Precisely what Dr. Pat needed.

Instead of breaking down, Ann handed a bundle to the tall Marine captain, who was always in heavy combat gear. Dr. Pat recognized it as Pintuck, a vaguely humanoid, hand-sewn doll with a button for a mouth. The eyes were long gone, and it was wrapped in a blanket. *Because it's cold out.* Saunders accepted it with a polite smile.

God, she's trying to make him feel better.

I'll see yer—

Nope! No more of that. Dr. Pat swallowed her entire emotional limbic system deep into her chest. It hurt, like squeezing a giant marble past her tonsils. But her head cleared, and the pressure behind her eyes vanished.

Her perspective on Ann changed immediately. Handing the doll—her security blanket—to Saunders became odd, disconnected from the purpose of the funeral. It was possible the permanence of death hadn't fully seated itself, and the child could not recognize how much she would need it in the coming days. Or perhaps the spark Mike had fired in her was still burning. That no matter how much she hurt, much in the way Mike had his whole life, she was driving on and no longer needed the doll.

Much as we all need to, Dr. Pat realized as her thoughts returned to her caseload at the clinic.

The ceremony ended with more fancy words from Benton. Then the empty box that represented the frozen bones of Gunnery Sergeant Mike Brines was interred.

"My lord," said Sergeant Orrugant as if his sloshing through the wet snow upon the allure did not suitably announce his presence. "Dalmore requests ye's fast return to the keep. A spire of uninked paper hath arisen only ye can smite."

Benton shared a smile with him. The former lieutenant of the old Portcullis Guard held much disdain for the charter and archival duties of office. The jabs had oftened when Benton assumed the offices of lord governor. They were dear, though, speaking to his heart as a man who longed for the road and the company of few chasing seasons and coin.

The sergeant joined his group—an unexpected gathering of Benton's sworn men from Oxhold and Lt. Maon of the Watch—atop the South Gate, watching the snow fall. What whitened Portcullis' streets in the early hours had since melted. Now even the high place of this wall was darkening to grey. A fell omen.

"Here now, Sergeant. Tell ye's master, Dalmore, our lord now holds his court in this pithy snow the like I hath naught seen," said Sir Thode trying to swell his chest beneath his white plate to match the former arena champion. Long ago, Orrugant beat Sir Thode in the unmounted melee, and a soreness had persisted ever since.

"Thode, by the cursed wraiths! What threat hath sprung ye from the warmth of Oxhold to the chill of these Widow's Tears?"

The knight's brow rippled with furrows. "What speak ye? Widow's Tears?"

"Aye," Orrugant opened a palm allowing the thin, wet snow to gather. "'Tis how it is called in Helidor. No doubt a man of the Palatine would know little of such." Orrugant was no knight of either the Ignes Glacies or the Palatine academies but still plucked their rivalries. The stout-hearted men of Ignes Glacies were forged in the south of Helidor, a cold place where even flame shivered. The Palatine was a product of the new age, placed in Durador with many vital institutions. Close to His Reverence.

Sir Thode blew out a puff of steam. His speech was oft slow to form and aided by waving hands and snorting. Orrugant allowed the dance to unfold with a smile beneath that black mustache. Finally, Thode regained control of his tongue. "Those banished to that dim realm are like to call all happenings and objects by their want for a lonely woman. Hath ye kin there? What name ye sword, Sergeant? Widow's Laughter?"

"Thode."

"Aye? And what be the sword's name?"

Benton hid his smile by facing out over the road south; the others rumbled with laughter. It worsened when Thode called for the name again, not knowing Orrugant had answered in earnest. Then it was unbearable when the knight demanded it as a matter of honor. The quarreling was a welcome reprieve from the city's burdens.

Long ago, the moments of men gathered in high spirits before battle, in victory, or staring into the night were plentiful. Benton walked with his companions beyond the confines of walls and courts. The wilds were rife with common and uncommon dangers, but they met those foes together. Never would they dream of gathering at a dry table to pass parchments filled with promises of aid in the form of one or two knives, a six of arrows (but no more), or two widths of fighting to be halted if rain should appear. They drank and ate around fire and spits, knowing the morning would bring strife, coin, and gnawing hunger for more.

"My lord," began Lt. Maon as Thode and Orrugant continued to spar. Benton kept one eye on it lest tempers begin to flare. Orrugant more than Sir Thode. "These ill-named Widows Tears are a strange sight after the Shade. Mayhaps the heat of Greth's Breath has blown into Ajid's Winter?"

It was a key concern. The unusual warmth, a boon in happier times, created the problem they had come to study. Only a few patches of white lingered before them upon the south road named Palings Pass. Each day the mountain roads remained passable gave the Genisans purpose to assault the city before spring. If they could move a sizable force into Galimay ahead of the heavy snows, no force existed to stop them.

Time. That is what a whitened road would give us.

Benton dared not let such a wish escape to the winds. Scianas was a world of miracles since the Retethering, and much could be made to fit the will and whim of people.

But not the weather.

The minds of rains and snows seemed close to man's reach, but to touch them, even lament them aloud, was fell. Forbidden. It invited judgment by a terrible power that cared naught for life, only to work undisturbed. "Widow's Tears," he echoed, diverting the talk from the greater pattern, "were so named because they fall wet but sparse and cold. Gone by morn."

"Naught of the warmth I should hope to marry," chuckled Lt. Maon.

Benton shrugged. "What we northrons see as a sign of false love, the stout of Helidor consider a strength. In such a barren and harsh land, a widow who cannot move on is a burden."

The young man, an educated sort from some forgotten tithe of the Rosses, gave a nod. "Aye, my lord. Still, methinks she might wait a tenday over the next morn."

"Aye, far too cold for my liking."

"'Twill freeze ye's wagging tongues sure as Thode's here," said Orrugant as Sir Thode entered a wordless spell of hand waving.

Lt. Maon tipped his head to the sergeant but pressed his interest. "Mayhaps these Widows Tears, much in the like of Helidor, offer us a beginning?"

The meaning was plain. What did desperate defenders desire most? Relief. Indeed, wise and appropriate, but such came with the entanglements that only years of experience in Galimay's courts could appreciate. "The coming days will tell much," Benton offered. Alas, Portcullis' allies had proven few.

The city's strength was nigh depleted. Former Lord Governor Elldren's estate—now in Examiner Creed's trust—had long been built of coin, not lands or men. Discussions with Council Lord Colm had deemed his forces were better positioned in the lower inlands to protect travel and trade. Lord Hamen Ross was dead, killed by Isllor Mortund, and his squabbling heirs could see naught beyond Tollshire's walls. And Benton's Oxhold had borne the brunt of Portcullis' tithe to Galimay's Fifth Army.

The Fifth Army that now laid decimated upon the slopes of Val'Narden. An entire generation of men was spent to feed the worms and brighten the ever-green grasses on the far side of the Dowdale Valley.

It was little wonder that Galimay now clenched.

The tell from travelers revealed that much of Greater Galimay south of the Palings was caught in the grips of fearful lords seeking to protect their own muddy plots. The Sapphire Branch remained formidable but contained within the cities to quell unrest. Durador sat mighty and silent with the vengeful Baylisses at its helm. Still, Ceal worked to fill the ears of any who would listen with promises of victory, coin, power, and rights. Alas, none had answered the call to defend Portcullis—the gateway to the world's last free lands.

And if they did, what might we feed them?

Since the withdrawal of the Sapphire Branch—Lord Artur Bayliss' Blue Cloaks—Portcullis had returned to a reliance upon its council lords—of which only two of five truly remained—for supplies. Bayliss had reaped Oxhold's lands during his oversight, and Colm sold much of his harvests in profitable markets south. In the now, thin soup would be hard-pressed to last them to the spring.

"Betwixt the Bark and the North Wall, Portcullis can hold against any assault," Benton added to the tone of hope. Thus, swords and boots mattered less than if only the roads would freeze. Then the Genisans would be forced to camp in the warmer north or even the season-less Dowdale Valley for the worst of Ajid's Winter. And time would be well in abundance.

Come spring, Galimay will be invigorated, and the armies shall come.

The thought was less rousing than amusing, a fine falsehood to keep hisself and men like Maon and Orrugant upon the wall whilst darkness gathered at their backs.

Sergeant Orrugant.

The former arena champion and lieutenant of the old Portcullis Guard did not come only to share jokes and news of piling parchments. "What was the sergeant's true purpose in joining us?" Benton asked now that the men had stopped bickering.

"Thought ye would never ask," said Orrugant before Lt. Maon could answer. "Teague and his lads said Examiner Creed looked inside the Vault. Said he found some foolery and wishes to speak with ye."

The Bark!

Benton's heart sank along with his hopes that a snowy road might matter.

———

"Clear, sir!" Sergeant Smith shouted back through the Vault's half-melted, half-blown-apart doorway. The air inside was a lot cooler and more breathable now. That massive gem was still disco purple, and the smooth walls no longer felt so close.

A tap on the shoulder let him know Saunders was coming through. The captain had been short on words during the ride over from the inn. Smith was feeling it too, and it had nothing to do with Benton calling them down here.

Gunny.

Him being gone was like the guests leaving after Thanksgiving. House got all quiet and weird, even though there were still plenty of people around. No one wanted to play hide and go seek or do much other than heat up leftovers. The spirit was gone.

"Want me to wait outside, sir?"

"Negative," the captain said, stopping at the sight of melted metal *and* stone. It was all glops of grey and coal with parts of the door and broken pieces of the quarried frame sticking out. Not hot anymore, hard as a . . . yeah, a rock. "Understood if you need some fresh air, though."

"No, sir. This hole kept us alive. If they was still writin' bibles, the Vault would be chapter one of the *Book of Smith*."

The CO didn't smile but let it in deep enough to say, "Without Ceal, that would've been a short chapter. Right, Benton?"

The statue in a white doublet and navy leggings—their version of a vest and some nice slacks—unhooked himself from that mesmerizing gem and said, "Aye, to mine great relief."

"Lost count of how many times she kept that fire off us. 'Preciate it, Benton," Smith said, wondering if he was cool enough to drop the lord part. When no one said anything, he chalked it up to some kind of privilege that came with all the Corsan Carre crap.

The Vault went back to library rules after that. Only noise was the murmur of Benton's peeps talking with Garcia and Light outside. Between the captain's grim demeanor and the city lord staring at his giant pulsing gem like it was their version of TV, the tension was two nuts too tight.

Smith opened his mouth to pop a conversation starter, a quick: *How's your dog, Palefang, doin'? He been around?* But the captain rallied and beat him to it. "So, would a fire-breathing, bullet-proof dragon that defies the physics of flight be considered . . . magic to you, Benton?"

Smith let the hint of a smirk play on his lips. The captain was a funny fucker when he wanted to be. Dry and rare like a fancy steak. Good to see it come out and well-deserved, too, considering these people were literally mages who scoffed at the entire concept of magic.

"Nay, my lady believes the Tel'racs wielded the Stochal Power. How could it be else? The Bark blocks the Quotidian, and the Base is wielded naught."

Even she doesn't know? Smith wanted to ask. Getting info on these Powers was tough since most locals who didn't have lord, sir, or *master* in their name were clueless. Kinda made sense being in medieval times. No internet meant the right people could withhold whatever information they wanted. But talking to Dalmore, who came and hung out for beers after taps a few times, had confirmed there were three Powers—two of which could be wielded. Leod liked to call the Quotidian the "Power of things." It needed a device to work, like electricity, but wireless and responded to voice commands. *Alexa, I got a magic wand. Can you hook me up with a fireball?* The Stochal was straight waggling fingers to make rabbits jump out of peoples' pants.

Ceal was jacked on Stochal, and everyone treated her like an absolute authority on the Powers. Her tossin' question marks was bad news.

"She hath spoken little of what was learned from the battle," Benton added. "Her mind and efforts focus upon the finding of allies."

"She doesn't waste time, does she?" asked the captain, moving toward the heart of the city's "magical" defense. It blocked the Quotidian, the system preferred by the Black Robes. The Quotidian also powered a lot of the city's lights, heaters, and indoor plumbing. Portcullis was apparently five-star before the Bark got installed.

Benton shrugged. "Nay. Ajid's Winter is yet warm and—"

"Same shit back home: it never snows. If you think that dragon or our losses have softened us up, nothing has changed. We'll make that abundantly clear."

Smith let the captain's conviction pump his chest and shoulders. *Ain't no question how much more we got to give.*

"Did you ask me down here for a SITREP?" Captain Saunders continued. "Our readiness and deterrence are outstanding. We are postured to outlast the enemy and the weather. Black Robes can't kill what they can't see. We can execute limited resupply and personnel transfers with Ceal to prevent us from getting siege-locked. And all that's before we add a brand-new perspective to warfighting: 500 years of tactical development tacked onto your swords and magic shit. And don't tell me it's not magic. To us, it is."

Benton sucked a shaky breath, and, for the first time, Smith noticed he was kinda pale. The purple light playing off his face wasn't helping, but homeboy seen a damned ghost. "Indeed, but so too does our design rely upon the Bark for protection and . . ." Benton's voice bled out, and all he could do was point.

A shiver rode the length of Smith's thick spine as he studied the Bark. It was like staring into a flashlight, but after some squinting, he spotted it. On the other side of the giant crystal was what looked like a hair resting on the surface. Practically invisible.

"Have you tried wiping it off?" asked the captain. Dead serious this time.

"It deceives. A crack through the sheath to the pith within. The Bark lives on only for a short time now. By Ajid's Spring, Portcullis will be defenseless."

Captain Saunders shook his head. "That scratch?"

"A fatal blow, in time."

Smith rounded the pedestal in case he was coming at it from the wrong angle, seeing just the stump instead of all the roots pushing up the sidewalk and climbing down into people's basements. Nope, just that little hairline.

Still, it made sense.

Back when he got his learner's permit, he followed one of those GU713 granite dump trucks too close and got a pebble pop in Mom's windshield. Tiniest chip ever, upper right corner. She didn't say nothing, so neither did he. A week later, it was a basketball-sized spiderweb, and they had to replace the whole damned thing.

Huh, maybe it's small enough to . . .

"Whatever Mendo did to it last time, Ceal repaired," said the captain, coming to the same conclusion. "Can't she do it again?"

"Isllor's damage was wrought of the Power; this is borne of material." Benton kicked a fallen stone beside the pedestal's base. "It cannot be repaired."

Smith eyed the stone, just something to look at. Then it dawned on him how much damage the ceiling had taken from the dragon. Cracked, fractured. Mom's windshield as fuck. It was a wonder the whole place hadn't come down on top of them.

Captain Saunders' jaw worked, maybe chewing up the first few words that came to mind as he connected the dots. It was easier to imagine some colossal strike from a circle of super mages channeling the incredible power of whoever this evil asshole Ajid was than falling debris. "So," the captain began when he found his voice, "all Mendo had to do was walk in here with a hammer and smash this piece of shit? Benton, man, we've got to work on layering your damned defenses."

Benton shrugged. "The days surrounding Isllor's return are dark, and I know naught of what stayed his hand. I think to approach the Bark, he first needed to usurp it, as he did with his wicked tool. But, when it was usurped, mayhap it served him to leave it in place?"

"Vault's a major security risk, sir," Smith said. He wasn't sure if the captain wanted his input, but he was pretty sure Gunny would've spoken up. Maybe not in so many words, but he definitely would've growled or something.

"Right," said Captain Saunders. "Benton, does this mean magic works here again? Are we facing an imminent threat?"

Smith felt a nip of adrenaline as every cubic inch of space suddenly became a potential enemy ingress. Black Robes had portals that could beam their asses here . . . anywhere. And if the past few weeks taught him anything, that's how they'd come if the Bark went down.

"Nay. The Bark holds for now, and I—"

"Smith," Captain Saunders said, voice cracking like a whip. "I want Marines guarding this installation around the clock. Two men, at minimum. Inside."

"Absolutely, sir." The guys were already running full days, but he could thin the over-cautious guard rotation at the inn. Probably set this pizza oven up with five, five-hour watches. Two guys could bullshit in here for that long before going crazy or needing to take a shit. One SAW or shotty in the rotation meant always ready to hold back some motherfuckery. Also . . . "Sir, could add overwatch right on top of this place."

"Good idea, talk to Francisco."

"Ah, Saunders," interrupted Benton. "The Corsan Carre are most welcomed here, but the Watch and Deadlies are capable of this duty."

"Benton, we're on an alien fucking planet cut off from everything we know. You, specifically your wife, are the only ones who can get us home. That makes our vestment in the Bark huge. From your talk of different cults and insurgent operations, I can't leave this to trust."

"The Anticult hath no power here!" Benton snapped. Smith reflexively took a step forward to make sure the lord governor bumped into 250 pounds of Kansas City street before the captain.

"As you were, Sergeant. Benton, two of your Watchmen and some Blue Cloaks are six feet under because of those *powerless* insurgents. Remember? That wasn't some shank after hours, either. They tried to kill PFC Licht in broad daylight."

"This disastrous deed happened when mine and my lady's gifts for the Sense were muted and dulled. Those rats were slain as they scurried to escape the quake of Isllor's fall."

"If your mental radar was so good, how did Mendo, Isllor, infiltrate in the first place? No, don't answer. I get it: sensing magic doesn't mean sensing intention. Point is we need to ensure no rowdy group of civilized folks gets it in their heads to put another dent in this thing."

Benton looked like he had more to say, maybe wondering what RADAR meant, but the captain had a good way of making his point even without having to understand every word. Gunny was good at that too, which was even better because the guy probably had the triple-abridged version of the dictionary as a kid. "We shall deploy a ten of Watch and Deadlies outside as another layer," was all Benton said.

"Great. Also, get a crew in here to make repairs and put a hard hat on the centerpiece of our defense."

"Aye."

"Next, we need a timeline. You said the Bark will fail before spring. My guess is that's about three months away. Uhh, twelve to fifteen tendays. Right?"

"Ceal will know more, but the soonest will be the deep of winter with our backs against the snow."

"That information does not leave this room. For now, the enemy threat is still conventional and ground-based. Between that wall and my Marines, we can hold. Nothing has changed. Got it?"

Benton nodded like a kid in a dentist's chair, promising not to eat any more candy. Smith figured that Bark had a lot more history behind it than he and the captain could understand. It'd be like showing Benton a picture of a burning cross and trying to get him to understand the generational horrors it represented in thirty words or less.

The captain stared at the lord governor for a moment like a dad hammering those last points in with his eyes. But he was done with this conversation. A million problems were happening at once, and the CO's mind was already moving into a new realm of damage control.

It was snowing again when they left the Vault, turning the medieval city back into a Christmas card. Garcia and Light were over by Benton's people. One of the knights—a dude named Thode, who Jersey liked to call Chode—was staring up at the sky like he had better places to be. The Watchmen were more grounded, studying the deep gashes through solid stone and the spots where the ground had turned to lava. Reverent. Apparently, that dragon was one of those legendary monsters they grew up hearing about.

And Gunny smoked it before getting swallowed by a mountain. Goddamn.

"All good, Sergeant?" asked Garcia.

Smith sensed the captain was in a rush to get back, so he made it short.

"We takin' over Vault security. Need you two in there, eyes open until I can get a proper rotation going."

"What? Yo, it's fuck-past lunchtime. How long we gotta watch this dandruff flake out?"

"Hour or two tops. Then we five-and-dime it and see how that goes for a couple days."

"Is another dragon coming?" asked Light.

"Naw. Remember them fools that fucked Licht? Captain thinks more of 'em is out there. Watch and Deadlies gonna work the perimeter, but the buck stops wit you. No one gets in unless cleared by the captain. Understand?"

"Ho now," said Sir Thode striding over. He had the swagger in that perfect ivory plate armor and sword hanging off his hip. It looked intimidating, but only because it took a 21st-century perspective to know the Pig could tear it all down in a second. "What sayeth our lord of this?"

"Benton's onboard," said Captain Saunders staring back at the giant stone igloo. The knight seemed to interest him less than the dusting of snow covering the scorch marks.

"Aye, with the stewardship of this great Vault. But doth he mistrust his sworn men to stand with the Corsan Carre?"

"Ask him, but guessing he has bigger plans than guard duty for the knighthood."

"Assuredly, Sir Thode," said Benton, breaking off from the Watchmen. "Be this weather Widows Tears or a proper snowfall, the Palings Pass is fated to close. Oxhold needs its steward, and Ajid's Spring shall need defenses risen and the able trained to fight."

Thode locked eyes with Benton. Instead of giving him lip, it was like they shared something. Then he said, "I shall depart this day, my lord."

Lieutenant Maon and Sergeant Orrugant were a harder sell because they started asking questions. Procedural stuff like *where we gonna get the men?* Benton iced it by saying he'd feed it through their chain of command, which was Chief Dalmore.

"Speak with Master Walram if ye wish canvass hung to make this weather bearable," he added before Lt. Maon left. Orrugant stayed back to organize the first watch while all the lowercase *j's* got dotted and *t's* crossed.

The march with the captain back to the inn was even quieter than before with the city noises muffled by the accumulating white fluff. Since there were no weathermen, weather reports, apps, or any sort of forecast, Smith could only guess how bad it would get. It also made him think about what Gunny's last moments were like. He hoped it was less like drowning in a frozen hell of icicles rammed into the throat, nose, and eyes and more like getting hit by a bus. Boom, done.

"Smith," said the captain when they reached the inn's front door. The day was getting grayer by the minute, and the temperature still dropping. Uumhrat's great room and that cow-sized fireplace were the only wants right now. But this was the Marines.

"Sir?"

The captain glanced over his shoulder before pulling him aside. "Wanted to take one and say you're doing an outstanding job. Brines is an incalculable loss, but you've naturally oaked up for the men. That's leadership, speaking man to man."

It was the *attaboy* Smith wanted, needed, but also feared. He reflexively stiffened his back and braced for the other shoe to drop.

"The enemy is up against a weather deadline. That dragon wasn't just a random hit. After weeks of ghosting us in the Lower Del, the Black Robes exposed themselves to support the attack. Maybe they hoped to drop the Bark and take us quickly like they tried with the Assembly Hall. Maybe Ceal was the target. Maybe it was all just to soften us up. Doesn't matter."

"They comin'," Smith said.

"Yeah. And when they do, it'll be the hammer. Benton and his people aren't ready." He paused to pan the quiet snowfall in the yard and street beyond. "Only ones looking out for us are us. You read? Team integrity and morale are critical."

"Yessir."

"As I said, you stood right up and filled the vacuum. But I want to make it official." He cleared his throat and straightened his already straight back. "Sergeant Smith, I need you to fill some hard-soled boots that were always two sizes too small."

Gunny. "Uh, sir. Pete, er Francisco, has a lot more experi—"

"He doesn't want it, need it, and it comes with personality conflicts."

Nickels. Also, some guys were a little nervous around Pete and his peculiarities. Great dude, super nice, but always like handling a loaded firearm. "Understood, sir. Uh, what about Captain Rath?"

"No. The men like you and respect you. Brines had that. He also knew when to take charge and when to listen. Existing rank structure will remain intact. You can rely on Corporal Nickels as your second or raise someone else. Your discretion. I'll make an announcement later when everyone is together."

"Won't let you down, sir."

"Right, let's get the guard schedule worked out. I've got a meeting with Ceal and then some council shit that'll drag till sundown."

"Sir, uh, one question."

"Shoot."

"What's our worst-case scenario here? Like with them Genisans hitting the city and maybe the"—he looked around to make sure they were alone; the captain didn't want the Bark to become public knowledge yet—"you know, our shields dropping . . ."

"We die, the mission fails, and Earth burns. Welcome to leadership, Sergeant."

CHAPTER 5

AMERICAN IDOL

"Is there a lunch?"

Dr. Pat felt a stomach rumble beneath a heavy bedding of flesh. "Shouldn't take that long," her voice spoke with the depth of a man's. Something was also wrong with the vocal cords. They were rough and dry, making the lungs work harder to get above a whisper. But her host didn't seem to notice or mind. His weight suddenly pooled in her legs as the elevator began to climb. "Besides, I didn't come to Dubai for the hotel lobster roll. There's a little hole-in-the-wall kitchen near Safa that I've been meaning to try. Tony says they make a ball aching kabsa."

"Do they serve alcohol?" asked the other guy in the elevator. Unlike the calamity of failing organs she had the pleasure of inhabiting, he was late thirties, clean-cut, and looking snappy in a gray, pin-stripe suit.

"Nah, but I'm sure they'll get you whatever you want upstairs. Fuckers are desperate. Hell, I walk in there and tell them I want some kabsa brought in by ten tiny slave children and fed to me by a member of the royal family, I'm betting we'd at least see a solid effort to get it done."

"Hand and foot for the privilege of inviting us into a trillion-dollar industry!"

A burning sensation came from the chest. Reflux. Dr. Pat had never felt such a thing, and the thought of spicy food made it worse. Still, the body and mind of her host were divorced from his failing health. He was confident, propped up by mountains of wealth. "Yeah, I been to a million of these pitches. All flash 'cause they ain't got nothin' under the hood. Probably spent their whole seed round flying us out here."

The younger man, black and gelled up top, stroked his sharp goatee. Then he froze and said, "You don't think they're . . ."

Laughter belched up, giving Dr. Pat a taste of what her host ate for breakfast. Something with peppers, and she didn't dare try to access the memory of it going down. "They better be. Only reason we're here is 'cause I wanted to see if that Kôz shit was bleedin' across the gulf. Remember Colonel Feyer, our consultant on the solid-state hydrogen project? Got a few bourbons in him last week, and let me tell you, no one has any fuckin' idea what's going on right now in Pakistan, Iran, or even Afghanistan. So, yeah, worst case, we get a little local gab on the way out. Makes for a cool story, y'know?"

"I thought we were here to get out of your wife's birthday."

The elevator bell dinged.

A team in business casual greeted them with warmth, handshakes, and solid eye contact. Perfect English filled with wit and trendy sayings came to their ears. The jokes were on point, and sure enough, the conference room had a full bar. Her host grabbed a bottle of water to cool the burn around his lower esophagus. His associate—an American named Robert Boyd—poured three fingers neat, gulped it down, and poured another. If it bothered any of the plastic smiles settling in on the other side of the table, it wasn't evident.

"Thank you for coming, Mr. Da Cunha," began the thin, middle eastern fellow directly opposite. He seemed Americanized, recognizable haircut, and there wasn't a trace of an accent. Dr. Pat found herself fascinated and impatient at the same time. Her host, however, was more focused on when he'd get a chance to slop down that spicy version of kabsa. "We promise you will find it well worth the trip."

"Right. And call me Allen, please. Da Cunha sounds too much like work."

They laughed at the joke and dimmed the lights. As the projector spooled up, Allen's eyes floated down to the slide counter. Three. Probably a 60-minute video jammed into a pirated version of Microsoft PowerPoint, *he thought. Dr. Pat agreed, but she'd rather watch a video than read bullet points.*

The speaker introduced himself as their company president and began a history lesson on goat herding in Pakistan. Robert poured himself another drink—with an ice cube this time—and Allen listened with thinning patience. The goat herders eventually abandoned their nomadic lifestyle and built a farm. The narrative was harrowing for Dr. Pat because the speaker omitted important nouns and transitions. Allen was confused as well, irritability rising. But he maintained a placid outlook, obviously a veteran of people testing his patience. His stomach, however, was the dumping ground for his anger. Dr. Pat wished she could get him to grab the bottle of Tums she knew was in his left breast pocket.

"Is this going somewhere?" Robert finally asked.

The company president folded his hands and smiled. "I just wanted to see how long I could keep fucking with you guys."

Allen shoved back and stood, face flushing with heat. "You guys a bunch of jokers? This some sort of prank?"

The president never stopped smiling, enjoying every moment. Allen turned and headed for the door, but Robert didn't move. Probably too hammered.

"I enjoy these moments of tension tight enough to snap steel," continued the president. "The peak when you think it cannot get any worse and then suddenly you realize something so extraordinary that everything is forgotten and forgiven. It goes from the pit of aching despair to your Christmas Day."

"The fuck are you talking about?" Allen snapped back at the table. To his surprise, Robert was still seated. He was studying a jar of blue liquid. Probably booze. "Rob, we're done here."

"You've . . . it's . . . it's stable? You've stabilized it?" asked Robert in as stone-cold sober a voice as Allen had ever heard.

The president lit a match and dropped it into the liquid, drawing a gasp from Robert. The flame hissed out, leaving Allen confused.

"Stable at standard temperature and pressure."

Allen's eyes flicked to the projector screen, now on the second slide. It was all a bunch of technobabble he couldn't understand. That's why Robert was here. But fuck these guys. Some blue liquid wasn't enough to—

"Holy shit, it's light," said Robert lifting the glass. "I mean, un-fucking real. Jesus, Allen, sit. This is, I mean, it depends on how you make it, but—"

"The process is proprietary, but collection and manufacture are solar powered."

"Scale?"

"We have seven rigs capable of supplanting 5% of annual global energy needs. In six months, another twenty rigs will be operating near capacity."

Robert whistled, and Allen returned to the table. Manufacturing was Allen's wheelhouse, in addition to capitalization. "Rob, why don't you tell me what it does before we start talking about how much we can make?"

"It keeps combustion engines in the clean energy game," said Robert.

"Impressive," Allen said. "So, let's say you really created some miracle gas-

oline and can eat the ass out of the market. What the hell do you need venture capital for? And why haven't I seen you on the cover of Time?"

"Because . . ." The third slide appeared, a redrawing of the middle east where Pakistan's borders had expanded to engulf Iran and most of Afghanistan. "Our brand could use a facelift."

Dr. Pat shivered; the last seconds of the dream still buffered in her brainstem. She rolled over, expecting a wall of warmth, but it was only empty sheets.

I'll see yer ass in the morning.

She squeezed her eyes shut. Mike's words were starting to bug her. They were like a nagging knee injury throwing her off balance at the worst possible times. Typically, memory association made sense: a stimulus—environmental or physiological—tapped on a particular nerve cluster and out banged the memory. Rain at the window meant soft flannel pajamas and stuffed animals held close. A psychologist would say Mike's last words came from the emptiness of her bed at dawn when he promised he would be here.

But that's not how it felt.

Instead, that empty pillow had shouted at her. Blasted through her mental defenses and smeared her face in the loss.

She wiped her eyes and whispered, "Mike, I promise I'll grieve for you later. Right now, I've got a job to do." And with that, she rebuilt the walls she'd placed at the funeral. After a minute of silence, she felt better. Mostly because his ghost jumping out of that pillow was a real possibility in this crazy world.

Micky was waiting for her at the Marine checkpoint by the stairs. She was in clinical uniform but somehow still looked slutty, twirling her brown curls as Captain Rath regaled her with a stumbling story. An elephant could invade the second floor, and Rath would never notice.

Ugh.

With Dr. Pat's mental defenses up, it was hard for her to differentiate a pang of jealousy from blind rage. Rath had a thing for Micky, which was fine and healthy. Most men had a thing for Micky, who, after a brief period of emaciation from capture, torture, and unbelievable trauma, was a specimen of perfectly placed curves. But this wasn't about competition or longing.

It was about the fucking guy who Mike died saving. Died saving because that was the chain of command.

"Dr. Pat!" Micky chirped, slipping away. "I was gonna let you sleep in, but hey, you won't believe it. I met this chick in the lobby."

"Not now Mi—"

"Pat. She does hair! Like, hair. It's a thing, and this afternoon we are getting fucking did."

So many questions and so little emotional availability. Yes, Dr. Pat once had a specific stylist she trusted to rein in her dirty blonde mop a few times a year. But MSF and combat zone cleanup tours shrank the need for frivolities. A reliable water purifier was worth a thousand haircuts. "Micky, there is no *after* work. Wake, work, sleep. That's the cycle until the clinic returns to treating tooth worm and dispossessed hiccups."

Micky snorted. "You ever watch NASCAR? It's the one where the racecars look like real cars, and it goes on for hours. All they have to do is keep going around a circle a hair faster than the other guy, and they win. But you know what? They can't carry enough fuel or tires or oil. Honestly, I only saw it once, and I was pretty drunk, but the point is they have to make a pitstop. Totally stop their car when they've been like an inch ahead of the guy in second place the whole time. Then they get buzzed, fueled, and shot back out of that cannon to try and catch up. It's necessary and budgeted, Pat. You need to refuel."

More sleep, not less hair. What would Mike say? *I'll refuel when I'm dead.* It didn't sound quite so motivational now. "Some medieval hack job is going to help how exactly?"

"Oh, uh, hehe. They do nails too. And uhm," she cut her eyes to Captain Rath, and her voice went deep sultry. "Think of it as a pitstop."

Dr. Pat's cheeks heated. "Micky!"

The girl took off downstairs, leaving no choice but to follow. It was that or stand in awkward silence with the drooling benefactor of Mike's sacrifice.

The inn's great room was packed. Since the Corsan Carre stuff started, the place had become a medieval A-list club. The only reason there wasn't a line at the door was because the Watch spotted what they called "wayward folks" a mile away and diverted them.

Missing, however, were the rich smells of fried dough and sizzling meats that would greet them back when the Blue Cloaks were in charge.

Uumhrat's pantry was low as anywhere else, forcing his menu to rely on dried grains and ever-thinning stocks of protein and fats. Still, between him and his now robust cooking staff, they worked wonders.

The spread on the buffet was appetizing, but an ironic emptiness had Dr. Pat feeling full, or at least intolerant of being filled. She could explain the psychosomatic physiology behind it in length, but that was also a waste of energy. Every ounce of her needed to go to work.

Outside, the front porch ended with her laced boots crunching into about three inches of snow. The air smelled clean, and it was cold—every shaded surface sat crystal-dusted. It wouldn't last. The sun—what the Portcullisers called Bergreth's Lamp—was already hard at work.

Half of the rascal rows of slate roofs populating the city had already shed the pale. Gates Street was melted down to grey cobblestones but still icy. Instead of salting the roads and wrapping their wagon wheels with chains, the Portcullisers just added extra horses.

"Pat, you have to admit that was cool," said Micky as Dr. Pat caught up with her by Uumhrat's wrought iron gate. Now they faced that dreaded daily decision: hail a carriage or hoof it. The streets were perfectly walkable and filled with people, but it would be a trudge through pure slush. No way was medieval footwear up to the task of staying dry.

"What was?" Dr. Pat asked. She caught eyes with Sergeant Teague overseeing the little guard post across the way. Understanding, he sent his men scrambling.

"Um, the dragon?"

It felt like so long ago. How many days had it been? "Right, we haven't had a chance to—"

"Talk. I know! And none of that henhouse crap Marie used to be all about, neither. Real shit. Adversity. You know? Everyone coming together and battling a freaking monster. We did that, Pat."

The doctor in her gave a polite smile. Micky was too scattered-brained to see the real-world consequences of that fight. Mike aside, it had taken a piece of these people to survive. Not just in terms of the hands-on fighting but the psychology of impending death. Back in the States, most mass fears were of economic disasters or disruptions in cold-chain supply lines driving a run on yogurts at the supermarket. It was stressful and demoralizing, but mortal terror was rare.

The fear here was real.

The streets had gone from vibrant and bustling to quiet and suspicious. Every day brought more drunks stumbling through the alleys. Robberies and fights over food had spilled out of the Sticks and reached the polished steps of Eastside Rise. That any of the Portcullisers kept to their routines was impressive.

"Milady, ye want a ride to the post?" called Watchman Stebbin from a two-horse carriage.

"Might fine morn fer it," said Micky, trying to mimic what she heard when the locals spoke. It had taken some sleuthing to determine how people on a different planet could speak English. Turned out it was an intrinsic property of their magical—but not really magical—mineral Renderstone. One of its basic functions was to act as a translator, somehow conveying a speaker's intended message in terms the listener would understand, which was variable too. Ask someone else, and they might've heard Stebbin say, "Miss, would you like to travel to the post?" Same meaning, but different. Still, it was a step up from social media, where everyone just heard what they wanted to hear.

Dr. Pat expressed her thanks to Sergeant Teague.

"Anything," he said, helping her into the carriage. "For the *Corsan Carre*."

That last part almost got a tongue-click.

Was it insane to hope that Sergeant Teague was always this accommodating? Or maybe appreciated her and the Marines' efforts to help the city through a bad time? At the very least familiarity from their daily commute by now. But no, none of that applied here.

"Fucking Corsan Carre," she muttered after the carriage started rolling.

Micky rolled her eyes. "Girl, of all things."

"What? Profiting off a lie?"

"Technically, you don't know that for sure. But even if it is, what's wrong with owning it? If everyone back home suddenly made you the face of the . . . I don't know, the Afghan relief mission. Not just a doctor, but the chick in charge. If your image landed a flood of funding and support for the displaced, would you kick that out of bed because it wasn't completely true?"

"I . . ." Micky had a point. People rallied behind flags, symbols, leaders, and heroes. Not because these things had innate power, but because one-day society decided *that's our cause!* The Corsan Carre stuff was a cause looking for a willing victim. Victims like a group of survivors from war-torn Pakistan who had crossed worlds. The perfect outsiders.

"Exactly. Benton and Ceal get to promote us for their Procult, and we don't have to slosh through the snow."

My kingdom for a taxi! "You don't see the problem?" Dr. Pat asked. "What happens when the threat of war wanes and people start digging into the Corsan Carre bullshit? I mean, if the Church back home named a new Jesus or even Anti-Jesus, the world would tear into them, looking for flaws and threads of corruption. That's what people do, Micky. So how long before all those mighty lords with huge armies come looking to shut down some cult riling up the masses?"

"The Procult is about as close as Galimay comes to religion, Pat. They won't dig because they believe. And the naysayers aren't much of a problem until they come over that wall."

"What if they want me to turn water into wine?"

"Sergeant Smith could do it. I mean, he needs grapes, some vats, and a little time but . . ."

"Any miracle, then."

Micky's smile faded, and those brown eyes intensified. "Depending on who you ask, it's already happened."

Ceal.

It always came back to that woman. On the outside—now that Black Robe Mendo/Isllor wasn't living in her head anymore—she was likable, poised, and proper. She was a movie star, the one who took the time to sign autographs and pose for pictures. TMZ had zero dirt on her, and everything she did was for charity.

All fake. Anyone who dared look past the presentation could see a pattern of behaviors that told a different story altogether.

Lady Ceal was a puppeteer. Every action, every second of her day, worked toward a hidden agenda. Sometimes there was overlap with other people's interests, but often there wasn't. Oh sure, she made it seem like her efforts were on behalf of everyone, but then, poof, she'd be asking for forgiveness as the cosmic scale tipped in her favor again.

And no one else sees it!

The woman could cover her tracks like a career congressman, but Pat wasn't about to forget what happened on the South Wall. While (allegedly) under the Black Robe's dementia spell, Benton had tried to throw Ceal over the side. It was only because Dr. Pat rushed up and pleaded for him to stop that Ceal was alive. Bam, timely intervention saved her life.

Except.

That didn't fit the narrative, especially the part when double-apeshit Benton tried to cut Dr. Pat in half with his sword. Instead of owning the mistake, Ceal spun the story into some extraordinary event that coincided with Benton kissing her awake or breaking some spell or whatever.

Fairy tale stuff.

Because Dr. Pat happened to be nearby, Ceal coolly called it the fulfillment of Prophecy, slapped them all with the Corsan Carre label, and cemented them into a world of unknown obligation.

"You could learn a lot from her, Pat."

"Who?" she asked, refusing to acknowledge any occupancy of thought by that woman.

"I love it when you're catty. But you can't ignore her forever. We're on their turf operating—as the Marines would say—at an extreme disadvantage. Hell, most born and bred Portcullisians have misguided notions about the magic stuff. Half of them don't believe, another half see something happen and rationalize it against the sun rising and trees growing. Then the other half is rich enough to know Ceal's the queen bitch of magic tricks."

It was aggravating when Micky started slinging numbers that added up to less or more than the expected sum. And that's why she did it, to get under her skin. "Put me in the don't care group."

"Oh girl, you care. When Benton tried to take off your head, something happened you can't explain. Benton is no joke; that sword should've landed. But it didn't."

"Ceal probably—"

"No. That moment humbled the fuck out of her." Micky drew closer and lowered her voice. "She may not be your bestie, but she's the rock-solid authority on superpowers. And you've got her ear. Don't piss that away."

The carriage creaked to stop before Dr. Pat could push a solid counterpoint through tight lips. "Sorrier sight than it used to be," shouted the driver, "but here we be at the Provincial Post."

The former keep of the Sapphire Branch Blue Cloaks still bore plenty of majesty with its soaring bluestone and arched windows. It was only on closer inspection (or after looking up) that the damage was apparent.

The top three floors of the central tower had collapsed, reducing the building to a five-story cube. That much stone rubble was concerning at first, but Examiner Creed's people found the structure sound if in need of some interior gutting. The clinic operated out of the first sublevel, where the air was reasonably dry. Patient rooms were being added in the upper portions as the cleanup efforts progressed. Unfortunately, there was much more work to do than had been done.

Micky thanked Stebbin, dipping her chest just enough to get the guy's brain into a tug-of-war between duty and objectifying a Corsan Carre. Dr. Pat imagined the internal struggle like a prominent churchgoer checking out Jesus' backside. *Ass is ass,* was what Mike would've said.

I'll see yer ass in the morning.

Dr. Pat shuddered at the lapse and hurried through the slushy, dripping streets into the keep. A wood fire burned in the soot-streaked atrium, a necessary use of fuel to make an otherwise horrid waiting room tolerable. The girl, behind the little reception desk, Pechel, waved. She was a young, pimple-faced thing. Yet somehow married and nine months pregnant.

No way she should be working.

Wisewoman Alena had even let it slip that the birthing plan involved a six-width break from work to push the baby out, and then she'd finish her shift. Horrified, Dr. Pat argued it up to a half-tenday. The Portcullisers laughed, they all laughed, but Pechel was more smiles than bloat face since.

"Pleasant morning," said Alena, emerging from the dark stairwell. She had that end-of-a-double-shift hunch, and her forehead was straining to hoist the load from her eyelids, but her face was bright as Christmas. "None were taken in the night."

Dr. Pat nodded. While she was dreaming about investment opportunities in Dubai, Alena was here chewing her nails over their severe burn patients. Most were out of the woods, which meant providing aftercare for people who would've typically died. A multi-disciplined approach involving skin grafts, surgical relief of contraction, and physical therapy to restore mobility was required now. Dr. Pat had a good portion of the knowledge but few of the tools. Fortunately, they had some time to stitch leechdoms and best clinical practices into workable treatment plans. Cooperation was key.

"Before I am sucked into the softness of a bed, one of the . . . one of your fellows is here. David," said Alena.

Dr. Pat felt a prick of adrenaline. "Why? Has Licht's condition changed?"

"I think nay, but still he waits above. Shall I come?"

PFC David Licht had sustained heavy trauma during the Assembly Hall fight. Easy enough to repair, but because this was a world of magic, his presentation was unusual. It was a situation for which modern medicine was ill-equipped. "Please."

Buontempo was outside the patient room chatting with one of the Wisewomen. Josina was a younger version of Alena, non-parous. If she was seeing anyone, it was not evident as she giggled and fidgeted at the Marine's every word.

Mike's memories stirred beneath Dr. Pat's professional mindset. He had been clear about the men "keepin' yer dicks in yer own hands" and "not fuckin' any aliens." He was never sold on the Portcullisers being entirely human.

Now he's gone, and both Saunders and Rath have bigger fish to fry than keeping a bunch of hard-bodied Marines away from the ladies.

Alena frowned at Josina, but before she could open her mouth, Micky blew past, words flying. "Hither do we wandereth with thine vows muted and honor soldeth for a peck and a pence, Buontempo? And ye. Josina, be it? Lusting, sinful eyes seeking to planteth the serpents kiss to destroyeth the Corsan Carre? Why dost thou forsake us, motherfucker?"

The Marine cocked his head. Josina, however, went white. Like, severed a major artery, white. "I . . . I . . . milady, I knew naught of . . . I beg thee, we hath only spoken kind words to—"

"Corrupt." Micky walked a circle around the quivering girl. Dr. Pat wasn't sure what prompted the outburst, but her number one fan's eyes were playful. "You wish him powerless, on his knees before your glory so that you might be lifted higher than the Corsan Carre."

"Never!" she dropped into a low curtsey. "I only—"

"You like the rush. His face, his jokes, his attention."

"Aye, I admit joy when he spake to one such as myself. But—"

"And now you've ruined him."

"Micky, come on," began Buontempo.

"Look at how he grovels! A beggar ye hath made of thim!"

Thim? Dr. Pat wondered how that fake word translated.

"Nay, oh how I . . . please, I meant nothing. Nothing! Alena, ye know of me; I know naught of the sinister," Josina said, but Alena's expression was unreadable. She probably had no idea what to make of this exchange. Josina turned back to Micky. "Please, is there naught I can do?"

"One egg of a hen whoeth did be stretched by the mightiest yard cock. Two jars of vinegar—one in which the egg goeth and the other to sear the cloacal sin from your face and hands. Keep the egg in the vinegar for a ten-day. Then you gotta eat it."

Josina nodded, furiously committing the disgusting details to memory.

"And keep your distance from Buontempo, no matter how he might beg your approach."

"Aye, yes, as ye say, milady. I . . . I must . . . I am needed," she stammered before running for the stairs.

Buontempo reached after her, mouth agape, but let it go. "Goddamn, you chicks are territorial," he said.

Micky ignored him like the whole thing never happened. "Do you need me to stick around and help with Licht, or should I check in with the Wethands?"

"We're fine," Dr. Pat managed. The display was weird, even for Micky. It's not like Buontempo and Josina were making out or wrapped around each other. Just some flirting. *What the hell?*

As Micky sashayed down the hall—*crazy!*—Dr. Pat forced her thoughts back to the reason they'd come. Patient Room Four used to be a doorless cubby that slept three Blue Cloak guardians. A couple of wooden tables, a chair, and a pile of boiled cloth now resided in the place of bunks and armoires. Inside, PFC David Licht was sitting in the chair, face still scrunched from trying to process Micky's tirade.

"Reason you're here?" Dr. Pat asked Buontempo.

"We were just relieved from the Vault, and Licht mentioned needing a checkup. Thought we'd stop by before hitting the, uh . . . well, I was going to make a joke about medieval clubs, but Micky kinda killed the moment."

Dr. Pat smiled as a legitimate medical explanation came to mind. "She's just helping everyone minimize the transmission of xenopathogens."

"Xeno—what?"

"Alien STDs," she said. It was witty, but the concern over infectious disease was real, considering they were all immunologically naïve to Scianas. So far, they had done well: two incidents of emesis after Nickels and Fischer ate lunch at a pop-up stand in the Sticks, and a mild upper respiratory infection passed through three weeks ago. But there were no guarantees going forward.

"Yes, ma'am." The way his eyes were shifting back and forth meant he would at least consider the possibility before unzipping.

Unlike hypocritical Micky. But that was another story.

PFC Licht brightened when she finally entered. Most patients did, but only because they'd been waiting so long. It was one of the constants between here and back home.

There was no chart to examine, or computer prefilled with patient information. Just him beneath the warm glow of four tall-flamed lanterns and Dr. Pat's working knowledge of his condition. "Sorry for the delay. It's a mess out."

He stomped his wet boots. "I think my toes are still frozen."

"First big snowfall?" she asked, inspecting his eyes and complexion. Licht was a Florida native. Not a military brat who spent some time there, but a lifer who went 0-18 surrounded by heat, swamps, and oranges.

"When I was a kid, we'd head up north to see my aunt in Cedar Rapids. One Thanksgiving, we got snowed in. I remember it being a lot of fun, not so much the cold and wet."

Complexion was good, pulse steady at 60-65 beats per minute. Of course, it quickened after she touched him, but she managed to grab the initial rate. Tidal breathing was regular, and the faint bags under his eyes indicated an early start to his watch. "Dad moved us around a lot," she said. "But we would home base in upstate New York whenever he was assigned to an unaccompanied posting. A foot or two of snow was common."

"Not for me. Any bit of cold, not even freezing, turns my fingers white." He held up his left hand where the pink flesh ended at the distal interphalangeal joints. The fingertips were ghostly, but she ruled out frostbite immediately.

"It's Raynaud's Syndrome. Your blood vessels are hypersensitive to cold and tighten up when exposed. Hand warmers help, but you can try swinging your arms around if they're unavailable. It forces blood into the extremities and reopens flow."

His eyes widened as he flexed the pale fingers. Then he flicked his hand a few times and looked at them. Deep red overtook the white. "Cool."

Overall, PFC Licht was in good shape. After the penetrating and compression injuries he received from the Assembly Hall collapse, he would not be here if not for multiple surgeries and Alena's Apperis Sap. But the real question was whether he would be here tomorrow or ten minutes from now.

Dr. Pat sucked a breath. *Time to check the foreign body.*

Alena stepped in as the Marine lifted his tan t-shirt. "Master Smith Tityrus lent me his Tap-Crystal," she said. "It tells him the purity of infused Renderstone in tap-finished works. Mayhaps, it has a Sense for this injury." She pulled out a smooth six-by-one-inch iron rod with a clear crystal somehow fused onto the end. If not for the weight of solid iron, it could have passed for a dollar store toy.

She held the Tap-Crystal above the two-inch scar on the Marine's trim, mid-lateral abdominal region. The muscles rippled beneath the skin, tensing in anticipation of the crystal making contact. Neither the kid's abs nor the supra-splenic scar was what held their attention, though.

It was the faint green glow emanating from beneath it all.

The intensity had diminished over the past month, but it still looked like he had swallowed—well, maybe not *swallowed*—a green lightbulb. It was insufficient to cut through his clothes and give away his position—a concern Mike always had—but sufficient to make a nighttime swim awkward.

Best they could tell, it resulted from the initial attack the Black Robe launched on the Assembly Hall. Captain Saunders described it as a white hula hoop expanding suddenly and ripping through the city's leadership. Everyone it touched turned to ash, with a lot of boiling fluids and smoking flesh along for the ride. Everyone except PFC David Licht, that is.

"Keep wondering if it's radioactive, you know?" said Licht.

It was one of the first things she had investigated. By a minor, practically useless miracle, the Marines had salvaged several dosimeters from their wrecked helicopter. "We kept the badge on for 24 hours, nothing."

"Maybe it comes and goes?"

"Radiation toxicity would present with readily identifiable symptoms. Also, in a world where my physics classes still matter, radioactive decay is a constant, predictable process. But since there may be other emissive phenomena here on Scianas that we cannot identify, maybe Alena's instrument will be informative."

The Marine nodded as Alena swept his abdomen. She was methodical, almost following a gridded search pattern. "If this greenish glow is of the Quotidian, the metal will cool," she said. "If it is the Stochal, it will warm." The frown that followed said it all: the spirits weren't talking. "Methinks we are too far from the splinter within. A chill or bit of heat may go unfelt."

Dr. Pat wanted to roll her eyes. Magic or not, Alena was throwing shit at a wall hoping something would stick.

Everything changed when the crystal touched Licht's scar.

There was a noise, like ice popping under a heavy pour of bourbon, but it was lost as Alena cried out and the tool clattered to the floor. The whole ordeal sent Dr. Pat a good foot backward.

To be clear, Dr. Pat's recoil was not out of fear but in response to an outburst. A totally normal physiologic reaction. Evolutionary. People who didn't jump back got the horns of an alien tentacle popping out of a human patient in a non-terrestrial environment. The second she composed herself, questions and some choice phrasing piled up behind her lips.

Then she saw the Tap-Crystal.

A sleeve of white frost encased the iron rod. Easily another parlor trick if not for the look on Alena's face as she stared at her hand.

Frostbite.

"Jesus, what the hell did Master Tityrus give you?" Dr. Pat asked, grabbing a boiled cloth. "It's dangerous. Let's get you downstairs and—"

"Nay, the hand is naught," Alena said, waving away the cloth. She fixated on PFC Licht. "Ye should be dead. A burst of frigid blackflame. What . . . what creature can hold such potency within the self? What Power keeps ye's flesh bound?"

The Marine did not chuckle at the display as perhaps some of his brethren would've. He went bug-eyed. "Like a bomb?" he asked, poking at the area. With Ceal's help, they had determined that whatever might be in there was indistinguishable from his tissues. Either it was trace foreign bodies—like buckshot—that were too small for Ceal's magical x-ray vision to detect, or a sort of latent capacitance. Dr. Pat figured the latter was his best bet because it would discharge over time, like an old acid battery stored on the garage slab.

"No, it's . . ." Dr. Pat began, accustomed to having her brain churn up an immediate and correct response. But nothing came. Alena also looked surprised that her lips weren't spouting advice, truisms, or even round-about comfort. If anything, she was resisting the urge to step back in case the bomb thing wasn't completely insane.

"Fuck do I do? Is it gonna blow? I could . . . I mean, I can't go back to the inn. Can't be around people. I—"

Dr. Pat grabbed his bare shoulders and looked him squarely in the eye. "It's been two months. If you were going to explode, it would've happened when it was glowing much brighter."

He nodded, extrapolating that the dimming process meant it might disappear one day. It was enough to stop the hyperventilating, at least.

"Alena," she continued, "this Tap-Crystal is usually used on metal, right?"

"Aye. Never upon flesh to mine knowing."

"Right, so not calibrated for living tissue. That's a good reason to take these results with a grain of salt. We'll report it to Captain Saunders, but . . ." She trailed off again. Nothing here was going to convince Saunders that PFC Licht was safe. More importantly, Alena's face said it all: he should've exploded. So why didn't he?

The words *Corsan Carre* spilled across her neural folds into a hole that medical and scientific knowledge couldn't fill. Hell, those two couldn't even dig this hole in the first place. But it felt fake, like shrugging off weather patterns to acts of God or mental illness to demons. There was another explanation; she just needed to consult with someone who understood—

"Lady Ceal must advise us," whispered Alena as if there were no greater authority in all the world.

Dr. Pat opened her mouth to let fly the backlog of venom collecting in her tonsils when Pechel appeared in the doorway. She was wide-eyed, breathing hard, and did not seem to notice her heavy stomach dragging her shirt's neckline down to expose her plump, vascularized breasts.

"Something hath happened. The streets are taken to madness!"

CHAPTER 6

ORDERLY

Captain Saunders wasn't late. Running behind, delayed, and prioritized elsewhere were better equipped to explain why he missed the Meet.

The morning was stacked. Not quite at the level of packaging a rifle company for deployment, but people were pulling him in more directions than usual. Dalmore's request that they inspect the North Wall had topped the list because it was foundational. It also involved a relatable product of sound engineering and physical principles that gave their defense plans a common frame of reference.

It is a wall of stone and some tricks, Dalmore had said. *As tricks battle tricks, we can but hope men and metal battle the stone.*

The mighty structure spanned the canyon leading into Portcullis, which contained the only practical route through the Paling Mountains into Galimay. Its strategic importance could not be understated and while it looked sturdy enough to hold back the great flood and a well-aimed asteroid, nothing beat a hands-on inspection. Especially after Benton and Examiner Creed had verified it as a point of failure during the First Battle of Portcullis a year ago.

Saunders enjoyed the walkthrough. It was ten stories at its height, giving an incredible sense of power over the fields, rocks, and road below. They were high enough to see the distant valley beyond, making it hard to imagine a fighting force arriving fresh after the long climb up the mountain road. The wall was also tiered, offering defenders multiple points of elevation to rain hell on the enemy and ostensibly cut the knees off any attempt to scale.

What if they try to gain entry through the lower tiers? Saunders had asked.

The answer was evident when they stepped out onto one. The exterior access points were flanked by iron cages which soldiers could poke spears through. Farther out, the battle promenade was cubbied with wooden shutters and braziers. About half the fighting positions could be closed to enemy fire. The other half had waist-high racks of iron spikes ready to hinder climbers.

Dalmore admitted that fire and steel could breach the shutters, and hooks could tear down the spikes. But the effort to secure and prosecute that approach would be greater than focusing on the main gate in the first place.

And the main gate was no joke.

The entrance to Portcullis was a tunnel running through the deepest part of the wall. It was secured by a series of heavy steel grates. The walls were lined with hidden doors that could launch entire rooms full of soldiers and sharps into the claustrophobic tube. The high, arched ceiling was impregnated with firing ports from the second tier. Arrows, gunfire, spilled coffee, and piss alike could rain down with near impunity.

Of course, in the first battle, the enemy had flown over the wall when Ceal's people—or maybe just her, it wasn't clear—faltered in their defense against what Dalmore called *tricks*. The Bark stopped all that, meaning unless the enemy waited until spring, they had to face the whole wall with pre-gunpowder, medieval tactics.

God help them into their early graves.

He and Dalmore had grunted and nodded their approval of the formidable structure over a hot cup of Ormcafald, the local approximation of coffee. Habanero coffee. Equally agreeable was their café: the massive command bridge jutting out of the top three stories. The locals called it the Ripolis Barbican, but for clarity purposes, internal Marine discussions had labeled it the NWCC, short for North Wall Command Center. It was essentially a stadium skybox, something the emperor of Rome might've occupied while watching the gladiators fight, except hardened and wired for war.

Whether it was the spicy stimulants or the commanding view over a raked and primed battlefield, Saunders felt good about whatever might be coming. The feeling lasted almost a full minute before Sergeant Orrugant had rushed out of the stairwell, breathless.

The city.

"Make way!" panted Dalmore in the now. Two of his Deadlies in full plate armor plowed ahead with five of Orrugant's white-tabarded Watchmen trailing in a wedge formation. It was slow going but faster than a carriage with all the chaos.

The streets were a four-alarm fire drill with no exits. Arms, legs, bumping bodies, and trampling trotters. It was mass confusion, herd panic. No one knew why they were running, but others were, and that was enough.

The Watch Keep, where Benton's Meet was supposed to occur, was barricaded when they arrived. No one in and especially no one out. Fortunately, Dalmore's indomitable presence and impressive command voice got the Watchmen at the gate to unshit themselves.

The courtyard was riotous, snapping Saunders back to his younger days of crowd control and mass casualty cleanup. These people would no longer respond to reason, just force and direction. Orrugant caught on fast and drove his Watchmen into affecting absolute compliance. Through barks and effective use of the trusty sticks the Blue Cloaks once issued instead of real weapons, they managed to open a hole.

Inside the keep, people were quieter and more confused. Merchants, city administrators, and the financially influential wandered aimlessly, hands out like they had lost something. Saunders sifted through those of increasing civic importance to find someone who could give him a clear answer as to what the fuck had happened. He refused to believe that missing one meeting had torpedoed this whole damned arrangement.

A shriek cut through the feral din. It was a different kind of anger than that coursing through the streets. Darker, deeper. A woman scorned.

Saunders found Ceal upstairs outside the main hall staring at a blank wall. Alone.

"Leave," she said, not bothering to regard him.

"Tell me what happened."

She spun, face molten and fists ready to crack bone. For a split second, the front-slung MP5 became a legitimate option in case she was possessed again. But through some force of will, she managed to bottle that toxic brew of rage and resume her usual placid posture. "Ye are late," she said.

Saunders' nerves flared. It was a button his wife Sarah liked to push, knowing his penchant for punctuality. On the rare occasion he arrived after the mark, she dug that shit in. Reminded him of it every time she wanted to tear him down. Ceal didn't know, it wasn't the same, but it got a response. "Fuck's going on here?"

Instead of dropping into the reverent Corsan Carre act of begging their forgiveness and offering a calm explanation of why the day turned to shit, she threw her arms wide. "Ye's delay proved disastrous. As ye and Dalmore knocked mugs atop the North Wall, Benton stood before the council of his own making. He"—she winced, suppressing a grimace—"believed himself among friends and spoke plain."

Saunders waited for the rest, but a few seconds of staring at blazing emeralds indicated she'd already dropped the mic. *Spoke plain? What could he have . . . Fuck!* "He told them about the Bark?"

"Without preamble or forethought."

That explains the chaos. Like the president announcing Russia just launched their nukes. "You think I could've stopped him?"

"The presence of the Corsan Carre might hath dampened the outcry. He needed support to bolster trust in the leadership that hath never failed them in dire times. Their faith in Benton hath hung upon a bare thread these past tendays. The terror of the first battle is reborn."

Saunders held up a hand. "The finger-pointing can wait; damage control is the priority now. Is there an immediate, external threat to the city?"

"Nay."

"Okay, then we need to reroute the extra men Dalmore stationed on the wall and position to secure supplies and administration before this turns into a full-blown riot. Then we use the Watch to restore order in—"

"This a fire no water can quench. We cannot hope to contain the people of Portcullis through force if we are to stand even one day more as a beacon of freedom."

"Contain? This is the same situation that followed the fight with Mendo." A shitshow that took a week to *contain.*

"Isllor."

Because the dead Black Robe's name matters right now? "Fine, but last time we had an active and persistent threat from the Anticult operating in the city. According to you and Benton, that's done. So, right now, it's just mayhem. You don't want people to get hurt? The Watch needs to set up security zones and herd people back to their homes. We can use the Criers for rumor control. Extra rations can't hurt either."

She shook her head without a single brown strand falling out of place. "There is no force soft enough nor words strong enough to stem the tide. The people do not rage against the council or some simple upset in their lives. They flee. Flee from a death now certain."

Corporal Nickels kneed LCpl Buontempo. "Get confirmation on Benton's exact words. For the historical record."

"Say again," Buontempo said into the headset, trying to hide his smile.

Damn right this shit's hilarious, Nickels thought.

The city gone wild was a welcome break from the intrusive mental crap that came with boredom. When City Square first went from parade ground on a Sunday to a swarm carrying chairs and fighting over carts and carriages, Nickels was relieved to find himself white-knuckling his SAW. Had to be a fucking dragon, Black Robe, or Horsenocerous. Maybe all three glued together on one body coming for this Vault again.

But it was just the locals breaking stupid.

Smith then radioed from the inn, saying the Watch was deploying to the Wall. *Fuckin' A.* But then it was a recall, no wait, they were going back. Next, the Market District. No fucking word from either Captain Saunders or Rath. Then it was radio silent for an hour before getting the deets on a limp-wristed Benton announcing the city was doomed.

"Doomed? I hear about the world ending every fucking day of the week," Nickels said, glad to have somewhere to channel his energy. "Back home, it's a super volcano or dick-sucking Nazis. Here, the big invisible Second Stochasm. Don't see me looting storage units." Nothing anyone was carrying had any value whatsoever. At least a riot back home involved liquor stores and high-end electronics.

Buontempo looked up with his Hollywood grin. "Well, now they know it's supposed to happen before spring."

"Dickheads should be on their knees praising Cromm for pulling the plug before that shitshow season. Fuck the grass growing, allergies, animals fuckin' . . . fucking. Nastiest time of year."

"Might be different here."

"Whatever, but, I mean, what's the exfil plan? Run through the mountains when the roads are already turning to shit? One blizzard, and they're double fucked and sewn shut."

"Apparently. Captain said the South Gate is hemorrhaging. Lotta people were like preppers—ready to go on a moment's notice."

"Hoarders, you mean. Fuckin' cornucopia-packing motherfuckers with so much shit it packs *them* up." Nickels strolled past the glowing Bark to the Vault's entrance, where a new iron gate had been fitted over the melted steel. It was far from blast-proof, but plenty against a mob. Outside was still a flurry of shouting and shoving, but the Watch was pushing in, and no one was throwing flaming bags of shit. People wanted out, not a fight. "Fuck is the big deal anyway? Let 'em go. Tired of fuckin' louts eyeballing me and every chick with a full set of fingers and toes being pre-married from birth." He spun and aimed a finger at a chuckling Buontempo. "And they take that shit seriously, too. They treat the entitled fuck like his dick is made of solid gold. I could be swinging ten inches of pure muscle, and it don't matter 'cause Midas ain't rubbed it out."

Buontempo squeezed his eyes shut, laughing hard. Nickels had been saving that Midas joke; it wasn't a spur-of-the-moment thing. Fit perfect around here with the rigid social customs. Everyone was taken or destined for something. He thought back to Master Gol's kid, Jon—the skittish, medieval nerd. Didn't matter how much of a loser that guy grew up to be; his parents decided he would be a knight at birth. Kid's short fucking existence was spent trying to be something he couldn't. And then he was gutted because no one could see how special he was.

"Goddamn, these people should've left weeks ago," Nickels said, forcing his thoughts away from Jon. That was the path back to self-loathing and rumination. "Months. Fuckin', you think Manhattan or fuck, LA would be just chillin' if a full division of Chinese was sitting over the horizon? Like, 'Hey, *ching chang chong*, America. Save the fucking date 'cause we're coming.'"

"More like San Diego, but yeah," said Buontempo. "Same time, I'd expect major deployments from Camp Pendleton and Miramar in and around the city. Anyone who didn't leave would be forcibly evacuated. Then we'd have the Pacific Fleet coming in from another angle, reinforcements left and right, especially if it was the gateway to a foothold in California."

"Instead, we got a buck fifty of Leods and five companies of Blue Cloak mercenaries. Fuck, why haven't *we* bailed yet?"

Buontempo got up and stretched. After a long look at the red and blue swirls in the gem they were protecting, which protected the whole city, he said, "We've got nowhere to go."

———

A wisp of blue cloth signaled Ceal's return to the hall.

The remnants of the council and those who stayed to rage were still thick as horses in a mounted charge. Some were merchants—the few who retained a line of supplies to the city gasping for life as the rest of Galimay deafened to Portcullis' pleas. Others were of Eastside Rise, whose many weights in wealth were stored in stone vaults beneath their manor homes. The rest were listeners—shouters on this occasion—for the many wards and neighborhoods that supplied the city's workers.

A piercing, jade stare bade Benton slip away.

The damp chill thickened as the stairs wound to the dungeons beneath the Watch Keep. The shouts and cries of a people flamed by the truth of the city's fate fell to the silence of their footfalls, and still, she led him deeper. Benton wished to ask plain, but his wife's calm was a bottled storm. Oft, he opened his mouth to provoke the torrent in small gusts but always did his tongue recoil from her silence.

His thoughts turned to Master Gol, who, before departing this morn to press Lord Colm for aid, had offered a stern warning: "Tell them nothing. Deny the Bark's woes till the stone of this place rains upon their heads!"

The aged Knight of Ignis Glacies was luck incarnate, having survived the Assembly Hall when many city officials fell to the scythe's swipe. But in the stead of lauding good fortune, he blamed his house guard Brogan for insisting the Resplendent Chainmail—a gift of the old Knighthood—be worn beneath his tunic. Alas, in light of Isllor's attacks that claimed the life of Gol's firstborn, Jon, and left his secondborn, Able, apallic for nigh half a season, mayhap he was right.

Oft ye prove right, mine old friend.

Ho, how it now burned to reject his sage advice. After much mistrust and deception from Lord Bayliss and his ilk, Benton had yearned to give his people—not by blood, but bond and charge—the truth.

"For what gain?" Gol had returned. "Telling a man the mistakes he might make only drives him to make mistakes ye cannot foresee. The common folk care little, know naught of how armies move to ensure their stomachs do not ravage the countryside. Nor understand the terms between lords that might spare a city the torch. Foreknowledge issues no comfort, only fear!"

Indeed.

The worst was when Ceal's mouth had opened in a protest lost to the rising outrage that overtook the hall. She had arrived late, but Benton minded it not. He was confident in his speech and the livened discussion that would follow. He anticipated worry, but those who could not accept the danger had fled long before the ending of Almon's Shade and the start of Ajid's Winter. Those remaining were sure to be bolstered with the same determination and strength that defied the Tel'racs. The truth would make the city fierce, a place to terrify the Genisans when they finally came to claim it.

Alas, he was wrong.

At the keep's lowest level, where wet floors of crushed rock and muck lay, Ceal turned to face him. The Stochal filling her eyes lifted the torchless dark with the blues and greens of a sucking sea. Benton did not step back but wondered if she wished to harm him.

The glow dimmed but brought no promise of relief from her fury. "With a twitch of ye's tongue, we are doomed," she said.

What was to say? "Shall I speak false as Gol wishes? What of stout hearts and defiance against the enemy that hath crushed the world?"

"How doth an army break? By the few or the many in mass?"

Benton's mind returned to the lessons learned upon the shores of the Seafill River west of Estmaw. 'Twas the earliest landing of the Genisans, met by the First Army under King Haberviel. War against such strength of men was new to Galimay then, and fast did King Haberviel's center ranks collapse. They broke as a crumbling wall altogether after the first cracks appeared. Trained soldiers, hardened from years of small skirmish and battling the Gra'nuul, gave to fear.

"Do mine words terrify as though spoken by the enemy hisself?" he asked.

"Nay, the Tel'racs terrified them. It was hope that gave them the strength ye perceived. And with but a whisper, their lord stole it from them."

The truth was a barb, and this was a battle he could not win. In what had not yet happened was the only refuge. "Then it is a great panic I hath caused. But so too will order return. Dalmore moves to reinforce the South Gate with bread and steel. The Criers sing mine assurances that we are no closer to danger today than yester."

He expected her to hiss and decry his words, to unfurl the frustrations she reserved for the private hours when none looked upon her. Instead, she sighed.

"All was according our plan," she said. "Balanced upon a spindle, the Bark did bar the Obantum. Then, as the Bayliss court wasted their venom at ye, dear husband, I was free to strengthen the Procult and begin rebuilding our Stochists."

Me?

Her features softened. "No other could bare such weight as to distract so many from our schemes."

Benton swallowed in remembrance of his many pains. A year of banishment and disgrace among lords and common folk alike. Those whom he dared call friends recoiling in horror. Calls for execution, a wake of bodies, and a city nigh lost . . . *This was by her design?* "Many others than I hath suffered . . ."

She hardened again. "All shall suffer now. Would that Isllor the Betrayer had not struck me s . . ."—he knew she would not say the word *simple*—"feeble, this spring would witness the birth of the means to counter the Obantum and halt the Genisan advance. Alas, as the seeds we planted in Portcullis scatter to the winds, ye force me to the child's task of chasing leaves as our supporters flee south."

Benton wanted to smash the wall, to kick that rotten barrel that some fool had stored down here with no mind for the damp. "Ye's thoughts quicken to a distant end! Mine mistake is oft made by the mightiest lords and the reason they keep men at arms in abundance. Order shall be restored, my love. Winter will set and give us time to correct the plan. The few who hath taken south along the road will collect in the villages and castles beyond the Palings, as they did when the Genisans first came. Mayhap fewer mouths is a blessing."

Ceal pursed her lips to respond, but then some power stole her voice. Her features slackened, and she stared as though in thought, but Benton knew it could also be into the depths of another world. There was naught different between what the Uplanders called a Vision—a result of her Gift or an ancient curse—and concentration for her.

Time passed, and she remained still.

Though Benton longed to pull her close to share in his warmth, he did not wish to disturb this trance. If it was indeed a Vision, the touch of two worlds would cause her pain. If she was building a new design for the fight to save Galimay, it would only compound his mistake.

"There is else," she whispered, returning to him and the damp of this low cellar. "Ye's ill-spoken words spread faster than quickened breaths could carry them."

"To mine eternal lament. But we—"

"Listen, husband. I speak now of those among us. Those who smile and appear as we but hold no fear of what shall come to pass. No fear of the city's fall and fertile lands of Galimay given to rats and murder."

It struck him the same as when he learned of Isllor's return. It was the truth behind her anger. "The Anticult," he said.

"To mine eyes come no faces, but the like of water's weight behind a dam. My love, they are stronger than we ever dared believe. Order is not enough when we are set upon from within."

"We need more men upon the walls, patrolling the streets, standing watch over our stores," he said.

"Portcullis rots and darkens beneath our very feet," she whispered, silencing him. "No matter our oaths, our charge must be moved."

PFC David Licht stared across the table as LCpl Andrew Light gave a slow nod. Then Drew set down his spatula-like utensil that substituted for forks, knives, and even tactical sporks around here. He didn't quite turn green; no one ever turned green without face paint or alien magic shrapnel. He stayed beige, the new green if you listened to the drill instructors ramble about Marine Corps history. But it was clear he was done eating.

"They can't take them out?" he asked, leaning back a little. Not pushing back from the table, satisfied with a gut full of food like Sergeant Smith, but edging away from someone who might be contagious.

"Nope," Licht said. "It might be magic splinters around my spleen; they don't really know. The sergeant thinks it's like Ironman. Uh, something about shrapnel giving him powers, I think."

"You fucked that up, PFC," called Sgt Smith from the next table. "Ironman got created 'cause Tony Stark had them metal shards in his chest. Needed a super magnet to keep 'em from tearing up his heart. Had some power left over, so he invented a powered exoskeleton suit to kick ass like Superman."

"Right," Licht said. He'd seen one or two of the movies (maybe two halves of the same movie?) but it was a long time ago during a sleepover at his friend Rebecca's house. Minimal retention.

"And that's what you got goin' on too, dawg. Someone gonna pull a suit outta their ass and be like, 'fuck, wish we had Rudolph wit his nose so bright.' Then, boom! PFC don't stand for private first class no more. Pure Fuckin' C-monster, baby."

Sergeant Smith was awesome. He had a talent for diffusing tension, and Licht couldn't help but laugh. But Drew kept staring like he was deciding whether to cut the blue or the red wire. Maybe he was right; despite assurances, the doc had reacted to that rod freezing up like this was a job for EOD (explosive ordinance disposal).

"Dibs on the power suit," said Cpl Nickels.

"Naw, son. Licht's."

"Fuck you suckin' his dick for, Bone?"

"Rights to the origin story."

Cpl Nickels launched into some tirade about dibs, calling dibs, rank, and the associated kickbacks. Same old crap. Now that the corporal was involved, PFC Licht was invisible again. Well, except to Drew, who was still trying to increase the distance between them.

Returning to his food board, Licht sliced into what looked like a long tree root stuffed with mashed potatoes. It tasted like ham-wrapped fried chicken.

"You ever . . ." began Drew in almost a whisper. PFC Licht set his spatula down, not wanting the sound of his chewing to distract the fidgety guy. LCpl Light was particular about a few things, and food noises were high on the roster. ". . . ever think about what it's like to die?"

Every time I brush my teeth with the last toothbrush I'll ever see.

"Uh, sure. Used to think it'd be quick. Sniper, thermobaric drop, nuke. But, ha, now everyone's got swords. So, it'll probably hurt for a minute."

"No, not *how*, but like *when* it happens. Do you think you'll be alone?"

In PFC Licht's short history of near death, surrounded by death, and otherwise terrifying experiences, he'd never been alone. When he was on trial at the Assembly Hall, just before he'd gotten this green thing in him, he felt alone. But even then, the captain was there tossing him nods as a reminder that brother Marines had his back. "I hope not. I mean, maybe? You thinking of Williamson?"

"What? No. No, not anything like that." Drew flinched like he was physically evading the memory.

Williamson's death had hit them all hard. At first, it was straight terror. Dude got ripped apart in his bedroom within this very building that was secured top-down by a half dozen Marines. No one heard or saw a thing until Captain Rath started screaming. Then Rath went catatonic because he glimpsed what everyone was calling the Monster. Totally crazy. Once they killed the Black Robe responsible, the whole ordeal became this weird wound. Not glowing green and scary, but something worthy of a flinch.

"Gunny?"

"No!" LCpl Light checked over his shoulder to see if the outburst caught anyone's attention. The inn's great room was less crowded than usual but still at 70% occupancy. The locals who'd smartly decided against storming the South Gate were all heads down in their meager rations. Smith and Nickels were still arguing over the power supply to the Terminator suit they were designing.

"No," he continued in a whisper. "That . . . I mean, that's probably how he wanted to go. You know? Taking out a dragon with a shoulder-fired missile and saving an officer from an avalanche. That's hero stuff; they'll remember him forever. Gosh, I . . ." He shook his head. "I had a dream."

"One of *those* dreams?" PFC Licht only asked because they were supposed to report anything unusual.

"Don't think so, hope not. I was dying. I was really old; in a bed surrounded by people I know. Some of my friends from home, my dad, and sister. I think my mom was there too, but . . . I don't remember her face, and of course, it couldn't have been her because she died because I was born. It was more like she fit a role. Like . . . that thing that's missing inside. Y'know?"

Believing everyone had some gaping hole within them was something Drew should be telling a shrink, not a brother Marine. But Portcullis was lagging on psychology graduates, so, at one beer ration a day, brother Marine it was. "Doesn't sound too bad."

"For sure. Like, I couldn't get up, but it felt really good to see everyone. Especially because, y'know," he panned the inn's wood beams awash in flickering lamplight, "because we're here and maybe won't ever see any of them again."

"Can't think like that." But everyone thought like that. This was the tour from hell.

"It was just a dream."

"Copy."

"Anyway, my older sister asks this nurse, 'How long?' and I start thinking: *hey, I'm not gone yet.* When I try to tell her that she needs to calm down, only this scratchy sigh comes out. Then it's hard to breathe like I'm choking. Everyone looks at me all . . ." He stopped, frowning.

"What?"

"Hopeful." A short pause sank it beneath the manufactured egos and hero-of-your-own-story bullshit to the sensitive underbelly of insignificance. The world only cared about what you could do for it today and tomorrow, not what you did yesterday. Not what you gave. Sensing that indifference sounded like the worst kind of death. "Then I could breathe again," he continued. "It felt so good, but everyone just sat back and started checking their phones."

"Can't be easy seeing someone . . . uh," Licht said, not knowing what to say.

"I just got this really weird feeling of being alone, even with everyone around me."

Is he trying to say he feels lonely? Licht wracked his brain for something reassuring. Andrew Light was a private guy, excitable, and often when he did start talking, he'd shut down as if too much human contact blew a fuse or something. Still, that story was more than a little haunting, especially considering some people were having dreams that somehow connected with reality.

"Bitch, the only thing you gonna feel when you die is a man pressing in from behind," said Cpl Nickels, suddenly standing over the table. "Hot breath in your hair, maybe whispering shit like, 'call me daddy.' Know why? 'cause he is your daddy, son."

"Is it you?" LCpl Light whispered. He was so damned sincere there was no way to tell if he was bantering back or genuinely trying to assess the situation.

"What? No. Hell no, I ain't—"

"But what if it happens in the snow and it's really cold? You need my body for warmth . . ."

Nickels stepped back. "Get in line, bro. I got Bone over there."

"Both o' you get some fuckin' blankets," laughed Sergeant Smith. "And let up, Jersey; Gunny still fresh, dig?"

Cpl Nickels gave that sly smile that said he had the perfect comeback but then stopped like his brain bumped into a wall. Drew was still processing the necrophiliac hypothermia scenario and didn't notice.

Seems like everyone's got their own mental version of a nuclear green alien thing stuck in their side, Licht thought.

The last two months had been busy, filled with new friends and firsts, but underlaid with total loss. The lucky ones who boarded that chopper out of Mina Bazar were now cut off from everyone they knew and loved. Hell, every*thing* too. Right down to the toilet paper.

And the captain's plan to get them home amounted to pointing at an empty bottle and declaring it filled with hope.

It reminded Licht of a TV show he binged over junior year's Christmas break because he was grounded for pulling the fire alarm at Applebee's. It was about a group of mercenaries and scientists who stepped through a portal to another dimension. Same Earth, but a different evolutionary path. They spent five seasons running and gunning through a mix of humans, evolved dinosaurs, and weird zebra-riding makeup monsters trying to get back home. Instead of all that paying off in the last episode, they learned they had all died on contact with the original portal. The entire show was just the last forty-two microseconds of the main character's brain stretched out into 50 episodes.

Total waste of time.

Of course, here in the real fantasy world, Dr. Bowman had debunked the end-of-life dream scenario. The process of dying didn't create new realities to live in. If anything, it released memories and sensations in flashes as different parts of the dying brain gasped for life.

Kinda like what was happening to the city: people sensing their demise were throwing everything into a desperate chance to survive.

A glance out the front windows showed an empty yard and street beyond. An hour ago, it was packed with carts and foot traffic. Fights, people getting knocked down. Not Portcullis' finest hour. Although, after those crowds moved out, little groups arrived to carry away the people who'd been trampled. So, not a complete shit show.

"Hey, Sergeant," PFC Licht said, breaking the silence that had settled over the great room. Maybe his brother Marines were starting to dial in on the situation's absurdity. "There an update on the South Gate?"

"Yeah, the fuck aren't we out cracking heads?" asked Cpl Nickels as if chowing during a riot hadn't struck him as odd until this very second. "Watch and Deadlies ain't got near enough people."

"Anything I gotsta say is just guessin', same as you," said Smith. "And my dawgs know somethin' about that, don't they?" He put on a big smile, but that was the senior NCO talking, not the guy with a reputation for every conspiracy theory and rumor passed around after taps.

"No word on whether they got it under control?" Licht asked. Bare minimum, the sergeant should be able to say whether he knew something or not.

"Local issue; local forces," said Smith. It was his version of name, rank, and favorite cereal.

"Fancy. Brines woulda just told us to *shaddap,*" said Cpl Nickels, imitating the rasp in Gunny's voice. And just like Brines was still here, everyone got quiet. Even the murmuring locals at the other tables stopped.

Hearing his name at more than just a whisper was refreshing. Even after the funeral, the subject of Gunny was super hush-hush. It was weird because Gladstone said there'd been a ton of remembrance for Williamson. He was all people talked about for a few weeks, everyone suddenly being an expert on him and all the gaming stuff he was into. That's just how it was when one of the team was lost. People spent time saying goodbye by remembering.

This time, it was like everyone was in shock. Maybe denial, somehow. Gunny Brines wasn't easy to connect with. Still, he was the team anchor, the reason Marines requested duty with a rifle company that called itself the C-monster. He was confidence, even here in an impossible reality.

The hole Gunny left behind made everything seem less real. Less important. No one would ever admit it, but they were vulnerable now. No amount of 21st-century gear, guns, or tactics could change that. Licht didn't want to go dark, but watching the team stare at their food, it felt like a switch had been flipped, and LCpl Light was right.

Everyone was just hollow company to keep until it was your turn.

"Uumhrat, we need the room for half a width," Saunders said, hoping that was enough to pull ten minutes from Portcullis' half-assed sundial clock.

"Aye." The burly clerk set down his dishrag. "The lot of ye out back with me. Wood canna carry itself to the stoves." Grumbles, but the stragglers, still pushing food around their boards in the inn's lobby, complied. Saunders didn't mean Uumhrat needed to go too, but it was probably best. This was Marine talk.

Everyone born on Earth, minus Francisco and Rath on Vault watch, casually grabbed seats by the capacious fireplace. The assembly was pisspoor, even under these circumstances. Mike would've had the men off their asses and straining for attention like the first one to crack a sternum would find a porterhouse steak under his pillow. Sergeant Smith wasn't failing his duty, he'd get the Marines there if ordered, but he was still young. He was Brines before the scars and medals. He still saw more living people in the ranks than ghosts.

"I'll make this quick," Saunders said, taking a spot before the fireplace. It was throwing the dry warmth needed after a day of wet snow and wind. "Today's riot is a direct result of a miscommunication." He left out the part about Portcullis' *rat* problem, which Benton had finally acknowledged in private earlier. "It is a local issue where we have zero responsibility or culpability. I don't pretend to fully understand the Corsan Carre thing but, after consulting with Ceal, concluded that our involvement would introduce an unstable element."

"Did Benton really threaten to kill people, sir?" asked LCpl Gladstone.

"What?"

"That's what Sergeant Teague heard, sir," said Gladstone. "Benton announced the city could only make it to spring if it had less people. Get out or get cut."

"Probably said: *get out, I got the gout,*" muttered Cpl Nickels.

"The hell that even mean?" asked Sgt Smith.

"I bet gout is really bad out here," said LCpl Light.

"Yo, you see that homeboy in North Ward with the blocks for feet?" asked Garcia.

"Thought he was wearing them for shoes," said Nickels.

"Nah, somethin' ate his shit off. The blocks are splinted up his legs."

"Wouldn't it be easier to crawl? We should give him some kneepads," said Light.

"Bro, we should give YOU some—"

"Enough," Saunders said. "Consider street intel unreliable right now. Benton's singular malfunction was revealing that the Bark is breaking down. Period. In fact, his riot response specifically called for a zero-threat, zero-harm policy of containment and assurance."

"So, he double-shit the bed, sir?" asked LCpl Buontempo, eliciting more than a few smirks.

"Negative. Situation diffused."

"It's not over . . . is it?" asked Gladstone as if disappointed.

"You hankerin' for a revolution?" drawled LCpl Fischer.

Saunders cleared his throat. "We're in a holding pattern. South Gate got hammered, and the Watch was losing containment. Rather than letting it come to blows, Dalmore stood Sergeant Batoth's people down. As the crowd calmed, he got their ears working and reminded them they're part of something bigger. The speech worked; exodus postponed."

Nickels frowned. "Permission to ask a question, sir?"

"Go."

"Why not let them leave? I mean, fuckers can't feed the people they got. That whole Sticks shitshow is like dragging a fat chick on a hike. Why are we hauling *her* water and cooler full of deli meat?"

"'Cause she yo momma," quipped Buontempo.

A few chuckles but more nods suggested a general agreement with Nickels' philosophy. It was easy to dehumanize under stress, but that was when humanity and compassion were most needed. "Ann lives in the Sticks. Is she dead weight?"

Silence.

"We considered evacuating the city a few weeks ago when the last of those Block Lords were put down," Saunders continued. *Block Lords* was Cpl Nickels' phrasing for the gang leaders who cropped up after the Assembly Hall fight. Mendo's forces trashed half the city, and opportunists raced to fill the power vacuum. The Block Lords who resisted long enough to be captured now resided in the dungeon below the Watch Keep. Eating food, taking resources to guard, but treated humanely. "Problem is, there's nowhere for these people to go."

"I thought they had all these lords with castles and villages and stuff, sir," said Gladstone.

Saunders shrugged. "They do. But here, the Portcullisians have roles and lives. They're productive. Anywhere else, they become refugees. A burden. Also, Ceal considers them *her* people. Protecting them is easier if they're all in one place."

"Yeah, but now that the Bark is all janky . . ." said Buontempo.

"Right, never a better time to leave," said Nickels.

"Counterproductive to our interests," said Saunders. "Our mission isn't here; it's back home. Keeping Portcullis whole means we have continued access to Ceal and proximity to our point of arrival. Presently, it looks like the Bark will last till spring. Ceal says she's made progress in understanding how we came here, and a few more months should be enough to engineer a way back."

"We're just going to leave, sir?" asked LCpl Light.

"Pull back, regroup, and return. Fleet needs our intel, and Galimay needs fire support. Think a dozen Corsan Carre is great? We'll come back with 2,000 Marines and the horses they ride in on."

"Oorah," said the men. Dr. Bowman *harrumphed*; Micky wore a polite smile.

"Point is," Saunders continued, "we have an equitable agreement that almost blew up on us today." Micky leaned in, suddenly interested. "If Dalmore hadn't performed a miracle of crowd control, then we'd be dealing with a baggage train wandering off to find their icy graves."

"But still . . ." began Nickels, confused.

"Because Ceal cares, dawg," said Smith picking up the slack. "While the people are here, she's here. If they leave, there's a damned good chance she will too."

Saunders gave a stern nod in affirmation and kept his eyes steel. Still, he wondered how much weight the old "for the people" story really carried.

Magnus Smallfoot, safe in his home, closed his eyes.

He could feel the writhing of bodies wishing to be free of their skins as the cold dark beyond Portcullis' South Wall beckoned. He could taste the snaps of their gnashing teeth, smell the jealous sweat of those ill-prepared, and hear the howls of wolves and screeches of unnamed horrors ripping through the night as the frantic flight was set upon well beyond the city's aid.

Except, it was false as any dream or wish.

When Sergeant Segar—one of those Blue Cloak fools—had come knocking, he said that in the stead of stampede, the crowds were calmed and returned to the homes they had lusted to abandon. The glorious terror that swept them toward the unfriendly wilds was dispelled.

Smallfoot drained his cup and shuffled through the mess of his fevered work to fill it again. The hearth lay cold and dark as he had spent his wealth of fuel firing the forge. That, too, slumbered for the night, glowing embers tucked deep within a bed of ash. And so it would stay, mayhaps never to light again.

Flat beer dribbled from a forgotten barrel. Found buried in the piles, stacks, and waddings of Smallfoot's possessions, it once belonged to Master Mesaulius—the famed weaponsmith of Caranusca slain two seasons past. Together with the swept and scented bedroom, they were all that remained of Smallfoot's former master. The rest was sold to fire the smithy.

"Because ye showed me naught of the craft!" he howled at the shelf of unsold, unworthy wares. Breathless, he found his cup had fled his hand and lost itself in the clutter that nigh reached the rafters. His throat turned parchment from shouting at the ghosts of Mesaulius' house, he found another beneath a rotted street sign that he thought to shape into a serving board. Filling it, he dared to glance again at the one-room kept sparse. The former master's chambers.

It was first kept as a memory of Mesaulius, a shrine of sorrow and guilt. He was slain in bed as he read by candlelight. A howl that Smallfoot would not soon forget marked the moment. In the stead of rushing to Mesaulius' aid, Smallfoot sank to the buried depths of his own bedroom. On the next morn, his courage gathered, and Mesaulius unrisen, he found the great craftsman in pieces like so many of his wares. In the like, so too did Smallfoot fall to pieces, cleaning and doting upon the room in the hope of forgiveness.

Blind.

Since those the Procult now named Corsan Carre came to visit, Smallfoot's vision had clarified the truth. Mesaulius was a magnificent blacksmith, but a selfish, fell fellow. Greed drove him, nurtured the hunger that bade him outdo the last magnificent blade or drape of mail. Rare was his praise; ever rarer did he stoop down and reward those who abled him. Apprentices like Smallfoot came and went, serving only as coals to keep the forge hot. Never would they name their works nor stand proud among Portcullis' famed blacksmiths.

Smallfoot spat, the taste of his groveling before that horrid man now vile and venomous. Truly, the Monster—Isllor Mortund in the guise of Lord Benton's wolf, Palefang—had done a service in killing Mesaulius. Torn the tarp from the ground and given the seed a chance to flower.

Stepping through his mounds, Smallfoot approached his worktable. Unlike the rest, it was reserved for only one of his treasures—the greatest. He set his cup down and stared at the black cloth covering the blade. His blade. The product of maddened dreams sprouting in newfound freedom.

A Peerless Work.

It was widely believed the artistry of Song Forging was naught more than the inspiration of excellence into smithing. A way to focus the work, time the heat, strikes, and quenches. True quality only came later from the infusions during Tap-Finishing.

Fools. But till now, naught of the living world had produced Peerless.

He tugged the cloth—the fur covering a magnificent woman awaiting his warmth at the end of a dark night—and teased himself with a glint. The blade held a faint radiance beyond the dim lamplight's reach. Would that the famed Caranuscan weaponsmith still lived so he might tremble before the might of legend.

"He would tear his eyes for not seeing mine potential!" Smallfoot screamed.

And see it can naught be repeated, whispered his thoughts. Heat gathered about Smallfoot's face despite the cool air.

Pride.

It bade Smallfoot believe the Peerless Sword was his work alone. And, but for a speck on the sheen, it was!

The Corsan Carre were the problem, his last visitors before the miracle. They laughed at him, whispered malus at his treasures, and fawned over the preserved leavings of Mesaulius. If they had simply left, no worries would linger in their wake. But the one, the leader, committed an act so innocent that none but the Corsan Carre could stand accused.

He touched this unfinished sword. Only a touch, nothing more.

Later that day was when it happened. When the work sang with Smallfoot's wonderous song and burst with such light and glory that it left an eternal spot upon his eyes. It was him, his, but always his thoughts returned to the strangers and that touch. When he failed to make another, he hired a Secret Scryer to learn the truth of their meddling. But she found these Corsan Carre dead to the Arts.

"Is it they who now walk with the power of sight and foreknowledge?" he asked aloud to banish his fears. "Nay! I am the master, the Song Forger reborn. Unto mineself I hath—"

In a flash, the worktable and the piles adorning his home faded to a greater visage. It was a Vision, one of the gifts he believed granted by the Peerless.

The South Gate loomed large and white with frost against lit braziers. Open flame in the night air was surprising at first, a waste of fuel benefitting none. But then he saw them: huddled and shivering, not all had returned home as Sergeant Segar said. Many were of the Sticks and mayhaps had no homes better than the cold cobble.

Though their anger had cooled, the vigil gave hope for the coming dawn. The heat of Bergreth's Lamp might refire their hearts toward their doom. *Vermin.* Smallfoot wished to return the spit they had so oft flung at him. Alas, he knew they would be warmed by precious wood and coddled by soft Watch—

A shadow pulled free from a dark place between fires and slipped into a shivering huddle.

Smallfoot gasped, but as more shadows came, he rippled with excitement. They were the like of men in dark cloths. They seated themselves beside those seeking warmth, passing steaming drinks and sweet whispers. Soon, those whispers returned as shouts, and the shivering stopped. Men stood, pointing at the South Gate, decrying the Watchmen as captors.

Louder.

Louder, their voices grew, and the night erupted.

Smallfoot covered his precious blade as the Vision faded and considered another beer. It was easier to think when the mind was freed of the world's weight. And the more he drank, the quieter the dissent to his becoming the smith of legends who forged the weapon of his own skill.

"Then why can I not make another?" he asked another pile of cold steel he had hammered upon over the many intervening days. "I must remember the trick!"

He poured from the keg wishing it were fresh-drawn from the tavern naught a quarter width's walk. But that would risk seeing the other smiths. Hearing their laughter and jokes about his "boasts."

I will forge another, he vowed.

Still, scoff, not respect would ring through the air if he showed them this blade and its magnificence.

He slugged the stale beer in one gulp and considered his plight.

Almon's first brew since the Genisans struck yesteryear, now filling mugs at every inn and drinkhouse in the city, was a great work. None questioned the brewmaster's talent to repeat. The old man was experienced, consistent, and respected. If he produced a liquor that promised to restore youth and infuse the strength of the Vissl, he would be lauded and welcomed in all the lands. If the great Master Smith Mesaulius had forged this Peerless Work, His Reverence himself would bow before its glory.

But for such a great weapon to fall into the hands of an outcast, lowest form, barely cooled smith like Smallfoot, it was a curse. He could not claim maker without producing another and another before their squinting eyes. Nay, a hundred Peerless Swords could not sate their envy, ire, or greed.

"I refuse ye!"

The rampaging thoughts calmed as he drank more. *Another. I must make another.* He poured and drank. *They will come hither. Down from their courts and thrones begging to see what kind of smith I am*, he thought, the hurtful world drifting farther with every gulp.

What kind of smith* we *are, spoke a voice from deep within his addled mind.

CHAPTER 7

INFORM AND INFLUENCE

Weakness sapped fierce prowess. Aches and sharp pain ebbed a once sure stride, and a tight void within gnawed without relent. But it was naught against the thirst and quick breaths of his men all around.

Those who fell did not rise again. No whips cracked nor guards prodded. Failure to reach the next camp meant facing wilds at night. A once proud host of warriors now drove as lambs to their captors for protection.

Dr. Pat tried to lend her host some of her energy or willpower. It gave him nothing. His legs were too leaden, the world shrinking too fast into the confines of his body, which was no longer fit to lead.

"Lord Morhock," croaked a voice familiar and foreign. Where Dr. Pat heard English, this Morhock heard other sounds that twisted her brain. "A rest, the soldiers need a rest. By the . . . the Grenedels. See them there?" A grove of pine trees bulged from the dry tree line. "Beneath the ground is soft and warm. We can fashion boards to carry the—"

"Each carries hisself," she found himself saying. The pain of those words put everything else to shame. They gutted Morhock, but he delivered them with absolute certainty. It was law.

"Must we wait till ye fall?"

Their doubts had grown bold indeed.

The world spun and was ever dimmer in one eye as this Morhock squinted against the Lamp; still, he marched. They were in tall grasses knocked flat and white by winter. But there was no snow. Ahead was rolling, dead country. Behind, the tips of a mountain chain sank into the horizon. He suppressed a cough out of pride, but the nasty shit clogging his bronchioles could not be willed away. His wheezing breaths grew tighter. "The wastes of Helidor could not break me, nor shall this," he managed.

"We need not ye's strength of command bled dry by this infernal walking," said another who Lord Morhock knew as his sworn man, Sir Kenric. The white of his chest armor was buried in bloodied bandages. Hemorrhagic anemia, infection, and blinding fatigue were written across the knight's face. Yet, he carried himself high, back straight as a board. "Let our shoulders strengthen ye's resolve."

"This is mine resolve," Morhock spat, and Dr. Pat realized the truth of it. He wasn't just putting on a brave face for the long, weary line behind. It was built from confidence. Another step meant falling into a collapsing body for her, but he'd felt this way before. He was stable, if barely able. He could go on long after the sun sank below the once rich and free Caranuscan lands. "I hath paid for this march in oceans of blood, the screams of our brothers that steal our slumber. We are beaten low, but this is a journey. None hath sacrificed so much to come so far. The Lord Commander of Galimay's Fifth Army shall not be received by our enemy as a cripple!"

The discussion was over, and the march continued. Dr. Pat shouted reason into Lord Morhock's thick skull as they passed the pines and the beckoning carpets of soft, brown needles beneath. Then she screamed as she shared the pain of his body teetering on the verge of collapse. Paralyzed, mute, and trapped, she was forced to endure endless exertion without being able to pull a single breath of her own. He needed to breathe. She needed to breathe!

Dusk fell, and the damp crept into Lord Morhock's lungs, driving a hacking cough. Dr. Pat felt a new terror as she realized he could be minutes away from drowning in his own fluids.

A light appeared in the distance.

Morhock surged with renewed purpose. But it was less hope than urgency. Howls and clicks filled the air as the last of the day's color faded. Commotion erupted from behind, and the march became a stampede. She did not know what else was in the rising mists and darkness, but Morhock did. And he was afraid.

The light—their salvation and the promise of everlasting torture and pain—grew closer. Morhock's men were under his arms now, carrying his full weight. Through fading vision and a swimming head, the scene was desperate. Blood-curdling cries echoed through the night, and groups of men rushed past.

It was a scramble of limbs and legs. Trampling bodies.

Suddenly, all was still.

The darkness retreated, and two bright figures stepped out as if lit by a spotlight.

"Turan," croaked Lord Morhock, aghast.

Dr. Pat did not recognize the name or have time to dig through Morhock's memories to understand why his confidence collapsed. But she didn't have to. From the dark draping and purplish aura, Turan was clearly a Black Robe.

The one beside him was what caught her eye. Female, a head shorter in those same robes that had haunted Dr. Pat since Mina Bazar. This one was darker, as if the absence of light radiated strength.

And she was staring right through Morhock into Dr. Pat's eyes like a cat that found a mouse.

Dr. Pat sat up in the stillness of her room, body shaking as it remembered its vitality. She pressed a hand to her sternum—the pain was gone—and tested a full breath.

"Was it *that* steamy?" breathed Micky, that mop of wild brown hair just inches away.

"Ah! Get out of my bed!"

"I'm not in your . . ." Micky's stupid puffy lips drew back into a smile. "Oh shit, were you dreaming about us? Was I good? I mean, what did I do? Please tell me it was like my face on Schwarzenegger's body. His old body. Younger, I mean. Oh, who cares, the old one too."

Dr. Pat swallowed the hairball of tangled rage, disgust, shock, and morbid imagery. "It was a death march," she gasped. "Hours of feeling someone named Lord Morhock drown in his own edematous lungs."

Micky stared as if committing the information to memory. "Oooh, a Vision dream. I want to hear everything about Morhock, but we gotta get going."

Other than an oil lamp Micky must have lit, it was still dark. "Going?" A spike of adrenaline answered the question. Someone was hurt.

"There was another riot at South Gate. A bad one. I'll explain everything on the way."

The open carriage rumbled through the icy streets with Uumhrat at the reins. Their usual escort was unavailable because all the Watchmen were down by South Gate trying to hold the line.

Futile, Micky thought.

It was the timeless tradition of bailing out a sinking ship. Stubborn-assed Benton couldn't see that the city was a façade with overinflated sentimental value. Everyone else knew: his enemies, both on the horizon and back in Durador, and considering recent events, Ceal too. But he just couldn't pull himself out of the fantasy.

You can bet I won't be there to see the look of surprise on your face when you realize you're fucked, buddy.

"I thought Dalmore calmed things down," said Pat, turning the collar of her white overcoat to the night air. Dawn was still an hour away.

He'd done more than calm things down; he'd gotten 90% of yesterday's rioters back in their homes. The ball-numbing cold should have kept the remaining diehards from doing anything more than clenching their teeth against chattering. But somehow, the ass crack of midnight—what the Marines aptly called 25th hour—sparked a flame.

Bigger than before.

The rest was murky. The people Micky spoke to since were second-hand witnesses circling the same question marks with half-assed explanations. Ironically, her best bet for a primary source was to tag along with Dr. Pat since the injured would gather at the clinic.

"No idea," Micky said, "but it sure took the Watch a while to start pulling the wounded out. Francisco was there when the gate fell. He said it was like a flood of flesh heading out into the night. Crazy."

Dr. Pat massaged her temples.

Ha, you think you're stressed now?

"So why didn't someone wake me earlier?"

"The stretchers just started coming in," Micky said. "Apparently, it was a whole hostage situation in the gatehouse. Totally out of control until Ceal broke bitch, and . . . I mean, she's so fucking gorgeous. Right? Poised, sure, and capable. Snuffed that shit like a leaf blower on a birthday cake."

Pat's fingers dug deeper into those temples. *Good.* Now was the time to plant seeds. It would be too late at the clinic since Pat somehow destressed by wading through blood and guts.

"Anyhoo, we're just the cleanup crew," Micky sang, the feint before the haymaker. "The Marines can figure out what to do now that she's *leaving*."

Dr. Pat blinked, and the massaging stopped. "What?"

"Right? Locking everyone in so she can be the first to jump ship!"

Micky dropped a light laugh to let her know it was a joke. Pat usually played the game one move at a time and wasn't ready for a post hoc chuckle about things that hadn't happened yet.

"How? When? Wait, have you talked to Saunders?"

No. "Yeah, he said it came up. Maybe Ceal was just venting, but usually, she's so polished. Like she's got a speechwriter and everything." Pat had the lord governor's Lady pegged as a master manipulator when the reality was much simpler. Ceal couldn't announce her grand plans and expect immediate conceptualization and execution. No, they were too complex for the average Joe to follow. So, she spent her days dumbing things down to bite-sized, seemingly incongruent steps. Sometimes it took extra thought to parse out, but, for example, her half-hearted attempt to stop the efflux through the South Gate was a damned billboard. Something had changed in the past 12 hours; those dear, sorry souls were now her excuse to leave.

"We aren't"—Pat eyed Uumhrat in the driver's seat and lowered her voice—"leaving too, are we?" *We* would've been just the two of them a couple of days ago. Girl power! But with Brines dead, Pat had frustratingly grown more attached to the Marines—their would-be rescuers who couldn't quite deliver on the getting them home part.

"You kidding me? Saunders, like Benton, is fucking in love with that wall. His biological clock needs him to be here when the Genisans try to break it down. But, and I know you've got issues with her, Ceal gets it. Portcullis is a dry funeral pyre paying top dollar to suck-start a blowtorch."

Pat stared through the warm glow of an oil-fired streetlamp, breath puffing out in little starts. *Might need to drop a giggle in there for good measure,* Micky thought. *Teehee. Wars and guns are so silly!*

Leaving absolutely had to happen. The real problem was separating the doctor from her own version of the Benton and Saunders fantasies: the obsession with the city's healthcare. That clinic was the ultimate monument to denial, almost as bad as her working in that Mina Bazar infirmary for the same people who murdered and tortured all her friends at Hudud.

That was Pat, though, and in a different light, it was an enviable quality. Unfortunately, what they needed right now was momentum. Forward, as the Marines loved to say, involved moving deeper into the feudal fuckfest, not hanging around on its crumbling fringes.

That meant taking a chance with Ceal.

Proximity and promises weren't enough. They had to play *her* game, learn the rules, plant a piece on the board, and give Galimay's queen of magic a reason to advance a token. She wasn't all-powerful, but with the Stochal Power came knowledge and history. She understood all the prophetic crap, the political networks, who had and wanted what. Better yet, deep down she also understood the true motivations behind this entire war. Absolutely critical for getting back to Earth.

The next question was obvious: what's the game's ante? *How do we get Ceal to take us with?* Saunders figured their worth amounted to fighting men pissing a few thousand steel pellets into an invader who bookended the entire combat spectrum from swinging clubs to complete control over particle physics. His Marines, by the way, were somewhere in the middle.

No, what Ceal wanted was sitting in plain sight, draped in disbelief. Dr. Pat, the totally clueless chick filtering all these wonderful events through a childhood codex written on another fucking planet.

Miss, you are the player, the piece, and possibly the poker face.

That was a few steps ahead. Presently the focus needed to be simple: Ceal good; city dangerous. Uncovering the nature of that new danger, which unseated Ceal when dragons and unstoppable armies could not, was compelling too. Micky hoped the answer was waiting on the lips of those at the clinic.

"All I meant was . . ." Micky began when Uumhrat's draft horse let out a strange snort. Horses snorted at stuff all the time, but this one was more of a gasp.

It seemed the answer was closer than expected.

By the time the carriage caught up to the fact that the animal had stopped, Micky was already pulling Pat to the floor.

"Stop tha—"

The air sang, and pale moonlight thunked where Pat was just sitting. Then something bigger and heavier crashed through the cart's wooden side, leaving a sharp point between them.

Pat sucked a breath but didn't scream. Micky snapped the spear tip off with her heel.

Another drove in.

Then another.

Micky lunged for the broken spear, desperate to fight back.

Pain.

Something. Her back. She couldn't move.

Pat's foot shot out. A thud and deep grunt followed.

Suddenly, Micky was free. Twisting away, a river of warmth slid down to the crack of her ass. She managed to get some air and went for the spear again.

A pair of black sleeves and gloved hands reached in. Micky drove her wooden heel into one, pinning the wrist. The other came down on her knee, hard. But she held. "Run, Pat," she croaked.

Instead of leaping out of the carriage and running off into the frozen night, the doctor became a thrashing jumble of legs and arms. The glint of metal swept into Pat's thigh, and she screamed.

Micky kicked herself into the tangle, if only to act as a shield, but caught a knee to the face. She didn't blackout, but it was enough to put her limp on her ass as Pat was dragged over the side. Then arms hooked under Micky's, and a knife pressed against her voice box.

Hesitation.

These weren't professionals; actual killers cut quick so their work wouldn't come back to haunt them. Amateurs had to overcome the big question of whether it was okay to take a life. It didn't buy much time, but any amount was an absolute win when everything was on the line.

Too bad Micky couldn't speak.

A scream pierced the darkness from somewhere beyond the cart. It was that primal, panic-inducing cry that every member of the herd understood.

Male voices cried out in pain as shadows stumbled back. Then Pat was up and free. Micky tried to follow along and figure out how Pat threw off her attackers, but it was all happening too fast.

Instead of running, Pat stood there as if confused about what to do. *Run!* She took an unsteady step, then went down like one of her legs gave out.

Micky suppressed the urge to buck and thrash against her captor. Instead, she slipped her hand up to the glove gripping the knife. The blade pressed deeper, crushing her trachea and carotids. Air wasn't coming, heart hammering in her chest. With a light touch, she caressed that glove. She traced a finger along the back to the wrist and then forward to the knuckle again. Her would-be killer got the message, and the blade's pressure released. A cooling rush filled her chest, and her head cleared.

That's right. I'm human; I'm warm. You hold all the cards.

She continued tracing that delicate finger around the glove, down to the backside of the knife, and dropping below to the buttons of her overcoat. It was too dark for a show, but the arm across her chest relaxed. There was no question she commanded his undivided attention.

"Ey," came a voice to the right. "None o' that, now. Have her after she's bled."

The blade tightened against her throat again.

Oh, for the love of fucking—

The carriage lurched like it hit a pothole. *But we're stopped*... Suddenly, Micky could breathe. She rolled forward.

Then came the yell. The roar was as if every lion in the jungle had just broken the sound barrier. Someone was out there.

"At 'em!" shouted the one who'd ordered her assailant to consider necrophilia.

The carriage lurched again as a flesh-tattered gob of burgundy, bearing the semblance of a human head, crashed through the planking. Micky kicked it back through the hole. Instead of making solid contact with skull, the heel of her boot squished into what felt like a rotten tomato.

Cries and the song of swinging steel filled the night. Micky tried to get up, but her body felt heavier than usual, and the cold was nipping through her overcoat. Touching the hurt spot in her back spiked her pain level and brought back slick warmth.

Shit, I'm gonna go into shock. Gotta move.

Climbing over the side, her blurring vision scoured the dim light, trying to snag the contrast of Dr. Pat's bright coat. A few feet away, there was someone in white crawling away.

Or, trying to.

Pat stopped after a few lurches and started swaying on all fours. A few shakes of her head seemed to get her going again, but she couldn't quite get traction. Her left hand pawed at the cobblestones as her torso slumped and sagged as if exhausted.

Micky sucked a breath, trying to push blood into her brain to think clearer. All the fighting was behind her now, probably a whole patrol of Watchmen from the sheer violence of it. Pat was important. Pat was everything.

Pat collapsed and stopped moving.

"I've got a second team reinforcing the Bark," shouted Saunders amid the people jostling for position outside the Watch Keep's barred and barricaded gate. Dalmore and his Watchmen stood within, swords drawn. "Sergeant Teague's heading to the North Wall. We need a read on insurgent activity. What's your status?"

"Raise the gate; let the Corsan Carre through," barked Dalmore through the iron crossbars. Two Watchmen swept in from the flanks and made a hole for Saunders. Closer and without the screaming in his ears, it was easier to hear Dalmore. "South Wall sounds no alarm at last, same for North. Alas, our enemy is among us. Sergeant Orrugant's men tell of fighting in the streets. Many bodies, few with any need for Wisewoman Alena."

"Might be a diversion."

"Aye," said Dalmore as the iron creaked upward. "Wall watches hold their posts. No word to Genisa's greater designs."

Saunders, with PFC Licht on his heels, ducked under the grate when it was chest high. It slammed down behind them. "Good, keep this place on lockdown. There's no telling friend from foe." This was the shit he'd been trying to warn everyone about since day one. Insurgency. It was an infestation both Scianas and Earth had in common. "Still believe the Anticult doesn't exist here?"

Dalmore snorted, "We are needed inside," and started for the keep. He wasn't the problem; Benton was. Frustrating but understandable for anyone with an ounce of empathy left at this point. The Lord Governor's world was camaraderie among the troops while backstabbing and steel-sharpening-steel were left for the courts of nobles.

The Anticult was a new-to-Portcullis enemy. Infiltrators who were indistinguishable from loyal civilians and government personnel. They'd give you the shirt off their backs and babysit your kids until some mental switch was thrown. Then it was gut gut, kill kill. It was a lesson the US Military relearned in almost every conflict: restrict access, monitor communications, and hedge exposure.

A shiver ran down Saunders' back as that last part triggered the sense of forgetting something. "Licht, tell Francisco to get some eyes on the North

Wall, report anything unusual. Also, everyone sounds off. I want another headcount."

"Yessir," the kid said, slinging his SINCGARS radio around to work the controls as they walked. The courtyard was bluish in the early morning light, making the sentries and logistics workers appear bled out. *No kidding, the city just fucking hemorrhaged.*

"Please tell me we're not going into another meeting," Saunders said as the guards unbarred the keep's fifteen-feet-tall, double doors.

"Our worries do not end with the streets," explained Dalmore. "The city's backbone crumbles as a cake before the flowing tide. Come!"

The climb up to Dalmore's office—the unofficial city meeting hall—was made on numb legs as Saunders' mind chewed on that detail he was forgetting. Diversion was a possible insurgent motive, but pre-emptive strike felt much warmer.

Targets. Insurgents strike targets.

The Bark? No activity.

Perimeter? Secured.

Personnel? No pattern, no intrusion into secured areas. Government officials were all accounted for and under guard.

Ceal? Any military commander worth their fancy uniform would immediately prioritize her as a first-strike target.

But Benton had talked her down from the crazy idea of following the rioters south—*thank God*—and she was stationed at the Bark. With Smith's team reinforcing, the Vault was the most secure location possible. Everything else was locked down per the protocol Saunders helped Dalmore establish.

"Sir, Captain Rath confirms all Marines accounted for and says Uumhrat took Dr. Pat and Micky to the clinic an hour ago," huffed PFC Licht keeping the two-stair-at-a-time pace despite his full loadout.

Right, all bases covered.

Still, that nagging feeling persisted.

Maybe it was the fact that pinned down to the five-second choke-out, Portcullis' enemies could deploy incredible and dynamic capabilities. Super insurgents ghosting in and taking out targets of opportunity? Entirely possible even without a green screen. Maybe no level of preparedness would ever lead to sleeping well at night.

Saunders stepped out of the stairwell into hysteria. Sweaty bodies, flailing arms, and open mouths. This wasn't a meeting; it was a white-collar version of the riot outside. It was everyone too important to stay the fuck home at dawn o'clock but too useless to be out running damage control. Anger, frustration, and a bag full of broken administrative tools.

In his heavy armor, Dalmore plowed through the upheaval to the raised platform serving as a stage. It was a convenient extension of the hearth, which was seated a full foot off the floor due to an architectural SNAFU. With that fireplace that could fit two refrigerators behind him, Dalmore gave the crowd a glare that could bake bricks. It was that age-old message, in good times and bad.

The military is here.

When it got quiet, and it did get quiet, Saunders joined him. Examiner Creed, son of former Lord Governor Elldren, also wiggled his way forward. The PFC stayed by the stairwell, back against a corner and head on a swivel.

Saunders held Dalmore's flank with menacing eyes and MP5 submachine gun slung over his bulging chest armor. It was the same posture he'd taken at Lord Bayliss' hearing when the Portcullisians seemed like a rogue bunch of throwbacks living in the remote Pakistani mountains. From the uncertain looks, they still remembered no-bullshit mode.

"Where is Lord Benton?" asked Master Lobhar. He was a friend of Master Gol's, whose bald head would be a welcome addition to the feral crowd. Lobhar was softer, better suited to managing the local boys club.

"Peace, Lord Benton's duties are vast," said Dalmore. "This night hath seen enough terror to challenge that of Portcullis' first settlers."

"Aye," said Examiner Creed touching his chin, an indication he was about to flip into historian mode. "Those fierce men and women of legend carved a refuge out of these frozen lands and held ablaze a welcome for all who would travel to Galimay. They knew suffering and despair but never defeat!"

The audience shot back icicles. Corsan Carre, military command element, and patriotism didn't matter; they wanted their lord governor.

"Creed," Saunders whispered. "Find out what's keeping Benton."

"Aye," said the younger man, wiping the sweat from his brow and making no excuse to exit stage right. Creed was a fantastic academic, detective, and conversationalist at dinner parties. But he had a glass jaw when it came to negativity.

"What knew the first s-settlers of *daggers in the night?*" asked someone. The phrasing was strange, same terminology Sir Krue had used when describing the loss of the Fifth Army's Corund Corps.

"Same as we," said Dalmore. "And different. As theirs lay with Gra'nuul glass buried in their chests, ours suffer the blades of those we knew as friends."

Saunders tsked. Turning the crowd on itself to take the heat off leadership was a terrible tactic. It worked, sure, but also spurred disunity.

"Mayhaps those . . . in the arena? They are naught of Portcullis!" cried the same person. There was a familiar snivel to his voice. Every word not shouted came out like a meek apology. But nothing about this motherfucker suggested he was sorry about anything.

Saunders struggled to see who it was. The wild accusation had come from somewhere, nowhere. *Fuck it, no time to play sleuth.*

"No," Saunders said with a step forward. "The Caranuscan refugees sweat blood helping you all recover from Isllor's attack." That drew more than a few nods. At least they were still receptive. "The problem is bigger and more diffuse than any one group or district." He paused, hoping he wasn't about to pull a Benton. "Presently, we believe this night's violence to be the work of the Anticult."

Gasps. Commotion.

"The Corsan Carre believe . . . believe us to be of the Anticult. The low sh-shall not be saved!"

Saunders leaned back to Dalmore. "You see who said that?"

"Nay, but the seeds of mine folly grow fast." The Watch Chief gave a single clap, and his tarnished plate armor rattled the hall. "Mistrust is the enemy's coin. It is their sword, their power. It was the way of Isllor Mortund, and it was the undoing of the Caranuscan Empire."

"We must purge the enemy!"

"Nay," Dalmore boomed. "We must strengthen our resolve. Truth and honor shall bind us and squeeze this poison from our veins. The Anticult hath long-promised much to those brought low by strife. High lords and common folk alike are lured by its sweet song. It deals in falsehoods and misgivings. I deny it!"

"He's right," Saunders said, slamming his vocal cords down an octave and pressing the gas on the command voice. "The Anticult is weak. Strikes from shadows and thrives on chaos. Band together; work together. Wolves can't hurt the herd."

"To what hope?" asked Lobhar, probably with genuine curiosity but also inciting a new wave of feedback.

"Our fate is to be decided this day!" boomed Dalmore over the rising protest. The flame-lit, stone hall got pin-drop quiet.

Saunders dropped back to parade rest and switched to receiver mode. Instead of riding the high of their victory against the dragon, morale and carefully laid plans were crumbling. Yes, the frontlines were no place for civilians. But this wasn't a combat outpost zeroed by over-the-horizon artillery; it was a fucking fortress high in the mountains. Brines, *may his demons be trapped in hell with him*, had taken out the aerial threat. Between the Bark and Ceal, the remaining external threat was a frenzied melee charge, uphill, against the North Wall. As for the Anticult, counterinsurgency was the Marine Corps' bread and butter.

What was left to decide?

"Mayhaps, the breaching of South Gate, was driven by the Anticult, but 'twas an opportunity seen and seized by our people driven to fear," Dalmore continued. "That is the enemy we must first defeat. For the strength of Portcullis lies naught in its stoneworks, but in its host."

"Scant are our men at arms; great are our families and infirm," said Master Walram. He controlled the city's building supplies market with hands soft enough to make a baby blush. "What valor do ye hope will come from this host?"

"S-south, to Greater Galimay!" argued that one fucking guy Saunders couldn't peg.

"Aye, as when the Genisans struck before," said Lobhar referencing the near disaster a year prior. "To the castellums of our lords as Portcullis braves the storm."

"Ajid's Winter is not alone in the follies that await us south," Dalmore said, pacing. There was something to be said about that saunter with a sword on the hip. It had style. A slung rifle over the shoulder or across the chest would never look as intimidating. "Mine former brethren in the Sapphire Branch—law to the wilds and much relied upon by the lesser lords of many taxed lands—hath retreated from their duties. They gather in Durador and the cities."

"Then we sh-shall make for the cities!"

Saunders was sure that no one said that. He had eyes on everyone, and the voice had come from the crowd's center mass. Either the guy was a ventriloquist or . . .

"To the charity of whom?" Dalmore asked. "And what birds might prey upon ye along the ways no longer patrolled? War comes, and the sturdy people of Portcullis, champions of these dangerous Paling Mountains, fall to fear. Durador cowers, sending naught a single colored cloak to aid. What do ye expect from simple villagers? Ask the Caranuscans what they saw of their countrymen as the great houses fell. Ask if their cities and wilds were safeholds."

"Portcullis was our only refuge," admitted a man in a green tunic who, like Saunders, had a little more Mediterranean in him than these pale-faced Portcullisesians. Back home, it would have pegged him for anything other than heritage, but the racial makeup was more stratified here. Caranusca was farther north, which meant a more temperate climate because they were on the planet's southern hemisphere.

"Indeed. Whence we turn our backs, only running remains. Shall all Galimay hop from city to souther city until our litter of corpses leads to an over-burgeoned Helidor at the tip of our realm?" Dalmore paused, face twitching. Then he drew that sword and roared, "There is NAUGHT after that!" Saunders flinched. The guy could lay it down when he wanted to.

The assembly of the greedy and selfish dropped their eyes. For once, Dalmore skipped pulling the honor and duty card and went straight for the throat. And they knew it.

Retreat just meant last to die.

"So comes our choice that will shake fate itself. Shall we split, leaving both halves weaker than the whole? Spears at our backs and Ajid upon our necks?" Dalmore slammed his boot down on the wooden platform. "Or shall we fight?"

Fuck yeah, this is—

"Nay."

The word ripped through the noisy hall like a gravimetric wave. Heads turned toward the far stairwell. There, decked out in clean (no longer the norm) white plate, flowing cape, and that immaculate blade stuffed into a jeweled scabbard by his side, Benton loomed in the entrance. He wasn't a big guy: Saunders' height, but a little narrower in the shoulders. But he commanded a presence when he needed to.

"Portcullis must fight," said Benton. "But it cannot win."

Not this again!

Mike would've shot him. Snapped that rifle up and put three in the air before the first hit. *Ain't no three strikes here,* he would've said. *Once is fuck; two is you.*

Saunders forced himself to hold fast, muscles straining to discharge the desire for immediate action. No matter the reality, the first rule of reassurance was to paint everything in the context of victory. Retreat was regrouping, surrender was bogging down enemy logistics, disarming was a front to fund fights on alternative battlefields . . .

And Portcullis is a fucking bluff!

"We can hold the winter," Dalmore offered. It came across as confident, a clarification of Benton's message, but the CO of Portcullis' armed forces was reeling.

"M'lord," sniveled that one voice. Saunders saw who it was this time. A parting in the crowd and a head of reddish hair about two heads too low. *It's that blacksmith . . . what's his name? Smallfoot.* "What of Lady Ceal?"

Instead of assurance, Benton's confidence waivered, and Saunders' skull rang with the word *fuck*. Every worst-case scenario was converging into the perfect hell. Saunders opened his mouth to parry the blow, but it was too late.

"Many hath taken to the treacherous road already, unguided and unaided. Once beyond the walls, Lady Ceal can do naught but listen to their screams float in on the mountain breeze. What choice hath she?" Benton's jaw stiffened. "Simpler for the rest to leave than lure our lost back. She will ensure they reach the safety of Oxhold."

So, we're back to Ceal leaving. It sucked the air right out of the drafty room.

Dalmore turned for the first time since taking the stage and frowned. "Ye's ghostly enemy mounds its victories." A sigh. "Would that I had listened to the warnings of these . . . recusants."

"You did listen," Saunders said, mind racing to reconfigure his assets and liabilities to find the silver lining. The way heads were turning toward the exits, the food and fuel shortages would disappear. The long-term strategy also remained intact: weaken the enemy with multiple collapsing engagements and hit them with the hammer when their supply lines and morale were stretched thin.

But Ceal would be a devastating loss.

Fuck.

"A perilous trek becomes tempting to all," Benton cautioned the crowd. "Alas, all the stone and steel from here to Durador is naught if Portcullis is swept aside."

"But ye spake the city doomed to fall," said Lobhar.

"He didn't say when," said Saunders hoping Benton's switchback was part of some masterful ploy. Dalmore just stood there looking fierce, probably suppressing the desire to bash skulls.

"Aye, till the rise of Ajid's Spring, the Bark shall endure," said Benton, now in the crowd. "Lady Ceal will return when those ill of will or ability are delivered to mine steward, Sir Thode, at Oxhold. Five days. Any are welcome into her company. But the battle is here. Life is here. The strength of ye's backs, arms, and wills is worth ten of what ye can offer the lower lands. We must fight."

"Ceal will s-see us s-safe as whence with Isllor," goaded Smallfoot. The little weasel was a fuckfest dick sore. Two minutes ago, he would've been top priority for corrective action. The intel drop on Ceal was a lot to process, though. Five days didn't sound too bad, but as the crowd and Benton went back and forth, it became clear that the bulk of the city would run. And herds moved slowly.

"The safety of Portcullis' citizens is to be a planned affair, not a maddened dash," shouted Dalmore trying to prevent another stampede.

The more that left also meant that Ceal had less reason to return. Sheer numbers would probably overwhelm the resources at Benton's Oxhold. Then it would turn into Moses leading the flock around.

Need to talk her out of this.

Dalmore raised his arms to calm the commotion, to no avail. The hall was out of control, and people were leaving. The keep was on lockdown, so they still had a chance at keeping this quiet. But neither the Watch nor the Deadlies had the numbers to stop a rush AND scour the streets for the Anticult, AND guard the perimeter.

Saunders wanted to drag Benton outside and sock him in the gut. The hero swordsman could move so fast that the blow would probably never land, but it would feel good to try.

As Dalmore roared and reasoned with the crowd, beige stepped onto the stage. A tacked-up, born and bred American Marine, PFC Licht, was a welcomed sight. He had a SITREP from Sergeant Smith.

City Square and Bark: secure.

Ceal: secure.

Unconfirmed reports of more fighting in the streets.

Marines were operating on the buddy system with rifles condition zero, kill ready.

Before Saunders could issue an order for Smith to send a patrol to the clinic, Benton gave him a weird look and motioned him over.

"Licht, go find out what Benton wants," Saunders said, needing to hold his position. The room was a hair-trigger ready to explode. His hand gravitated to his sidearm as arguing became accusing, and the mob edged in on the stage.

"Resist death!" boomed Dalmore, and everyone jumped back. It jacked that fight or flight response better than a warning shot over their heads. The herd bristled but decided to listen.

"Mayhap there will come a time when all hath fled, and I alone stand to bar North Gate from the combined might of the Pandonis Immortalis and Obantum Carre," he said. "And with every width I live, so shall the all of Galimay enjoy a prolonged life. I ask, who would stand with me to give such a gift to so many?"

The hall's response was lukewarm, but no more shaking fists and spittle. It was an improvement that could allow time for calmer heads to prevail. The city needed troops, even if it was just bodies looking mean from up high. Just to intimidate the Genisan scouts long enough for the weather to move in. Then, Ceal would get her five, ten, twenty days and maybe return. *It could work.*

The crowd shifted to a more positive note: Dalmore and hero-talk instead of mystical Corsan Carre and Lady Ceal crap. It gave Saunders a breather to focus on Benton and maybe that asshole Smallfoot.

PFC Licht was right next to the lord governor, who was holding back the masses with a raised hand. Benton said about two words before the PFC turned that shit-hit-the-fan shade of white and started swimming his way back through the crowd. Less breaststroke and more grabbing and pushing. And shouting.

"What did Benton say?" Saunders demanded when he was close enough to hear.

"The—"

"M'lords!" gasped a white-tabarded Watchman stumbling out of the stairwell. It was Sergeant Teague who was supposed to check in with the Dawn Guard and assess the North Wall's security status. Before anyone could ask if he needed an oxygen tank, he said, "The Dowdale. The enemy marches!"

That was when PFC Licht managed to report that Dr. Bowman and Micky had been violently attacked.

Saunders' nagging feeling of forgetting something disappeared, and suddenly nothing else mattered.

CHAPTER 8

A PART

Smoke hung in the air without odor or taste among wreckage and ruin. Stone, meant to be straight-line stacked, laid in heaps beneath the cracked fragments of once sound buildings. Silence floated down still streets; Dr. Pat was alone.

She studied her hands; they were the same as she remembered from her waking life, down to the chewed nails from a habit she tried to break but always backslid.

A lucid dream? *she wondered.*

They were the best: fly high into the sky, swim to the bottom of the ocean, or live out any number of fantasies. Total control over reality. Usually, she opted to get laid because they never lasted long. The dreams, anyway.

Reaching out, she commanded, "Bourbon." Getting laid could wait.

"I'll see yer ass in the morning."

It thundered across the heavens scaring her worse than any nightmare. Suddenly, the battered and destroyed city of stone pulled her in. Instead of a drink in her hand, the ruined streets became a million shadows hiding eyes, teeth, claws, and malice. Smoke brought burning tears and spasmed her bronchioles. A black plume of unburned carbon billowed out of the white haze like a hand reaching for her throat. She pulled her shirt up over her face so she could breathe and broke into a run, stumbling and crunching over things she didn't dare look down at.

Around a corner and through an alley, she emerged from the enveloping smoke and the day brightened. A familiar sight stopped her cold. The ruins could've been anything, definitely medieval, but that one mountain towering above them said it all.

This was Portcullis.

Can't be a magic dream, *she thought. They weren't prophetic. Lady Ceal had said they offered glimpses of the past and present. Never the future.*

Beige.

It was loud in the colorless world of whites and greys. One of the Marines was sprawled on his back in the middle of what used to be City Square. Perhaps a casualty of whatever happened here.

"I need to wake up," she said, hoping the dream would listen. The gloom behind her was still coming, pouring out of the alley.

"Faaahk," growled the Marine.

Her heart jumped, and suddenly, the nightmare was forgotten.

She ran, pushed hard against the dream trying to treadmill her in place. That growl . . . it was familiar. Same as the yellowed teeth and little pinch on his cheek from that scar whenever he tried to smile. It was all just a dream, but she couldn't stop herself. She ran away from the terror building in the sky and filling the streets; she ran toward him to . . . just to . . .

She stopped short.

However she remembered him in life, he was now a ghoul in comparison. Those pale blues were sunken deep beneath a paper-white mask. His uniform was out of focus, bloodied as much as it was still beige. It was a monster, phase two of her subconsciousness trying to scare the shit out of her.

That head rolled to the side, eyes falling on her. The mouth started flapping, maybe remembering words through pure motor memory of whatever might be left of a zombified Mike Brines' necrotizing neural tissue. She searched for somewhere to hide. The government buildings that once lined the square were crumpled and dangerous. The clinic's lower levels are dug into the rock. It should've survived, *she thought, trying to orient herself.*

"Yer . . . yer . . ." the creature croaked.

She wanted to scream, but no sound came.

"Yer wearin' clothes," he finished.

"What?" she asked, dumbfounded. Zombies usually didn't speak.

*He sat up, dead head panning the ruins. "Fah *cough* fuck happened here? Fuck are we? Christ, why's it feel like . . ."—he stared at his pale hands—"Oh."*

Dr. Pat was unprepared for the rush of emotion that followed. The ghoul went from another decaying feature of this hellscape back to the shining bright spot in her heart. The thing she most wanted to touch, hold, and never let go. She shook, heat rising within. Mike was hurt, cold. He needed her. Tears flowed, choking off her words as her mind descended into a sense-filled deluge of need. Need to touch and caress his face. Hold. Warm. Be with.

"You uh, you ain't about to turn weird, are ya?"

Pat pulled back, realizing how ridiculous she must've looked. It was out of character on the worst days and entirely new for anything she'd experienced in a dream. "He's hurt," she heard herself say. But it was a child's voice, that little girl she kept locked away in her pink bedroom so Dr. Pat could protect her from the world.

"Fuckin' dreams," Mike huffed, climbing to shaky feet. "Sex ain't happening, so what we doin' here?"

Pat tried to answer, but a raging bundle of emotions she'd never felt before blew out to the forefront. Everything went white, and she cried out in . . . in what? Not pain, quite the opposite. It was like her bones were glowing, bathing her in light from within. Then it was over, and she could think again. If that was some sort of dream climax, it was the weirdest . . .

"He's hurt," came a voice to her lower left.

Ann. Complete with chestnut bangs and a gap where her right canine should've been. Dr. Pat sucked a breath full of wood smoke.

"Already came out the other side of hurt, kid," Mike said, sunken eyes locking onto something behind them.

"You're dead," Dr. Pat whispered.

"Everyone's fucking dead." Brines lumbered forward, fixated on whatever was stealing the light from their backs. Dr. Pat didn't dare turn around.

"We can't stop it," said Ann, trembling.

"Don't mean we gotta lie down and take it." He straightened his back, standing firm like he did in life, and said, "Get behind me."

Dr. Pat woke as it struck, heart frozen on its last beat. The dream faded, everything but that final moment, that glimpse of what was coming. It was the char of a burned universe.

The original evil.

". . . spear or something . . . missed the spine . . ."

". . . other options?"

" —kin' prison shanked, sir. . . . days we ain't got."

"I need to know if Micky will recover." *Saunders* oozed the voice recognition neurons.

Micky! Screamed the follow-on.

Dr. Pat forced her eyes open. Blurry and dim, the room was buzzing like it should've hurt but didn't. *Drugs?* Extreme sleepiness tucked the question away for later. She tried to form words, but her jaw just drooped; no need to close it again. At least nothing hurt. Everything was quite comfortable and fuzzy.

The lazy river of eternity continued until a new voice rattled its waters. It was an irritating woman sound, and all Dr. Pat wanted to do was roll over and go back to sleep. Trouble was, everything ached now. Her mouth was cotton, and head was . . . *OW pain ten!*

"Still, dear. The hurt is just ye sense comin' back," mothered Wisewoman Alena. Between that and the headache, sleep lost its appeal. Dr. Pat took another shot at opening her eyes and found the room back in focus, if bright. Being in the clinic, which was a basement, it was probably dark. Hypersensitivity. At least everything had stopped spinning, and thoughts were gelling a little faster.

"Wha . . ." Dr. Pat began before losing the action of her tongue to the glue trap on the roof of her mouth. Alena pressed a glass against her lips and liquid relief flooded in, calming the headache. "What happened?"

"Assassins, milady," rumbled Uumhrat scrubbing his hands in the corner. The big innkeeper was seated on a comically tiny stool, which made her giggle.

The memories landed a second later, blowing away the cobwebs in her head. "Micky!" Events were out of sequence, appearing in flashes. But dark arms and glinting metal at her number one fan's throat were crystal clear. Blood, blood everywhere. Dr. Pat stared up at Uumhrat in awe. "You made it. Are . . . are you okay?"

"I be fine, lass. Drove 'em off, I managed."

"Drove?" snorted someone in beige. Buontempo. "More like five confirmed kills with his bare hands, Doc."

"Micky took the point of a spear in the low of her back," said the wisewoman. "The Sap mends as she rests. There is naught of this to worry."

Dr. Pat sat up, emotions running wild, and gravity trying to pull her brain down through the back of her neck. "I heard something . . . something about the spine. How much blood did she lose? Where is she?"

"'Tis but a hole between the vital parts. I expect weakness to linger for days, but strength will return in time."

"Charlie Actual, this is Two. Doc's awake," said Buontempo slipping out of the room.

Dr. Pat huffed; her brain was three parts sludge and one part stuck in that fucking dream. It was too much to be picking up on subtleties from the Portcullisers. "Where is she?" she repeated.

"Ohh shit," croaked a voice from the doorway. Not one of the Marines or Wethands, but a sight to be sure. It was Micky wrapped in a blood-stained bed sheet. "Pat . . . you're alive."

"Dear, ye must rest," said Wisewoman Alena swooping in, but Micky slipped past her, grabbing onto the wall shelf for support.

"I'm fine. Your"—she winced and clutched her lower back—"your sap is . . . god, it fucking hurts. But it's working. I just need time." She came over to the bed. "Can you walk?"

Dr. Pat considered several possible answers, each addressing the problem through theorization of her physiological state and the narcotic-like substances saturating her brain stem. Instead of delving into a lengthy discourse, she swung her legs over the bedside and sat up. Her stomach flip-flopped, and she wanted to duck her head beneath an invisible sledgehammer, but balance was fine. She also noticed her legs were bare and . . .

"Clothes," muttered Micky to Alena. The fact that the girl wasn't using this as an opportunity to make her weird little innuendos was a testament.

"I be needed back at the inn," said Uumhrat keeping his eyes up during his hasty exit.

"Where's Saunders? I need to tell him . . ." Dr. Pat began as the wisewoman followed Uumhrat out. Her jaw was starting to throb as her head cleared. A vague memory of a fist popping stars into her eyes surfaced.

"No, we need to bail," said Micky, plopping beside her. The way she grimaced suggested that sitting down was no better than standing. "And don't argue with me. This place is not what Benton advertised. It's about to be a warzone. All those promises about winter delaying things were total bullshit."

Did Micky have a Vision too? "I think you're right," she said, following with a quick rundown of her dream. She walled off the specific emotional events; seeing a zombified version of Brines was something for the top tier of the ivory tower to pick apart. As Micky's unbroken stare seemed to agree, the highlights were the destruction, the dark entity that defied description, and the fact that none of it had happened yet.

"Girl," Micky said, not so much scootching over but more leaning into her, "You saw the fucking future."

"Maybe? I don't know. Ann was there too, same as she looks now. None of us were part of the future; we were more like . . . visitors."

"We need to tell Ceal."

"No." The word popped out on pure reflex. But it was the right one. Ceal would just pervert the Vision to fit her narrative.

"Pat, there's more going on here than we know." Micky waved her finger like cops did during a field sobriety test and nodded. "This wasn't a random attack. Those fuckers drugged you. That's intent to kidnap. Fucking Mina Bazar all over again. You agree we need to leave, right?"

"Yeah."

"Well, we can't hide out in the baggage cars waiting to get jumped again." She lifted the sheet to show the bloodied cloths wrapped around her torso. "A little to the left, and I'd never walk again. Not feeling my power button is unacceptable." She cracked a half-smile.

"The Marines can protect us."

Micky laughed, then cried, then finished her laugh. "Ugh, we're dropping like flies. Brines, Williamson, almost us. They're rifle people, Pat. Not shields. Not Ceal."

Mike's dead face flashed from the dream, and anger boiled up, eager to blame Ceal. Others would call it projection or some other psychological need to assign blame, but Dr. Pat didn't care. Mike was the only one not to come home on Ceal's watch. Even Captain Rath made it back, broken as he was. "Wasn't much of a shield for Mike."

"You need to put that shit to bed," Micky snapped. "Even if that savage bitch pulled his heart out through his ass, you need to let it go. This is pure survival now, and she's our ticket to getting away from this cartoon mountain town and tucking in with Galimay's *real* defenses. Their armies, their walls, their fucking wizards, and witches."

What happened to the happy-go-lucky Micky Toms, who taught kindergarten to impoverished villagers? The combination of torture, trauma, and then arriving here on death's doorstep was taking its toll woefully so. The

Micky of today was the rusted, salted, and barbed version of yesterday's "We should totally go explore the world!" She was also correct, but in that *don't do drugs, diet and exercise, less screen time, smile and be lady-like* sort of way.

Easier said than done.

Or was it? This Vision was different from those of the past and present because there was no host. Maybe because the future had no substance yet. *I'm nowhere near sober enough to think through it.* One thing was for sure: Ceal told Micky and Saunders that Visions never revealed the future. An absolute lie. More evidence of Ceal hiding stuff for her own sake.

Maybe the real reason she's leaving is that she saw the same thing.

Suddenly, Dr. Pat was back in Portcullis' ruins. The skies were grey, dark clouds rushing up from the valley. It wasn't a storm; it was the end, the primal source of all fear that had and would always scatter mankind's accomplishments before it.

An involuntary shudder returned her to the medieval recovery room. Micky was studying her, and there was no telling how long she'd spaced out. It didn't matter; Dr. Pat couldn't argue with that sort of terror. "Okay, we'll talk to Ceal."

"No," Saunders said, declining Comack's offered armchair. He preferred to stand, wet boots sinking into the plush carpet of Benton's private living room. It better set the tone for the coming discussion than balled fists and shouting.

Ceal nodded from the ornate two-seater, sipping at a cup of something thin. Not red wine, maybe white. Wasn't beer because he would've taken one. Not that he needed one, but his ship was shaking itself to pieces on the eve of battle. After the security lapse that almost killed the women, the bigger wave behind it was unfathomable.

The Genisans.

All force projections had grossly—by orders of magnitude—underestimated their numbers. And now they occupied the only spot on the planet that could get his Marines back to Earth.

"Welcome," she said in that calm, collected voice. Comack bowed out and took his post in the hallway.

Saunders skipped the pleasantries. "Your husband said that army assembling in the valley is the biggest single force of manpower this planet has seen." He gave it a second to set before slamming down, "Ever."

"Aye."

"Dalmore's calling it the *Last* Army. According to your scripture and beliefs, that means the race is on. Right?"

"Aye."

"Then they're going to come. Hard. If they break through the mountains, evacuation won't matter. The second that Bark falls, they will hit you and your convoy from a hundred different angles. The battle is not . . . not out there!" He pointed at the fancy window overlooking the backyard for effect. "It's here."

Ceal gave a practiced politician's smile. "The gem of Portcullis doth shine bright. Mine eyes were drawn to it long ago, enthralled by its charm and possibilities." Her expression darkened. "But it is an illusion that fast fades."

At least we're on the same page there. "No question Portcullis is getting short, but you agree it needs to hold until winter sets in. Right?"

"Which is why Benton chooses to stay," she broke eye contact.

"Why YOU should stay. That five days shit made sense this morning. Now we've got tens of thousands advancing on us." He walked to the window. Clear skies for a change; the high mountain slopes were all powder. Gorgeous. "Evacuation was inevitable," he allowed. "We're heavy on mouths and light on arms. Portcullis needs to drop weight. But not you! Anyone can command a caravan through friendly territory. Not anyone can control lightning."

She sipped her drink. "All is not as it seems as this day hath revealed. More than dust, rain, and rock lie in wait in the lower inlands. The enemy, too, hath prepared for a year to defeat the Portcullis they faced before."

"They haven't met us."

Penciled-in eyebrows popped up as if to say, *oh really,* before laying down a glossary of counterpoints. Instead, she changed subjects. "Speaking of the well-met . . . Dr. Bowman and Micky, by the Five Mercies, visited early postnoon."

An involuntary fist clench gave away his frustration. Uumhrat had demonstrated some latent badassery and protected the women while Saunders was distracted by the circus. Thanks to that medical sap, Micky was already up and about when he spoke with them. Problem was, as with most civilians, terrorism had done its job well. They wanted to leave.

Goddamn it, Ceal, use your magic to scrape that army out of the valley and get us the fuck home! he wanted to scream. Instead, he asked, "What did you tell them?"

"They needed little convincing to join me as Portcullis' fate is now clear in their eyes."

Don't explode. Play the game. "So, Dr. Bowman's Vision *was* of the future?"

"No." It was almost a shout. Ceal collected herself immediately. "Impressions in the like of tapestries or echoes can ripple through the currents of Power. Those sensitive to their wakes can relive brief moments of the past. Oft, the past as it transpires. What hath not happened cannot leave a ripple."

Instead of instilling confidence, it felt like a classic strawman argument—a deflection. Most of Saunders' "Visions" involved weird shit happening here on Scianas—Vissl and knights holding court in the Dowdale Valley, people moving through portals, mundane moments of lives long forgotten or too distant to matter—but a few happened back home. Dr. Bowman reported one where she saw the C-monster gearing up for another fight in Pakistan, allegedly now a denied area. Some of it was stuff he didn't want to believe—Black Robes subduing and brainwashing Russian special forces and legions of devout Kôz followers flocking to General Khel's banner—but it was too real. So, if seeing across lightyears was possible, why not the future?

"She was pretty adamant about some new enemy," he said. "*Primal* was her word for it. No physical description, more of a force. Sounded like a game-ender. A weapon. Is that some ripple from a fantasy rock, too?"

That smooth, creamy brow furrowed for an instant. "I believe she perceives the danger of and to our world. It is naught to dismiss, but neither is it more prophetic than our expectations of Portcullis."

"You're side-stepping."

Ceal set the cup down. "Much must be learned before I can answer. If we lend credence to her dream, mayhap this *Primal*," the word was drenched in accent as the magic translation failed, "is naught but Genisan governance after we are driven from this place. Or . . ." she let it hang in the air. Saunders caught it as *fucking Satan*.

"Okay, answer me this: Is there something worse than the Genisans out there?"

Benton's wizard wife, recently returned from the dementia ward by some mystical shit purportedly involving Dr. Bowman, pursed her lips. "No."

"Then, Dr. Bowman and Micky stay. The city will hold until you can—"

Her eyes flashed green, two traffic lights screaming *stop*, not *go*. "Do ye not see her importance?"

Her importance.

That statement sent Saunders flying back in time to Captain Strom's day quarters aboard the USS *Storm*. *Sea Monster* was a newborn "go," and Charlie Company was fresh-faced and ready to rescue 126 Americans from a psychotic rogue Pakistani general. Admiral Bowman stood with a demanding stare across that heavy, bolted-down wooden desk. Between them was a red binder labeled TOP SECRET and plastered with the restrictive caveats that indicated immediately actionable and ultra-sensitive information.

Within was a face and orders for priority extraction from Mina Bazar.

She was the singular reason the military had authorized the entire rescue operation. The reason—indirectly, he assumed—they were here in the first place. Despite all Saunders' Marines, capabilities, actions, and networking with primitive and alien cultures, he was nothing more than an escort. A bullet sponge waiting to get wet. "What does *she* want?" was all he asked.

"To change guardians, it would seem," Ceal said, sipping her wine, apparently fully aware of the situation. "We leave on the morrow's morn."

"If it was me, sir, I'da gone in wit him," Smith said.

Captain Rath sank deeper into the high-backed, velvet armchair that looked like it could barely fit one of Smith's shoulders. This little waiting area, more like a cove away from the formal rooms, was probably where Benton did all his serious talking. During the day, the bigass windows in front of them had a sweeping overlook of the mansion's backyard and mountains beyond. Rustic, soaring, and breathtaking.

It wasn't half-bad after dark, either, with those ghostly slopes backed up by the clearest, most brilliant cosmic spread anyone who wasn't on a space shuttle had seen.

No matter the neighborhood, the people with money always had the best views. Still, it was nice to be chillin' here with the officers, lords, and ladies. Best part was none of the locals knew that "sergeant" meant dick. Nah, Jason Smith was *Corsan Carre* here. Fuckin' Justice League superhero shit.

"Captain Saunders has a . . . uh, there's something he needed to discuss with her alone. I don't think he wants me around," said Captain Rath. It was a weird admission, more said to himself than anything.

"Don't know 'bout that, sir. Only ever seen the cap'n respect what people got to give. Shoot, if Gunny had his way, he woulda drummed out Jersey, err, Corporal Nickels, forever ago. Cap'n wouldn't let it. Sees somethin' in him."

Captain Rath crumpled at the mention of Gunny Brines.

"Permission to speak, sir?"

"Always."

"Ain't no lie Cap'n and Gunny was friends. Legit hell and back again, but you ain't the one who gotta carry it around."

Captain Rath stared through those windows, probably seeing more than shadows. "I get the impression people blame me."

"We Marines, sir. If we thought it was your fault, there wouldn't be no ambiguity."

The pilot nodded, even flashed a little smirk.

"Gunny died savin' people," Smith continued. "You, me, this whole city. That's what he always wanted. Not goin' out a hero but atonin' for all the guys under him who didn't come home."

"Like Williamson," Captain Rath said, shaking his head. He was the only one who witnessed it, but from the mess, there wasn't much left to imagine. "Him, Gunny, the Osprey flight crew, my copilot Padilla, and who knows how many more on the ground at Mina Bazar. I'd say I'm bad luck, but I guess curses are real here in magic land. Best to keep away from me."

"You pilin', sir. It's what people do when they go negative. Gotta shake that shit like one of them bogies up there, y'know?"

"Bandits."

"Yeah, okay. All I'm sayin' is it's a shit hand, sir, but ain't the last deal. Them responsible are comin', and that means we gonna get a chance to rectify some stuff. Captain Saunders' gonna need you; I'm gonna need you. The men need you. We Marines. Everyone else is just everyone else."

Captain Rath gave that trademarked officer nod of mutual respect.

Smith felt he said the right things but couldn't help but wonder how Gunny would've handled it. Probably would've growled and planted his knife into the wooden table between them. Smith had a knife, a standard-issue six inch Ka-Bar, but to him, it was like a screwdriver or can opener—something in the toolkit, not a reason to get up in the morning.

"Let's go," ordered Captain Saunders marching in. Comack, the butler, was trailing with a stream of apologies, urging them to wait until his esteemed Lord Benton arrived.

Fuck, Comack, Benton tried to hack you up a couple months ago. He don't deserve you.

The captain made for the door without looking back. When Watchman Stebbin offered his carriage out front, it was shrugged off in favor of hoofing it through the frozen streets. It meant another twenty before chow, but the reasoning wasn't hard to guess. More than blowing off some steam, the captain's agenda always involved the mission. Tempting fate with those Anticult motherfuckers prowling around came to mind. Three rifle-toting Marines were a much harder target than two women on their way to help sick people at the clinic.

Deep in the freezer-burned maze of dark buildings and alleys where it was just wind and crunching boots, the captain ordered a halt. Thinking they were about to take a detour, Smith got pumped for combat. Instead, the captain turned and dropped a freaking hammer. "Smith, I want you plus one to accompany Dr. Bowman and Micky with Ceal tomorrow."

Not cool.

First, it meant that meeting with Ceal must've shit the bed. Second, if this was Gunny or Staff Sergeant Carneal talking, they'd hear some words. Bad words, maybe pleading. The fight for this castle city would be heavy trigger action against a metal army of sitting ducks. There was no question Smith and his M240 light machine gun, *the Pig*, needed to be a part of it. But he held back, remembering that senior NCO meant functioning much higher than his current pay grade. "Sir?"

"They're pulling out with most of the city's remaining civilian population and headed for one of Benton's facilities at Oxhold. Their safety is mission critical."

Smith glanced at Captain Rath while keeping one eye on the shadows and the other on the crusted slush and icy stones at their feet. Anyway, it made sense. Operation *Sea Monster* was probably a closed book back home, but they were technically still deployed here. Keeping two hostages in a forward position was fucked in triplicate. "Why the split?"

"Two-prong protection: your team will have proximity, the rest of us will keep the enemy corked here so they can't pursue."

"Saunders," said Captain Rath, suddenly interested. "How about I take charge of Cork Team?"

The captain cocked his head. "To what end?"

Smith gave the two officers space and set his eyes on patrol mode. The streets were a combination of *it's fucking cold,* and *we're leaving in the morning* deserted. Watch posts were staffed, but patrols were hunkered around smoldering braziers. The oil streetlamps were lit thanks to insurgent activity but couldn't cover the gaps where those non-functional Q-lights were. If someone wanted to do them like they did the doc and Micky, there wouldn't be a better time.

"Continuity," said Captain Rath.

"You think Cork won't make it?" asked Captain Saunders.

"Unnecessary risk. I'm an ancillary element in this whole deal. You're planning, administration, execution. You're leadership, Saunders. I can tell riflemen where and when to shoot. I can't . . ." he trailed off.

Saunders cut his eyes to the shadows, maybe buying time to figure out what he was gonna say. Maybe he heard something. Smith gave them a little more space, just enough so it wouldn't be easy for anyone trying to kill three birds with one stone.

"Rath, this isn't a suicide mission or a sacrifice. Nor is it an excuse to go hog wild against an enemy who can't shoot back." Smith figured that last one was aimed at him. "It's the C-monster backed into a corner. We're a pot of shit shoved into a closet that needs to grow into a fucking fruiting oak. And that's what we're going to do. Rah?"

"Oorah," Smith barked. *Damned right.*

"I hear you," said Captain Rath. "Adapt, overcome, all that. But why send our civvies with an element we can't control?"

Saunders kicked an ice ball off the street. "The situation is evolving rapidly. I haven't had a chance to keep everyone updated, but yesterday's plan of hold and work the Ceal angle is gone. She's leaving, and we need to keep tabs on her."

"Right, and part of the deal is maintaining a presence here in the city. Accurate?"

"Yes."

"So that's it. The situation with Ceal needs a strong hand on the wheel. Cork Team can meet our obligations here with me while you—"

"Negative."

"Why not?" asked Captain Rath. "Sounds like a trust, not a tactical issue. Either you trust Ceal—someone who can literally become superwoman—to protect the civvies, or you don't. Two riflemen won't move the needle at all."

"So, you're saying we should let the women go alone?"

"I'm saying that it needs an officer at the helm. Let the rest of us execute Cork."

Smith liked that idea a lot less than escort duty. Rath might be able to direct the Marines, but he wasn't gonna pull some last-minute shit out of his ass when it mattered.

The RAG came to mind.

To the pilot, helicopters were meant to fly, not crash. He never would have ridden that shit into Mina Bazar like Captain Saunders. Plus, Rath wasn't in good with the lords, ladies, and whatever that guy Dalmore was.

"Cork isn't just a shooting gallery," said the captain. "It's entrapment and exfil. I can't be in two places at once."

"Can't you?" mused Captain Rath. "Ceal could portal people in and out. Right?

"No. Apparently, they're already interfering with magic travel." He cocked his head toward the distant North Gate. Beyond that, the road wound down into the valley where they'd first arrived. It was a sobering reminder that armies were gathering out there in the death of cold, a metal glacier slowly coming to crush them.

"Then that's it. Either you're here, trusting that the doc and Micky are safe with someone who could deflect an asteroid from hitting the planet, or you micromanage it. And trying to put the sergeant here on babysitting duty is a poor use of resources."

The two captains stared at each other through the dark with little puffs of breath coming out of their mouths. Smith widened his stance in case it came to blows. The tension was so tight that it was a good time for an assassin to jump out of that potted plant they were talking about.

Instead, Captain Saunders said, "What about you?"

Captain Rath gulped, but his shoulders didn't bow. "I've got some people skills, Saunders."

Saunders rubbed his jaw. "If we're gonna split the command, it'll be easier for me to give you a crash course on Ceal than the evolving situation here. I still need some assurances. Smith, belay evacuation detail for now. We're heading to the clinic." And then he stomped off into the night.

He trembled, staring at the darkness left in the wake of the Corsan Carre. Cold and quiet had reclaimed the street, but the air still sizzled from their presence. *Yes. Yes! I can sense it. I hath the Sense,* Magnus Smallfoot thought.

Voices from down the street drove him behind a barrel of nails. Shopkeeper Walram sold the nails to the sorry lot of builders that had cropped up after that snake Benton stole their ability to work with the Quotidian. Master Walram kept the nails outside because they were Seven Seasons Nails—such low quality that none would last a year. The builders loved them, and thieves were more like to steal the barrel itself.

A half ten of Watchmen stepped out of an alley two shops up from Walram's. They glanced down the street, blowing steam into their cupped gloves, before marching down another. As they walked away from the lighted streetlamps, the dying glow of their white tabards made Smallfoot think of how their lives would soon fade.

Silence returned, and he crept out, worn boots crunching in the ruts of hardened snow. The Corsan Carre had walked much quieter, he realized. Mayhaps taking care in their steps, or more the like aided by their wickedness. Smallfoot's musings vanished as glistening frost commanded his attention.

My prize.

Trash to the unkeen eye, it shone as might a marked tree to a strong-snouted dog. It was his purpose, another of Master's promises fulfilled. In moments, the cold ice the captain of the Corsan Carre had kicked was burning Smallfoot's bare palms. He envisioned a blue fire searing away the last vestiges of the fool Mesaulius tried to make of him. Smallfoot was the first in the new age to Song Forge. Now, with a new master who saw his full potential, he could go beyond the pithy works of his ancestors and change the world in one fell stroke.

The thought of the Corsan Carre returning to the warmth of Uumhrat's inn, dreaming of the morrow and their plans for war, made him smile. It was all as his new master had foretold. Fallen Lord Benton's witch would flee, and the rest would stay.

Forever.

"I just wanna know why it's all rings and amulets and shit," Nickels said, setting down his beer ration. Well, third ration. The regulation was probably more of a suggestion, anyway. How did it make sense that two Marines like Bone and that hypochondriac Light, at least a hundred pounds apart in weight, got the same half-pour and not one drop more? "If Williamson was here, he'd tell you we got a million stories. Fuck, a million games back home where you got all this enchanted bling, but it's always something you can find at Kay. You know?"

Leod slicked back that gorgeous black mane on his head and said, "There is naught but so many places a man can decorate himself and still be fit for battle."

"Lip rings?"

Sergeant Teague snorted. "In the like o' the Aventians? Mayhaps, but none I hath seen."

"What gains ye from odd placement?" asked Leod. "The same Quotidian flows through the metal of an ear, lip, and,"—he looked himself over for more spots to pierce like someone who never saw the inside of a middle school bathroom—"nose ring as with that of the finger. The hands one can shield. Is it so easy with the face?"

"Bro, we can discuss brown-bagging another time. Right now, I wanna shoot a fuckin' fireball from my nipple. Read?"

The Watchmen laughed. Fucking right they laughed because that shit was funny. And practical. Hell, it was tactical too.

"Not under the Bark," said Teague taking a swallow from his mug that left pure snow on his mustache. Bone was right about one thing; this brew was epic. *Delicious* didn't even touch it; it was exactly what the mouth, mind, and body needed from every sip to vacuum chug.

Nickels raised his beer, and so did the two Watchmen because that's what dudes did. *When one drinks, everyone fucking drinks.* "But you get what I'm saying. A Sock of Power. What up? No one sees that coming. Right?"

Leod stared for a moment, then brightened. Sergeant Teague took notice and slapped the table. "Ho, he wants we should tell o' the legend."

"Aye," said Leod sporting a wicked grin.

"Brodrapeds, I will fuckin' buy the next round with those coins that chick paid me to squirrel-nut her cheeks."

"It . . ." began Leod, either scouring his mind for the details or stalling to spin a yarn. Either way, Nickels didn't care. He was three beers deep and finally speeding away from the baggage train of emotionally draining, suicidal shit that had managed to keep pace across wars and worlds. "It is hearsay, of course."

"Of course."

"When the lands were as we are told to remember, at peace with grand nations working for the good of all as well as themselves, the Powers were but a small part of men's lives. Learned folk—the wise—were first to uncover the secrets of Renderstone. From cut pebbles that could answer modest desires to the ringing anvil that granted might and prowess, the early Quotidian trinkets served to amuse the high courts of Caranusca and Haquatia. Rings, as ye say, were concealed and made men appear as magicians."

"Women, too," added Sergeant Teague.

"Alas, as ye know, power only seeks more of itself. In time, Renderstone crafts became evermore fearsome. The low and common could wield the strength of a lord's finest company."

"Sorta shit government wants to put a lid on. Same deal back home," said Nickels.

"Aye. A clever Princeps of . . . ah, a fallen Caranuscan house—"

"We name it not, here," said Sergeant Teague.

"—decreed that a craft's weight with the Power should be evident in worsening sight and encumberment."

"Like a fuckin' serving dish stuffed in your lip?"

Leod smiled. "In the like."

"Where'd you learn all this shit? Last time we talked, you were like a half-page ahead on the magic stuff. Remember that? Truckin' up that mountain freezing our balls off . . ." said Nickels recalling the ruck up to that wolf cave. Everyone was complaining, but it was a nice, numb time. Lotta laughs.

"Aye, had meself wrapped in both arms to keep warm."

Laughs that ended with six Watchmen dead and Leod totaled. "No, bro. That . . . that's not what . . . I mean, I wasn't trying to that bring up."

Leod flapped his nub like the dastardly motherfucker he was. If the guy had his balls ripped off, he'd drop trou just to get a rise out of people. The missing arm probably haunted him at night, but that shit didn't matter in the moment. Nickels blew out a breath, recognizing the game. "Bitch, save it for the ladies and finish the story."

He straightened his face and said, "Examiner Creed oft visits our headquarters, and his wisdom is offered for the asking."

"Yeah, guy's a walking library. Bet his ass goosebumps read like braille."

"As he tells it, a mighty artifact was created. The maker, knowing many would lust after it, obeyed the Princeps' law of encumberment. 'Tis a chain, as ye say, that wraps the head and hooks to an orb held in clenched teeth."

Nickels almost spit out his beer. "A Ball Gag of Power?"

Sergeant Teague pounded the table, roaring with laughter. Leod was busting his seams too. Good chance it wasn't real, but that didn't make it less funny.

"What else? Anal Beads of lightning? Dildos that can crack concrete? I mean, I know the wise tribal elders are making wedding rings and power armor, but a twenty-year-old leaking high T from his kneecaps is gonna be thinking and working toward one thing. You know?"

Teague moved aside as Ann hoisted a tray of three mugs up to the table. Nickels grabbed one without making eye contact. That big smile and piercing gaze were a guaranteed trip back to the pit of despair.

After a healthy gulp, Sergeant Teague said, "Not in Galimay. Here, rendercraft be the realm o' the sanctioned few."

"'Tis forbidden to craft and," Leod stretched out the fingers on his only arm to show off a little silver band on the second finger, "wield."

"That finger cuff's illegal? What's it do?" Nickels asked.

"Naught beneath the Bark, but elsewhere it would keep the wearer warm as many furs in the brisk cold."

"If the Blue Cloaks saw it, Leod would hath a finger t' go with his missing arm," said Teague.

"Good thing they're . . ." Nickels trailed off. It wasn't a good thing that two thousand stacked and jacked dudes in plate armor and whatever else they hauled out in that wagon train were long gone. Before that thought could bleed through his buzz, the timeless Marine cattle-prod—the voice of the CO—took care of it for him.

"Not ideal," said Captain Saunders stomping his boots off at the door.

Bone, Captain Rath, and a limping Micky plowed in behind. Injured or not, the crazy kindergarten teacher chick was usually worth a look. Instead of sporting that home-grown cleavage, though, she was in a blue overcoat that was three sizes too big. It almost came down to her feet, leaving about six inches of ankle covered in those white pajamas they had at the hospital. The doc was conspicuously not with them.

"We're past ideal at this point, Ron," said Micky leaning against a table to catch her breath. Bone posted up beside her, but Nickels still felt that inbred, gentlemanly instinct to rise and assist. Problem was that the second he moved, it would draw the captain's eyes, and three . . . no, four beers would get questioned. "Anyway," she continued, "Ceal promised that once we're out of range of their . . . oh, what's she call them?"

"Disruptors."

"The Black Robe Disruptors. BRDs! Once we're far enough away, she promised to send us straight to Durador. Did I mention that everyone who is everything is there? Rome, Constantinople, and Durador. What possible argument is left on Earth . . . ha, or wherever, for us NOT to be there ASAP?"

"Benton believes it's inevitable," admitted the captain pausing at Nickels' table. He eyed the smattering of mugs but let it go. Probably understood that Nickels wasn't up for watch until what they had defined as 24:45 based on Francis' calculation that Scianas had a fucking 25-hour day. By then, the beers would be a distant memory.

Or he's gonna get senior NCO Bone to chew me out. The thought disturbed Nickels as much as it pumped him up for a friendly fight. Still, what the hell were they talking about? Why was Micky suddenly in the loop?

Bone refused to meet his questioning stare. *Great, trust issues again. They probably do think I'm drunk.* Nickels pushed the untouched fourth beer away. Leod and Teague had no trouble dividing it between their mugs.

"Assuming anyone gets out of Portcullis alive," over-informed Micky continued. "If you lose the heroic hardon, you can come with! All your problems are solved, and we can get some sleep."

I will sleep with you, thought Nickels. Leod and Teague were a little leaned back watching the conversation too. Or at least the correct side of it. Even in the coat, Micky was still top pick in Portcullis. Notable exceptions were Ceal and Gol's wife, who had some of that aged smoke going on. None of that child-bearing hips shit that was all the rage out here. Clear skin, legs for *widths—oh shit, drop that one on Leod*—and symmetry.

Micky actually had the hips, but no one was thinking about their future first-born male heir when she sauntered by.

"Benton and Dalmore can field 600 soldiers. Staffing the North Wall, they can hold against thousands, tens of thousands. Maybe more," said the captain.

Micky frowned like she was running a mental simulation of the upcoming battle. "And you'd like us to stay while your squad of Marines fights an entire army? From the exciting things Ceal has shown Pat and me, guns are not a great equalizer here."

Nickels finally caught Bone's eye and tossed him a *what the fuck?* Bone shrugged, also unsure why the captain was giving Micky any airtime. It had to be because they were attacked. Knight syndrome.

Chicks dig scars, and dudes dig active bleeds.

"Shock and awe, high-value target prioritization . . ."

Aww, he spelled out HVT for her.

". . . and we have no choice. Portcullis is key terrain until Ceal is beyond the BRDs."

Micky giggled. "I knew you'd love that acronym. And I get it, I really do. But the second they bring down that Bark, it goes to hell. I'm sure Ceal told you that, too."

"Only reason we're still entertaining your exfil."

Micky's brown eyes seemed to get swallowed by her pupils, and she said, "This *has* to happen. Long game, Captain. Pat promised to work her shit out with Ceal, so we get to ride shotgun with the most powerful person in Galimay. We'll be safe; there's no question. But also, there's follow-through."

Saunders scrubbed the back of his neck. "Explain."

"Durador. Remember what happened when you rolled in here like a bunch of growling assholes beating your chests and calling yourselves the C-monster?"

"C-monster oorah," boomed Smith.

"Oorah," said Nickels. Leod and Teague just raised their mugs; no *Bohu* this time.

"We can't do that again," said Micky. "A couple of cute Corsan Carre can utilize Ceal's connections and pave the way for your grand entrance. Those Baylisses, the family of the Blue Cloak lord you pissed off, rule Durador. We need a gentle, if not insidious, touch."

Fuck, maybe I am drunk. Is she . . . did someone watch too many spy movies or something?

The captain just nodded. "Nickels, tell Uumhrat to put on a pot of that Ormcaf stuff. If we're doing this, we've got till dawn to plot it out. Smith, Rath, Micky, 2000 hours briefing in twenty, shake a leg."

Nickels was used to crazy by now; Micky was a special breed. But captain taking any of that shit from a kindergarten teacher who was only here because the doc was her friend seriously got his jaw dropped like a motherfucker.

"You okay, babe?"

Saunders was surprised to feel his head turn, long strands of dark hair brushing bare shoulders, and offer a slow nod. He, or as the apparent emptiness in the crotch suggested, she *was in a car with a left-side passenger seat. Driver was on the right.*

European? *he wondered.*

The vehicle's interior was beaten to hell, an ancient Maruti Suzuki Omni rented and conscripted to an untold number of abusive masters. The terrain outside resembled the east shore of North Carolina, with a beach road running along the coast. But the beige, mud-brick buildings planted them in the Middle East. "Got me some butterflies," she said.

The clean-shaven black man next to her, Trey—a guy Saunders had never seen before yet radiated the same affection, warmth, connection, and history as his own wife on a good day—nodded. "It's real now. A whole new world, and I'm not just talkin' about the sandbox. Seen plenty of that. No, this is . . . this is what peace and freedom gonna look like, babe."

Military, *Saunders guessed. Or a contractor. But the guy had experience out here, wherever they were. The road signs were in a language neither Saunders nor his host—Victoria—could read. No English meant it was off the beaten path, and he would have recognized Arabic from his first tour in northern Babil, Iraq.*

Those breathy, up-pitched vocal cords came to life again. "I know, I know. I just wish we didn't have to . . . to sneak in this way." She checked the mirrors for cars following too close. They were on a highway, the same garbage infrastructure that usually needed to be swept for mines and IEDs ten times a day. "You know, be nice if we coulda flown in. Maybe tipped back a few."

Trey smiled, and Saunders felt Victoria relax. "Yeah, fuckin' world's clampin' down. Wish we coulda gone through Iraq or Armenia, but they're in bed with the US and those stupid containment policies. And there ain't no underground out here. Shit, if you think it's bad being Black back home, just wait till you show up in the sandbox tellin' everyone you converted to Islam." He laughed. "Shit, we crazy, babe. But this is where we belong. It's what America was back in the day. Opportunity. And this time, it ain't just for the boy's club."

"I'd feel better if we had met Mutanob Racer in person."

Is that a screen name? *Saunders wondered, wishing he could shout some sense into Trey. Whatever these people had gotten themselves into, it was obviously a scam.*

"Gotta protect what's theirs. Shoot, it's only been a year since General Khel freed Pakistan. They makin' moves: Iran, most of Afghanistan, but it's like an eggshell. If America gets wind of what Mutanob showed us, that super fuel shit, they ain't gonna be content on the sidelines. They gonna invent a reason to come heavy and take it all away. So, borders on lockdown, and information gets passed on the blockchain—y'know, the ultra-dark internet. If we wasn't friends with Rob, we never woulda got the hookup."

Images flashed in Victoria's mind. Land, lumber, hundreds of cranes rising high over a gilded city of copper and gold domes; people from all walks of life and ethnicities shaking hands, sharing food and laughs. It was the timeshare pitch from hell because it looked damned good.

Saunders forced himself to ignore the fantasy and focus on what happened in Pakistan. Mina Bazar wasn't a year ago, or was it? Why was Iran involved? But the half-assed minivan began to slow. A multilingual border checkpoint was ahead: **Now Leaving Azerbaijan.**

"You sure he's gonna be there?" Victoria asked, stomach knotting up again.

A hand on her thigh brought comfort and even a slight tingle in the toes. "Yeah. And the address checked out too. It's a done deal, babe. Ain't like we freestylin' the Rio Grande, neither. They want us to come."

The Azerbaijan outgoing checkpoint was staffed. Odd. *Two guards in bright green scatter pattern BDUs with black AK-74Ms slung over their shoulders motioned for Trey to roll down the window. Victoria's heart hammered in her neck; this wasn't supposed to happen.*

"English," said Trey. "There a problem?"

"Ah, very good. Ah, no. We are warn all travelers re-entry from Iran not possible," said one of the soldiers.

"You ain't lettin' anyone back in?"

"Azerbaijan welcomes all."

"There a long line trying to get out?"

The soldier glanced down the bridge to the opposing checkpoint. It was hard to see, but there was zero activity. "No," he admitted.

Trey smiled and patted her leg. "That's what I figured. Ain't no one lookin' to leave."

Victoria's body shuddered like someone with a healthy fear of heights stepping toward a thousand-foot drop. "You don't think that's weird, baby?"

Trey turned back to the soldier and said, "No one can get in through Iraq or Armenia. Right, my man?"

"Yes, we are only border open for travel south."

"But they can get out that way?"

A frown, maybe realizing their tourism industry was taking a backseat to war-torn Iraq. "Yes."

"See, babe?

She nodded. It made sense to Saunders too. Any concerted effort to prevent emigration to Iran meant US or European involvement, which explained cooperation in Iraq and Armenia. If you wanted back into the free world, Iraq was the most direct path, not driving up through bum-fuck Azerbaijan.

The soldiers stepped back and waved them past without further discussion or even a cursory inspection. They didn't care, just there to deliver their lines.

The three-cylinder engine groaned as it dragged the car—loaded down with everything they hadn't sold, given away to friends, or stored in her mom's barn—across the bridge. The river winding deeper into greenish countryside was comforting. Victoria always thought this part of the world was one giant desert. Saunders wished he could tell her it was. It really was.

Water was just decoration; it had no purchase here.

Instead of the usual smattering of drab military vehicles and rifle-toting soldiers, the Iranian checkpoint was a campus. Brand new buildings sporting solar rooftops, antennae, satellite arrays, and a fuckload of one-way glass loomed over a sizeable lock-gate system. It was a security specialist's wet dream, gorgeous and futuristic. Nothing like this had ever appeared in any of the briefings on Iran.

"What'd I tell you, babe? Money," said Trey pulling in behind another family in a similar minivan. A dark-haired man in the passenger seat caught eyes with her through the side-view mirror and waved. It was like they were all in line for an amusement park.

Victoria's enthusiasm was building, but Saunders couldn't get over the fact that the Iranians were somehow conning American citizens to immigrate. Has a year really passed back home? Are we losing?

The vehicle ahead passed into the first gate lock, and three guards approached it. Two were in what could've been Iranian dress uniforms. Not the standard beige battle utilities that most of the sandbox's soldiers wore, but tan blouses and slacks with shiny black runners. Black leather belts and brass topped it off. Everything was starched to fuck, too. The third—the officer—was in all black with silver buttons and clasps. The cloth wasn't just matte, either. It had a familiar reddish sparkle that would've raised the hairs on Saunders' neck if he were in his own body.

Smiles and laughter were all around as the guards waved the other minivan through. Beyond was six lanes of black blacktop, spacious and orderly. Everything was new, just like Trey said.

The two guards in tan beckoned Trey forward. It was all congratulations, welcomes, jokes, and sincere desires to connect.

"Coming to visit or stay?"

"Meeting anyone?"

"Of course, drive straight for a kilometer, and you will find the visitor center. Good coffee and hot Quottob."

What registered to Victoria as perfect English, however, Saunders heard with that almost imperceptible delay found everywhere in Portcullis.

Before he could think, the officer in black came over and shook Trey's hand. "You will find a home here," he said with a smile. Victoria's cheeks began to hurt she was so excited. Visions of what they might find, what Mutanob might look like, or where he might take them floated by.

Saunders could see the officer's uniform a little better now. It was like the fabric was coated in ruby dust. No, silver dust emitting a reddish glow.

Renderstone.

Alarm bells.

Suddenly, the officer was eyes wide, staring at him. Not Victoria, but straight through to Saunders.

An angry shout.

The left window shattered.

Something wet splattered all over Trey, and Victoria's head hurt. Her head hurt so much; everything numb. Confusion. Dizzy, dark.

Hurt.

Saunders woke in a cold sweat, returned to the silence of his dim room. It was still the dead of night; he couldn't have been asleep for more than an hour. He shook his head, trying to clear the sensation of someone's brains being blown out. "The fuck is going on back home?" he asked no one.

Dawn shone upon a dirtied city.

The streets emptying Eastside Rise were lined with animal droppings from the early and orderly departure of armed caravans. From South Ward west, long trails of people were bent forward by the burden of bedsheets and blanket bundles. Refuse became their wake as the weight of even meagre possessions was felt.

Behind them, the Sticks sat empty. Houses left open were ransacked and burned by miscreants without family or stead. Mayhap the Anticult themselves. As morning cooked off the high mists, the remains of the Korigi Carre were set to task.

To the north, a more chill wind blew as Song Street—the city's harmonious heart—sat silent. A paltry sum of smiths stayed, mayhap wishing their hammers could mend the brokenness they felt within themselves, but most fled with their lives to rebuild elsewhere.

It was the telling tale, the true goodbye for those remaining at their posts. Yesteryear, when the enemy came with crashing swords and skies of fire, the fighting spirit of Portcullis roared back, defiant. Now it gasped and flailed against one foot sunk in a cold mountain tomb.

In the spite of doom driving heads low and sending fearful eyes to the skies and dark alleys of their beloved city, people held a dignity, a humility from a bloody yesterday. Calm and order held fast against gnashing teeth and wild fear. The strong aided the weak, and forgiveness triumphed vengeance. No longer taken by maddened flight, the people flocked to the safety of caravan and convoy.

And all expressed gratitude for their Lady Ceal.

Of the city's armsmen, seven Watchmen and forty-two of Dalmore's Deadlies asked to leave. Chief Dalmore resisted in the way of the Sapphire Branch, threatening death for breaking an oath, but to oath breakers he was speaking, and Lord Benton had no use for those who would flee at first chance. The group was instead armed, named Honor Guard, and placed under the command of a fuming Sergeant Orrugant.

If ever a man could roar at denial on the cusp of all his desires granted, it was the former arena champion. Still, crashing rage and drawn steel were calmed by Benton's careful appeal to the man's greed for battle: *Ye's will be the greatest charge of all. Protecting the Corsan Carre.*

And it did no harm to add: *Mine wife as well!*

As the great caravan made ready to pass beneath the South Gate with Lady Ceal and a small retinue in the lead, it was discovered that many of the Caranuscan refugees refused to leave. As a group, they had been the last to cross the Dowdale Valley by way of the Twin Tithes, the last to carry memories of a free world left behind. But Lord Bayliss had stopped them from moving deeper into Galimay, resigning them to a retched purgatory within the Portcullis' modest arena. It was a cold shanty, tended only by the Watch, that made the Sticks seem grand.

With the Criers also departing, news once more traveled by foot. When Benton visited the arena, he found the refugees—men, women, children, and aged—with their backs straight, defiant against the enemy who had taken their homes. They wished to aid, to fight.

They offered themselves in totality.

It was a noble gesture, but so too, a sad reality that most were unfit for travel. Benton accepted them and led them from squalor. It was the least he could do to let them occupy the empty homes and comforts of a once grand city. What they might find in ransacked cupboards was a pittance against having extra eyes to watch the shadows.

It was cold, but a dry cold.

Holding his nose against the filth of unwashed people and animals pissing and shitting, LCpl Gladstone squinted against what the locals called Bergreth's Lamp. The sun never bothered him back home, but here it was agonizing, worse by the day. Being a different star, maybe it was brighter than what his 4X space strategy games called *Sol*, but he really had no idea. Nor did he care. It was a distant problem, a distraction.

"I don't need a gun," said Dr. Bowman pushing away the snub-nosed .38 Special in Captain Saunders' outstretched hand. Her reaction was more than a distrust of firearms, though. That was Gunny Brines' weapon, the one he used to hurt . . .

Master sizzled a whisper just behind Gladstone's ear.

. . . the Black Robe.

"Suit yourself. Micky?"

Micky was a sight; the only color in the grey, drab world of horse asses, staggering bundles, stone, and fucking cold mountains. Her flowing red dress with white lace and elbow-length white gloves wasn't the sexiest Gladstone had seen her, but it put her in the same league as that prima donna Ceal. Micky was every part a lady oozing youth and grace from a sleek body beneath.

Dr. Bowman, by contrast, was like an old scout mother: bundled for warmth with dark circles under her eyes from worry. Gross.

Still, they both looked good, considering they got mugged yesterday.

Micky's eyes doed over, and she purred, "Ooo, put away the snub and bring out the cannon. You know what I want."

Captain Saunders didn't react.

Wife must hold the pants, the whip, and the balls in her purse for a guy to stonewall a girl like Micky. Gladstone would've given anything to take Captain Rath or Buontempo's place in the convoy. If only to keep Benton's witch off Micky's back. *God, her back. Ass that could nest a man's head like an egg.* Rath liked her too, but he was so obvious that Dr. Bowman—the prude—cockblocked him at every chance.

Micky pulled back with a viperish look. *God, she could melt rock with those eyes.* "I wouldn't want some big strong man to take it from me and accidentally hurt himself."

The rest of the disembarkation team—Captain Saunders, Fischer, and PFC Licht—chuckled. Gladstone forced himself to join. It wasn't unfunny, but the air of his joy had gone flat a while ago. Except when Micky was paying him attention, or his thoughts drifted into the forbidden spot in his head.

Hello? he called out, testing the bundle of his darkest and most brilliant desires. No answer came, but one day it would. And with it, rapture. Kinda like keeping after that hot girl in math class: worth the wait.

Gladstone panned the sprawling South Ward. The city's loading and unloading zone for inbound supplies and travelers was now a disordered parking lot of wagons, horses, and thousands of people and their belongings. The rich, like Master Lobhar, had wheeled carriages with fresh paint and pack animals. The rest had wheelbarrows and packs, and then some had only the rags on their backs.

There.

The serving girl, Ann, and her parents.

Gladstone stared. Not so much from familiarity or that she mattered, but because it tingled that dark spot in his head. Probably just a memory of how Master used to look at her, but the register gave him hope soon, someone would answer his silent pleas.

Though it pained him to look away, the true prize of the day was over by the gate complex with at least fifteen feet of clearance yet still looked like a cartoon mouse hole within the larger South Wall. In glorious arrogance, she was standing on the raised driver's bench of a pearl-coat stagecoach attached to a team of four black stallions. Her blue robes floated on the breeze coming through the gate tunnel.

Lady Ceal.

The whole setup was impractical for what was the mountain version of *Oregon Trail*, sans guns. But it looked great, and that's all witches cared about. That and waving to make a big political show.

She's leaving. She's leaving, he reminded himself.

The dark spot quivered.

"Oh," grunted Dr. Bowman clutching her stomach.

"Did our baby just kick Pat?" asked Micky slipping in with a hand. Ceal and everything else in South Ward became a distant memory to the two women touching.

"Just a cramp," she said, swatting away Micky's advances. Gladstone wished his stomach hurt.

"Not too late to change your mind, Doc," said the captain.

"Pat, you've got a really sexy six-pack under there," cooed Micky.

Two women—even if one was comparatively haggard-looking—having a little tummy time was too much. Gladstone tried to remember the last time he got laid. It was two months before the Pakistani hostage situation kicked off. So, about four months. The Queen of England would look good brushing her teeth right now. He needed a cold shower.

The thought of a shower did not help his trousers.

"I'm fine," insisted the doc. She gave the captain a look. "We'll see you in Durador." Then she spun on her heels and headed for the witch's wagon.

Micky kept smiling, but it was that plastic, upside-down-frown smile. "She's just peeved that Wisewoman Allena gets to stay behind. Gotta heal them all, ya know." Gladstone got the Pokémon reference, but the other Marines blanked through it. Then Micky's beautiful, brown eyes became stone. "Remember what Ceal said: five days. That's us safe. That's when you pull the plug."

The captain didn't *yes ma'am* her; why would he? But he nodded, and that was goodbye.

"Hate to see ya go," whistled Fischer under his breath, watching Micky's backside like she was wearing yoga pants. That red dress amounted to being draped in the thick curtains Mom hung to darken a room: nothing to see. Fischer was just being stupid, trying to be all buddy Marine. The PFC ignored it, and the captain wasn't interested.

I'll play . . . buddy.

"Remember that time she went AWOL?" Gladstone whispered back. "Eastside Rise . . ."

Fischer's fleshy face lit-up. "Dude! When she came runnin' outta that loft, bits flopping all over the place in the moonlight. I said goddamn." He smiled at the memory. Smiled at . . . Gladstone's memory: something special and private turned into another late-night pair of titties being passed around barracks. "Did we ever figure out what she was up to?"

Another pang of jealousy hit.

Rumor had it she had been sleeping with one of Master Walram's relatives. Some kid. Well, not a child, but no one checked IDs in Portcullis. Maybe he was hung like an elephant, but probably not, considering she never went back.

"Stow it, guys," the captain said, lidding the issue. He was watching Micky and the doc go too but with the hard stare of a battleship commander watching his prize disappear over the horizon. Gladstone only knew the guy was in over his head. If Saunders had any clue, he would've been chasing after Ceal, begging her to take him too. The returning after five days thing was laughable.

Ceal was never coming back.

Horns blew, and cheers erupted. Everyone was waving, shouting. Then as Ceal's sleek, white stagecoach pulled out, the tears began to flow. People were leaving their homes, their childhoods. And anyone left behind, standing stoic and waving, were ghosts to them.

Except me, Gladstone hoped.

Sergeant Orrugant's vanguard consisted of two open-air Watch wagons. Most passengers were grey-plated Deadlies with a few Watchmen—no tabards—wearing battle chainmail. Two beige forms, Captain Rath and LCpl Buontempo, sat conspicuously among them. They tossed a wave, and LCpl Buontempo pointed at his radio pack to remind everyone that he would call before bedtime.

Gladstone wanted to toss back a middle finger and somehow beam a promise of suffering and death into Captain Rath's mind, like Master. But Master was killed for being impulsive.

Long game.

Micky could go, but she couldn't leave. When the dark spot glowed bright again, they would be together.

South Ward emptied slower than Mom's shower drain after a major shedding. Gladstone held parade rest with the others, nodding to the endless stream of people pleading for a Corsan Carre blessing as they passed. By the time the rear elements were lined up for the gate, his back and legs hurt like hell.

"We shoulda brought some chairs, y'all," said Fischer bending his knees when the last stragglers ambled by.

"Walk it off," said the captain. "Fischer and Gladstone, you've got your assignments. Sergeant Batoth is in the gatehouse. Let's get the city buttoned up and get a count on who's left. Licht, you're with me."

PFC Licht glanced over, maybe to wish him luck with trying to run a security sweep with a bunch of medieval Watchmen in a city this size. His eyes dropped right away, though, knowing he wasn't welcome.

David Licht wasn't a total loser. Hell, he was buddy material in a former life. Good mix of smarts, wit, and he had a glowing magical shard stuck in his belly. Real spice of life shit.

But right now—Gladstone eyed Fischer and the smiling face of someone who knew too much—those chummy efforts were committed to keeping enemies closer.

Gone.

The silence should have calmed Smallfoot. Song Street had fled to Durador, where they would find themselves low in the place of the high. Their wares and works, rubbed so long beneath his nose, would know the pain of rusting upon high shelves. A fitting end, but ill of comfort.

He crossed the empty floor of his now barren home. All that did not serve him—once precious leavings and treasures—was gone, tossed to the Sticks and other places that found value in refuse. The new Master had given him a far greater appetite than the petty squabbles of men.

The sword.

It was finished now, affixed with a silver pommel and a blackwood handle. The blade wicked into an impossible edge that could bite tap-forged Rendersteel. But that was paint upon a canvas serving the eyes less the arm.

The true worth was within, that which made it light as a bird with the heft of a boulder and beyond deadly. It was the dream of all smiths; the legend made living.

The Corsan Carre reached out and brushed the metal. In surprise, he drew back. "Shocked me, man," he said, looking at his fingers. "Feels it'll be a great piece."

"Even the Corsan Carre fear mine Power, Mesaulius!" Smallfoot shouted in defiance of his past and sureness of his morrows. His new Master knew his worth. Magnus Smallfoot was the chosen, a Greystone smith of legend reborn at the birth of the Second Stochasm to arm the Last Army.

"And this is mine first, the deadliest that shall strike the deepest cut." They were Master's words, Master's promise. The sword would bring sure victory to the Anticult in one fell stroke.

Scratching in the walls scattered his thoughts, and the cold loneliness of Mesaulius' common room returned. It was just a rat, a resident that Mesaulius would never have tolerated. Still, it pierced the great architecture of Smallfoot's ambitions, leaving him where he began—short and uncertain.

Suddenly, the blade was dangerous.

It was not made by Song Forging but imbued from contact with the Corsan Carre and poisoned by the Master.

The ice touched by the Corsan Carre, the ritual, the Peerless. Evil, all evil!

The metal was sick; streaks of black rot gripped the polished silver. So too, was this city doomed. If Smallfoot left now, he could catch up to the exodus and surrender his madness to the higher powers. They could hide him from the enemy, and he could tell them of the blade. They would not blame him. They might reward him for bringing this magnificent weapon, for in the right hands, mayhaps it still was.

They will blame you, whispered the shadows.

He shook his head. The pithy slights of his fellow smiths were naught more than the jokes men played upon each other. They . . .

They laugh.

A lifetime of scorn and dismissal slammed down. Smallfoot snarled and the moment of weakness passed. The blade glowed beautiful once more.

Soon you will be the hero of all.

His heart fluttered at Master's attention, and he drained the mug of beer he did not remember pouring. With wet lips dribbling, he answered, "Yessss."

Soon the silence outside his home would roar with the clinking and clanking of thousands, his closest friends. Men and women who would credit him in prying the Procult ilk from this place. They would listen to his stories, dream of his songs, and buy his wares with gold stamped by the mightiest realms.

Magnus Smallfoot would be honored, at last.

CHAPTER 9

PORTCULLIS DEFENSE COUNCIL

Peter Francisco, covered by the special Watch-issue ghillie, hugged the ground. Sergeant Orrugant had said the unassuming cloak would match surrounding colors and patterns. Considering how well it blended with the brown detritus of the forest floor, that was a solid 10-4. Back home, the government would've called it Active Camouflage and made the Corps wait in a ten-year line behind Army and Air Force. But here it was just one of those available, quality-of-life upgrades. The perfect concealment.

With his .50 caliber custom Barrett XM500 'Bullpup' fire-ready to his right, he panned the spotting scope over a break in the ridge separating the Lower and Upper Dels. That little wheelchair ramp was how any ambitious patrols or scouts would approach. For now, the enemy was confined to the valley beyond.

Like water was confined to the oceans.

"I ain't never seen that many people," muttered a pile of leaves two meters left. LCpl Fischer. The barrel of his M40 Marine-issue sniper rifle stuck out like a stick, moving almost imperceptibly as he panned the masses in the distance.

The valley was still lush and green, untouched by the winter's bleach affecting the surrounding mountains. It would be a great vacation spot except for the endless rows of black tents, cookfires, block formations, metal troops, horses, wagons, glinting steel, and the simple machines of a dangerous enemy spreading as far as the aided eye could resolve.

This wasn't an army; it was a population. Hundreds of thousands.

"It's like ten sold-out sportsball games," Francisco told his former apprentice.

"Didn't know you were into sports, hoss," said Fischer. "Oops, forgot we partners now. Ain't gonna call you partner or bro. But I'll figger somethin', don't you worry."

Partner would at least match the southern drawl. The kid had scored his 0317 MOS right after joining the C-monster. He had the eye, the nerves, and the will. Saunders saw his potential, and boom, Francisco had a new "spotter." Having a student was hard for a loner, but it was worth it. Today, Fish was a brother. Not just a brother Marine but blood-bound kin in a world where first-strike antipersonnel capabilities were king.

"Any other time or place this would be a no-brainer," Fischer said, switching back to shoptalk. "'Hawk, this is Hunglong Actual, foot mobiles spotted *en masse* and exposed. North o' my position, only spot that's got some green. Time on target, fire for effect, drop everything ya'll got.'" He laughed. "Hell, it'd be like a cow shittin' on ants."

The vernacular was still a work in progress.

"Maybe. But we're not here for them." Large infantry formations always looked impressive, but the common soldier's story was sad. Kids with rifles—or swords—were dressed up pretty and told they were dangerous. Then waves were sent to batter the enemy while the real war was fought in the stratosphere, cyberspace, or a negotiation table filled with bottom lines and fuckall. The ants were destined to eat shit, even without Fischer's cow.

Of course, the enemy had their own cows. Steers. With horns. Unicorn fucking horns.

A B-52 bomber from Fischer's fantasy might get lucky and drop part of its payload on the unsuspecting legions. Vulture Group also survived the first ten minutes of Operation *Sea Monster*.

But then the game would change.

Some wizard would set fire to the skies or squish those gray fuselages between their fingertips. That was the danger that catapulted snipers into the top tier of capabilities. When Francisco dropped the Black Robe in the Assembly Hall, it was with a single well-placed shot, a .50 caliber bullet clearing the guy's skull. Effective for one reason alone: surprise.

"Bravo Romeo," announced Fischer. *Speak of the devil.* "Pan up from the edge at 11 o'clock. Maroon circus tent."

Francisco found it immediately. A walker in black robes followed by a 4X6 column of dark-mailed soldiers. As it pulled back the tent's flaps to enter, a glimpse inside sent a chill up the back. A blackout snake cult of shitheads on steroids.

"Whole goddamned nest of 'em," whispered Fischer.

"Get a count and keep searching."

It wasn't long before they'd marked four more posts just like it, each with ten to fifteen Black Robes. Considering the damage just one had caused at Mina Bazar, Portcullis was in big trouble.

"What say ye?" asked another pile of leaves. Watch Lieutenant Maon.

Francisco marked their locations on the grid he'd scrawled on some parchment. "We need to wrap this up." Perfect concealment or not, seeing those Black Robes left him naked.

"All them soldiers dressed in black and grey looks damned evil," said Fischer. "That on purpose, or they plannin' to hit us at night?"

"Of the tales I hath heard from those who fled Caranusca, the Pandonis Immortalis stormed the fields in glinting mail and cloths the like of bone and Grethwood," said Lt. Maon. "They dress dark now for warmth during the harsh Galimay winter, as do the Coals."

The Coal Cloaks were Galimay's professional military. An actual army as opposed to the Blue, Red, and White Cloaks that comprised law enforcement and specialized combat units. The Coals—the Fifth Army—were obliterated a few months prior in a foolish gamble to strike first. So, this horde was completely unopposed save for—

"Make's 'em easier to spot. I woulda worn white, myself," said Fischer.

—the few, the proud. The only.

"Methinks the white would stand equal against the Dowdale's lushness," said Maon.

"I mean when they git on up into them mountains."

"Mayhap Lord Benton will command they die in the valley?" Maon appeared to retort. Between the translational vocal artifact and cultural differential, it was tough to tell if he was serious. Believing it was within Benton's power to dictate the outcome was not outside operating parameters.

"Got another cluster, one o'clock, two klicks in," said Fischer. "Maon, y'all think Benton's got his finger on some big ol' button ready to finish it all?"

"He waits till they are gathered. Else what serves our purpose here?"

There it was.

Lt. Maon had proven himself the superstitious, conspiracy theorist type on the hike down. To him, talk of losing the city was just a ploy. It didn't matter that an incalculable force was arrayed before them. Benton did something extraordinary once, and past results *always* predicted future performance.

"We doin' what they call *quantifying the fucked factor*," said Fischer. "See, the captain and them know we're fucked, but that don't fit into the analytics well. They need a solid on the fuckification multiplier; how many times dead we gonna get. So, here we are."

"The like of knowing the Gra'nuul chop and chew their enemies long after death?" Lt. Maon asked. "Sucking and slurping the bloat and decay over days, never a proper burial."

Brines.

Francisco knew the avalanche got him, and word was these Gra'nuul were trapped in their subterranean realm thanks to some wizardry. But when the locals looked up into those mountains, they weren't seeing ski slopes like Saunders. The visceral image of Mike going out as cannibal kimchi was stomach turning. "Enough. Fischer's right: Black Robe presence is all-factors overwhelming. Let's pull it and report in."

"'Bout time. Gettin' the heebie-jeebies out here."

Lt. Maon was smart enough to let Fischer's big ass take lead as they slithered back from their hide site quiet as satin bedsheets.

Francisco wanted to put distance between them and this spot before radioing in. According to Maon, they were still beneath the Bark here, so conventional tactics and threat assessment applied. But that didn't ease the sense of building urgency.

He tucked the spotting scope back into its case and started to move his rifle, but something compelled him to take another look.

The Nightforce SHV 5-20x56mm's ultra-transmissive lens coating afforded him a brighter picture of the sprawling enemy camps. Security and patrols were disciplined and orderly at the front near the tree line, but the deeper bivouacs were lax. Soldiers gathered in small groups without helmets or in various states of armored dress. Tent flaps were open, and the usual handwaving antics and belly chuckles surrounded little cookfires. It was the sort of camaraderie expected from soldiers, eve of war or not.

A Black Robe in the mix stopped him cold.

The narrow, hairless jaw suggested it was female. The woman, more of a damned creature in human form to Francisco's eyes, wasn't partaking in the meals, the laughter, or anything. She was standing there, alone among many, staring back.

Master Turan Rilseri, High Councilor of the Obantum Carre and Order of Eyes Presiding, finished his missive to High Axi'arch Tiem Cemeho. It was a simple instruction of when and where the legions were expected. The true maneuverings of this battle would happen well beyond the farthest horizons of the Pandonis Immortalis. Still, the soldiers responded to Cemeho, and his throat needed to be wetted and full of clear-sounding voice when the time came.

The tent flaps fluttered as a warm breeze, and Moderator Bela Rastaw entered. The cloth of her Pan'jid Mantel seeped about as a black fog. She spoke not, head bowed beneath her dark hood. Unlike that fool, Isllor Mortund, she minded the manners of respect.

Turan cleared his throat, and a quick-footed messenger in tanned leathers retrieved the sealed letter. The servant kept his eyes low, bowing and reeking of fear as he backed toward the exit. A small *ask* of Quotidian could deliver the letter to the High Axi'arch's desk—Turan remembered the location well—but sending the simpleton, one of the conscripts from these conquered lands, would carry that lingering stench of fear. A reminder of the proper authority here in the field.

"Moderator Bela," Turan said.

"My Master," she said, so perfectly polite. "It is as we feared. As we hoped. There can be no doubt now that our thralls speak truth."

Her certainty was enticing. The great army covering the Vigil Valley outside his tent tilted between two places in history: the mediocrity of another victorious campaign or the Last Army that would echo through the ages. Indeed, rattle the very stars. "Tell me."

"I saw one."

"Another Vision?"

"In life."

He stood. "The Corsan Carre are *here*? Why do none cry alarm?"

"Far, cowering at the Barrier's edge within the forests."

Of course, they dared not step outside what the enemy called the Bark. Turan relaxed. Moreover, Bela's Sense of the presence behind the eyes of the enemy commander Morhock at the prison camp was real. "A true taste of their essence, at last. The minds of the Tel'racs and the enthralled could be deceived, but not you. Bela, you surpass Isllor in more than just civility. Your power and prowess are often discussed among the council. They envy the advantage you bring to the Fist."

"The Fist is my home, but the Eyes are my privilege."

There was more behind her words, but greater curiosities commanded the moment. "Indeed. Tell me all. Was it," he licked his lips, "was it the One?"

Bela cast the stare that could wilt men by the crop to the plank-on-canvas floor. "No."

Turan allowed his disappointment to deepen the creases of his face. Twice now, they had been thwarted, making the final step seem the entire journey's length.

"But," she continued, "the men have found that which will satisfy other needs."

The . . . *men*. Those of the Stretched Guard were an exceptional breed but still of High Axi'arch Cemeho's mud trekkers. "What other need?" he asked, hopeful the low had proved useful. One concern lingered beyond verifying the presence of the Corsan Carre—warriors prophesized to threaten even the might of the Last Army. It was a petty need, gnawing and impolite. Bela knew it was precious to him, though. Knew it was his only genuine regret after so much flesh spent saving the world. "Something of the Three?"

A nod.

Turan trembled as an ancient sensation rose within. He recognized it from a life lived long ago.

Excitement.

When the Three had chanced to cross the place-between-places in search of the Corsan Carre's home, Turan was left behind. It was decreed the Council's will, but more the pettiness of Veris Loar, First of the Three. Loar was an equal, a rival. As High Councilor of the Fist, he took poorly to Bela's fellowship with the Eyes. With Turan.

For all my disappointment, old friend, it could never match my curiosity.

Who were the Corsan Carre? What splendors did their world contain? Were the Three alive or taken and enthralled into devious designs?

When the first whispers arrived that the Procult had found the Corsan Carre, Turan writhed. Had the Three failed? It consumed him.

He followed Moderator Bela out of the tent into the stench of brining salts. There was no escaping it. Thousands upon thousands of meat barrels were scattered among the endless camps, and meals were always in some state of preparation for the insatiable legions. The odor was rivaled only by the dung pits.

"The Stretched Guard was first to the find," Bela said, raising a glinting Renderstone bracelet to her lips. It was a new trinket, one Turan had not seen before. Maybe it came to her in trade, but she was still sifting through the spoils of the Caranuscan House Carnifex. "They will look to you for praise." Her lips were violet beneath the hood, almost brushing the gem as she asked it to aid their journey.

"They shall have it," he whispered, breath stolen by from the sight of her. The upstart pupil who tripped and fell upward through the Obantum's savage ranks had blossomed into a glorious visage. Lethal in the Powers, her wiles could sew doubt in the stoutest of hearts. She stalked the world, crumbling towers and bleeding lands dry with an unassuming presence that even he, in all his mastery and position, envied. And here she was, limitless potential devoted to his ends alone.

Of course, her soldiers would be rewarded.

They stepped through the *Quick* to another part of the valley, near the center. Stretched Guards stood ready, glinting Quotidian red in their Renderdust Plate. They were numerous, encompassing, and not lax as elsewhere.

They guarded a secret.

Within and beyond their encirclement grew the Vigil Valley's cursed green grasses, ever untouched by the world. But beyond that, there was nothing special.

"I do not—"

"See," she breathed, and a cold wind blew frost through the greenery.

The Stochal!

She had demonstrated her prowess in countering an *Origin* as the Tel'racs scoured the gate city for weaknesses but to challenge Taichleach's Vigil! It was a day of awe, indeed. Enthralled by her mastery, he watched the grasses fall to winter's brown and retreat. The soil beneath was black, smelling of strong drink and lamp soot.

"This place was touched by flame," he mused, sensing a strange familiarity with his surroundings. His gaze drifted up to the sharp peaks to the south, which were always white. As they edged north around this great bowl, a smoothness overcame them. Memory forced in. Last time, they were green and bright with the life of summer. "We have been here before," he said, searching for the exact spot the Three had entered the place-between-places.

"Not here, but close." Bela pointed north to a place a man's eye would see as lush and green despite the winter raging in the mountains all around. The device to scry the truth of the valley's center had taken a team of Master Rendersmiths four years to complete. Truly, their success was more happenstance than else. Much work and strife for a single stroke of harmony, an instant where their songs joined in perfect pitch. They Song Forged, an accomplishment unheard of in this age. Alas, the consequences of Song Forging Renderstone were disastrous to them. Worse, the Scry was later lost when the Isllor Mortund went mad and struck Portcullis at the height of its power.

"Fool," he spat.

"Soon, the Scry shall return to its masters," said Bela, knowing his thoughts.

Turan cooled; she would see it done. Her dark boot kicked something free from the scorched soil, and his eyes feasted. It was bright as a flame, orange as Bergreth's Lamp sinking into the endless horizons. He almost asked if this was the fire that blackened the soil, but the shock faded. It was woven. "Cloth?"

Bela knelt and sniffed the scorched edges. She recoiled with a sharp cough. "Poison," she said. "As when the Waxleaf burns."

He extended a palm, and a guard hurried to dig the oddity from the ground. Turan made a point to thank the soldier as gratitude to Bela. The orange cloth fit loose over what felt like impossibly supple leather. Straps of waxy weave hooked to black latches bearing metal's smoothness and the weight of feathers. *A garment?*

He rotated the ensemble envisioning how it might fit a man.

A vest.

His fingers fiddled with a protruding cord that made no fashionable sense. "Strange are their styles," he said, tugging at it.

The vest hissed to life in his hands.

He threw it down.

The orange fabric tightened as the strange leather beneath bloated and bulged. A taste of the terrors Turan knew from the night creepers of his childhood bade him call for flame. Bela held up a hand, begging patience.

Upon the black soil, the hissing vest twisted as it expanded. A vision of it growing to endless proportions tried to pry into the calming pool of rationality within Turan's formidable mind. He again resisted the urge to burn it, and the hissing stopped.

"There is more," Bela whispered.

His thoughts spun like a great loom throwing out blood orange weaves and hissing vests. He reached out with the Sense, asking and commanding the Powers to reveal themselves, but only dull clay came from this place. Impossible, unless . . .

"They are constructed," he said.

"Metal," she said, revealing a great sheet beneath the soil with the aid of her bracelet.

A shield for giants? It was rent, blackened, and punched with strange nails and metal bits. Two guards hoisted an edge showing the like of sheared wool on the other side. When she asked the soot back into smoke, cleaning the metal, the cold of Ajid's Winter raging beyond the valley finally touched Turan.

"I have seen this before," he said, voice failing to rise above a whisper.

He knew not its meaning, but the smooth grey paint had come to him in a message from Isllor Mortund. The retelling of a Vision. Riding on thunder, metal ships sailed the skies as men below ran in terror. It was the like of the Tel'racs, but the men were no cowering villagers. They spoke with the same thunder, and the skies flashed and dust swirled. The message ended too soon as something distracted Isllor. Until this moment, it had made no sense.

The Vision was from one of the Three.

"What?" she asked.

"Tell me," he said, scouring the white mountains surrounding the valley. "You saw one? One of the Corsan Carre?"

"Yes."

"But Sensed nothing. It was not the one we seek?"

"Yes." She pressed those violet lips together, succulent and poisonous. "I did get a strange feeling that he could see me . . ."

"By what Power?"

"None. He was as mute as my soldiers. The one we seek is beyond, moving deep through the mountains as we hoped. Worry not we—"

"If naught of the Powers, what dares remain to face us in the city?" He stared at the weight of the metal, wondering if it truly rode upon thunder. "Reach to your spies. We must know the truth of Isllor's death. And these *other* Corsan Carre."

———

Benton turned his ears to the echoes of his footfalls—the loud cries of barren floors and walls within his empty home—rather than the damning words that now haunted him. The truth upon his wife's lips at their parting embrace.

Comack had left the cupboard well-ordered and stocked. Pouring two cups of blushing strawine, Benton half believed the butler might sweep in behind and re-cork the bottle. Alas, he had departed ahead of Ceal to join the house guards and staff in Oxhold.

The house—its cellars, bedding, sitting rooms, and places closed off for heat—was always overlarge. It had once been Lord Elldren's summering place for members of his court. The grand furnishings and tapestries, chosen and placed by the late Lady Elldren, were from better days. Reminders of Elldren's sympathies and generosity when the Procult needed refuge in Portcullis.

This was always more camp than home, he thought, returning with the wine to Chief Dalmore at the Smallmeal table.

"Thought 'twas beer we drank at Highnoon," grunted the chief in his unadorned blue and white clothes. The breaking of tradition did not stop him from a swallow, but he did raise an eyebrow, swirling the pink liquid. "Is it . . . watered?"

Dalmore's surprise brought a smile. Benton, too, was once dragged from the dirt and rough to a clean table with odd rituals of eating and drinking. "The Blue Nellon grape oft bloats with juice permitting a bountiful third pressing. Atop that, they add a soak so it is not so . . ."

"Tart? I find it quite refreshing."

Benton sat and sipped from his cup as if it was his first time tasting the common drink. Sweet dew floated florals and a whisp of leather just beyond the tongue's grasp. In summer, it was served from cool cellars and drank as water, but now with the harsh winter upon them, he preferred it at body warmth, which also lent some flavor.

"Mayhaps I can taste the bitter." Dalmore frowned as his eyes wandered the Smallmeal Room. Taking in the two wooden archways leading one to the hall and the other to the atrium where guests gathered afore meals and mirth, he said, "I long thought through service and sacrifice I would earn the privilege to sit at a lord's table."

"Was not such earned with Lord Bayliss?" said Benton. "Many a day, I saw a low Blue Cloak lieutenant seated at a table with commanders and lords. Tasting second, mayhap first pressings." He gave his cup a tap.

Dalmore stared at the thin wine. "I would know little difference. But with Lord Bayliss, aye, 'twas so for a time. Alas, naught of courage or duty rose me to his side. Blind incompetence. 'Puppet be closest to the hand,' mine father liked to grumble. He was a sour man with oft biting truths. Some of it useful."

"Duty and courage hath brought ye to mine table, meager as it might be," said Benton.

"I thank ye, my lord," said Dalmore with the same grin worn by men as the world cracked from the First Stochasm.

"*My lord*," Benton snorted. "Ceal is gone, the city council a band of appointed folk without entitlement, and Portcullis lies still, a severed limb of the great Galimay. There are no noble men here, mayhap never were." Cups knocked, and they drank in agreement.

Benton's time as a titled lord with lands, a court, and fine tables filled with delights was exciting when new but ill-fitting in the end. Its best purpose was strengthening the Procult through Ceal's work upon the courts and their games, which she played well. When the High Varigan Court of Durador, His Reverence presiding, struck Benton's name from the roster of lordship and cast him down to the position Chief Dalmore now served in impeccable capacity, it was a blessing. Benton enjoyed naught of the shame but the freedom from poise.

"If ye will take no offense," began Dalmore once more solemn, "I hath found our drinking together, walking the battlements and such, to hold the companionship of a fellow soldier."

"It heartens me."

"So too ye's mislike for the talking and endless battle of truthless words driving men like cattle rather than joining their arms for a cause." Dalmore dug into a bowl of the yestermorrow mash Uumhrat had sent. A mouthful and a nod affirmed its quality. "It hath tempered mine own ambitions. The glory of commanding a great army is horrored by the attachment of a retinue."

"Familiar words."

"I do not envy ye's renown: Hero of Estmaw and famed or ill-famed Companion of Dominus Redwick. Mayhaps even the catalyst for the Retethering if all stories sung 'round the campfires are believed."

Benton listened but gave no answer to the unasked question.

"Indeed, keep ye's secrets. Such a burden is greater than mine, and ye's station cannot be tossed aside. The might of His Reverence and the Varigan could not keep these people from naming ye their Lord Governor. Thus, I dine at a lord's table and call him *my lord* when it pleases me." Dalmore then stuffed a heaping into his mouth to hide a smile at his cleverness.

"Aye, burdens upon burdens."

Dalmore swallowed and flushed with wine. "So, why come to Portcullis?"

Abrupt, but such was to be expected. Few could see how Portcullis benefited the Procult over Durador. There were many answers, most rehearsed to the like of heroic songs that would rouse young blood to war. The truth, of course, was bereft of courage, grandeur, and foresight. "A forced move born of many disasters," he admitted.

"Which?"

"The fall of the free realms, lost companions, a dire expedition to the White, the Procult chopped down and lessened at all turns . . ."

Saddle-tanned eyes narrowed. "Else?"

He wishes to discuss that which is high treason to speak aloud.

No tightness came to Benton's chest as when others pressed him. It mayhap spoke to this pocket of freedom from the tyranny that gripped Galimay. Or he was worn thin on pretense and the weight of words. Still, care was needed. "Why did ye turn from Lord Bayliss and his Sapphire Branch?"

"I hath spoke of it afore," Dalmore said. "Dearest is the vow to avenge mine brother's death, but so too the losses we hath suffered amid blind leadership. The Bayliss' are owed no allegiance from the true fighting men of Galimay."

"Ye speak such freely? Ye are not in poor company, but it catches mine breath."

"In the Assembly Hall, Sergeant Teague declared for Dominus Redwick before Lord Bayliss and the City Council. That is what moved me from safety to the outnumbered side of the Watch and Corsan Carre. Powerful moment."

Benton nodded. "Indeed. Then mayhap ye will enjoy the truth of why we came to Portcullis with a touch of history."

"More than beer, wine, women, battle, and to see Uumhrat one day take up his ax again, I long to hear it."

Benton laughed. "Be grateful ye know Uumhrat *the Innkeep*. Anyhap, it began many years ago when the Fourth was driven from Val'Narden. It was not the first defeat, but the first and, mark me, only city of Galimay to fall."

"I know this pain well; 'twas where mine brother was slain."

Benton shook his head. "Aye, a dark day for all. But worse was how it empowered the serpents in Durador. Lord Tethredon Bayliss used the failure to usurp Dominus Redwick from stewardship."

"Different from the tale widely told."

"Indeed. Dom's name was muted from the voices of Galimay, and the record amended to show him as a villain, nay a servant of the Anticult. Such fear did and doeth Teth Bayliss command among the people that the sullying of Dom's name only worsens."

"Be it all lies?"

Benton offered a shrug and said, "As it is the truth I share, I admit that Dom's guilt and punishment were much of his own doing. His, ah . . ."

Dalmore studied his face and gave a nod. "His wife."

"Lady Lanal." Benton drew deep from his cup to blunt the stinging memories. There was not enough wine in even Agrannidor to quench such. "At first, the war in Caranusca was going well. The Fourth Army was the fiercest host of men and horse ever raised, and they threw the Genisans back with blinding speed, nigh to the edges of Lumberland. They stopped for naught of steel or rendercraft. House Carnifex, under Princeps Noniam, rallied and laid siege to reclaim the great Caranuscan cities of Drethanum and Hastadonia. Haquatian Savagers took to the enemy lines; Stochists from Ceal's academy countered the Obantum Carre at all turns. Even the Corund Corps, then just . . . scholars with rendercraft, helped reclaim parts of the Uplands."

"The histories fail me, for I know only of the Fourth's doom from poor provisions and training," said Dalmore repeating the common story.

"The Fourth was magnificent. Till," he did not wince, but Dalmore caught the pause, "Lanal." Benton finished his cup and went to pour another. "She and Ceal, it was their academy. Did ye know that?"

Dalmore shook his head.

"After Lanal went missing, a search found a letter written by the same hand that took her life. Her own. The words spit fire at Dom, Ceal, the Procult. Questioned us, hailed the Anticult for their interpretations of the prophecy. I . . . I should hath seen it false, but we were taken with grief. By the time we learned that Isllor the Betrayer had been the one to strike her down, Dom was already maddened beyond hope."

"The same Isllor as Commander Mendo?"

"Aye, with a different face than ye remember. He was a student, quite gifted in the Stochal, and brilliant with the Quotidian. He helped make the Bark, which is how he was able to usurp it."

"So, he fled to the Obantum Carre only to return years later?"

"He fled but returned much sooner. After His Reverence removed Dom, Isllor struck against the academy. By sinister means, he roused the Gra'nuul from their caves."

"Against which the Power is naught," reasoned Dalmore.

"Aye. The loss of life and talent was immeasurable; Ceal herself was bested and beaten by Isllor amid the slaughter. The remaining students threw themselves upon him in a blast of Stochal and sacrifice. We thought him dead; we were wrong." The horror of finding his love clinging to life surrounded by the char and blood of her hopefuls and friends did not leave Benton's lips.

"But . . . he is dead this time. Aye?"

"We burned the body and passed the smoke through renderweave bedsheets. Then buried the ash deeper than most beneath the Doormat. If he can yet again be made whole, it is by no Power we or the Corsan Carre know."

"Mayhaps we should hath pissed on the ashes as well, but no matter. So, the enemy poisoned Dominus Redwick through grief, and the Caranuscan front collapsed?"

"Dom raged and snapped at the Genisans in vengeance. Great losses to gain useless ground. In time, the Fourth's maddened thrust struck steel and was driven back twice fast. Teth Bayliss turned the court's favor against Dom long before Val'Narden fell."

Dalmore snorted. "And in the like of a sinkhole, he sucked in all those closest."

"There were trials, purges. Teth restored the old kingdom under the pretense of councils and voices. Mayhap, this title Reverence is higher than even a king; certainly, he acts as more than a lord of lords. But as those dire days compelled us to flee, they doth not speak to why we came here."

"I nigh lost interest against the backdrop of such history. Well, was it the North Wall or the mountain air?"

Ceal's last whisper, her lips brushing Benton's ears, floated past a tightening throat. Just yesterday, his words would have been truth. "To battle the enemy," he managed. "To show their Obantum Carre could be countered. We believed such success would rally Galimay."

"Did it not?"

The slanderous lies and endless parade of lords claiming victory following the *First Battle of Portcullis* spun bitter and burn in Benton's chest. "Aye, the Fifth was risen and sent forth, but with no greater mind for strategy than the Fourth during Dom's madness. It was as if the spirit of our victory was poisoned and spent without regard."

Because we pursued else, he did not add.

Dalmore listened to the silence, mayhap deciding for himself whose hands were drenched in the Fifth's blood. Then, creaking back in his chair and resting a hand upon the hilt of his sword, he said, "And through all that death, ye plucked the prophesied Corsan Carre from Portcullis. Happenstance?"

No.

"Aye."

Dalmore rapped the table. "Then it is ye's lust for battle that brought ye, keeps ye, and will aid us in the morrows to come. Though, it would be nice if the Corsan Carre brought a miraculous weapon to aid us. Mayhaps they will reveal such at our meet this aft'nun."

Benton kept his face lax. "Captain Saunders believes a strategy is key. His relics are unique but still the like of thunderous crossbows. When he exhausts his bolts, he will be as we are."

Dalmore waved it off. "Bah, it is as I hoped. No ancient prophecy can stand in the stead of a united Galimay."

United? It was a laugh. The cities, towns, villages, and lone wandering lordships of Galimay paid homage to Durador and shared likeness and stamps upon their coppers, silvers, and gold. Beyond that, they feuded. Were it not for the threat of the Gra'nuul, Portcullis' South Wall might be grander than the North.

"His eyes narrow," laughed Dalmore. "But mark mine lowly words ye shall see something of men unbound from lords and ladies."

"I am intrigued."

"No doubt ye hath seen the report of the Genisan host?"

"Aye."

"The force that struck Portcullis yesteryear was but a vanguard, a sword touch in a polite duel." He leaned forward, eyes wild. "This is the thrust, Benton. The Last Army."

The Last Army.

Those words drove chill bones and a quick heart. It was the thrill, the guilt, and sight of dark days to come stuffed into an egg and sat upon by the great bird of hope in the hearts of men. What would hatch from it? Doom or glory? "All are promised to fight . . ." Benton whispered from memory.

"Aye. We shall spread the word and smash the grips of old lords and tired traditions. Galimay will resist death."

"But who will come before the fifth day after so many hath left?"

Dalmore shrugged. "Some, few, many. But come they will, and they must find a position of strength. We few shall hold. We and the Corsan Carre." Dalmore reached across the table and clasped his wrist with a swordsman's grip. "To the fifth day and more. We resist death."

Benton remained silent, recalling Ceal's suspicions of the Corsan Carre's true talents. Dalmore saw only the soldiers, but she saw their charge. One and only one stood to fill the destined needs of the Procult.

On her parting, Ceal had leaned in close and whispered, "I hath what we need."

It had but one meaning: her search was ended, and the wealth of Portcullis spent.

By some means, the enemy knew the Corsan Carre were revealed. Mayhap their Anticult spies, but so too through the eyes of the Tel'racs. Now, they rallied. All their might gathered and poised.

Dalmore was right; this was the Last Army. The surge to stop or trigger the Second Stochasm. It was all happening.

Behind Benton's surely wild eyes echoed the last of Ceal's farewell. A single word that spoke of the fates of Dalmore, the remaining Corsan Carre, and the many fine folks who deserved more.

Flee.

In the small study off the Watch Keep's main hall, Saunders fumed. Spread out on an angled drafting table was the map of Portcullis that Examiner Creed had provided.

The deployment of defense forces was as obvious as risky. The North Wall was wedged into a natural bottleneck—the ass of the narrow canyon leading into Portcullis. It was a primary obstacle to enemy ingress and position where defenders could inflict maximum damage and deterrence. It was also a tactical myopia.

While everyone is lining up at that wall, I'd be swinging around back.

He let the scenario play out in his head. Skirting the North Wall meant a ton of mountain climbing and single-file movement. A special operations team could do it, but then what? A small unit incursion needed force-multipliers like artillery or air support to cause effective damage. At face value, these guys had neither the tech nor the capability.

That left sappers and assassins, but after dealing with the Watch's hindrance net of observation posts, they would find the city's high-value targets locked down and guarded. The rest of the sprawling wards and districts were empty, and infrastructure decentralized. Setting fire to the Sticks would be a nuisance, but not like hitting a substation and knocking out power. Stealth intrusion worked best far behind lines where security was laxer and supply caches richer. Portcullis was emaciated and mean; only stone, steel, and flesh to find here.

Sneaking a larger force through the mountains and hitting the South

Wall was demonstratively infeasible. If they could do that, they didn't need to take Portcullis in the first place.

Mages and wizards could slip through, though.

The Bark negated their magic—at least type Q, or Quotidian—but only while it remained online. It would be an HVT, no question. As such, the Vault was postured against pack and lone wolf attacks. Unless the enemy had another dragon, they were stuck with in-horizon, ballistic kinetics—catapults or similar mechanical throwing devices.

Which they'd need to bring through the canyon across a killing field called the Doormat.

That circled the main action back to the North Wall. Still, there was no guarantee the enemy's nuclear-option magic shit was offline. Ceal could use her Power—type S, the Stochal—in the city. So, if the Black Robes had another asshole like Mendo/Isllor, they just needed to flash him in behind the South Wall and keep him alive long enough to hit the Vault. Then, it was game over.

So, actuate Smith's idea of a sniper team on the Vault.

Saunders needed clarity on whether anything was stopping that Type S Black Robe from rolling right up to the North Wall and tearing it down. Dalmore had mentioned that supernatural materials were woven into the stone but didn't include efficacy. Could a Black Robe hammer it into submission if given enough time? No way to know, and any intel was probably based on second and third hand promises to calm fears.

Also, Bark be damned if thousands of plate-armor soldiers managed to enter the city. His Marines didn't have the ammo, the manpower, the anything to slow that down. Let alone hold for five days.

Five days under the best circumstances where butterflies lighten loads and people can be trusted.

The image of Ceal and Benton's final goodbye popped into Saunders' head. The swordsman, thin and hard in his form-fitting ivory armor and white cloths, was engulfed by the silken blue robes of the Lady who could shoot fire from her fingers. It was touching at the time, but now it reeked.

Not them or their stoic separation.

It was that they had that moment.

My big goodbye to Sarah was three parts fight and one part begging forgiveness. No contact, no fucking backdrop of a great stone wall holding back the hordes. Just the gray bulkhead of a warship and an earpiece. It was jealousy, plain and simple, but damn it if Saunders couldn't indulge himself for a minute before presenting a 21st-century operations plan to a hodge-podge of former adversaries and two-dimensional thinkers.

Benton, of all people, had been getting laid on the regular for the past two months. It was beautiful, really. His wife, pulled from the abyss of a Black Robe's dementia and restored to full health, was a true miracle. Saunders remembered his own homecoming after being declared KIA in Iraq. Sarah looked at him with such . . . gratitude. Anyway, it was a honeymoon times ten.

And dammit, I want that right now. Sarah!

He sighed. Maybe it all came down to Ceal. She left, and with her, the mission. Brines was gone; this whole place was about to get stomped. Everything felt futile and fake. *The hell are we still doing here?*

"Sir? Everything alright?" said LCpl Garcia poking his head in. Typically, PFC Licht would be attached and running comms, but fresh rumors about that weird green shrapnel in his side were making the rounds. People were on edge, which put a microscope on every obscure facet. The last thing Saunders needed was this briefing derailed by irrelevant superstition and disproportionate focus on minor details.

Hopefully minor.

Garcia was a good kid, though. His south Texan drawl was (usually) peppered with Spanish from his upbringing in a bi-lingual house, and all the pop culture crap was on point. Parents probably came up across the border before he was born. Strong work ethic, funny, and he was, apparently, perceptive.

Hell with it. Only the British looked good bottling everything up and letting it age. "Ever wonder if you're in over your head?"

Garcia panned the study. Dusty plank and furs at their feet, stacked stone and thick wood all around, and a raging mountain draft that only abated around the massive fireplaces. Guards out in the hall with swords and chainmail. Horses. The contrast to his hometown in hot and flat San Antonio could not have been more evident.

"Nah," he said with a wry smile before adding, "sir."

Single-source, external validation. It should not have made an impact, but it hit like a war horn. The Marine motto *Semper Fidelis* wasn't a loyalty program at a hotel chain. It was an oath.

Fuck the odds; hold to duty.

"You're a good man, Garcia. They ready in there?"

"Yessir."

"Then let's work the plan. Come on."

Sergeant Smith stared into the distance at the Watch Keep, a stone block poking through a crop of slate roofs, and wondered how the briefing was going.

City sweep identified over three hundred holdouts. Guys with families tucked away in basements planning to stand their ground with hammers and shit. They got a big green splotch on their door, and a quick talk about heading to the Watch Keep when those bells on the North Gate started ringing. Then there were the Caranuscan refugees, who Benton said could have their pick of the houses.

Ain't no one want their pick of the Sticks.

The stampedes into Eastside Rise and North Ward were epic. Sorta thing Smith didn't want to see get shut down. But the Watch could field a force when they wanted to. It lasted about an hour and a half before everyone got to somewhere they could deal. Then it was smooth sailing.

Until it came back that the sweep had not identified a single insurgent.

It meant two things: the insurgents were hiding, or they went with the evacuation to take out targets of opportunity. The second one made sense, but time in Afghanistan said it was the first. Hiding out rather than going on organized, secret missions.

The captain was not going to like that. He wanted names, faces, bodies. Not promises of operatives within the wire.

"You guys are cold too, right?" asked PFC Licht rubbing his arms and pacing the walkway.

Smith would never admit it because he had to set the pace but fuck the cold. When the mercury dipped, these Kevlar plate carriers went from sweat factories to paper-thin. Add some wind, and it was evident that they needed to discuss winterizing the MCCUU.

"It's not even below freezing yet," said LCpl Light staring at PFC Licht's white fingers. Apparently, the kid had some issue where his fingers would get even whiter in the cold. *Gotsta be fuckin' frostbite,* Sgt Smith thought, reaching into his back pocket for gloves.

"They're not frozen," said Licht, flexing his hand.

"It's like Mr. Freeze," said Light.

"Shit ain't Mr. Freeze," Smith said. Not even a little bit. Mr. Freeze was specially adapted to cryogenic conditions, meaning he needed to be kept cold, not got weird in the cold. Handing over the gloves, he added, "Motherfucker's more like . . . Green Lantern."

"Thanks, Sergeant," Licht muttered, probably not in the mood to joke around about the glowing stuff in his side. He also handed the gloves back like they weren't worth shit.

"You best be thankin' me. You gonna need a sensei when you get them superpowers."

"Are you a sensei?" asked LCpl Light.

"Fuck you askin'? Keep yo eyes downrange, dawg. The boys talkin' here." Smith turned back to the PFC, who was focused on the job, watching out for the riders supposed to report back on the convoy's progress. "Yeah, bud, superpowers. You gonna go all dark thinkin' you turnin' into something nasty. Then . . . boom, you're a fuckin' swinging dick Lady Ceal. Shoot, maybe it does turn you into a chick. Won't matter, though, 'cause superpowers. Dig?"

LCpl Light wandered to the South Wall's edge. The road was quiet now; the neighs and shouts echoing back up through the mountains were gone. After running around all day, this was a cake babysitting job on an expired target. If only it wasn't so damned cold.

"Anything stuck inside you ever end well?" PFC Licht asked.

Smith laughed. "Good thing Jersey's on Vault right now, or we'd spend the next thirty in the gutter."

Licht finally cracked a smile. "Yeah. I think I'm past fearing it; I'm not worried if I don't think about it."

"Didn't mean nothin' by bringing it up; was raised not to dance around shit, you know? Gotta talk it out like working a muscle. That pain means you fixing things, gettin' stronger."

Licht stared at Light, who was now waving at someone down below. Probably the gate guards. "Stronger for what? I mean . . . after what Francisco reported . . ."

There it is. Ain't no fuckin' bullshit about glowing shrapnel or cold fingers. "All fun and games when we got the guns, and they got chamber pots, right?"

"Yeah."

"Now they gots a hundred, a thousand times our number. You gotta kill a thousand fucking guys, and so do I. Shit, so does my dawg over there," Smith said, pointing at Andrew Light. If there was ever a source of distracting levity, Light was it. "Man, Light, we gotta git you a name sometime. Fuckers will think I'm callin' for a lamp or some shit out on the field. How about . . . uh, Bulb? Ain't no way that's in the Portcullis dictionary. Bulb, you cool wit that?"

"Sure, Sergeant," said Bulb.

"Done. Anyway, Licht, we ain't got the ammo or the hardware for every guy in the city to kill a thousand."

"Right," said the PFC trying hard not to smile at Bulb's new name.

"Right? Fuck we doin' here when we could tuck into a mountain somewhere? Live off the land poppin' heads from a mile away. Let those hundred Black Robes have this shit. We'll rig up some IEDs for a little surprise and book."

"Why isn't that the plan?"

Smith's chest walled up. "Because the C-monster don't give up, don't give ground, and don't give a shit. They built us to win. That's what we do, dawg. The cap'n ain't gonna take any action that doesn't bring us, the United States Marines, closer to victory."

"How does all of us dying help back home?"

He blew out a breath that steamed in the air. It was getting colder, but they only had to hold out for another 45. "Gunny'd probably have a good answer for you. Truth is, I don't know. But we gotsta trust it. Right now, they runnin' a briefing for Benton, Dalmore, all them. Bringin' 'em up to speed on the battle plan and exactly how we win. They don't like it, we book. Simple. But if they do, then it's the right move. Protecting all those people, maybe Ceal, maybe the doc, and Micky matters. Hold for five days."

"We'll be lucky to last five—"

"Guys." LCpl Bulb was leaning over the edge with a hand cupped to his ear. "Do you hear something?"

Chief Tybalt Dalmore marveled at the gathering.

Watchmen, freed Blue Cloaks, a half-ten of Coals who survived

Val'Narden, threadbare sergeants from the Caranuscan refugees, and a mix of able men who had sent their wives and children down the Palings Pass filled the hall.

They were few, but they heard the call.

It was not the host promised by prophecy nor the battle that would avenge his brother, but it was first crack at the Last Army. Mayhaps that was enough.

The Corsan Carre captain, Saunders, stood as marble flanked by one of his and Lord Benton atop the hearth platform. If there was any hope among this sorry lot, it was there, as it once was with Lord Bayliss and his false splendor.

What drives confidence up those ever-straight Corsan Carre backs? Dalmore wondered.

Lt. Maon had confirmed the reports from the northern overlook. It was naught a trick of the eyes, the entirety of the Pandonis Immortalis—the endless legions that had defeated Haquatia, the combined might of the Caranuscan Houses, Galimay's own Fourth and Fifth armies, and the like of other minor states and tribes whose names were not known—had come. No doubt remained; this was the Last Army.

And dribbled atop was the Obantum Carre.

During the *First Battle of Portcullis*—so named because all knew it another was inevitable—the enemy ranks comprised but a single legion and a half-ten of Obantum Carre. Together they wrought destruction unseen no matter how many winters a man had lived, driven back only by the Bark and reinforcement from the Sapphire Branch—2000 men who barely held the North Wall against 10,000. Now, it was fewer than a thousand against . . .

Uncountable. All the waves in the seas.

"Chief, methinks we deserve more coin," said Sergeant Segar, a stout fellow whose face bore likeness to a punched pillow. Under Lord Bayliss, he had distinguished himself in keeping the Dawn Guard timely and well-accounted. He also had a wit that could lance a boil.

"Are some getting coin?" asked Sergeant Aldun, a fit and well-bred stock from a tithe near Kelnmaw—Dalmore's place of youth. In the days leading up to Commander Mendo's treachery, Aldun had given the ill-ease within the Sapphire Branch ranks a voice. It was he who suggested Dalmore break into the Forecrypt to learn the truth of the Corsan Carre.

"Nay, I hath kept all the coins—stamped, smudged, and bitten—for meself," Dalmore said. "Such glorious riches this post delivers to me. And that flattened bread . . . Ye know the kind, when the baker has naught in his cupboard but water and grinds to make paste."

"Aye, fires hard enough to mend stone," said Segar. "And the taste, what do they put in it?"

"'Tis of cracked teeth bleeding," said Aldun.

"Har!" said Segar. "Mayhaps we are better biting down on these invisible coins Dalmore keeps. Eh, Lieutenant?"

"'Tis chief, now."

"Tell it to the Genisans; mayhaps they go home?" said Segar.

"Fear mights the sword. Dalmore hath come! Chief Dalmore of . . . ah, the fallen and the folks with the serving aprons," said Aldun.

"Nay, Chief of the Corsan Carre. Gore them with the bigger horn."

Dalmore allowed his amusement to show; the mirth of men on the eve of battle was naught to ignore. "Drape mineself in that ugly orange eye, and they shall cower." Lord Bayliss was to blame for branding the Watch with that foul tabard. In the spirit of unity, the Deadlies adopted it when they split from the Sapphire Branch. It lasted naught a tenday.

"The laughter alone will shake Almon's Peak down upon them," said Segar.

"Aye," muttered Aldun, sharing in the joke, but his eyes swift-moving to deeds and duty. "Think tell of their number is true?"

Dalmore considered speaking false. Their path was chosen, worn down as a great river through screaming canyons. What mattered it to know how high the fall off the water's edge at the end? "Aye, from North Overlook and Lt. Maon's own eyes with the Corsan Carre scouts."

"As it was told so long ago?" asked Aldun.

"The Last Army. All are oath-bound to fight," Dalmore said.

"Few are the all, methinks," said Segar. "Better pay down south."

Indeed. The lapping luxury of a nation propped by rich lands and a world of vaulted treasures blinded Galimay to the true threat. Portcullis went unaided for the sake of His Reverence's disdain for Benton. Pithy, mayhaps disastrous.

But there was naught to regret. "I came hence to avenge mine brother," Dalmore said. "A good man fallen in defense of Val'Narden. If too I may serve in the vanguard that faces the Last Army, no greater purpose can bind mine death."

"Resist death," whispered Aldun.

The words floated quiet through the din but snared ears as the Tel'racs' roar.

"RESIST DEATH," answered the gathered Deadlies. So too, did the Watchmen carry the cry, and the Corsan Carre captain beamed as if their spirits were all the riches of the Palings, Durador, and the lost Isle of Oban.

When order was restored, Captain Saunders—not Lord Benton—stepped forward to speak. "You folks know why we're here, so I'll get straight to it," he said in the perfect tongue that made his true words known to all ears. "My people are coordinating with the Watch to sweep the last of the city, but a few stragglers aside, we're lean. Portcullis is now a forward position, a combat outpost. That's it. Forget Examiner Creed's histories; it is a tool of war. Five days. We need it to give us five days."

Shouts flew back at the man, if the Corsan Carre were indeed men, protesting the task of rats helming a mighty battleship to war. Dalmore smiled. Lord Bayliss had oft said the ranks would complain in victory and defeat, great tasks and small. Silence told only of crushed spirits.

Captain Saunders showed no doubts, nor dismay. He did not wait until their voices calmed but spoke sudden and powerful. "The mission is to leave the legions lame. To give them pause. Right now, they're king shit out there. Unstoppable. We'll wet their beaks on the nightmares waiting for them in the lands of castles and steel beyond."

The last were Benton's words, good words that never failed to fire Galimay's heart. The Caranuscans and Haquatians, though built of strife in their ways, spent naught of 700 years battling men, the Gra'nuul, and the Southron Storms that roared from the White to strike crop and people alike. Galimay possessed a matchless strength, or so it was hoped.

"No doubt the enemy fields a superior force, a massive fucking army that will not take no for an answer." Grumbles rippled through the ranks, but still, they hung upon his words. Dalmore mused at "fucking" as it came to his ears raw in the strange sounds of their language. He liked it, but it was used so oft he could not gather its meaning. "But their size makes them obvious. And we have a plan."

Captain Saunders then wove a vision beyond Portcullis, where defeats were piled upon defeats and suddenly hammered into a golden, victorious statue. It was well-versed, but Dalmore listened through the promises to the placements and usage of not only his men but also the Corsan Carre.

Archers.

Benton spoke true. For all the shifting sands, Captain Saunders' men were simple marksmen. Quite welcome, yet missing were the likes of Ceal conjuring fire from the skies or other fearsome events. The noise their relics made was impressive, but to the damage of a crossbow, they were confined.

Sergeants Aldun and Segar heard it the same and stood eager for more. The question could not go unasked.

"A sound plan," Dalmore announced. So it was. "But is there naught else the Corsan Carre might bring to surprise our great enemy?"

Lord Benton cast his gaze to the floor as Captain Saunders answered.

"Back home, we've got some stuff that would smash the valley five times deeper and score the Genisan cities off the map. At the end of the day, it's all bullshit." He rapped his chest. "Heart's what matters. Us. Boots. The will to get it done. All we gotta do is bring the pain."

———

Bring the pain?

Captain Rath was glad LCpl Buontempo's radio didn't have video because the look on his face would have the assembled cast of Hamlet running for the hills. To think, he was rambling about taking charge of Cork Team last night. It could've been him standing up there in the Watch Keep shoveling bullshit into a crowd of outnumbered and frightened soldiers while Saunders sat pretty in this rocky carriage listening to the broadcast.

The transmitter was near Saunders on the other end, so while he and Benton's voices came through clear as high-flying skies, the crowd was muffled. Still, those were cheers Rath was hearing.

That lame-assed one-liner had somehow struck a note.

But to what end? From memory, half of those medieval knuckle draggers were meth-addict thin from hard labor and food rationing, and the other half were mountain hicks. Not unusual, most rag-tag armies looked like shit compared to the professional ranks of first-world countries. But when coupled with their tiny numbers and vanishing capabilities, no amount of motivation would matter.

Five bucks says they stand down and leave Cork holding the bag.

Rath made sure not to say that aloud because Buontempo might jump out the back and ruck it back up the mountain to die gloriously with them.

Rather than capitalizing on the tough-as-nails ground commander's momentum to slam home their promised victory, Benton's voice jumped in to clarify a few points. Maybe it was the magical translation being weird over the radio, but the *hero of this, that, and the other* sounded meek as hell.

Hey Benton, you should hear yourself on the radio. What an awesome mindfuck that'd be.

The important stuff fed into Saunders' plan to hit enemy logistics. The fundamental assumption that the bigger they are, the harder they fall wasn't stupid. It sounded great, really resonated with the people who couldn't do math. It was a classic football jet sweep where the bulk of the teams got locked in the middle while a receiver delivered the package to the endzone. It was just missing just one tiny detail.

We don't have any fucking players.

Rath, Captain Rath—same O-3 pay grade as Saunders with better training and a 95th percentile on the ACT—was tempted to open his trap. Unless there was a secret plan—which happened with this group—Cork Team was facing down impossible odds for the sake of living up to the Marine Corps killer spirit—the race to die, get a foot in the grave before Death could blink and steal credit.

Problem was that Rath didn't have a Plan B.

"The old paths are shored and fortified," Benton continued. "For those new to our city, they were dug to fight the Gra'nuul whence they still roamed the surface. It was how the few of what is now Old Towne fought against such fearsome numbers. After the Gra'nuul were driven to their caves, much fell into disrepair, but the paths shall serve us once more. Naught of an army's size can matter up there; one man can hold hundreds."

"One Marine could bury thousands," thumped Saunders.

Rath wanted to scream. There wasn't enough ordnance in the entire expeditionary force that launched Operation *Sea Monster* to even dent the numbers Francisco had reported, let alone what eight Marines with small arms could do. And that was before factoring in magic.

He flashed back to the cockpit of his AH-1Z Viper over Mina Bazar.

The display altimeter was spinning, confirming the readout on the HMD. The ground was rushing up at them. No warnings, no malfunction.

Physics fucked.

Mayday. Mayday. Mayday.

Freefall.

His weapons officer—Gurka—on the com shouting for him to get control.

Blackness.

The AH-1Z Viper attack helicopter could decimate a mass formation of medieval infantry. Rake back and forth all day with total impunity. But these Genisans were ready for that too. Back on Earth, just one of those Black Robes took on 30 Vipers, a hail of cruise missiles, and a company of Marines storming through a smoked-out burning hell. The only thing that stopped it was . . .

Well, fuck, Saunders does have a point. All the fancy tech and gear were bullshit; Brines bagged the first Black Robe. Francisco took out the second. Maybe . . .

"M'lord!" came a gasp through the radio. Then commotion.

"Fuck," muttered Rath. "Can we ask what's going on?"

Buontempo shrugged. "Not until Garcia lets up on the mic."

As if hearing them, the radio came to life with Garcia's *mexas* drawl. "Exodus, this is Cork." Radio protocol was stupid on a planet with only three radios. "One of the Watchmen, uh, Sergeant Batoth, just came in like he tripled timed the ten-miler. Something's up. Over."

Silence meant Rath could finally talk, but now all he wanted to do was listen. He grabbed the mic. "Standing by."

The radio came back with Captain Saunders shouting, "Make a hole!" More shuffling noises and commotion followed. Someone called for quiet. Buontempo stared hard at the radio as if that might help pick out the transmission better. Rath found his own heart thumping a little harder in his chest. Excitement? Or was it fear that the line would go dead, and he'd never find out what happened?

Sergeant Batoth, he assumed, came across as if his lips were grazing the mic itself. "A host presses from the south!" And then all hell broke loose.

"Garcia, Garcia. Shit, let up on the button," Rath shouted at the radio.

"Did he say south? Did we pass an army and not notice?" asked Buontempo grabbing the controls and switching frequencies. But all they got was Vault Team screaming for a SITREP amid panicked locals.

Rath sat back, wondering if the entire concept of corking the enemy was bullshit from the get-go.

The Corsan Carre scrubbed their hands against the chill air, but Benton found it comfortable in a simple doublet. More, an overcoat or armor with its soft padding, would leave him stricken with a moistened brow and longing for the breeze within South Gate's tunnelway. It was sure that these men who dressed as the desert sands came from a land of heat in the like the Genisans. And had never dared a voyage to the White, which would forever make ice warm to the touch.

"My lord, they hide their numbers beyond the road's bend," said Lieutenant Maon sweeping the Palings Pass with a sight glass.

"Lance Corporal Light spotted 'em first, Cap'n," said the darker Corsan Carre, Sergeant Smith. This Lance Corporal Light, the like of Sir Gol's firstborn son Jon, gave a boyish smile but kept his stare past the wall. Young, yet stoic as any soldier. It was a discipline Jon never had the fortune to learn. "They rolled up and held out of, uh, arrow range or whatever," Smith continued. "Just give the word, sir."

"Stand down; let the locals handle it," said Captain Saunders. "PFC, update Exodus on the situation. Find out how we ended up with zero early warning."

Benton ignored the content of their words as finding meaning oft begged much of his time. He considered climbing atop the South Wall's defensive crenulations to get a better view but saw all he needed to. The six riders awaiting parley bore the welcomed sight of the red skull banner, but what appeared to be their leader wore the Reverent Armor of the Diamond Branch. "Our northern brothers arrive from the south. From Durador," he said.

"But do not hail our gates nor reveal their strength," said Lt. Maon.

"You think they're here to arrest you?" asked Saunders, mayhap also seeing the knight's importance.

Benton could give no answer.

"If so," said Lt. Maon in his stead, "may they also possess a decree to occupy this besieged city. If they can take the South Wall, their numbers are great enough to hold the North Wall for five days."

"Or they just drag us out of here and leave it a ghost town," Saunders said.

Maon's chuckle rattled his battle gear. "Forgive me, my lords, but I jest. This is a boon; the time of ye's despair is ended."

Benton shook his head. Maon was a fine soldier, but his eyes tended to the flowers, not the thorns. "His Reverence hath struck clever once more. Be this army to seize or aid, so too he wishes them buried with me. Their greens and great crossbows mark them as Caranuscan, and they bare the sigil of House Carnifex. But who leads them? What treachery hath befallen mine dear friend Princeps Noniam?"

"Real question is whether we stack this wall and get ready for a fight," said Saunders.

Flee.

"Nay," Benton said. "Of mine few and scattered allies, these are the last who might condemn me no matter the puppet in command. Sergeant Batoth, invite them closer!"

"Aye, m'lord." Shouts for formation and arms followed below.

Benton turned to Saunders. "Alas, they hath given and lost much in this war. I shall send them away. Portcullis will drink its fill of blood without theirs."

Lt. Maon turned north, where a dark cloud hung over the Dowdale. "Is not every man needed?"

Flee.

Benton dismissed his wife's dire plea. "Here in a place we only wish to hold for days, the remnants of House Carnifex matter little. Elsewhere, on grander fields sewed with the finest iron seeds, they might avert disaster."

The six of riders approached unhurried. The two banner bearers and three cohort captains wore the deep leaf green of Caranuscan marksmen, but it was the white knight at their head who commanded the South Wall's attention. They were met by Sergeant Batoth and a full ten of Watchmen in glinting mail and sharp swords.

"Is that . . ." began Saunders as the knight dismounted and revealed a mess of wild black hair beneath his helm. He squinted up at them, wearing a smile of broken teeth.

Benton's heart sank. It was a dark hound in knight's white. "Lord Bayliss' sworn man, Sir Rampo," he said.

"Dickhead has balls. Didn't we tell him we'd fuck him with cinderblock if he showed his face around here again?"

Benton did not remember such a threat, but much was lost in the chaos of Lord Bayliss' departure. Sir Rampo, surely the foulest of Bayliss' ilk, was a fell omen.

"A mountain rises, Lord Benton," Sir Rampo's voice echoed up. "And ye stand upon its peak."

CHAPTER 10

THE CONSUMPTIONS

How long have you had the dermal ulcer?" Dr. Pat asked, hoping the polite term for the gangrenous mass chewing the flesh down to white bone would be conveyed through the magical language translator. The man—thin, pissing sugar, and riddled with peripheral neuropathies—had walked on it for ten hours straight. He only allowed himself to be loaded onto the back of a flatbed cart after blood started gushing over the top of his boot.

"Comes an' goes. The boots. Ma, tell her the boots be tight, rubbin'." He reached down with dirty fingers to massage the pale, fragile flesh around the necrotizing cauldron that was once his heel.

"N . . . no, don't touch it."

"Muh boy speak true," said the white-haired woman who'd flagged down Dr. Pat. She appeared to be in her eighties from the stoop and crackle in her voice. But she was still spry, joints running smooth as a 50-year-old's. Her life's story was a leather coat left out in the sun. "Them shoes ne'er fit. No stretchin' that hide for 'im neither. I told 'im: 'drink less boil an' ye will 'ave some coin for new ones.' He ne'er listen."

Whatever "boil" was, it sounded like a major contributor to the decline in this fellow's quality of life. "The ulcer is because your feet are numb," Dr. Pat explained, poking the non-necrotic skin. "You can't feel where the boot is rubbing, making the wound worse."

"I likes me feet numb."

"Likes yer 'ead numb too?" asked his Ma with a smack to the back of his skull.

"Do you not . . ." Dr. Pat began but cut herself off. This was a society bereft of self-inspective education and social programs. The body was a tool that worked until it broke. Foot falling off? *Gamgam had that happen in her 40s; guess it's my time!* "I can stop this from killing you, but it's gone too far. We're looking at amputation. Do you understand?"

He lost color. "Me boots . . ."

"Lass, a drop o' the Sap is what 'e be needin'."

Antibiotics and surgical debridement, *yesterday*, were what he needed. Still, a few slugs—a pharmacist's nightmare for dosing—weren't out of the question. The problem was potentially the same as with the burn victims; the wound might not have functional blood flow. The supply was also limited since Wisewoman Alena had requisitioned most of it for the troops in Portcullis. "For now, we can irrigate with hot vinegar and bandage—"

"The Sap," insisted Ma.

Sigh. "We're going to try the antiseptic soak first," Dr. Pat said as if denying a pain med script. "When we stop for the night, maybe we can get you on the priority list for Sap."

"Luck be mine," said the man pointing over her shoulder. She turned. The long flow of carts, draft animals, and walkers was pooling where the road elbowed into a mountain river.

They were making camp with daylight left to burn.

What the hell?

Dr. Pat found Micky helping—supervising—a group pounding tent stakes into the ground. By then, the wagons were circled with hundreds of little camps forming on the bulging riverbank. A group of bare bodies splashing by the shore caught her eye—not that she was looking—and gave her a solid shiver. It felt colder down here than up in the mountains, and that ice water was not inviting. She gave herself a ten count for composure and then asked her number one fan, "Where is Ceal?"

"'Scuse me, boys," Micky said in a sultry voice. "Gotta check in with the tower." Whether the roustabouts understood her was unclear, but they missed a couple swings staring at the swish in her ass as she sauntered over. Stopping two steps too far into the personal bubble, she swept a hand over the camp of tan tarps and pointy blue tents. "Might fine afternoon for a refugee camp, eh gubnah?"

"Right. *Afternoon*, not sundown like we planned. Where is she?"

"I'll give you one guess."

Dr. Pat clicked her tongue and marched off without further discussion.

Having someone point out the obvious was the worst. And the blue and white striped *pavilion* was fucking obvious. Two Watchmen flanked the entrance looking weighed down by invisible packs filled with shame at jumping on the lifeboats with the women and children. Sergeant Orrugant was on his way out as she entered. Their eyes met, his dropped. *Get over it; no one is judging you.*

The canvas flaps transported Dr. Pat from the crunchy gravel and frozen mud of the floodplain back to Ceal and Benton's manor in Portcullis. It was such a detailed replica of Ceal's top-floor study that Dr. Pat checked over her shoulder to ensure she hadn't actually translocated. Micky was right on her heels chatting up the two Watchmen. Beyond them, everyone they were trying to save was still out there.

"Dr. Pat," Ceal said without looking up. Rather than having a desk, plotting wall, or a bean bag surrounded by hand-scrawled pages of a dirty manifesto, Ceal had a dining room table. Black, single slab, it was a showpiece that could seat eight if it wasn't piled with parchments, books, and unidentifiable dust collectors. Impressively, it was arranged precisely how it was in her old office, down to the little pyramid of stacked scrolls.

"What is this?"

"Shall I spend a fortune in widths explaining the heap of knowledge upon and within this world, or will ye ask again with precision?"

So that's how it is, huh? Step away from the city, its lords, and the Marines, and the façade of pleasantries dropped. Not surprising, but directness begot directness. "Why have we stopped?"

"It is eventual that all motion must cease as it is exhausted of impulse."

Words piled up on Dr. Pat's tongue, a textbook on Newton's laws of motion about to slam down on that table of lies and fairytales. But arguing with the ignorant was a game impossible to win and only served to piss that *fortune of widths* down the drain. "Pretty sure we still have enough impulse and daylight to get us another few miles."

"Crack the whips, and another half-day we might make. To what end?" Ceal still hadn't looked up from the yellowed paper in her thin, uncalloused hand. Dr. Pat wondered if this was how Master Gol treated Jon. The old man behind a desk at the end of a long, narrow study never bothering to regard his son. The height of arrogant displays.

Was this the last five minutes of Jon's life? Standing there trying to reach his father, tell him about the mysterious team from another world he met. Pleading for his dad's attention until his hoarse throat was ripped out by a shape-shifting psycho.

"We have soldiers covering our asses so we can reach this so-called safe point," Dr. Pat said. "Every second we delay is them dying in that city. A half-day? That's a long freaking time!"

Emeralds replaced eyelashes. "Oh, hush. Ye demean yeself. To fight against the Last Army, even in defeat, is the dream of every Galimayan boy. They chance for glory, to see their names carved upon the stone of Durador's white walls." She chuckled. "Until they too crumble."

Unbelievable. "That doesn't mean we should abandon . . ."

"We possess what we need." She went back to that fucking paper. "Our pace will quicken once the walking piles of rags begin to die off. Alas, leaving them behind now is much too early; they might limp back to the city and raise alarm."

Dr. Pat knew her blood couldn't boil, but boy did it flush hot as it hammered into her head. "YOU are a goddamn—"

A bump from behind.

"Hey, quit blocking the door," said Micky. Sliding past, she whispered, "Careful, Ceal's got a little more bite than Alena."

Rage.

Whether it was justified or that twenty gallons of everything from Hudud to Brines stewing in a cauldron, it didn't matter.

It erupted.

The physiological manifestation was a flash of light. Raw emotion electro-chemically conducted through Dr. Pat's brain, overstimulating the visual receptors, the cranial nerves, and the entirety of her senses. And then, everything was different. Anything in the world was possible. Every thought and whim were real as stainless steel.

"Oh fuck," came a voice in the distance.

"Dear, quick: read the letter I hath valued over yeself," shouted Ceal.

Curiosity beat defiance. The text was hidden beneath a blanket of blue light pouring out of Ceal and probably in a different language, yet the contents came to her clear as day:

Dear Pat,

Made ya look!

Love,
Micky

Shocked that she'd read that stupidity out loud, a wave of fatigue crashed down, and Dr. Pat's thoughts faded to whispers. "What . . ."

"I totally wrote that," blurted Micky.

Ceal sat back, breathless, and folded her hands. "Indeed. And naught of mine strength could keep it secret. Well done, Dr. Pat."

Sir Rampo.

The knight, clean and polished even by Marine standards, leading his troops through the South Gate was a classic frontline moment, a triumphant parade of saviors. Fifteen hundred soldiers in green plate strapped with crossbows, quivers, swords, spears, and little packs pounded the cobblestones in step with their chests out and heads high. But the reception was cold between the Black Robes, dragon, malnutrition, supply shortages, and a triple serving of all that times ten waiting beyond the North Wall. The spectators lining Gates Street amounted to a smattering of ragged uniforms and glassy-eyed stares.

The hope the Caranuscans brought wasn't lost. The refugees cheered at the sight of their countrymen. Watchmen, Deadlies, even Saunders' Marines warmed to it, but like a rock outside the fire circle, they never got hot.

Combat Stress Reaction is what the Defense Health Agency called it. Brines had different names, but it all came down to stress and wasn't always a product of how many bullets or arrows were flying. It was that vice grip on the chest tightening a half turn every day, always and forever preventing that freeing breath.

The frontlines were an additive hell.

And then there's the asshole from regimental HQ who comes down dressed to impress, thought Saunders as Sir Rampo goosestepped his way into the Watch Keep.

The keep had been cleared of all non-essential personnel in the same way a skeleton crew could be stripped of their marrow and secured. Sergeant Teague's ten held the courtyard and only admitted Rampo's six-man parley unit. Francisco and Fischer had the rooftop. Sergeant Smith's fireteam, with a full combat loadout, was stationed in the upstairs hall where the reception would take place.

Trust is earned.

Sir Rampo was one of Bayliss' men. Letting these 1500 "greens"—not even part of the esteemed Galimay Emerald Branch but foreign nationals from up north—into the city felt like another occupation. Especially since Portcullis had just gotten rid of the Blue Cloaks and hopefully flushed out the Anticult insurgency. Still, Dalmore had that *more meat for the grinder* gleam in his eye, and that's why it was being entertained.

The handshaking—more wrist-grabbing and fist-to-chest salutes—phase dragged on for what must have been hours. As oil lamps and raw flame took over for waning daylight and more green personnel were allowed up, the tension began to dissolve. Private discussion groups broke off from the large format grilling sessions. Laughter replaced Q&A.

Saunders smiled and nodded as necessary, but he and his Marines were given a wide berth. Some greens cast sidelong glances; others stared with unfaltering scrutiny. Clearly, the Corsan Carre thing wasn't an instant sell with everyone. And that was fine because the Marine thing could be an instant hell for anyone.

When the daylight was bled out, Sir Rampo had food brought up. Fruit, salted meats, dry-packed crackers the size of pavers . . . Saunders refused to be bought but had to admit it was a goddamned glorious sight. Rib-sticking mess hall mass after weeks of splitting MRE field rations and drinking pre-pissed water. If there was one—and only one—redeeming quality of Lord Bayliss, he never let anyone go hungry.

Watchmen took the place of the usual servants, which was a top profession in feudal Portcullis. Grunt service was familiar to Saunders, though. Comforting, even. In the Marines, from front-line to the rear, everyone was a rifleman. Everyone reliable. So, the guy baking that pecan pie or the woman slinging those potatoes were all an *oorah* away from menacing and murderous. Likewise, he and his men had all spent their time doing the shit jobs. It was just—

"Captain Saunders."

He turned to find the polished clearcoat of Sir Rampo's white armor glistening in the flamelight. Fifty pounds of enameled plate beneath the flowing cape that had to be at least 5,000 thread count was mildly intimidating up close.

Rampo's pocketed cheeks pulled thin lips into a smile. "I bear tidings from our Lord Bayliss."

To the right, Sgt Smith tensed, wallpaper turning to brick.

We're friends. All fucking friends.

But friends who don't talk to each other. "I'll direct you to our customer service rep," Saunders said. Smith stepped forward and flexed, dwarfing the knight despite layers of armor and padding.

Sir Rampo snorted, an approximation of a laugh. "A fine specimen. Am I not worthy to face ye's second?"

Saunders stared back.

"Brines," he clarified. "I did join mine sword to his relic whence we drove the enemy's Stretched Guard from South Gate. Such did his weapon thunder! But 'tis naught before his lust for battle. Few are the men who inspire me; fewer are those I do owe an ale for mine life."

Saunders remembered Mike muttering something about Rampo. A weird grunt of approval that was lost in the fact that the entire Bayliss shitshow had tried to kill all of them. "He's dead."

Sir Rampo didn't flinch, but men like that didn't flinch. They braced, took the bullet like a block of ballistics gel, and waited for the next. They never bothered looking down at the holes and just kept going until one day, they were found cold on the garage floor surrounded by broken bottles. Or drowned in an avalanche.

"How?"

The words came hard. "The dra—, uh Tel'racs." Saunders stole a breath to regroup. "Gunnery Sergeant Brines took him out."

Sir Rampo absorbed the information, face impossible to read. Fucker didn't owe Brines a beer; he probably came here to pick a fight. *Say the wrong fucking thing, scumbag. You're not a tenth the man he was.* But Rampo nodded, thumped his chest in salute, and said, "A hero who will go unsung in this world, as might we all." Then with a sparkle in his eye, he added, "But so we must fight unto and through the weakness of this flesh the worms and wolves seek to claim. We live only to resist death. For ourselves and all."

They were good words, strong words. An unexpected homage with as much sincerity as Saunders had ever heard. That was also Dalmore's line: *resist death.* Nothing Bayliss had ever said. Saunders, speechless, returned the salute, and so did Smith.

Then Dalmore was beside them, and Sir Rampo hardened. Saunders considered hanging around for moral support since the two men clearly had beef. Betraying the mighty Lord Bayliss had a way of dropping enemies on your head. But the congestion of people, wood smoke, and scents of cooked meats and ripe fruits were getting to him. He needed air. Not the courtyard balcony, that was . . . that was where Mike would've gone with a stogie. Instead, Saunders had Smith take charge and headed down to the streets.

Brisk cold hit his lungs. One thing about Portcullis was the mountain air. It brought him back home: Boulder, Estes, the Rockies. Not identical, but for anyone who knew the mountains, it was family.

The commotion and traffic jam of a parade endpoint with no dispersal plan were hours gone. Sunset usually put Portcullis indoors, and from the racket coming from the Market District, Rampo's people had found their primary bivouac. The noise and cookfires wafting through the frigid air made it seem like there was a large, zero-music concert in the distance.

Aside from the Watch Keep gate guards, Saunders was alone.

The buddy system was still in place, so he couldn't wander far. The plan was a quick walk down the street, always in shouting distance of the Watch. He just needed a reduction in external inputs. Time to collect his thoughts.

Brines.

Portcullis.

The dreams of that strange religion—Kôz—spreading across the globe back home. Sarah. Tommy.

The mission.

Fighting was easy. Dangerous but easy because it was the job—something all-consuming. A distraction. Dr. Bowman's distraction was healing people. If Sarah were here, God forbid, her distraction would be helping Benton run the city. If Saunders and his men were a team of plumbers, they'd probably be out 24/7 laying the fuck out of some pipe for Portcullis.

Working overtime to make the Shitchairs™ flushed and the faucets squirted. All the while missing better opportunities.

Is that us? Are we just doing what we know, like salmon swimming upstream to the waiting net?

His own intelligence was not an asset in answering the question since it sought to justify rather than criticize his actions. It was the same back home. The whole world was struggling to deal with a threat in a conventional, justifiable way. Even if the Pentagon had an inkling of what these Black Robes could do, which they certainly did not, it was a good bet no one in Washington had the stomach to listen.

Instead of taking the most direct paths to get home and warn the world, Saunders was burning through Marines and ammo for a sack of empty promises. Not just that, but the sole reason they'd launched Operation *Sea Monster*, the VIP, was riding deeper into a medieval world of feuding lords, cultish prophesies, and typical third-world shit.

I've lost control.

A counterargument struck fast: *Doubt is your enemy; stay the course.*

So much truth. Hesitation and uncertainty didn't care whether the action was right or wrong; they just wanted to stop it from happening. Maybe he should've forced Ceal down into the valley at gunpoint a month ago and made her figure out how to send them home. Maybe they never should've left the chopper.

Maybe, would, should, could, what if.

Fact was they were here, and the price to move forward involved pissing time and giving ground.

A shadow brought Saunders back to the cobblestones and cold. He'd walked about a half-block; the MP5 was in his hands, condition zero, ready to *resist death.* Ten feet ahead was a void between the lambent streetlamps. The lighting gap was staffed by a non-functioning Q-light, but there wasn't enough space to hide an assailant. And it backed up to a length of wrought iron fencing between now abandoned buildings.

It was just a standard security snag: check all corners. But something about the Q-light called to him.

Unlike the oil lamps lit tonight with the fuel from Sir Rampo's troops, Q-lights held a fist-sized crystal where a standard floodlight would go. Pretty much the same concept as electric light bulbs. The power supply was

Quotidian, which the Black Robes controlled with Harry Potter-like magic wands. In the same vein, the city was "wired" like an electrical grid to "conduct" magic to various Q-devices.

Fuck it, probably the same thing as electricity. Saunders hadn't seen the generator yet, but none of it worked with the Bark in place.

It was tempting to click on his barrel-mounted LED and take a closer look at that crystal. Still, the combat veteran wasn't eager to give away his position. Something had caught his eye in the shadows, and there was no shortage of potential enemies in Portcullis.

The warmth and muffled cheer of the Watch Keep wafted down the street. It was another case of the rich dining while the grunts bathed in darkness and anticipation. Saunders understood it, even accepted it, but it wasn't his deal. *Hand me a beer, and I'll pass it down the line.*

At that moment, he realized two things:

The men need a beer.

And . . .

It wasn't the shadows that interested him, but the potential. The second the Bark was destroyed, that crystal—silent and waiting—and all the others like it were going to . . .

Reactivate.

Neurons clinked together, and something new formed.

An answer.

A fucking awesome answer to one of Saunders' biggest problems. He spun, excited thoughts bursting the dam of anxiety and doom. He needed to grab Benton's or Examiner Creed's ear. One of them would know—

Movement. This time it *was* the shadows.

The MP5 snapped to his shoulder in *high ready,* and the sights locked onto the darkness before his eyes could register the shape.

A kid?

The target was short, like an ex-psycho girlfriend who didn't have to drop her guard for a nut shot. It straightened, gaining an inch in height, and stepped out from behind the Q-light. There was no way the light pole was wide enough to hide behind.

"Show me your hands," Saunders barked, checking his flanks and the grassy alley beyond the fence. It was dark, and if he missed the classic bad guy hiding behind a beanpole, then he could be surrounded. The Watch Keep gate was just out of sight but not earshot.

"Ho! I mean not to frighten," came a familiar, sniveling voice. It was the little blacksmith who was talking shit yesterday morning. Smallfoot.

"That's close enough."

"Yes, milord," he said with a bow.

"Over there."

Smallfoot slinked into the flickering light of the flanking streetlamp while Saunders stayed in the shadows. Hands were empty and out. Nothing else was moving; good visibility all around. An enemy could have him covered with crossbows, but assassins wouldn't usually hesitate.

"Turn around."

The mess of a person spun, looking even worse than he had the other day. His half-assed beard was somehow quarter-assed shaved, a mess of reddish stubble and tufts. At least they matched his bloodshot eyes, which were knocking around in their sockets like a high-speed game of Pong. Oh, and he had a sword strapped to his back.

"I only s-seek—"

"I'll ask the questions," Saunders said, head on a swivel. "How many with you?"

The little troll twitched. "N-none with me. I could not come close before."

"None with you?" He clicked the LED on, blinding Smallfoot in clean, white brilliance. "I'll ask one more time."

"Milord!" he cried in shock. "Please, I . . ." he covered his eyes. The other hand groped at his back for his sword.

"Touch the weapon and die."

Those little hands dropped. Struggling against the LED firehose, he said, "I bring ye aid, milord."

"What kind of aid is the Anticult passing out today?"

Smallfoot's eyes widened, then slammed shut. "Nay! I am nothing of that filth, milord."

"No? Just yesterday, I saw you pissing lies into an already pissed-off crowd."

"I speak only of concern for the low! So oft are we forgotten in the great contests of lords."

There's nothing to discuss here, just him stalling. "Tell it to the Watch. Move."

"I shall go to them," he said, shuffling in the correct direction. "To mine misery, I am here when all others hath fled. But it was for good purpose, milord. A gift, I bring ye. A great boon which ye's coming hath afforded me. Please! As I walk, consider. The sword I carry is unlike any ye will find in the lands of Galimay. Do ye know the legend of Song Forging?"

"No. Keep moving."

"The song harmonizes the metal as it reddens and mashes. A true master can create such harmony that the steel breathes in an ancient Power. It is legend, but milord, grasp such in ye's hands. Ye hath touched this sword once before. Do so again before casting me, and mine works to the prisons of a doomed city."

People would say anything to get out of cuffs, but they were coming in sight of the gate guards, and disarming the guy wasn't a bad idea. The sword was semi-familiar, and Saunders remembered touching a metal hunk during their brief encounter a few months ago. He could get a read on the sword from Benton later. "Unbuckle it," he said, allowing a solid ten feet of space between them. It'd be enough time for the MP5 to react.

Smallfoot pulled the black scabbard off his back and held it in outstretched arms.

"Show me the blade." Steel flashed in the white LED beam. Beautiful and sleek, the sword was a definite killer. *Mike would love this.*

"Milord," Smallfoot said with another bow. He rested the weapon on the cold cobblestones with the care one might have for a newborn and stepped back, head low.

Saunders kept his rifle leveled at the blacksmith's chest as he squatted down to the supposed gift. It was all sorts of weird but somehow compelling. Maybe it was that little bit that Brines left behind, that obsession with knives and swords reaching out from the grave. Smallfoot also didn't strike him as anything but eager to please. That and someone who didn't wipe their ass after going four rounds with the Shitchair™.

The visit to Smallfoot's home two months ago came to the forefront. The piles of garbage, trails of food that missed the mouth, and rancid smell . . . Micky had howled with laughter afterward. That trip to the end of Song Street was one of the top stories she told people. Despite it all, the smith's wares were pristine and handled with reverence. Maybe the shitshow life was just the price of perfection?

Saunders grabbed the dark wood handle. It was warm, but probably only in a relative sense. Wood was terrible at transferring heat, which was why people could grab logs out of a fire—so long as they weren't burning—with their bare hands. Touch that metal poker, though, and instant sear.

Smallfoot sucked a breath, eyes wide as Saunders raised the sword to test its weight. The balance was incredible. He'd swung a few yard sale replicas with friends as a teen, but this could crack like a whip. Zero training to slash, parry, thrust, and the deal with flinging it around overhead and slamming that power strike. He also got the strangest impression that no matter how many swings he took, his arm would never tire, just get stronger with each hack and slash.

No wonder the sword was the dominant form of small arms for over a thousand years. Made. To. Kill.

A white puff billowed from Smallfoot as he exhaled through a dropped jaw. His expression was strange, a mix of wonder and disappointment. "Was it supposed to do something?" Saunders asked.

"N-no, no milord." His eyes told a different story but flashed to pure craving in the next instant. "I only ask what ye will do now."

Turn your ass in and forget about this shit.

It was the right move. Then again, the little man had come crawling to pay homage to the Corsan Carre like a little kid running away from his parents to see Santa Claus. "Do you have means to leave the city?"

"Aye," he whispered, trembling with sudden excitement. "This night. A strong horse and few burdens, milord. I shall join the rest and not see ye again."

The street was quiet, the air still enough to crystallize the scant humidity into a feather frost web ensnaring the city. Smallfoot was a distraction; Saunders had men who needed a break and plans to make. "Thanks for the sword. If I catch you here come morning, you won't be leaving."

The hot mess backed away, bowing and . . . groveling. That's what it was, fucking groveling. When he was gone, Saunders slung the sword and returned his attention to the darkened Q-lights.

From the ashes of Brines, Williamson, a city in flight, and his chances of ever seeing Sarah and Tommy again, a new battle plan had risen.

———

Moderator Bela Rastaw stepped from her tent, bare skin basking in the moonlight. Her personal guards, Samer and Adrad, flanked the entrance and offered the slightest tips of their dark *croftas* in tribute. Their eyes never moved from their watch of the darkness.

She bade them stay with the tent and all the worth within. She only needed the candle and the cool air of this rare occasion.

A cloudless night in the Vigil Valley was a gift few would know, and fewer could profit from. The other black tents, shadows in fading campfires, were still. Her brothers and sisters—those of the Heart, Eyes, and her own Fist—rested as if sleep would better prepare them for battle. Their minds knew only the summit ahead, nothing of the gems at their feet.

Patrols passed as she searched for the proper locus, but few heads turned toward her sleek, desirable form. Those that did were quick to find interest elsewhere as recognition took over. The low—legions of men long into campaigns away from the comforts of women—were not with lack of need and want. Nor might she deny them in the proper setting. But apt were they to the danger, the torment upon their desires. None would dare invite her into even their wildest fantasies lest she take root in their minds leaving a thrall to rise in their stead.

A flat place of fresh grass far from the tent clusters and rattling armor of patrols suited her.

Kneeling, the soft blades of Vigil's Meadow tickled her inner thighs as she planted the silver-veined candle. It lived in a renderstone holder stamped with sigils from the seven Caranuscan houses. A trophy. Also, a reminder of power unused. This trinket spent much of its life condemned to a display case within the Caranuscan capital of Novantum, longing for the command of flesh and a curious tongue.

The night air stilled as she spoke light to the wick. A solitary violet flame rose, a successful merging of Quotidian red and Stochal blue. Few among the Obantum Carre could wield both with mastery. Isllor Mortund could, so too with the Three. The candle was a reward from Master Turan for breaking the Caranuscans. Still, he had not known of its ability to merge the Powers. Such powerful rendercrafts were above her station. Forbidden.

But to rise in the Obantum was to dabble in the forbidden.

The southern mountains glowed white in the distance. She asked to see more, and a brilliant red orb appeared in their stead. The Bark. She knew little of its construction, only what Isllor had allowed when pressed. It made deaf the Quotidian to questions and stole its voice of answers. Isllor had known enough to make his questions heard unaided, but she was not so adept.

She whispered to the candle. "Show me."

The white mountains returned as the Stochal slipped through. It was the Procult's arrogance in believing their Stochists unique in mastery. She peered through the thickening red haze and heavy stone until her heart fluttered before an incredible gem.

The Bark's physical manifestation.

Swirls of Stochal and Quotidian teased and danced around the device. The crystal planes drew them in before smashing them together to create the nullifying reaction. Impressive! But the focal point remained hidden; thus, its construction remained a mystery.

Her real prize was upon the Bark's surface, a crack that blazed fire against beautiful violet.

Bela struck with *command* and *ask*, voice rattling as her adornments baked against her skin. The full fury of her might, focused and strengthened through the candle, smashed into the crack. In one decisive moment, she would end the Procult and outpace the enemy.

Nothing.

The Red and Blue swirls still flowed in, and Violet poured out. The mountain dome still glowed red where the Quotidian sparked against the deadening effect of the Bark.

No matter. Else would claim the Bark in time. Bela turned her gaze to those wrapped in the oily tendrils of her Enthralling. Her spies. Some walked, awake and smiling with their brethren. Some slept. Others were far from the city.

She focused first on the surprise, a leftover from Isllor. One of the Corsan Carre themselves! It was a breakthrough she shared with none, one who resisted at every chance, unknowing. He was celebrating, cheering with the others, head filled with defensive plans and odd flickers of a world she could not grasp. Unlike Isllor, she found no pleasure in tormenting him. The bond was strong, if uncomfortable, and she knew he would act when the time was right.

The next was entirely her creation. A weakling who could hide in a crowd and none would care to discard. His crimes would earn him a quick death and few questions about his motives. The perfect messenger.

She plucked the black tendrils woven through the light of his being. The mind responded with true affection. He had been willing, hungry for the enthralling. A creature devoid of ambition craving only acceptance. She purred for him and asked if he had planted the pivotal seed that would destroy the Corsan Carre.

His answer turned her veins turned to ice.

NO! she screamed into his mind as the memory showed the wrong Corsan Carre receiving the sword.

Fear, shame, and a need to please floated back with the words: *I gave it to their leader, Mistrus. The leader of the Corsan Carre, as ye commanded.*

In a stroke, she could silence the creature forever but knew the error was hers. She had assumed the most capable would lead, not some . . . *second* with a fraction of the potential. Still, to destroy the one called Smallfoot would be another mistake. The trap could not be undone or repurposed, and the prey caught in her snare was no small prize.

Instead of foiling the Procult in one fell swoop, she would have to settle for two.

"Dawgs, you should see the shit infantry gotta put up with back home," Smith said, somehow the center of attention to the Caranuscan staff officers. The rest were outside camping in the cold. Which was weird because the city had plenty of vacancies. The only reason the Marines were still here at the inn was because moving sucked. Plus, Uumhrat was a good cook. Otherwise, one of those stone mansions with perimeter walls up in Eastside looked good. Defensible, private, and plenty warm when a fire got going. "Most times, you ain't even get eyes on the dude tryin' to kill you. He might be, shit, like this motherfucker right here." He caught Fischer on the shoulder. "A mile away and a minute from droppin' you dead." Fish gave a thumbs up without knowing what the hell they were talking about and waded back into the crowd.

The senior group member, an old soldier the captain had introduced as Dux Herms, shrugged. "Your enemies fear the same, yes?"

Just like that, Smith felt like a rich dude complaining about overpaying for a can of green beans. Mina Bazar was probably the only pitched battle in the past twenty years where most of the exchange was through iron sights. Everything else was called in and rained down. "That's right, but it don't—"

"We, the remains of strong houses, vast cities, and shared history, have no reciprocal," he said. "As we lack talent in the Arts, so are we leaves in the storm of war struggling to hold on."

"Leaves nothin'. Thought anyone could use them magic wands?"

Herms, weathered with salt and pepper scraggle coming out of his face, shared a smirk with his buddies. "When Caranusca stood strong and free, and Haquatia took a knee, our Princeps vowed to wipe the Genisan threat from Nuada's shores. The houses joined and turned their riches to scholars who promised great weapons of war. But who marched?"

"The legions," cried every green-armored dude in the room.

"Who won battles?"

"The legions!"

"And when the coin and promises turned to air, who bled and fell to protect those scholars?"

This time no one shouted. But the silence said it for them.

"And of all the riches," Herms continued, "spirits, oceans of blood exhausted through the years, no price too high, no sacrifice unjust . . . What provisions were spared to the ground, to the true wealth of our homeland?"

"Boots," answered a green.

"I just got the one," said another, pointing down.

Smith couldn't help but look at the guy's feet. Both his leather wrap jobs were dirty, but one was cracked to fuck with a big hole where the toe had worked its way up through. That or the guy got stabbed in the foot.

It was probably a smart idea to let them win this round. Still, no television, phones, or porno magazines meant conversation was the main form of entertainment. The crazier, the better. "What about that fancy armor?" Smith asked, poking Dux Herms in the chest plate.

A tense moment of people drawing back like he'd just picked a fight followed, but then Herms busted out with, "Found the goblets after the wine was poured!"

Laughter all around.

Even the edges of Uumhrat's mustache lifted a little before he turned back to filling mugs. Smith nodded like white people did when they pretended to understand something.

"That there like fixin' the ol' wagon after the horses come home?" asked Fischer coming back around. It was refreshing to see some beige emerge from the wrong color of green.

"Stable, bitch," spat Nickels, following him. Jersey was definitely deeper than the two beers authorized by the captain for their one-night shore leave. "Fuck horses gonna do with a wagon? You gotta fix their house, or they'll start shitting on the floors."

"What you think happens in a stall, hoss? Floor's all they got. But yeah, my bad. Gotta fix the door, or they'll get out."

Dux Herms took it in, thoughtful. "Both serve, I think," he said finally. "We returned from war to broken houses and mucked floors. We found ourselves sapped of the strength to stand tall. So, we were rewarded. Elite, they now call us. And so too do they drape us in colored metal." More chuckles, but these were dark. *We made it here, and we don't want it.*

"But they couldn't give your boy here another boot?" Smith asked.

Real laughter this time. "The Princeps bought us boots only a war ago! They have another two, three Last Battles before they wear through." Herms raised his mug, yanking every green arm in the room up as if they were all connected. "To lives lived to bloody the Last Army!"

"Rocan!" cheered the green chorus. Smith dropped an *oorah*, but glassy-eyed Fischer and Nickels were still trying to catch up with how the conversation turned serious.

"Okay, okay," said Smith as they settled down. "So, like we was sayin': infantry tryin' to fix the world with broken wagons. Same here as back home. But your disadvantage—them juju motherfuckers—is rare. Mostly, you get to look the dude who gonna kill you right in the eye."

Dux Herms pulled a foamy slurp of Almon's White, tightening Smith's malt buds. "Few possess such an affinity for the Arts to use them in war," he conceded. "When I was a young man, battles were contests of muscle and steel. The crush of men and beasts in the like of the stories." He took another drink. "Then came Bedinch."

Somber nods joined him from some of the more seasoned soldiers.

"Fuck coulda happened there?" asked Nickels, leaning in with reddened cheeks. It was probably time to yank the leash and slow down his drinking, but Jersey usually leveled out once he scored a solid buzz. And the captain did say this was the calm before the storm. Smith let it be. That two beers limit was with a wink and a quiet, *don't get wasted,* anyway. Plus, he fully intended to join in when his shift ended in sixty.

"It was when the skies themselves became every soldier's enemy," said Dux Herms.

"Well, fuckitty fucktardia," said Nickels. "That's buy-in, bro. We got shit fallin' from the skies too. Bombs blowin' our asses up, fire, fuckin' chemicals that'll piss your lungs out the ass, and then there's always a chance that someone will go big and drop a nuke. Can't top that."

"Nuke?" The word fell out of the Caranuscan's mouth like a three-year-old sounding out his first vowel.

"Yeah, dawg," Smith said. "Bomb so big it'll pop a city like a wet piece of fruit."

"Did y'all just call Nagasaki a melon?" Fischer asked.

"Hush it."

Herms leaned back against a table, contemplative. His armor flexed with his torso like plastic, but it had felt like steel when Smith poked it. Batman pulled that same kinda suit out when he needed protection without the weight. Except his was black, not green.

"As ancient Pandor suffered the *nuke*," Herms mused. "We are now of shared danger."

"Yeah, but you guys got some Corsan Carre motherfuckers running around who gonna save you."

The sarcasm translated, and the Caranuscans, all of them, roared with laughter. Herms had to put his beer down as two of his guys took knees like they were proposing to each other. Then came a wave of jokes where Benton's name was the only thing recognizable.

S'what I thought; Corsan Carre don't mean shit to them.

Meanwhile, Jersey whispered something in Fish's ear, and then they slapped each other five. *Damn, when did they become bros?*

"Well met," said Herms extending an arm. Smith grabbed for the hand like it was a shake but got the usual wrist instead. Rather than hanging on, feeling pulses, and staring into each other's hearts, Herms let go, and they wrapped knuckles. It was almost cool. "Long have we endured Benton's—"

"They call him lord here, Dux," shouted the green with the one good boot.

Even Smith laughed at that one. He didn't know Benton's history, but Smith's parents hosted plenty of rich-people parties back in the day. The ones who didn't fit were easy to pick out.

"Might they call you Lord too, Otum, if you last the morrow," Herms said. "*Lord* Benton has overstuffed our heads with tales of the Corsan Carre—great masters of horse and beast wielding the Arts with veins of ice and silver. Hearts pumping raw Tri-source so their glow might outshine Bergreth's Lamp. Relieved I am to find men who call battle a terror and find solace in fine beer and may even fine wine."

"Bone will fuck you up with beer, bro," said Nickels. "He brews that shit himself." It wasn't wrong, but stacking his homebrew up against Almon's White was the ultra-light featherweight, 65-pounds-and-under men's division against a 250-pound concrete cracker.

"Yes, as custom in Sabara," said Herms.

"Paint their walls with harvest grapes, they do," added Otum.

"Yeah . . . nah, it stays off my walls," Smith said. "But we regular folk like you. Ain't no mythical warriors or—"

"Well, Gunny," said Fish.

"Big difference between legendary and mythical, dude," said Nickels. "But uh, yeah . . ." He trailed off like he lost the energy to make fun of it. Probably no one else would or could notice, but Smith knew how attached Jersey got to people. Even guys like Gunny.

"Point is we got heart, and that's what's gonna matter up on that wall tomorrow," Smith said, filling the void.

Dux Herms' eyes flicked to the strapped-up M9 pistol. Either he'd gotten the low down from Sir Rampo, who'd witnessed guns in action a few weeks ago, or he was just an old soldier who could recognize a weapon in any shape or form.

"Yeah, dawg, that too. You gonna love bein' on our side."

A refreshing belt of *oorahs* backed it up from everyone in beige except Gladstone. But he'd been quiet all night.

Saunders set the SINCGARS mic down and dismissed PFC Licht to the party below. Some sort of music was floating up the stairs, a rhythm of thuds and whiny strings. More interesting was the warm glow coming from the window beside his bunk.

The festivities had spilled out into the streets. Twinkling lines of torches stretched all the way from the Caranuscan bivouac in the central Market District. Laughter and roughhousing were rampant and rising in the inn's front yard. His Marines had orders to keep it to two beers, which translated to whatever it took not to be visibly drunk. Still, he wondered if he'd made a mistake.

Turning away from the temporary distraction, Captain Rath's report laid heavy and wet on the mind. First, it seemed the Palings Pass was not just a straight shot out of the mountains but had several branch points. That was how Rath missed Sir Rampo's army. Leading up to that revelation, there were serious competency questions that would've undermined the entire operation. Second, the convoy was making shitty progress.

Naturally.

They had too many infirm and not enough wagon capacity. That five days to reach the safe zone was already stretched to seven, maybe more. He suggested that Rath push Ceal a little harder or that they break into fast and slow groups as they'd done with Bandit and Snowman when crossing that valley. The response was essentially that the women were running the show, and no one was getting left behind.

No one left behind means our people, not all people!

Saunders glanced at Mike's pack by the wall for a distraction from events he could not control. But the sword beside it took the stage.

The hell am I going to do with you?

He resisted the urge to pound a perfectly good fist into one of the thick bracing beams along the wall. It was becoming clear that no matter how much he wanted to, he couldn't just throw the sword out. Once his Marines were out of ammo, they were in the same boat as all those Caranuscan refugees: sharps and spit to throw at hardened legions.

Not while I'm in command, he vowed, tossing a blanket over the sword and Mike's stuff.

One step at a time.

The Rath situation was irritating, but a project for tomorrow. Right now, there were bigger boulders to nudge. Saunders buttoned up his MCCUU blouse, strapped on his vest, holstered his sidearm, and headed downstairs.

The "four-hour, two-beer shore leave" had turned Uumhrat's great room into a full-moon frat house on Halloween. Costumed characters in white, green, and the earthy civilian garb of the refugee conscripts mixed and mingled. Everyone had a drink or two in hand and were trying to out-shout each other in red-faced attempts at conversation.

And right in the middle of it were his Marines, still in their gear, partying. It was damned criminal, but he wouldn't report it if they didn't. Same time, he'd gladly take the heat of a full-on court-martial or anything to be back on Earth.

Saunders smiled, wading through the sweaty bodies and locker-room musk that marked so many a sausage fest. Uumhrat offered him a mug, white foam slopping over the side. It looked delicious, like an answer to the anxious tug in his mind. He thanked the innkeeper but kept going.

"Okay, okay, so . . ." came the rhotic voice of Cpl Nickels somehow above the din. He was at the head of a table with some notable characters: Acting Sergeant of the Watch Teague, Dux Herms, and the gilded knight Sir Rampo in a clean white tunic with gold embroidering. Saunders probably needed a half-hour with each of them, but this was the wrong environment to talk shop despite what the private sector might say. "Say this big Stochasm happens, but it ain't like last time."

"If it happen different, be it still the Stochasm?" asked Teague.

"All hypothetical. We're just fuckin' . . . like *what if.* Okay?"

"Aye."

"So instead of blowing up the world or cutting this big galactic energy cord or whatever, it neuters every fucking dude on the planet."

The men shifted in their seats uncomfortably. *The hell does he come up with this shit?* Still, Saunders listened if only to grab a little more background on the Last Army, Stochasm, and Corsan Carre Rescue Rangers nonsense going around.

"Which . . . ah, ye mean?" asked Teague, hands working as if the air were two orbs of clay to be molded into clarification.

Nickels cocked his head sideways, but then Sir Rampo clarified, "The shovel or the seed?"

Laughter.

"Oh man, that's why I fuckin' love you guys," cried the corporal, slapping the table. They all raised their mugs in toast and drank. "Fuckin', just to keep it simple. The seed sack. Poof, gone."

"Since this fate is spoken by the Corsan Carre . . ." began Dux Herms with a smile.

"No, bro, I ain't legislating this shit. This is just a *what would you do?* Okay?"

The men nodded.

"Okay, so every dude on the planet EXCEPT you. Boom, still got your shovel, the seeds, the needs, and you are the one guy who can knock a chick up."

Sir Rampo stroked his chin, pondering some evil fucking thought. Probably no more evil than whatever Nickels was about to say, though.

"You'd be the world treasure, right?" said Nickels. "The hottest dude in all of history. EVERY girl would want some. And . . . and that's not gonna just be you dragging your seed-laying ass through fields of triple-plowed wenches, neither. Alpha female beauty contest winners'd be questing for your gear. Tryouts, fuckin' talent contests, entire Olympic events weeding out the best from the best. The kinda game you'd get would be unbelievable. Chicks who could get a whole room of dudes to blow their loads with just a look. Sex-fucking-magic."

"You said I will be this great king of fertile men, yes?" asked Dux Herms.

"Only if ye survive the coming morrows," said Teague.

"Legends will sing of the great Dux Herms fleeing the South Gate before the Last Army, ass bare in anticipation of saving us all!" laughed Sir Rampo.

"Guys, let me finish. There's a catch: you're married. Like, soulmate and said all your oaths and vows. Fuckin, so you got all that game lining up outside your house, the ultimate jackpot. What do you tell your wife?"

"We hath company, my dear," said Teague.

"I would vanish to some far place and live to the last days holding the future of men all to mineself," said Sir Ramp. *Fucking deranged.*

"Dux, you in for the ganger?"

"In this fate you speak of, my wife yet lives. Such joy would be more than a thousand youthful pleasures," Herms said with a sigh. Saunders would've stepped in right there, but Nickels, by some grace of God, pulled back, remorseful.

"Oh, I uhh . . ."

"Thus, I would be true to my lady... and allow her to watch." Dux Herms winked. "For the fate of us all, of course."

The men, and Nickels, howled, pounding the table and their mugs together.

Close call, but everyone was bonding better than expected. The decision to give them all a night was still yielding positive. Same time, that anxious tug was growing. Easy to dismiss it as that type A part of Saunders' personality writhing at downtime, but there was more. That part about Herms running for the gate triggered something deep, a thought or feeling that needed to be unpacked but was buried in an avalanche of other shit.

Avalanche.

Saunders tossed the group a nod, then caught eyes with Smith. The big sergeant excused himself from Lt. Maon and came over to report. Situation was under control; Nickels' drinking was being monitored, and no one had thrown any punches.

What I need isn't here.

The gravel yard out front had a fireman's fair atmosphere. Soldiers were clustered around burning braziers roasting salted meats. Hot breath blew as much steam as smoke into the frigid air. Watchmen on duty remained at their posts, casual like cops along the boardwalk. They might break up a fight or ask someone to tone it down, but they weren't there to plant bodies.

The city walls, outposts, and observation points were well-staffed too. Not everyone drank; not everyone could relax on what might be their last night. Francisco was out there, somewhere. He'd taken a Watchman and a radio. If anything was going to happen, they'd have a solid heads-up.

The timeline to enemy contact wasn't a concern. The Bark was an assurance against the Black Robes; the perimeter prevented incursions and the depopulated city limited insurgency. Everyone was going to see it coming.

No, the kinetic reaction to contact is the problem.

Saunders needed to speak with someone knowledgeable about the city's infrastructure. Heading down to Benton's was an option, or maybe the Watch Keep, which was now the city's de facto tactical operations center. But, like General Harrel at a state dinner, the ground combat commander of the Corsan Carre didn't just walk invisibly through the crowd.

"Hullo!" shouted a jovial Examiner Creed. The flickering light registered a healthy redness to his cheeks, but he wasn't slurring his words yet.

He'll do.

"Examiner," Saunders said, taking an offered meat on a stick. Kabob, maybe. "Regret not evacuating yet?"

"Nay, the city remains quite comfortable. Indeed, mine father would be most disappointed if I abandoned our interests in such a time of need."

It became clear to Saunders that Creed was the son of former Lord Governor Elldren at the mass funeral they'd held last month. As the dead from Isllor's attack were interred, Creed knelt before Elldren's crypt and . . . well what wasn't obvious from how these people used or didn't use family names became blindingly clear. Of course, the truth about Elldren's death was another layer, but the point stood. "It'd be a little more comfortable if Lord Colm or whatever's left of Ross was jumping in to reinforce us." It went without mentioning that Elldren's "assets" were committed elsewhere. Kinda like World War II when every allied nation went after Europe and left the Marines to hold the Pacific.

"Tollshire reels from Lord Ross' demise," said Creed shaking his head. "Succession has been invoked by his half-brother, his firstborn and rightful heir, and his minister of war. It is a mess of legal entanglements dancing upon the blade's edge. Lord Colm commits his host elsewhere in agreement with Lord Benton."

"Right." Saunders had a vague memory of the Lord Colm update. The guy had stalled and ignored requests for support, fearing winter would trap his forces here in the city. So, he got to go after Europe too. Grand strategy and all that.

"Anyhap, it's a bit of sport, is it not? We shall bleed the Genisans, then whisk away through the South Gate when the advantage is lost. The true risk is only if the Bark falls before we can withdraw."

Withdraw.

The tug flared. *That's what's pissing me off.* Portcullis was a solid defensive position, but more correctly, a cork with an expiration date. The planned retrograde was a tactical necessity to reposition a capable fighting force. Fight hard from the high ground, then find new high ground. But everyone was treating it as an opportunity to take a couple of shots and bail.

Fuck that. This wasn't the time to start shouting sense into people, though. A more immediate part of the plan needed his and Creed's attention. "Hey," he began, tone casual, "so about the Bark." He pointed at one of the dark streetlights looming over the reveling masses. "Guess those will snap back on when it fails. Right?"

Creed swiveled his head. "Not in absence of the Q-stone. It was parted from the city lattice."

"Why?" Saunders imagined this Q-stone was a big plug or battery. Something to connect the raw torrents of capacitance—or whatever one might call a reservoir of "not-magic" Power—to the grid.

Creed chuckled. "These small lamps deceive, but a great Power within the stone drives Quotidian through the city. To work, it needs the talents of many applied through careful ritual. Else, there might be a surge."

A surge. "Tell me more."

LCpl Gregory Gladstone stared at his beer—flat and flavorless like the party.

It had sounded fun: a night off and a chance to forget about duty, service, guilt, and a mountain of mistakes. But as darkness settled, the color of cheer turned gray as the rewards circuits in his brain were flipped. First feared and resisted, he now embraced it as a new truth.

Downtime was opportunity.

His former life was always uncomfortable, fake. The American ideals of freedom were caked on thick to hide a world that didn't give a fuck about people. Succeeding meant picking himself up, learning to swim, and somehow rising above the other guppies. Simple! People would only help if they thought catch a ride on his coattails. Beyond that, it was millions playing single-player gamers in the same room. No talking unless someone found a better way to cheat.

Here, he'd discovered something different. Care, concern, and the opportunity for a guaranteed path forward. It wasn't *follow orders, and maybe we'll review your performance one day.* It was an upfront negotiation, an agreement bonded and sealed in a way no contract on Earth ever could be. Souls were collateral, and the rewards beautiful.

It also took the guesswork out of what might happen tomorrow. There was no question whether Gladstone would come out of another combat zone dead, alive, or paralyzed from the neck down. Now he knew exactly where he'd be, what actions to take, and when he'd feel Master's embrace.

Or, should I say, Mistrus.

A group of half-armored green fools burst through the door, laughing and tossing tufts of snow at each other. *Odd,* he thought. *Mistrus didn't mention any inclement weather.* A peek out the window showed every open flame swarming with flurries. And everyone was hoisting and toasting the snow they believed might delay their enemy.

Childish and unworthy of even Gladstone's contempt. If anything, significant accumulation would speed up the timeline. Regardless, his place and actions would be the same. So, he bided his time staring through the gray world at his brother Marines bullshitting with the doomed.

"We got errything we could ever want back home," said Sergeant Smith beside the huge fireplace. He'd returned his rifle to the armory and now had a beer in hand. "Sit there, scratchin' your balls, and order it up. Poof! Arrives next day, sometimes same day. Anything you can imagine."

"It be true magic," said one of the astonished listeners. Gladstone had the vague realization that Smith was talking about online shopping and was almost tempted to interject. No way was the sergeant equipped to adequately explain or connect the ideas of button clicking, credit cards, and home delivery.

"Ain't magic; distribution," said Smith. "Like wit you. You know my boy Uumhrat over there, right?" As the group looked over, the oversized innkeeper tipped his head from behind the bar. "Yeah, so say you want a saddle. You go tell Hat: 'set me up.'"

"Mayhaps Master Walram," said Watchman Hull. The old Gladstone might've laughed. He had an app that scrawled the markets and found the best price on the best match to his needs. His mom, however, had some weird loyalty to Amazon. It's like once she gave them her payment and shipping info, they were exclusive. If Amazon didn't sell it, it didn't exist. Here, a guy named Walram was the new Amazon.

"Yeah, well, let's keep it local. Cool?" asked Smith.

"Ha, what serves the innkeeper as a saddle fetcher?" asked the first guy.

"'Cause he charges you a shipping and handling fee. Right? Money talks. Anyway, he goes to the saddle shop, grabs your shit, delivers it to your door. Might take longer here, but there it is. That's how we used to roll back in the day too. But then we got global. So now it ain't just saddles, but anything you can dream up. Want a sword made of some dude's teeth? Someone somewhere's got the hookup. And you ain't gotta do shit or see no one. Just send a message from the butt print of your favorite chair."

"As with the Long Voice?"

"Sure, hoss," said Fischer coming over and wrapping an arm around Smith's broad shoulders. "But we call it the internet."

Gladstone tingled. Fischer was brilliant color in the drab, muted world of distraction. His mind raced, thoughts of his own and Mistrus' blending and ripping at each other. A shotgun blast, ages ago now. Second Lieutenant Weber's blown-apart face flopping back into grainy darkness. Terror, fear, guilt. Fischer coming up behind, pulling him back.

He saw.

He knows.

A flood of alien sensations, Gladstone's tormented soul resisting like a stubborn anorexic clinging to a diet. Then, the acceptance. The soothing. The confidence and knowledge.

A full stomach, guilt-free.

The inn's front door swung open, and another rosy-cheeked bright spot walked in, rubbing his hands. Captain Saunders, real as life, but like an old photograph. A before picture to those who could see what was to come. Some distant part of Gladstone felt almost nostalgic, but it passed quickly.

The captain gave him a hard stare. *Fuck.* But rather than leveling accusations, he flashed the rally-on-me signal. Something was up, something Mistrus hadn't quite seen or mentioned. Probably minor but interesting.

Gladstone snapped a mental photograph of Fischer enjoying the night with his asshole friend Corporal Nickels. Then, forgetting about the beer, he joined the captain outside.

———

PFC Licht fetched a fresh cup of water from the bar. Too many times he'd seen his dad getting ready for a big day the night before, swearing up and down he was only having a few drinks to calm his nerves. Then the upstairs bedroom door would slam shut at two or three in the morning. Next day he'd be late, red-faced yelling at everyone. And things would only get worse from there.

Not me, Licht vowed.

The way most in the great room were staggering and slurring, not too many were thinking the same. Weird because as the night wore on, the rumors about a possible attack at dawn were getting some legs under them. Francisco's last report detailed a shift in the Genisan formations that got the Watchmen nervous. Then there was the snow that everyone thought might save the day but now was more like a wakeup call to anyone hedging their attack plans on the weather.

There was no way to know, but one thing was sure: tomorrow would be a reverse trainwreck of people slowly unfucking themselves and getting back in gear.

Licht raised his cup as another round of cheers erupted. *Maybe not everyone's like Dad,* he thought. Right now, it was like Christmas Eve. The guys in green were slapping backs with the off-duty Watchmen. Deadlies and refugee conscripts were toasting to old ghosts, and everyone was friends with the Marines for a change.

Sergeant Smith and LCpl's Garcia and Light were straight, enjoying the party for the company. Fischer had a little red in his cheeks, but maybe that's because he was smiling so much.

Dad never smiled when he drank, just got quieter. That is, until someone made too much noise or walked in front of his TV. Then it was a bad night.

If anyone looked like they would have a bad day tomorrow, it was Uumhrat. He was the still waters hiding thirty gators. Looked okay to the tourists, but anyone in the know knew.

Uumhrat probably represented what everyone was feeling deep down. This ramp-up to battle wasn't like Operation *Sea Monster* with rock & roll blasting, the brass shouting *oorah* and *get some* over the ship's 1MC, Marines loading up under cover of *The Marine's Hymn,* and swarms of attack choppers launching off into the night. Frightening, but what a rush.

No, this is what it was like to be in Mina Bazar, knowing death was coming.

A happy couple bumped into the table. Two guys in refugee rags. "Apologiessss . . . ah, milord?" said the one trying to lead. Licht guessed they were dancing.

"No problem," Licht said, raising his water cup. They swung back into the thinning crowd, and it was hard not to smile despite everything. Outside of tonight and a few beers here and there, it'd been work, work, work.

"Gonna ask the sar'nt about that, bud," Fischer said, plopping down at the table.

Corporal Nickels followed with *another* full mug. "I call Smith's beer Bonebrew, bro. It's good, but it ain't what Uumhrat's got on tap." He emptied the entire thing.

Looks like we'll be missing him at assembly.

"You talking about Sergeant Smith's homebrew?" Licht asked.

The corporal stared back like a phone taking its time to focus the picture. "Yeah, Fish was wondering if he could make this almond crap when we get home."

Almond? Probably meant Almon, the old man they named Almon's Peak after. He had a brewery high up there on the western side. "Think he could? I mean if he knew the recipe?"

Fischer laughed. "Can't tell ya. Maybe it's like sayin' I could make a bourbon with my backyard still."

Nickels shrugged. "Shit'll make you go blind."

Fischer slammed down his beer. "How many times I gotta tell you we pour off the crap? It ain't medieval, man. We got standards."

"Yeah? Well, maybe you gotta get medieval sometimes. Fuck, I'm dry."

"Shine ain't about goin' blind or medieval," said Fish. "It's about evading taxes."

"Buy your booze in Delaware. Tax-free."

"Dammit, it's a family tradition."

"So's this. Uumhrat, another!"

Fischer laughed but didn't follow the corporal to the bar. Instead, with eyes a lot more focused than his demeanor suggested, he said, "You see where Stone went?"

You mean after he was too busy staring at that beer he didn't drink to talk to anyone? Licht knew he should've let it go a long time ago; Gladstone was friendly, once upon a time, for like a day. Then it was all cold shoulders, which would be fine except there was sometimes that glimmer of hope, a desire to reconnect, in the guy's eye. Then, poof, it got shut down. "He and Hull went with the captain."

"Yeah, just thought y'all were buds, and he mighta said what was up," said Fischer.

"Not really."

The country boy pondered the plank table for a moment. "Been gettin' the same treatment. If I didn't know better, I'd think I hit on his chick or something." Brightening, he moved closer. "Dude, I think he's got a thing for Micky."

Licht almost laughed. Chilling over beers trying to get inside a buddy's head while living an old Roman Empire movie, and somehow it still came down to girls. "Who doesn't?"

"I tol' you about that one night, right? When she was rubbing all up on Cap'n Rath trying to rouse him outta that Black Robe spell. Fuckin', that is the wallpaper of my spank bank, man. Creepy as all get-out, but if you'd been there . . ."

"She gets around." Licht checked his flanks; the next admission felt a little stupid, but *what the hell.* "I kinda dig the way she and—"

"The doc? Don't even say it, dude, or I will NOT be shootin' straight tomorrow."

Licht's cheeks heated up like he'd just aired some dark secret. But if the other guys were picking up on the same thing, then it wasn't a malfunction. "I feel like she does it just to torture us. Maybe Gladstone's taking it personally?"

Fischer blew out a breath. "Few months ago, I never woulda believed it. Met him on video game night right after we left Dubai. Small group of Charlie and Bravo. I got invited 'cause of my MOS. Don't get me started on how holdin' a rifle proper don't mean you can work some buttons with your thumbs for shit. Still, I ain't half bad at them shooters. Greg, though. Dude, he's a wizard. If you made a gun like an Xbox controller, you and me would be out of a job. Maybe even Francisco. Anyway, we got to talkin', and it became regular."

"He one to throw down the controller and punch walls and stuff?"

"Naw, that's just it. Cool as ice with that stuff and all the social shit in general. Told me about some of his past girls and how they'd dump him over the video games. It was a big shrug for him, like a dude gettin' a blow job on the couch during the game. Take it or leave it, but I ain't gettin' up."

"Maybe *Sea Monster* bothered him."

"Reckon that's when it all changed. Learned him a potty mouth and started switchin' hot and cold like my momma's shower. Couldn't be the transportation to an alien world, though."

"No, couldn't be that." Licht laughed.

"Tell you what. Captain has us paired for Vault duty tomorrow while y'all get to watch the most epic fuckin' battle on top of that there wall."

"They probably won't even come."

"Hope not. But I'll have a chance to talk to him a bit, just me and him. Think this is one of those times. Y'know? Intervention-type shit. And I think you done lit a fire under me, boy."

———

An hour after receiving his new orders, the cold night was soaking through Gladstone's fur overcoat, plate carrier, and MCCUUs. Frost gathered around his collar, nipped at the cuffs of his gloves, and pissed ice on his toes. Beyond the orange umbrella of Watchman Hull's torchlight was an ocean of darkness. They were alone, a raft blindly bobbing in the waves, never knowing if the next would capsize them.

"Dark work we tend this night," muttered Hull.

"The enemy has eyes everywhere," said Gladstone, parroting a line he remembered from a *Lord of the Rings* movie. It sounded creepy and explained why they needed to operate at zero dark.

"Aye." The Watchman squinted into the shadows of the rocky hillside. "Methinks there still be a Monster out there. Mayhaps more murderous than the agent of evil that stole the likenesses of Palefang and Commander Mendo."

The Monster. It was that classic case of a supernatural serial killer turning out to be bigger and badder than anyone could imagine. A god in wolf's clothing. Master Isllor.

Gladstone groped around the base of the boulder bottling up the larger slide above. Most of the stones were pinned, but one rewarded him with a wiggle. He pulled it free and reached into the little channel beneath. It was deep enough to fit his whole arm. *Perfect.*

Feeling playful, he turned to Hull and said, "Back home, we call them copycats. Killers who get off on killing like other killers. Fits right in here with Portcullis, don't you think?"

"Sergeant Abhan be sayin' the same. That the true Monster be preyin' by many a name: Genisans, Obantum, Anticult, Blue Cloaks. Anything that be givin' rise to our misery."

Gladstone lowered his night vision goggles, and the rockslide brightened to full daylight. They were standing beneath megatons of broken stone where the mountainside had collapsed. Outside the slide were smooth slopes rising into the whiteout elevations. The angle could've been steeper but workable. It just meant he needed to use a little more explosive than planned.

Hull wasn't looking up; he was staring down at the goggles. That faint battery whine probably got his cheeks puckered, which gave Gladstone a wicked idea.

"What about us? The Corsan Carre." Gladstone said, hiding his smile in the shadows as he fished through his pack. Seeds of doubt were all too easily planted.

"Huh? Nay that would . . ."

"Group from another planet slipping into your midst while your civilization faces annihilation? We're literally alien invaders, advanced weaponry and all."

Hull scrubbed the back of his neck. "I trust those who hath read the prophecies. If there be such danger, it . . ." he paused, trying to collect his thoughts. *That thing you're trying to leap over is what we call a logic gap, son.* Everything he believed reasonable in his life was synched together by the same awful threading that had plagued mankind since day one: faith. He never considered that his religion—or belief in a godless prophecy containing idols and supernatural occurrences—was wrong.

"I mean, we're a patchwork military unit," Gladstone continued. "Back home, we're all brother Marines because the machine keeps us in line. Here, there are no court marshals, military police, or chain of command to nip at us. We're just guys like you with the same asshole thoughts. What are the odds one of us might be fucked in the head? Like, he's here to kill because he likes killing. Not because he's fighting to stop the Stochasm."

Hull shifted his feet as if steeling himself for a peek around the curtain.

Gladstone set everything the captain ordered out on the ground. Bricks of plasticized RDX, detonators, transmitters. Hull had no idea just how bad the Marines were.

"Do ye suspect one of yer own?" Hull asked finally.

Gladstone shook his head and waved it off. But there was power in knowing that he could turn Watchman Hull to the dark side with a few words and a solid handshake. That wasn't what Mistrus wanted, but it was a tool in the kit. Gullible people were useful people, and a small part of him wished there was a path forward for everyone. But there wasn't.

Rigging the north road up from the valley to block the Genisan advance had been expected. Classic military move, and it happened a month ago with that toxic fuck Fischer standing beside him, drooling drawl over a perfect opportunity for sabotage. But Mistrus knew the danger and would work around it.

The 11th-hour mission to blow THIS pass, though, was downright diabolical. Something unexpected from the unflappable Captain Saunders.

Gladstone studied the finished device, a simple, radio-triggered bomb, and wondered if the old him would've obeyed these orders. It was sick, savage, and an about-face on people they considered allies. If Hull had any idea the real reason they were out here . . .

The new Gladstone flipped it on and packed it deep into the hole.

Mistrus will be pleased.

CHAPTER 11

HEARTS

Sorrow.

It simmered as a gravy pot in the back kitchen, lending taste to the air. Though the many courses of meal and fine drink could mask it, it always returned after the laughter fled and candles burnt low.

This night, life pulsed through the floorboards of the First Inn of Portcullis as the city's famed hospitality flared once more. The Caranuscan host was welcomed and toasted, driving away the sourness of gravy pots and frightful memories. Nigh by the Power did the eve sparkle as snows dusted the streets and rooftops. Alas, as darkness thickened, so did the risen spirits ebb. The snow stopped; the empty cups piled. Grumbles of the morrow and duty drove men to their places of slumber.

And so returned the sorrow.

War was coming. War unlike any fought before across the realms. It would be the might and minds of men in contest beneath a frail umbra holding back the great Powers. No matter the skill, strength, or number slain, all would fight balanced upon the finest point. At any moment, the Bark could fail, and naught of strife or victory would matter.

"Hat, that keg kicked yet?" asked a voice so clear in the tongue it could be mistaken for naught but passing through the Arts. By some mercy—mayhaps the Five, or one less sung—Benton's Bark never stole the Quotidian's common voice. The lights, warmth, and water of peoples' homes, aye, but still, all could hear their cries.

Uumhrat turned to regard the stout and stocked Corsan Carre whose browned skin—but naught of custom—bore him kinship with those in the Port of Aventia. Sergeant Smith.

"We come to the last of Almon's White," Uumhrat said, refilling the pottery mug with frothing snowmalt. "Soon it be but a few casks of wines from hidden cellars to sustain us."

"That you goin' dark?" said Sergeant Smith, mayhaps scenting the simmering pot of sorrow.

Uumhrat forced cheer into his cheeks. The Corsan Carre knew little of the land's lore, less of the true mountain that held Portcullis aloft. The bodies and hardship stacked and packed tight beneath their feet.

Going dark?

The journey had long been so. The blood that set Portcullis' foundations was the same lying in Uumhrat's wake. 'Twas their commonhood. What drew them together in understanding and the promise to make better morrows.

Whilst Uumhrat long believed that promise would ride evermore upon strong backs after age finally dragged him to the crypts, 'twas now as Benton had oft foretold: *smiles make quick ashes.* "Nay lad, wine drinks same as any. I think more to the mess, mine floor stained red by sloppiness."

The Corsan Carre sergeant tipped his head and turned to watch the last of the merry folks dancing and cheering to their demise. Uumhrat saw only the coming lightless shell of his inn filled with still shadows and sticky floors, snow pouring in through shattered windows and a rotted doorway, weeds poking through the planks, and walls webbed with vines. None would remain to tend the sheets, all stained and bitten by pests, mayhaps fire. The stone pillars bracing the walls and the fireplace would be the last standing memory of his dream.

"Y'all," said the one called Fischer leaning into the counter. This one was smaller and paler than Smith, yet wise enough to wear some winter fat. Many of the Corsan Carre walked lean as scavengers no matter the weather. "I tell you I got like what you might call a feelin' about tomorrow?"

"He cut off," said Smith with a finger aimed at Fischer's chest. The fair lad was still steady upon his feet and could surely stand a few goes at a boil bucket, but even that would do little to lift Uumhrat's heart. "You got somethin' to say, Fish?"

"See, I got this theory," he said, knocking his mug against Watchman Teague's. "Bohu bitches!"

"Bohu!" cheered the last revelers this place would know.

"So now you into theories, huh?" asked Smith with a smile Uumhrat wished could be trapped to a tapestry.

"Yeah. Whenever we get ready for an OP, we get a uh, a send . . . uh, no. Food, yeah. We get some special food, right?" Fischer took a long draught. "And beer is food, right?"

"Fact."

"Yeah, so we goin' to war tomorrow." Fischer dropped onto a stool.

"Fish, man, you're a little bitch, you know that?" said the Corsan Carre Nickels elbowing to the counter. His words came clear but from a head spinning faster than his legs. Mayhaps Smith had meant this lad be the one finished with the night's drink. "And no one parodies Bone but me, read?"

"Dawg." Smith's word had no meaning to Uumhrat's ears but was in the like of the endearing terms between friends. "You gonna need a bigger—"

The mailed arm of a Watchman, his only arm, slapped upon Nickels' shoulders. "I hear tell a war comes this morrow!"

Smith gave him a great hug, lifting man and mail with ease, and said, "Leod!"

"Thought you were on watch," said Nickels.

Sergeant Leod tilted his head. "Did ye think I would not join the last festival on the eve of destruction?" He slipped out from Smith's grasp and grabbed a fresh mug. "'Tis our duty to drink the remains of Portcullis' stores lest the enemy know the fine taste of Almon's beer. Aye, Uumhrat?"

"To ye's returned health, lad. The Last Army sleeps ill this night with ye on patrol."

"True that, Leod," said Smith. "Good to have you wit us." He glanced at the missing arm. "Man, you was fucked up when they pulled you out of that wolf cave."

"Aye."

"Been meanin' to ask, if you don't mind, how you came back from a beating like that."

Leod took a long drink of the snowmalt and said, "Thirst clings me to this life."

"Hells yeah, son."

"Well, we gonna pay it back, tell you what," said Fischer. The oath stirred the pot, and Uumhrat glanced at the ax above the fireplace's mantel. It did not go unseen.

"What's the story behind that wood splitter?" asked Nickels. "Gunny always thought you might get it down one day if someone pissed you off."

"Sorrow of Dusk."

"Huh?" asked Fischer.

Another night, Uumhrat would chuckle and cloak the truth in jest. Say 'twas a gift from a lost love or bestowment from a father whose face he could no longer remember. But this dire eve of ending mirth brought the memory forth.

"Once a young Upland Joc found hisself in small debt to a troop of wayward folk. They asked only for what he could spare, though in great need they were." *Needs of the body, needs of the mind. We were animals. Animals,* he wished to say. "The Joc held many riches but would spare none. In their stead, he had simple weapons pounded pretty with an ore common to the Uplands. It was Renderstone. Hath ye heard of it?"

"Uh, ain't that the stuff with the Power in it?" asked Fischer.

"You guys heard about the Ballgag of Power, right? Fuck you; I'll tell you later. Keep going, Uumhrat," said Nickels.

"The Joc believed he had created weapons of false beauty and illusioned value. He cheered himself as wise for repaying his debts with *stonecoin*." Uumhrat sighed. "Were that it so. To Lord Benton, the Dawn of Mourn. To Uumhrat," he pointed, "Sorrow of Dusk. And to the world, a terror of men and might."

"Told you this tight-lipped mofo has a history," said Nickels as Sergeants Teague and Leod only nodded. "Bro, you should walk around with that thing strapped up."

"Complaint department 'round back," said Smith.

"Heyooo!" said Fischer.

Uumhrat offered only a smile. The smile he had practiced with longer and harder than that ax.

"Chief," said Lt. Maon entering the side room now serving as Dalmore's study. The quiet quarters were humble, hidden on the second floor of the Watch Keep, and near to the main study taken by the public as a receiving hall. The lieutenant stepped into the desk lamp's light and pressed a fist to his mailed chest.

Dalmore set down the birdbone quill and missive. He knew it best to finish his thought, but it was late and found his mouth less tired than his hands. "Report."

"The Genisan mass slumbers within the Dowdale, but their scouts hath crept far. Dark eyes lie upon the Doormat and North Wall."

Dalmore nodded. "Strike posture. Still, the Twin Tithes is a long road, and the Corsan Carre hath set a welcome in their strange ways of war. The enemy will find it unfriendly to cart, horse, and boot."

Maon brightened. "I shall take to North Overlook at dawn in hopes of sighting the magics of a Corsan Carre welcome."

"They would laugh to hear it called magic," Dalmore said. He flattened the square of parchment upon the desk. Neither sword nor shovel so ached his hand as this ill-sized quill. Might be it was made for the hand of a babe if he did not know Benton used it oft. "If that is all . . ."

"Nay, the Dowdale hath struck against the enemy."

Dalmore froze, the missive forgotten as a trove of possibilities birthed before him. Ancient Powers beheld to mysterious masters were said to rule in the Dowdale Valley. Was it possible Portcullis had an ally?

Alas, Maon's dour face emptied all hopes. "Was it the warmth or green grasses that bloodied the Genisan host?" Dalmore asked in jest.

"The Corsan Carre hunter sent tell 'twas the Vigil. He saw the fabled horses."

Taichleach's Vigil.

The old story never spoke to sense. Lord Taichleach was long ago steward of the valley, guarding it against all the lands. Or was it the contrary? Anyhap, all his knights and those monstrous Vissl in their service were seared into eternity by the flash of the First Stochasm. Forever bound to their duty.

But now, only the ethereal horses remained. No knights. Still, there was truth to the Vissl. The Corsan Carre had brought two grand hides without like from the Lower Del. Both were stollen by Lord Bayliss upon his leaving, affirming their worth. "Do they not appear on all nights?"

"I know not," said Maon. "But where the mists flowed among the Genisan camps, terror and destruction followed. A nibble, but still a victory against the likes of the Last Army."

"Indeed. Though I suspect if the waggling of wine-drunk tongues is true, the remnants of Taichleach's Vigil will not join our fight. The Genisans wrought their deaths from the Vissl by striking against those horses."

"Aye!" boasted a voice from the door. The gleaming white of an armored knight entered. Not Lord Benton, but Sir Rampo. "As they sayeth: Make ye no move swift or laggard against Taichleach's steeds lest ye long for a hard horn between soft cheeks."

"Do ye wish I should stay, Chief?" asked Maon stepping back from the knight. Two Watchmen were in the hallway, and more could be summoned from the lower floors and yard. Alas, none would arrive in time should Sir Rampo be on a mission of his own justice.

"Nay, rotate the men and scavenge what sleep ye may."

Lt. Maon bowed out, eying the knight and the bluish sword at his side.

"Armed and armored," Dalmore said, aware how light his shoulders felt without his plate and thick padding. "To what do I owe this occasion?"

Rampo ran a hand through his black hair. His lack of helm was of small comfort. "A knight and his arms are never apart. A knight standing upon the wall is one sword, a hundred beacons. A knight's honor makes those who follow him unbreakable."

"Oft lofted oaths of the Palatine," Dalmore said. "Do ye now speak them to cloak misdeeds?"

Rampo cocked his head. "I thought mayhap this new Dalmore I stand before might enjoy remembering the falseness of Durador. The place that would forge men for battle from pillows and spiced wine. The old Dalmore was always so . . . daft. What misdeeds?"

"Are ye here to kill me?"

"Blunt!" Rampo spat. "Did not high society teach ye the dance to asking such? It is a serenade that would take us round the Almandine Throne twice, through the Great Hall, and down to Serve's Alley in the late of night. There, alone in Durador's guts, we would find the answer in a flash of brilliance."

"So . . ."

"Nay, Dalmore. I come in earnest, even if I was not sent so. Lord Bayliss rages at ye's treachery, but so too his humiliation." Rampo unbuckled his sword belt and set it upon the window table. Then walked *away*.

"Does that amount to violating the codes?" Dalmore asked, transfixed by an untended Reverent Sword.

"It does," said Rampo, dropping armor and body deep into one of the three low-backed chairs across the desk. "But I would need it not to kill ye. There are unseen daggers throughout the Reverent Armor and mine hands adept in the craft of death."

"Mine comfort wanes."

"Ye seem quite terrified," Rampo laughed. "Nay, our talk must be of Lord Bayliss and this boon he hath provided."

"Boon? There can be no more offensive word. Three cohorts of northrons to answer the oaths sworn by all free men? The Last Army is here!" Dalmore slammed his fist down. "Do not speak of boons. Speak of why Galimay fails to rise!"

"The Sapphire Branch hath withdrawn to the safety of the cities," said Rampo studying a stray thread on his cuff. "Talk of a Sixth Army of Coals stalls on the tongues of lords who gave much to the Fifth. Mine brethren in the Diamond Branch nurse wounded pride, and fear hath spread that the Corunds are weak to the enemy's tricks."

"Weakness and fear asunder before the oaths," Dalmore said. No Power held men to these words they spoke as boys. Nigh did friendship or kinship, yet all were bound. "What of Lord Bayliss' lands? Can they not loft a mighty host?"

"Aye, the backbone of Bayliss power in Galimay. They will be the last to see battle."

"So, He sends Princeps Noniam's soldiers in the like of scraps tossed over the wall." His Reverence's mislike for the Caranuscans was well known. He blamed them for the loss of the Fourth, the madness of Dominus Redwick, and many other transgressions that helped him achieve and retain control over Galimay. It was falseness upon falseness wrapped in peaches.

"Indeed. Meat to the dogs. How could a savage in the such of Sir Rampo resist?"

"I believe that is what *drew* ye here," Dalmore admitted. Rampo lived and breathed the misery of men beaten down to their lowest. It was where he thrived as if pain and suffering were his Apperis Sap. "But not why Bayliss *sent* ye. If Galimay will not fight the Last Army here, what serves Portcullis? We fight only to protect the lives of—"

"I come for truth, a weapon for mine lord to wield."

Dalmore was tiring of the games. "Speak plain."

The knight leaned in and whispered, "His Reverence hath named the Corsan Carre agents of the enemy."

The world went flat.

It was a mother lost, a fortune stolen, a brother's memory wrung dry of deeds and sopped in muck. It was Dalmore's drive, ambition, and the sole purpose behind every breathless action and toil plucked away.

Unspeakable.

The Corsan Carre, the rallying cry . . .

Condemned.

Rampo leaned back, lips curling into the sneer he wore so oft at Lord Bayliss' side. "'Tis why Portcullis finds few friends at the end's dawn."

Dalmore steeled himself. Oft lords and their courts saw only the grand tapestries of battlefields, and so knew naught of how the tinctures of blood and dirt were mixed. His Reverence hated Benton and would oppose any declaration. He saw naught of the Corsan Carre defeat the Obantum Carre and pull Lady Ceal back from the depths. None who witnessed such could believe them false idols!

Nay, there must be more to this story.

Dalmore unclenched his fist, crumbles of the birdbone quill that he did not remember grabbing falling to the desk. Rampo was here with soldiers friendly to Benton, not a ten of Red Cloak questioners. "So what worth is this dying appendage of Galimay? What truth?"

"Lord Bayliss disagrees with his father."

The impossible.

Sir Rampo spake it as if commenting upon the Lamp's rise, or children fighting over unstamped coppers. Naught of his voice, posture, or composure shouted the fury of this quarrel that could crack open the last of the free peoples and bleed them dry long before the enemy's blades found them.

"Truly, in part, I am here to view the shock of it all upon ye's face."

Dalmore recovered himself. "And the rest? Out with it, man, what does Lord Bayliss seek?"

"Mine word that the Corsan Carre are genuine," he said with a wicked smile. "Tell me, when this battle is done, what plan hath ye? Die upon the wall, or lure the enemy into a great Palings trap in hopes Galimay will one day come?"

"Ye know we fight to the fifth day. Beyond is a dream."

"Aye, and in this dream, ye will need Lord Bayliss' support. That makes me ye's savior and Lord Artur Bayliss ye's debtor."

Dalmore opened his mouth to protest, but no words came. To lash out and reject Bayliss' aid would serve him, but not the many.

"Ye did not think the only burden of station was a cramped hand, did ye?" Sir Rampo sneered.

Benton stared at the mess of his home. A company of officers and city officials had followed his beckon from the Watch Keep to finish their discussions. The remnants now tracked throughout the rooms, and many a serving board lay streaked with jams and cheeses. It was heartening to see life returned to these walls one last time.

Flee.

The whisper struck sudden, tearing free his sense of place. The strength of her command carried such compulsion that he wondered if she had laced it with the Stochal. It would speak to broken trust betwixt them. The lagging ache of Isllor Mortund nigh destroying their love with nary a fight.

Isllor, who bade mine arms to push mine forever love off the South Wall.

The horror of that day stayed muddled as a dream but still stung deep, and Benton wished to be free of it. His mind was not his own whence, but . . .

"It was mine face she saw!" he shouted, and a cup he did not remember throwing clattered against the back wall.

Breath came fast. What of him was worth her trust? He was healed, severed from the black vines of Isllor's corruption, and so was she. Still, the rent halves were not whole. Stitched together, mayhap, with jagged edges clinging to each other in desperation, but the tear remained.

Flee.

It sounded to reason. The city was emptied, and their (her) plans for it exhausted. Ceal had extracted the one true gem of this expedition giving the Procult their salvation.

The Corsan Carre.

They were born of a prophecy he dared not doubt but long beheld as less a people and more an oath-bound promise to inspire the Procult. Benton's surprise when they strode out of the Dowdale seeming as mortal men had no measure. Indeed, a whole world of them awaited beyond the valley and mayhap the stars if Captain Saunders' words were believed.

Time. Ceal knew only the promise, not the use of the Corsan Carre. Their existence changed none of her grand plans, supplanted none of the Procult's hard-earned resources. Allies were needed now more than ever to guard against the insidious Anticult.

Our haughtiness allowed them to strike at our very salvation. Benton lamented. *To force blood onto Uumhrat's hands once more.* He could feel only a pinch of his friend's pain and longed to bring comfort as fire-side companions were wont. Alas, one weighed little against many, even he of Uumhrat's size.

Ceal needed Lord Benton of Oxhold, former Commander of the Ruby Branch and head of the Procult. Only through him the hope and power of Galimay could rally. Not Bayliss nor his father could stop it.

So why stay in this city whose importance was fast shrinking against looming designs laid in motion over 7000 years ago?

Captain Saunders stood out against the whispers to flee. *Honor.* It beheld the mighty and the low alike, even those who had crossed worlds. Saunders said he would stay, and so he did despite holding no allegiance or oath to Galimay.

Is the bond stronger than the will of your beloved?

Benton dared not answer, instead knelt beside the crumb-covered couch that had held many great lords, ladies, and emissaries over the years. Collecting the giblets and discards that fell beneath came from his childhood. His mother would oft say a left mess made mice. Ceal disagreed, but the habit remained. Behind a spilled cup, his hands found purchase on a prize: a corked bottle of wine.

The label was old but new to his eyes. Rare and, if such could be believed, sobering.

A Seic'al red.

Not a vintage produced from House Seic'al's lands after the other Caranuscan houses had cannibalized them, but from *before* Bedinch. A time when Nauda was young and the Corsan Carre just a tale told by Ceal around campfires.

A message from the Princeps.

He set the wine upon a trestle bench. The Caranuscans were long a centerpiece of disharmony that found unity only at long tables in their capital of Novantum. Before the Genisans came, Caranusca was a land of opportunity for Benton, Dom, and their young band of companions. Coin and blood overflowed their cups as houses and cities traded thrusts in the shadows. Riches mattered naught against position and winning, no matter the foolishness of the game.

Bedinch was the climax of that culture. All were threatened when a terrible force left a score of ruined villages across Caranusca. In the stead of uniting, the great houses postured and bickered. They waited until House Seic'al, the strongest, stepped forth to battle. In a beautiful moment of honor and sacrifice, brave patrons and warriors turned from the old ways to embrace the defense of all.

Benton sighed at the remembrance. Heads craned upward, sword and spear tips finding no enemy. Then death. Death for the sole sake of sating a horrid appetite. 'Twas the mate of the Tel'racs, Heb'azile. A force no host of men could stand against. Much of Seic'al's strength and the city of Bedinch fell to ash before Ceal could attune the Stochal and deflect the beast.

But the damage was wrought. War was forevermore changed, stolen from the common man's grasp, and a new likeness of terror gripped the Caranuscan Patronage. The houses availed themselves of Seic'al's weakness to pounce. Accusations. Trials. A storm of hate and blame that only the husk of Seic'al could satisfy.

Else came from that solemn day. Understanding the lessons of Bedinch better than any, Princeps Noniam turned from a lavish life to embrace the true runnings of a country. He protected what little of Seic'al he could and cloaked those the other houses hunted. He made those tables in gilded Novantum longer and more oft filled. Through tireless talking, assuring, and plenty of drink, ancient feuds fell to shared purpose. In time, even bits of fellowship arose. When the Genisans came, they expected fracture but met the whole of Caranusca more oft than not.

They are the answer, he realized.

The Caranuscans, beaten and destroyed, had naught to care for Portcullis. But they were here. The wine was a reminder that weakness was not an opportunity to sacrifice but to strengthen.

So too, Benton could have fled Bedinch when the enemy's guile and a new way of war were revealed.

Mottrel where death itself demanded his kneel.

Estmaw.

The White.

And the many tests of his mettle. Princeps Noniam, Lord Dain, Dom, Lanal, Ceal, Uumhrat, and all the rest stood with him because he did *not flee.*

The floorboards creaked as he hauled filthy serving boards stacked with cups into the kitchen. The mess was worse here. In their haste, Watchmen took to the work of butlers and cooks. Most were young and still tended by their mothers instead of wives. Service in Portcullis' disbanded Guard and now the Watch taught them to keep a clean and orderly camp but naught about the inside of a home. It would be a night's work to wash and put it all away if Benton still cared to keep house.

Uumhrat would.

Outside, the mirth and glow of the Market District beckoned. Captain Saunders had sprouted the infectious idea of celebrating the coming battle. Mayhap it was his custom, and it was well-matched by Portcullis' famed hospitality to weary travelers.

Benton might have gone but for Sir Rampo.

Flee.

The shining examples of stoic Caranuscans faltered as Bayliss' schemes darkened all horizons. It was a truth that a history of victories ensured nothing of the morrow. Mayhap to stand now when all else had fled was to be his folly. Ceal would be left alone, the last of a mighty company of heroes. Could she forge onward? She would, as was her spirit, but in grief and despair. And without the blood of Benton, doors would close.

Wrath found him as a visage surfaced of her standing before Durador's gates. The great weight of steel bars veined with Renderstone sat lowered and barred. Ceal's pleas went unanswered as the warring world at her back pressed in.

Benton bristled as the tell Dux Herms brought came once more to his ears, clear as the North Wall bells. *His Reverence has declared the Corsan Carre false and issued an edict for their capture.*

"I cannot prevail in both places!" Benton shouted, pounding his fist into solid wood. The column, wide and thick to fill a grown man's arms, cracked with a terrible noise. It did not fall, but the house groaned as it settled its weight on a new lame leg.

In the stead of shame or remorse, he lamented. Dom would have loved to see that.

Benton snuffed the lower lights and started for the stairs. Rest. The decision to flight or fight could wait till dawn. Mayhap his dreams would lay down his worries and his path. The steps creaked loud in the emptiness, and the chill deepened. He longed for a fire.

Scratching.

It unsettled the fresh darkness in the like of mice. Large mice. The hairs upon his neck rose, his mother's warning now haunting.

The scratching turned to thumping. *Something at the door?*

Back down through the dark, Benton strode—not crept—to the atrium. It was naught, he told himself. Dalmore with a bottle and fired spirits from meeting Sir Rampo or Lt. Maon with a custodial worry and no mind for his proper superior.

As Benton arrived, the heavy door shook. The sight froze him as a cat caught by torchlight.

Naught storms of the south nor the pounding of heavy Blue Cloak fists in the late of night had ever rattled it so. Thoughts turned to the Anticult, its poison reaching ever far into the hearts of Galimay. *Might they think me alone and vulnerable?*

Hinges blew dust against another blow.

In truth, the distraction was welcomed. Benton felt not the fear of others as they stepped forward to combat. His was the work of a seamstress upon an oversized cloth. Ribbons needed cutting, and a hip dagger would suffice. If they were many, the formidable Dawn of Mourn was within heartbeats. He swung open the door, eyes keen.

White fur and jaws rushed for his throat.

The dagger fell astray, useless against the onslaught. The great wolf's paws fell upon his shoulders, tongue swiping at his face.

"Palefang," Benton cried, embracing the dance, "I thought ye long gone from here."

The White Wolf—once thought murderer of innocents and possessed by a wicked evil—oft came and went from Portcullis by his own will. But he had not been seen in many tendays. The absence was felt because, with the defeat of Isllor, Palefang was restored as a harbinger of hope to the city. The beast born in the White's depths, the like who could save the legendary Lord Benton from death, was naught a trifle. He had even earned the respect of the Corsan Carre.

With another lick and a gaze from those glacial eyes, Palefang released him and stalked into the house.

Questions rose, enough blush the whole of the Ruby Branch: *Do ye hunger? Where will ye go? What of the morrow?*

Palefang went to the sitting room, his white fur lighting the path with trapped moonlight. It was here where the house oft gathered and enjoyed sundry talks. His great head reached the fireplace's mantle and nuzzled the Dawn of Mourn. The blade that had born Benton through years and battle was still sharp and glinting as the day the Uplanders forged it.

Then darkness overtook those blue eyes, and Benton knew. The wolf had not come to visit, to roll in the yard under the warmth of Bergreth's Lamp. The Everwinter monster had come to aid his friend once more.

And at last, Benton had his answer, a way to satisfy honor and protect the world's fate. "Not here," he whispered.

Captain Case 'Padilla' Rath walked a patrol through the moon's pale light.

Is it a real moon or some giant alien tanning its ass out in space? he wondered. It looked spheroid, but being farther away and brighter than The Moon made it hard to tell. Also, it was either full blast or not, with no half or waxing crescents. On one night and off the next like a light.

Or pair of pants.

The fire pits were doused, and the wagons buttoned up. Thousands of tents were packed into the camp, which was planted haphazardly out in the open in the middle of an icy flood plain. Not ideal, especially since Rath had this nagging, irrational feeling that the darkness was watching them. But anywhere else along the road would have stretched out the camp making it harder to secure.

Quick feet crunched across the frozen ground by a tent cluster at 9 o'clock. He tensed until little giggles followed. Kids. They probably thought this was a big adventure, not a damned exodus from their homes.

Rath checked his watch—functionally just a timer since the 24-hour clock was bullshit. An hour until LCpl Buontempo relieved him.

Gotta find something to do other than think about the moon being some dude's ass. Worse would be to think of it as a chick's ass because that would lead him down a needy rabbit hole.

He stopped to chat with the two Watchmen manning the southern approach. All clear and quiet. Talking turned out to be a waste of hot air that could otherwise be blown into freezing hands. The distraction was short, and Rath moved on, cursing the life of an infantryman.

The ass moon caught his eye again as it ran for the horizon. He squinted as his brain superimposed a little cleavage into that plump pale. It was enough to tighten his trousers.

The moon did not just become porn.

The damage was done, and he found himself scanning the camp. The prehistoric, burrowing mammal within wanted nothing more than to find Micky and crawl into her warmth. He knew she was just a big flirt, mostly tease, but rationalizing it didn't remove the hooks.

Not an option, he told himself. Hundreds of women throughout the camp would welcome a legendary Corsan Carre if he needed to get laid.

Like those pilot's wings, it takes all the fun out of the hunt.

No, Micky was what he wanted. He could deny it, but that was only damage control for every time she flirted with other guys, even women.

Was she sleeping around?

She had every right to, but he'd made a point of tucking the women in tonight to ensure they were alone. If Micky and the doc were sleeping together, that wasn't a threat because it was a different category than men. Right? He wasn't sure, but he found himself back at their tent before he could figure it out.

Don't go in there.

It would be like walking into the girl's locker room. What he needed was a way to coax Micky out. Maybe throw rocks at her window, grab a guitar, and play until she swooned.

"The night weighs upon ye," came a whisper.

Rath's spine cracked like a whip, bringing his situational awareness up to *rotors burning.* Ceal was sitting just five freaking feet away, working her hands over a bowling ball-sized rock. *Was she there all along? Fuck, can she read minds?* "Uh, ma'am," he managed, heart racing. "Thought you'd gone to bed. Just . . . just making my rounds."

The freaking rock burst into crimson flames like charcoal doused in lighter fluid, but there'd been none of that. "I require little sleep," she said. "Sit; I wish to hear ye's tale."

The reddish fire seemed a better alternative to the biting cold, so Rath sat on the larger rock beside her. M4 carbine stayed slung across his chest for easy access. "My tale?"

"We hath a commonality," she said, brushing her hands through... THROUGH the flames. "Isllor's touch upon our minds."

Rath forgot about the fire. "Yes, ma'am. Still having nightmares, if I'm being honest." He wanted to be honest. Ceal was trustworthy, like Micky but different in a way he couldn't quite target.

"Tell me."

"It's like I'm sleeping, but the darkness has substance, and it starts pushing into my mouth, nose, eyes, and ears. Feels like hands wrenching things open, reaching inside. Crap you'd see in a horror movie." He paused. "Uh, read in a horror book? Story?"

She passed her hand back through the flames and studied him. "Ye are different from Captain Saunders."

Yeah, it's called having marketable skills. Rath gestured at the open night around them and said, "He's a little more agoraphobic than I am." When she didn't react—obviously not everything translated—he added, "Afraid of wide-open spaces."

"It would seem to beckon others to our fire, no?"

Nope, Saunders isn't winning this one. "Well, ma'am, from what Sergeant Orrugant tells me, the threat level around here is low. Long as Portcullis keeps the Genisans bottled up, our biggest worry is the weather."

A cold wind blew between them, and Rath couldn't help but shiver. "We are safe," she said, the words crystalizing frost against his core. Another shiver. "But only through fear and Greth's lingering grace."

"You're gonna need to explain that one. I thought the Genisans weren't operating in this area."

She clicked her tongue and gave him a dark look. It wasn't meant for him, though; more like she was seeing someone else she wanted to scream at. Instead of blowing up, she said, "I can help ye." Her hand passed through the red fire again. "Remember the cliff. Before the snows fell."

The air warmed as Rath relived Gunny Brines' last moments. The ice and rock were shaking, an impossible drop just inches away. Rath clung to the rope, life flashing behind his eyes, and pleaded with Brines to follow. But all that came from the stout gunnery sergeant was a shout and a boot to the chest.

"There," she whispered.

He saw it. Behind Brines, a . . . something humanoid made of green glass shards. It was waist-high, stalking toward him. "I remember . . ."

"What ye see is his killer."

"N . . . no, the avalanche must've . . ."

She let silence crush reason. Suddenly, the creature was an assassin, striking in those last moments just to ensure Brines bit it. A decisive blow to Marine morale. More importantly . . .

Gunny Brines' death wasn't my fucking fault.

"They are the denizens of these Palings."

"The Gra'nuul?" he asked. It was a name he heard often from the locals. A briefing with Benton's people confirmed they were real and dangerous but dormant. Still, a new wave of terror crashed down. Spiders were tiny and scary; this was a giant, four-legged spider, an ice spider with no fucking soul.

She cast her eyes into the stillness beyond the perimeter, and her features tightened in anger. "Long a plague upon Galimay, the Gra'nuul possess but a single drive to consume warmth." She pointed to the fire. "Naught of true heat, but the warmth of life."

"They drain people of their warmth?" Like the opposite of him cracking open a cold beer in July.

Her eyes sparkled green. "They thirst for what appears to some as a light shone from all beings."

"We call that infra-red; it's how we target . . . uh, you know. Sometimes it's dark, and we . . ."

"Castles and stoneworks, mighty armies bearing armor, steel, and renderstone were necessary to survive the onslaught. Centuries of strife, fired by the hearts of an indomitable people, forged the strength of Galimay. So too was it quenched in ice given evil life through ancient Power." She pursed her lips, staring off into oblivion. Whatever memory haunted Ceal passed after a moment. "In time, the proper wards were crafted to contain the Gra'nuul beneath the rock and snow."

"Then what about that . . . the one that I saw?"

"That is why I wished us to speak."

"But you said we're safe out here."

She did something with her hands, but her eyes were so demanding he didn't dare look down. "We are. They feed upon warmth and will find none here."

That damned breeze again. He wanted to excuse himself and update Saunders. Everyone back there thought the Gra'nuul were long gone. Also, Buontempo was probably ready to tag in. But like a pothead, Rath couldn't care enough to get off the couch. A couple of furs on the cold gravel never sounded so good.

"Their hatred will hath them seek other prey in hopes of hurting me." She bored into him. "Tell me of Benton."

Rath felt a thrill. He couldn't wait to unzip that file. "Last report said he was having trouble deciding who should do what. But after some soul searching, he's decided to take full command."

"As I hath guessed." She pressed her fucking palm into the burning rock without so much as a flinch and said, "The Corsan Carre must remain with him."

"Yes, ma'am."

"No matter the hardship," she added. "Keep Benton safe."

Rath nodded, feeling good about their chat. Saunders didn't know what the hell he was talking about; Ceal was cool. And this wasn't just the ass moon beaming him with weird vibes. She was best friend material, empathetic and compassionate. No judgement. He could tell her anything. And Benton was definitely getting the full concierge Marine Corps service so long as Captain Rath had anything to say about it.

She passed her hand through the flames again.

"Wait," he said, head clearing. Was it ever not clear? He tried to remember what they were just talking about. Ice creatures? *Must be.* "So those Gra'nuul. What's to stop them from attacking Portcullis?"

"Are there vultures upon ye's world?"

There were, and he didn't have to ask her meaning. Saunders' entire plan was to bug out the second they lost containment on the North Wall. He wasn't expecting to find an army of flesh-eating ice creatures waiting for him.

"I need to go make a call, ma'am," said Rath excusing himself from her satisfied smile. He started toward the Watch tent with a strong stride and intent. Any plan that did not involve colossal troop formations and a ton of metal armor was fucked with those things out there. It would be like sending a platoon through a crocodile-infested swamp. Shark-infested swimming. The Gra'nuul that killed Gunny Brines came out of nowhere seconds before an avalanche hit. How could anyone fight that?

I need to warn Saunders and . . .

He stopped.

And tell him . . . what? Pull out? Reconfigure the retrograde from small-group scatter into a massive formation that couldn't possibly exfil? Start selling him on a wild new explanation for Gunny's death with zero evidence?

It'd turn into a shouting match at best; at worst, Buontempo would get orders to zip-tie him to a wagon for observation. Saunders was a stubborn fuck who did not respond well to 11th-hour challenges to the plan. Tough-as-nails infantry commander would pull out that back pocket list of perceived derelictions and failures. Brines, Williamson, Mina Bazar.

No, Rath had to think in terms of the mission. Cork Team remained in Portcullis to buy time for Micky and Dr. Bowman and protect Benton at all costs. That was it, period. *Keep Micky and Benton safe.*

Spotting LCpl Buontempo coming out of their tent, it was clear the mission could only go forward if everyone did their part despite the danger. It came with the job.

Escort the women to Durador, ensure Benton stays safe, and await further instructions. Keep Benton safe.

Rath never made that call.

CHAPTER 12

THE PORTCULLIS LINE

Lips.

Lush and hungry, they pressed in as fingers raked hair. Breasts slipped across bare chest, and thighs wrapped his waist.

Now this I can get used to, *thought Saunders, heart pounding and hands kneading the firm flesh of a woman. The kiss broke, and his mouth pecked down her neck. Her breaths quickened to shuddering gasps, driving wild thrills. Hot hands on his backside pulled him closer.*

Urgency rose. The passion was sizzling, desperate, and overwhelming, like it was his first time with the first set of boobs he ever saw.

A life-changing explosion.

An instant of all impossible desires realized.

They fell to the satin sheets together, panting. Somehow, his host wasn't done and reached a hand up to massage her chest. A moan escaped her lips, and teeth nibbled his shoulder.

Desire.

She wanted him. Bad. As need returned, he wanted to sprint through the finish line. But god, she was so worked up. He wanted to stay here forever, enthralled in hot flesh, dynamiting through a mountain of tension. It was real-life, interactive porn, and he did not give a fuck who these people were. Just that he was the dude, and that mess of blonde hair was bringing the animal need.

Slick thighs parted and pressed against his manhood. A moment of resistance, then a return to the primordial creche. His hips drove her into a long sigh.

It was good, amazing, the best experience of his life. After a minute, Saunders remembered his body was not operating under his control. Still, the woman reacted so . . . so amazingly predictably that it was glaring when the guy missed a mark or failed to anticipate a tempo shift. Where Saunders would slow things down, he sped up. Her intensity faltered a couple of times, but the sheer passion of it all made up for it. Everything was forgivable, just as it'd been long ago.

Lungs drew deep as Saunders and his host rallied for the home stretch. A deep twinge, a rush of excitement and strength signaled the point of no return. Suddenly, expectedly, she wrapped him in a bear hug as her moans crescendoed into breathy cries. She was so tense, so tight, and he was . . .

Staring into a pair of eyes he knew better than his service number.

A battering ram of confusion and ecstasy slammed into Saunders' brain. He wanted to cry out her name, tell her a hundred things, caress her face, and share everything with the woman he loved.

But most of all, he wanted to . . .

Those blue eyes widened in horror, and she shoved him back into oblivion.

Captain Saunders snapped awake, breathing hard, electric with excitement and disorientation. "Sarah!" he gasped, arms, abs, and legs jerking as his body reconnected with his brain.

His hand only found empty, woolen sheets beside him. *So real.* He'd had sex dreams about his wife before, even after years of marriage. But they were always brief, just a flash of skin and the sensation of their connection. This was a trip back to the early days of mad passion and love. Before the kid, the fighting, and the interplanetary thing.

He stood, the cool air of his room smelling of snow. Deep, early morning blue spilled in from the window, but the streetlights were still bright outside. Maybe a half-hour before sunrise and no alarm bells were ringing.

Just a dream, he told himself. It was the pre-operations sendoff every guy who ever stood at attention needed. *God, I was with her.* He could still feel the warmth and pressure of her palms and smell her $60-a-bottle, citrus-infused shampoo. *Why didn't I notice that right away?*

His lizard brain oozed out an answer, like when Mike would grunt in absurd satisfaction. *Right.* Plus, it was a dream. All sorts of weird shit happened during dreams. There were no rules. It probably was a different girl initially, and that last part was just the mindfuck. Like strolling into class and just then realizing you're naked.

Jesus, babe, you could've melted cast iron with that kiss. He shook his head, pulling on his trousers and boots. It was fucking perfect, a solid reminder of why they got married. *We are good together.* The only ding, coming from his Type-A analytical personality, was that weird sensation that his body wasn't his. Not unusual for dreams, but here in Portcullis it . . .

No.

Her eyes widened in horror . . .

Saunders was half-dressed with a mountain of readiness actions, battle-plans, and protocols about to crash his waking brain. But Sarah's reaction, the look in her eyes, shoved the fate of two worlds to the distant background. It wasn't shock or fear . . .

It was surprise. Recognition.

The dots connected faster than he wanted.

He searched his neck for hickies and teeth marks. It was clear, but hook him to a polygraph, and he'd swear they just made love.

Was it one of those *dreams? A Vision?* It made sense; they were happening more frequently now. The content gave no sense of their ultimate purpose, but it was always a ride-along in some other person's body.

Someone else.

The noise vanished, leaving only a pure, terrible signal.

"Did I just fuck my wife with someone else's dick?" he demanded from a world that seemed hell-bent on screwing with him.

Lance Corporal Fischer didn't wake up so much as he came to. All at once he was squinting against the washed-out daylight in the windows and trying to get his bearings. Last he remembered, it was cold, dark, and Nickels was on his ass. *Outside. We were looking for Gladstone.* Then Uumhrat was there, and poof, a quiet room and soft bed.

He shifted on the coarse sheets, still in uniform. He'd also slept in his boots. *Shit, it's late.* Last time he got up after dawn without being sick was eight years ago. Straight slept in, and it took a cold bucket from the creek to get going.

He rolled his head to the side, bracing himself against the swift retribution of a skull-crushing headache, but it never came. In fact, he felt great, which was usually a bad sign. "Ugh," he said. "I think I'm still drunk."

"Morning already?" mumbled Cpl Nickels sitting up in his makeshift floor bed.

"Morning," said Gladstone. He was already dressed and standing by the window with a steaming cup. "Was tempted to let Uumhrat tuck you into that bed together, but I did you a solid."

Nickels turned red. "Bullshit. No way I was that hammered. My turn-gay number of beers is bigger than your mom's waistline."

"You put us to bed, Stone?" Fischer asked, shaking his head. Still no pain or hangover spins. He wished he could remember what happened, what he might've said to Stone when drunk.

I was gonna hammer him about being a flaky dick lately.

"Captain wasn't happy about it but said he'll file the paperwork later. Big day today."

Fischer stood and tested his balance. Steady as a cow on grass. "Welp, feel like a new man today. Glad I didn't get *that* hammered."

"You were shitfaced," said Gladstone without turning away from the window.

"I'll check my gear later to make sure you didn't give me a good night blow job," said Nickels getting up and smiling at his ability to stand.

Fischer sucked a deep breath of morning melt and three-dudes musk. "I'm like crystal clear. My eyes red?"

Nickels shook his head. "Musta been drinkin' the good shit last night."

"The sar'nt called it 'magic beer.' Hell y'all, I'm a believer."

"Dude, remember the brewery plan?" said Nickels. "Hangover-free beer, bro. Cocktillionaires. We'll need special ladders to climb our stacks and count the cheddar, feel?"

"Yeah," said Fischer fancying a job without people shooting or stabbing at him. "Just gotta get the recipe. Cake, right?"

"Corsan Carre Corps, bro. We'll ask nice, then turn our gats sideways and ask again. They ain't got capitalism or IP protections here. Ripe for the plucking."

"Stone, you sure the captain ain't pissed? Why'd he let us sleep in?"

No answer, just more staring out the window like the horses were about to come home. Nickels cocked his head. "What's up? We say something stupid?"

Fischer shrugged. Gladstone, as usual, was hard to read. It was best to poker face it until last night's memories rebooted.

Nickels, however, wasn't one to close the door. "Stone, you gonna answer him? And by the way, where were you all night? It gets fuzzy after circle jerking with Uumhrat over that ax, but you bugged out long before that. Where were you? And what the fuck are you look—"

Boom. The room shook, and the bones inside Fischer's chest rattled. Something big just went off. A Tuesday in a forward position, but this was Portcullis. From the strained look on Stone's face, it was one of the rock-slide bombs they'd rigged up a few weeks ago. Hard to tell if he was happy or pissed about it, though.

Right, we got ourselves a war today.

"Of all the times to not have a weather app," said Micky, face pressed against the coach's window. She was all over the place this morning, chirping about the clouds, humming, and flirting with everyone. Somehow the lower Dr. Pat felt, the more amped up Micky got. Like a negative energy vampire.

Maybe that's what keeps her around. I'm a fountain of pessimism.

Dr. Pat summoned the strength to look outside. A dark front was rolling in, and her heart sank even further. There was no outrunning it in this creaking, clopping, luxury coach pulled by four horses that could get passed on a sidewalk. They also couldn't afford to stop and take shelter.

All those people out there . . .

"It is good fortune it approaches from the west. It shall shroud the city and favor our defenders," said Ceal from her desk. Yes, that desk fit in the fucking carriage while the ridiculous tent rode bundled on the roof. Meanwhile, the thousands limping along outside went disregarded.

We can make a faster pace once the walking piles of rags begin to die off.

Scrooge could not have said it better himself. Was that the real Ceal poking through? Or just provocative for their "experiment," like Micky suggested.

"Oh, the west," said Micky as if finding the perfect distraction to the torrent of human suffering this storm would unleash. "No one ever talks about it. Always *north this* and *south that* like everyone is living on a big, long—"

"I think I'd like to get back out there," Dr. Pat interrupted. Their hypocrisy was making it hard to breathe. "Probably a few dozen within earshot who could use a ride more than me."

"Let us discuss ye's dream again," said Ceal pulling a fresh sheet of paper—actual paper, not dried animal skin—from beneath one of the many piles on the overcrowded desk.

"Oh, that dream was wild," said Micky in a breathy voice as if it was somehow erotic. "I just can't believe I wasn't in it. Doomsday? No problem. The vibrant tightness of a dead boyfriend with just a hint of fabric softener? Yes, please." She put a hand to her mouth. "Oh gosh, Pat, I'm so insensitive. Seeing him must've messed you up. Wait." She tapped a finger to her lips. "Have you . . . uhm," she let out that little, privacy-invading giggle, "taken care of it yet?"

A mix of insane impulses threatened to explode from within, but Dr. Pat iced it down with liquid reason. She wouldn't let them provoke her to experiment with this . . . whatever it was that let her read the letter yesterday.

Gaslighting.

That's all it was, and it wasn't hard to figure out why: the people in Durador were much less gullible than Portcullis. They'd see right through the Corsan Carre act to the wayward group just trying to unfuck their own situation. So Ceal was desperate to create some caricature or fantasy to sell it. What better way than using supernatural manipulation to make Dr. Pat a believer in her own divinity?

I'll see yer ass in the morning.

And then there was the lingering echo of Mr. Ultra-Macho Type A planning out his next piece of ass.

I'm done being used by everyone.

"Yuppers," Dr. Pat said, mimicking Micky's high-pitched bird voice. "Like old shoes on a washboard." *Yeah, it doesn't take a terminal degree to live in the gutter.*

Micky clapped and laughed. "Oh god, I love it when they resist!"

"Time enough for that later," said Ceal studying her. It was the same scrutinizing look Dr. Pat had once given a mouse shivering within a plastic tank. The fact that the data they collected became a vital contribution to the characterization and treatment of Sickle Cell Disease wasn't lost on her, but *fuck being the mouse!*

"Those visited by Visions are oft silent Stochists," Ceal continued. "Their Gift in the Power is small and unwieldable in the waking world. But at night, they live history. The most adept can witness events as they unfold. Never before hath any seen that which hath not passed."

"I was drugged," Dr. Pat reminded her tormentors. The dream was unusually vivid, but not being an experienced drug user, maybe that's how it was. "It wasn't like the other Visions. I was in my own body and . . . I mean h—" she wanted to say Mike's name, but the pronoun came instead, "—his . . . body, goddamn. It couldn't be there either. Right? No resurrection or anything." *Right?* She stared into those melanin-depleted lime irises hoping for a hint of shiftiness. Micky listened with an equal level of interest.

"None return from death."

Well, she's either a great liar, or that's this world's equivalent of a peer-reviewed textbook fact.

"But Pat isn't Stochal," said Micky.

Ceal pursed her lips. "No. Much was not known of how the Corsan Carre would present themselves. Whether they wielded great Powers, new Powers, or if their sole purpose was to appear and herald the beginning of disaster."

A rumble in the distance served to mark that point.

Micky spun and shouted, "Boo!"

Caught up in the moment, Dr. Pat practically jumped out of her medieval skirt. A sharp pain dug into her skull from the wooden paneling behind her. Fight or flight hit hard, demanding satisfaction from the ill-timed prank. But she was wise to their schemes now. Through sheer will, the cauldron cooled, and she did not throw any fists.

"Oh man, totally got you."

Smile and don't reach back to see if your head is bleeding, Dr. Pat told herself.

The episode didn't get so much of a blink out of Ceal. Instead, her attention was on the window facing the northern mountains where her husband and the Marines were facing incredible odds. A wistful sigh followed.

"Probably just thunder," Dr. Pat offered.

"The dream," Ceal said. "The city was in ruin, yes?"

"It was wrecked with blown-out buildings and rubble splayed in every direction," Dr. Pat said. She did not add that it resembled other places she'd visited back on Earth as part of an MSF (Doctors Without Borders) emergency aid team.

That it resembled the aftermath of what artillery could do to civilization.

———

Flurries floated through the stone arrow slit and ambled toward the fireplace like moths drawn to the light. Midway across the chamber, they crashed to the planks as if they were rain all along.

Saunders watched the fatalist show with passing interest, hoping it was a metaphor for the Genisans.

The new Marine Corps home was cold, cramped, and situated off the North Wall Command Center (NWCC in milspeak). They were eight stories above the canyon—aptly called the Doormat—leading to Portcullis. He could've stared out that narrow window into the gathering snowstorm for hours, letting his mind play out a hundred battles. But right now, all he cared about were the two packs leaning against the cold stone.

Sergeant Smith had facilitated check out from Uumhrat's inn before sunrise, loading their entire supply depot into two Watch carriages. When the Marines first crashed, they'd salvaged and hauled a ton of shit from the wreckage, well over a hundred pounds of gear per man. Fortunately, the Dawn Guard helped mule it up eight flights of twisting stairs. Now, PFC Licht was in an adjacent room working on bug-out packs with everything they needed for a week or two in the mountain wilderness.

Not everything could go.

Weapons and ammo were prepositioned along Tier Three, most of which would be expended during the fight saving a ton of weight. Not ideal since resupply was infeasible but necessary for the plan. The rest wasn't a matter of need but priority. They could make insulation and find food; they couldn't fabricate electronics or explosives.

Saunders stared at the two extra packs—Brines' and Williamson's.

Both were full, but one was empty.

The discovery was made during pack-out. Sergeant Smith had darkened the doorway with Brines' ruck in hand. Saunders started to say it was an unquestionable priority . . .

Just askin' if you got it with your stuff, sir.

Got what?

Saunders didn't wait for the answer. The special operations capable Marines weren't big on personal, identifying symbols for OpSec reasons. But Mike was a force. He had the medals, the presence, and the scars. No one dared say shit, and everyone loved to talk about it.

The knife.

It didn't have a name, no special story other than him hammering it out in his mom's backyard with a piece of steel and some animal bones his grandfather left him. But it was distinctive. It was Mike.

And it was gone.

Theft was the suspicion, and the list of suspects limited. Only three people outside of Marine personnel had access to the armory and that pack: Uumhrat, Emlin, and Ann. Uumhrat denied it with the sincerity of a wounded kitten. Ann and her mom Emlin were with the refugee caravan and unreachable. The thought of sending Captain Rath to conduct an interrogation crossed Saunders' mind, but it was more trouble than worth. According to Buontempo, the guy spent his time puppy-dogging after the women. Which was exactly what the mission needed right now.

Of course, in a world of magic, everyone was a suspect. The aggressive timetable was not amenable to an investigation, and there wasn't much of a point. It wasn't like they lost a firearm or the solar charger keeping all their electronics working. Just some sentimental shit.

Mike would agree, but it wasn't much of a comfort. At least they didn't take the guy's stogie. Saunders rolled the oil-black stick between his fingers. Half smoked, it was a . . .

Goddammit, man, we both knew you wouldn't see 40, but no one ever deserved to live more.

. . . a symbol of hope from someone who could not collect.

It was stupid, irrational, and emotional, but Saunders put the cigar in his pack anyway. It helped; felt like he was moving forward again. Strapping that two-foot sword in its black scabbard to his side made him feel better too. A lot better. Maybe it was Mike's soul giving a nod to the upgrade.

With a straighter back, Saunders left the quite room for the bustling command center.

Aboard the Marine Corps' amphibious assault ship USS *Storm*, the Landing Force Operations Center (LFOC) was a hive of neural activity. Circuitry and displays were filled with information being pulled, distilled, and integrated from all over the planet. It was alive as anything back on Earth, but physically unobtrusive. Operators were seated at terminals wired up for their respective roles, and command staff were clustered in usually quiet discussion as the operation progressed. Occasionally, it got rowdy, as he imagined the scene had unfolded during Operation *Sea Monster*. Otherwise, it was calm.

The NWCC was heavy on dumb metal and stone. Cold air blasted in from the observation deck while fireplaces baked asses. It was smokey, noisy, and bodies were in constant motion. Sweeping overlooks, messengers, bannermen, and horns were the battle informatics and actuators. Ropes on pulleys were the radios, and soot-on-slab was the whiteboard.

It was a sheer organ of human power.

"Sir, Francisco for you," said PFC Licht bringing the SINCGARS radio in on his heels.

The company sniper's message was simple: the enemy had anticipated the Twin Tithes rockslide and brought a prefab wooden causeway to bypass it. That didn't mean they got out unscathed. North Overlook had spotted the enemy's vanguard at dawn, and three widths (an hour) later, the lead elements were in the kill zone. Saunders didn't hesitate.

Fortunately, good ideas rarely traveled alone in the C-monster, and they'd rigged a second slide higher up on the road that would take a lot more than some boards to clear. But that was for later.

Along with so much more.

Gladstone's mission last night roared to the forefront, twisting Saunders' guts. He could already hear the screams of betrayal, see the horror on Benton's face as the cost of winning came due.

It was cold, but it was war.

Shaking it off, Saunders clicked the mic and asked, "Back roads still clear?" He hadn't personally walked the mountain trails that bypassed the main road. Still, reports indicated they were in decent enough shape to allow incursion units cliff access. That would give them elevated firing positions on the North Wall. What they might be firing was another matter, but in no world, realm, or reality was Saunders going to give an inch of high ground.

"Clear and all positions secure; will apprise if it heats up," said Francisco.

"Roger that, out."

Benton and Rampo were staring at him, warfighters ready to do work. They were both carved from marble in their white armor, but Benton had an edge in the way that two sports cars could look similar, but only one cost two grand for a brake job.

"Enemy moving up the Twin Tithes," Saunders announced. The NWCC fell silent.

Benton nodded and opened his mouth to say something.

"Sir!" shouted PFC Licht pressing the radio receiver to his ear. The rest was lost in a wild clap of thunder. A tremor passed through the NWCC, and all eyes went to the ceiling as everyone realized that wasn't the weather.

Saunders let his experience and training, rather than his intellectual curiosity, direct him to the stairs. He took those winding stone steps three at a time and burst out on the top tier where the bulk of Sir Rampo's ranged forces were congregated. The air was swirling with flurries, and the towering mountain peaks were already swallowed by the white.

Rows of archers in green stood easy among the parapets, staring up at the same spot on Almon's Peak. Saunders grabbed his binoculars and spotted a black spec in the snowy slopes.

A little impact crater.

"There, milord!" shouted a green.

Saunders caught a glimpse. It sailed up from the valley, over the city, and cracked off the rocky slopes lining the road south. It wasn't much to look at, but it must've been a car-sized boulder from the report.

Artillery.

Someone down in the NWCC recognized the danger a moment later, and the North Wall bells began clanging, bringing the city to full alert.

The war was on.

"S-sir," called PFC Licht from the stairwell, breathless. Sir Rampo came right after him, white armor blending with the worsening storm. "Francisco again, urgent."

"I see no throwers," Rampo called from the crenulations along the edge. Another thump suggested a rock landed short, maybe on the far side of the western slope.

"Go ahead," Saunders said into the mic at a normal volume. The wind should've been whipping up this high in the mountains with this kind of weather rolling in. But it was dead calm amid the ranks of stunned medieval troops scanning the skies for the next bomb to drop.

"Take it you're reading some incoming?" said Francisco as if this were a casual discussion.

"They're lobbing boulders. You got eyes?"

"Origin is a camp three klicks northeast of where the road inserts into the Lower Del. Bunch of Black Robes working in teams, a pile of rocks. No physics; magic. The usual."

And we've got no mortars, no air, no rocks, no response. Fuck! "Wait one." He ran back down to the smokey NWCC, where Benton was calming a mass of blue, white, and green officers and sergeants.

"They seek to avert our eyes and vigilance," Benton said. "'Tis all! Tired tricks of yesteryear to shake our resolve."

"Be it our doom to stand fierce only to be crushed?" asked one of Dalmore's Deadlies. Sergeant Segar.

"Nay it . . ."

"Benton," Saunders interrupted from the deep parts of his lungs. "They're using mag—uh, the Power to launch these stones from the valley. Why isn't the Bark stopping it?" Saunders had a guess but needed everyone on the same page before connecting the dots.

"The Bark reaches not the Dowdale," Benton answered. Then, his mind shoved something right behind it. "But it doth strip the Quotidian enchantments, so they are plain rock when they fall."

Great, the asteroid has no explosive warhead. It's fine. The information was still helpful. "That means they're ballistic," Saunders said. Confused looks all around. "They're firing blind. Look at the weather out there. The valley might be a different story, but we're just a big cloud up here to them. They've got no zero and no spotters. They'll be lucky to hit the city, let alone a specific target."

"The Corsan Carre speak true," confirmed Benton. Did he really understand? It didn't matter as murmurs of agreement followed, and the sergeants headed out to spread the word.

Saunders found PFC Licht, and Francisco confirmed the assessment. "What's more, sir," Francisco continued, "they've been at it for a while. They were setting boulders on fire, making them glow red and all sorts of stuff. Then they'd fly them toward the city, only to have them suddenly drop out of the air. Only now did they figure out that the rocks retained momentum after passing through the Bark. Unclear if they can develop that Redleg math to put one on target."

"Can't assume ignorance. It's only a matter of time until they refine the process."

"Roger that. Also, ground advance now on hold. Looks like they got wise to the utility of pounding fixed positions."

"Or they're sending engineers to ID and clear our explosives. We'll deploy to tighten the spotter net on the backroads. Maintain visual on our second line of ordnance and keep me updated, out."

———

Nickels thudded down the stairs, geared up and ready to face the shitshow.

Situation normal.

Instead of finding the house trashed and someone's car in the pool, the First Inn of Portcullis was spotless. Not just picked up and swept, but Uumhrat broke out the polish. From the sweet smell of baking bread to Bone and Garcia at the usual table by the fireplace, it was downright copacetic.

Fischer stumbled down after him and, like him, stopped for a double-take.

"Mornin' ladies," said Bone over his shoulder. The rest of those fuckers snickered into their feedbags.

"Fuck's all this?" Nickels asked in the authoritative voice drill instructors used to remind junior enlisted of the pecking order. "Teatime? You guys hear that bomb go off a minute ago?" Gladstone, and then Fischer, shuffled by to grab food boards off the counter. The clopping of their boots reminded Nickels of how empty it was today. *Fucking right; everyone else is at war.* "Bone, why didn't you wake us up?"

"Stone said you an' Fish needed to sleep in a bit," said Smith. "Thought you might be lockin' lips and stuff."

"We accept you, Corporal," said Light. Actually, Lance Corporal Bulb as he was now and forever known.

"Fuck that shit. This dough don't rise for the Y's," Nickels said, grabbing a seat.

"The donut," said Garcia.

"Powdered sugar, baby," said Smith.

All the fuckers laughed like there wasn't another care in the world. Gameday usually looked a lot different, even before gash-face Gunny would triple down with the motarded shit. Bone, for one, would be too caught up in his horoscope predictions for fooling around. And everyone would be in their heads, not snickering into their cups. "Fuck's going on here? They call the war off?"

Smith pulled a mug of that watered-down café picante crap to his lips. Big smile as he sipped, making everyone wait. *I ain't gonna beg, bro.* Nickels went to the front windows. Outside, Watchmen and green-armored troops were warming themselves around braziers. Some were eating. Minus the gray sky, flurries, and plumes of hot breath coming out of their mouths, it was practically a picnic.

Stone and Fish were digging into their trays when Bone finished the longest sip in history. "Garcia, download the corporal his intel."

"Captain blew the pass leading up to the city, yo."

It explained the boom they heard. "That where you went last night, Stone?"

Gladstone shrugged without looking up from his food. Fucker was pale as that sky out there; served him right for not drinking the magic beer last night. *Vitamins, bitch. Get some.*

"So, we got the morning off?" Nickels said, eying the food service bar for the first time. Not being hungover was hungry work.

"Nah, we workin'," said Smith. "But we special ops now. Oorah?"

"Oorah," said the swarm of lance corporals in the room. Bone and Garcia smacked their mugs together.

"We in what Cap'n called hypowar," said Smith when the commotion died down. Slowin' our roll till we gots a place to be. Locals pullin' the duty for now."

Nickels was fine not questioning it. Sleeping in before an OP? Unprecedented. No inspections or ball-polishing busy work meant an easy wait until the other team showed up. But then school was in session.

He grabbed a board and some bread smeared with the red fruit paste. More laughter caught his ear, and he turned to see Stone and Fish joking about something. Funny because Fish was all up in arms last night about Stone's biweekly (or bi-tenday here) PMS. Now they were buds again.

Something was still off with Stone, though. That shade of moonstone marble was stark even compared to Fish and his pale Irish sire genes. *Whatever.* The guy was up all night planting charges under the cover of sniper fire while the rest of them were passed the fuck out.

"Hey, y'all, we still up for Vault watch?" asked Fischer.

That put some color in Gladstone's gills. He spoke up fast, like Mommy just said she was taking him to the arcade *and* buying him a pony. "Hope so. Babysitting the safest place in the city isn't something you kick out of bed."

"Until a dragon sticks his dick in there," said Smith.

"Heh, god's honest truth," said Fischer. He looked around. "Wait, who's on watch right now?"

"Leod and Teague," said Smith.

"Stupid," muttered Stone, fidgeting. Weird that he cared, but he was also correct.

"Now we're trusting the locals?" Nickels asked. "Leod's my boy, but remember that time in Hell we let the Afghans handle Checkpoint Sierra? I forget the road, but it cut over to Garmsir from Dwyer. Bone, you remember. The second we turned our backs, they fucking wandered off into the field like a bunch of dementia patients. Shit was more retarded than a Tickle-Me Elmo in a bathtub of milk."

Food shot out of Fischer's mouth as he laughed. "The hell that even make sense?"

"Exactly. We've been sitting on that vault egg 'round the clock. Why pull us now?" Nickels asked.

Gladstone, practically hyperventilating, cut his eyes ever so fucking carefully back toward the kitchen door where Uumhrat was probably jackin' it into the next batch of dough. Then in a whisper, he said, "I don't trust them."

"Like sayin' you ain't trust a man with his own gold bar," said Smith. "Bark's their problem more than ours."

"If it breaks, we're fucked."

"Point, Stone," Nickels said.

"Hey, we last in line to get fucked. Bark or no Bark, nobody wants none of this. Read?" said Smith.

"Point, Bone," Nickels said.

Gladstone rocketed to his feet and pointed, *fucking pointed*, at the 250-pound, six-foot slab of muscle that somehow grew a head and knew how to brew beer. "You weren't there. You don't know what *they* can do. The Bark is everything. Everything, Sergeant!"

Nickels pushed back from his untouched food board. It was true; Smith missed the action in the wolf cave and the Assembly Hall. What those Black Robes could do was not easy to forget. Stuff of nightmares. Still, Gladstone was out of line.

"Come on, y'all, it's Leod," said Fischer stepping between him and Stone. "He ain't lookin' to lose another arm anytime soon."

"Wait, no. We're cool, Corporal," Gladstone said, hands raised like blades of grass that thought they could stop the mower. Smith's face was unreadable, but his shoulders were telegraphing like turrets on a battleship. "Look, Sergeant, we're on standby. Right?"

"What about it?"

"I'm just saying . . . maybe Fish and I go check it out while we wait."

Holy shit, he won't let it go.

"Twenty minutes, Sergeant. Tops. Security in layers, isn't that what the captain wants?"

It wasn't what Gladstone said, how he said it, the brazen disrespect, or even pushing it too far. It was the eyes. They were a mix of fiending and terror, like a man dying of thirst in that lifeboat about to stick his head in the sea and start gulping.

Before Nickels could get in there and correct the lance corporal, a report rattled the windowpanes. For a moment, no one spoke. Then the first dong of that heavy bell on top of the North Wall hit. Clanging followed.

It was the call to war: General Quarters on a ship; battle stations for Portcullis.

The picnic outside turned into a mad dash. Uumhrat came out of the kitchen and tossed his apron aside, but instead of grabbing that ax like a rerisen titanic badass, he stared at the collection of dirty food boards and spatulas like cleaning them would empty his balls.

"Garcia, Light, up top. Cap'n said he'd toss a flare if we needed," said Smith.

The two bolted up the stairs like it was a race to get topside. For Bulb, it probably was.

"Report to the Vault, Sergeant?" asked Gladstone.

"Negative. We holdin' till we see red smoke or—"

"Holy shit. We. Are. Under. Attack," Gladstone insisted, moving toward the door. He even had the nerve to wave Fischer over. Like the bitch was homo-actual of their little love nest.

Nickels was ten past done with the disrespect, but Smith exploded first. "Stone, sit the fuck down. We HOLDIN."

Gladstone froze, and then after his eyes did some back and forth in their sockets, he dropped into an empty chair. Fischer kept eating, and Smith started pacing in front of that big fireplace to walk off his anger. Nickels gave Gladstone the Stare™. A promise for later.

More thuds broke through the clanging. One sounded like an alley backfire. Soon everyone was looking up at the ceiling.

"Sergeant," yelled Bulb returning from the roof. "It's like meteors or something."

Garcia was right on his six with a less stupid report. "They're throwing rocks. Big ones, yo. One just took out a row of houses in the Sticks."

"What about the cap'n?" asked Smith.

The answer came striding through the front door a few minutes later. Captain Saunders. No red smoke or bullshit signals, just PFC Licht puppying after him hunched like he was ducking fire. Nickels acknowledged them the same as Smith: at the ready with his game face on.

Gladstone, however, popped right up in their business. "Report to the Vault, sir?"

There were no words.

Bone, no, Sergeant Smith, senior NCO of the fucking C-monster who commanded and deserved the same fucking respect they would've given Gunny, rocked his head back like Stone had just taken a swing at him. Then, that big chest beneath the plate carrier swelled as he got ready to use his daddy fuckdown voice.

"Negative," said the captain holding up a hand to silence Smith. Brines would've stomped through that shit and stopped the whole war to correct the problem, but Smith respected the captain's choice. Time was tight. "Enemy ground advance stalled. They're waiting for something, maybe their artillery to soften us up. We're pivoting to support Francisco in eliminating their spotters. Teams of two, Watchmen will take us up to the mountain paths."

About time, breakfast tasted like shit anyway.

"Sir, I been up there plenty," said Fischer. "Reckon Francisco's got the west all angled up, but there are some sweet spots up over Eastside Rise that give us a clear bead on those overlooks."

"Good, you and Nickels. Red smoke if you get in trouble. Since we're light on radios, three bells are recall. We just need to keep them from zeroing the city until the snow picks up, like Benton thinks. It's already coming down half-decent out there."

"We'll get it done, sir," boomed Smith, still fuming. "You all heard him: pair off, and let's git." A silence rippled across the tension in Uumhrat's great room before he added, "Stone, you with me."

Now you're gonna find out why we call him Bone, bitch.

Driving white flakes stung Gladstone's face. The carriage was moving fast, two horses at the front charging at a near-gallop through the deteriorating day. Boulders were crashing down; people dragging wounded through the streets. Anything not caked in snow was self-developing a layer of frost. And on top of it all was Sergeant Smith, itemizing and illustrating with hot breath and spit the C-monster creed of respect, discipline, and duty.

It would be enough to overwhelm Gladstone even without the flaming icicles ripping apart his brain.

Mistrus was angry he was not in the Vault.

While Smith ranted and raved about discipline, tactical positioning, and opportunity as the enemy hesitated, Gladstone had the weight of worlds on his heart and soul. An ocean of rewards was held back by a single, insignificant dam. The Genisans weren't hesitating; they were waiting.

On him.

Gladstone was out of excuses, bare to Mistrus' probing. Hell, he couldn't lie to her even if he wanted to. It was like fighting a warm breeze on the edge of a cliff overlooking all his heart's desires. He wanted to answer her, to please her. His worst pain was not the burning behind his eyes that clenched his teeth and dug his fingernails into the carriage's wooden bench. It was her disappointment.

I will disable the charges, he thought to the void in his head. The captain wanted to blow the second part of the pass. Blow the whole thing, maybe. *Give me time to clear them so they won't threaten the advance.* No answer. She had gone radio silent, hung up on him. He knew the explosives and the landslide weren't important. Only one thing: the Vault. But . . . but he couldn't.

Could he?

The question and the sergeant's speech bought him a moment to reconsider the insane shit going on in his head. Through searing pain and absolute conviction, he forced himself to quiet the urges.

"I won't," he whispered in a weak attempt at defiance. The words were empty, but he needed to say them; otherwise, he might try and think them, and she'd turn every memory he ever had into a raging inferno. Every single second since he was born, bedridden and on fire.

"Won't what, Marine?" asked Smith, probably thinking he was about to round off his discipline speech with a promise and a handshake.

Instead of an answer, Fischer's face flashed between them, and Gladstone's blood boiled a clouding steam into his skull. Mistrus knew him and his haunts too well. Her promises and forgiveness floated in on placid waters. Unlike the world, she was merciful, and he could not betray such beauty.

Tomorrow, he promised her as the horses reared up at the North Gate. *We'll have another shot tomorrow.*

Portcullis was white long before night arrived. Within the North Wall's Ripolis Barbican, what the Corsan Carre called the "command center," Benton listened to the stillness of men waiting in the dark. Fires throughout the city were doused so the living might hide among the sprawling emptiness. The promise of a ceiling and shutters was false against the like of falling rocks, but it made some brave, and so was its worth.

Benton chose to fix upon the roots rather than the leaves.

A crack, the like of a tree limb snapping, echoed through the swirling snows. It was the work of the Corsan Carre stalking the storm for Genisan scouts. Every *crack* was a small victory, a felling of another enemy. As Dalmore had made such known to the men upon the wall, so did the quiet erupt in cheer at each.

"I had a thought," said Sir Rampo when the clamor of the last kill faded. He lounged in a stone chair beside Benton picking at an absurd spread of food. It was summoned to him along with a short table to set upon. "The Obantum Carre need naught of scouts and armies to break down stone walls. Can they not fly over these mountains as they please?"

"As a bird might?" Benton asked.

"As these great rocks do."

"Fear of falling, mayhaps," said Dalmore cleaning a fingernail with the tip of a dagger.

"For some, but others might overcome such in the name of, say, the *Last Army,*" said Sir Rampo.

Benton guessed Ceal would know more, but much of the Powers remained shrouded for sake of none having explored them in such ways. Since Bedinch, the simple sates of war begged fire and batter of the Powers, while craftsmen fancied works of the ground over the skies. An easier discussion was found in Dalmore's assertion of dissuasion. "The Obantum knows little of Galimay's forces," Benton said. "A string of Violets could reside among the Palings, watching the skies. Ceal, too, lying in wait to command the air to flame. Mayhap it is our arrows they fear most."

"Then not soar above us, but the valley to look down at the city they rain rock upon. Doth that not steal the need for watchers and scouts sneaking upon our paths?"

"The storm," said Dalmore. "And their Arts cannot help them see through the Bark."

"What about the Stochal?" asked Sir Rampo with a smile that spoke his mind to be more of winning the argument than uncovering the enemy's designs.

"A hardship to those enthralled by the Quotidian. So says Benton's lady, anyhap," said Dalmore, meeting that smile.

Silence returned to the Ripolis Barbican. Then, Sir Rampo brightened at a new source of amusement. "Can Ceal fly?"

Benton had never seen her fly but change the air to the like of invisible rock and make heavy furniture float upon it he had. So, why not herself too?

"Poor form to ask the lord governor about the happenings of his chambers," said Dalmore.

Sir Rampo stood and dusted the crumbs from his fingers. "Are the great leaders of the Procult beyond reproach? I grow bored awaiting mine salvation by desperate people hoping the fight will outlive this battle. Let us talk of how the Powers might make a man's chambers the thing of dreams. Or nightmares."

"Mayhap we speak on the thefts of ye's Lord Bayliss?" Benton said, also tiring of Sir Rampo's long wait for death.

"Oh?"

"Hides of Vissl: gifts of immeasurable worth from the Corsan Carre. The adornments of Isllor Mortund that aided his usurping of the Bark. Ripped from this city in the time of greatest need. Speak upon that, Sir."

"Sir, ah . . . Lord. Lord Governor, I mean," interrupted the rendered tongue of a Corsan Carre entering the command area. Their style of speaking was distinct from others—such as the Caranuscans or even Dalmore, whose words fell to the Power on occasion—by their lack of familiarity with nobility. That and their many odd sounds that could not be rendered. Benton found it refreshing as he was oft illeased in dealing with the highborn.

"Licht, join us," said Dalmore, another who paid no mind to formality. "Sir Rampo is moments from speaking ill of our Lady Ceal and boasting of his prowess in thievery. After he is slain, his meal is ye's."

Sir Rampo leaned back to show his comfort with such, and Dalmore frowned as some unhappy secret passed betwixt them.

"What word, Licht? How fare ye's brethren in the night?" Benton asked.

The young man, a boy no older than Gol's son Jon had been, twitched as if hoping his captain would stride past and take lead. When it did not happen, he said, "Just got a report that they're withdrawing. The Genisans, I mean."

Dalmore rocked his head back. "From the Dowdale?"

"No, from the mountain road . . . the . . . the Twin Tithes pass. Near the rockslide," he stammered. Rendered language made the disfluency even worse.

"Indeed, back to their beds!" declared Rampo.

"What of these rocks they heave?" asked Benton.

"Still getting reports, but the storm's too thick for direct observation on the launch sites . . . err, to see the magic stuff. Uhh, the Black Robes. But . . . but they've stopped sending people up those back trails." The Corsan Carre smirked and straightened his back. "Guess they don't like getting shot at."

Shot was one of their words. Its meaning varied but centered around the action of their weapons. Benton nodded and walked out upon the brisk observation deck, where his boots sank to the ankle. The night beyond the thick snow, swirling and mixing, was black. He could scarce see five paces ahead. Drawing a deep breath, the ever-colder air tasted of the far western shores.

Hope.

Returning to the warmth and might of the Ripolis Barbican, he announced, "This storm is no trifle. It shall last days."

"That's what Francisco was saying," said Licht. "Ah, sir. Lord, I mean."

"An unexpected ally," mused Dalmore. "Ajid's deadly winter come to save us."

"Indeed," said Benton. "Ring thrice the bells, return all to the walls before they can find their way no longer." He looked out at the impossible boon once more. Winter was what they needed, but how much of it they could endure, he did not know. Could such foil the Last Army long enough for Ceal to reach Oxhold? Or was devious Ajid building their tomb out of ice in the stead of stone?

CHAPTER 13

SOUTHBORN

Is there a . . . chill to the air?" Master Turan asked, working the stiffness out of his gnarled fingers.

The aged always feel changes first, Bela thought. *No matter the enchantments and adornments that might prolong their lives, old's roots run deep.*

"An effect of the Nepitine Artifacts," she said. "Come, see what our patience has yielded."

Patience. It was a word spoken lightly now, but four days prior, Bela's fury was immeasurable. All was to plan except for the linchpin.

The Bark.

Her task of its destruction was foiled and failed. By some favored chance, the Obantum was merciful and agreed to let her try once and only once more. They cared not for the dark forces she would unleash upon the world to see Portcullis fall, only that it be done.

Turan and Bela left the tent and embraced the brisk air beneath heavy clouds. In the distance, the forested crop of foothills beneath the formidable Paling Mountains—what the enemy called the Del—was white as a newborn shearling.

When the Weathermakers of the Heart had learned they could not soon break the storm, they aimed the Nepitine Artifacts against the Vigil Valley itself. They succeeded in piecing the bubble of deadly paradise like a ground well, drawing much of the ill-timed storm away from Portcullis.

"Snow has not fallen in this place for thousands of years," Turan breathed. There was an edge of pride in his voice. He loved knowing the ancient spirit of Taichleach was beaten and bothered not pondering the consequences further. "Still, we stand at the dawn of the fourth day. Let us dispense with this council in haste."

They met the Pandonis Immortalis' directorate at the High Axi'arch's command tent. Bela followed them inside, head bowed within her dark hood. The round pavilion was cluttered with tables, clustered chairs, and the thick scent of stale beer and half-rotted meat. Beyond its purpose as a command post, it seemed to serve as a tavern. That is how Master Turan would later lament it, as his disdain for the High Axi'arch was well known. She, however, knew that eating in the place of labor was the domain of the busy.

High Axi'arch Tiem Cemeho was wearing infused plate so black and clean it showed as a haunting mirror. He stalked to the end of the long table, spun, and slammed his metal fist down. "Twenty more riders were slain at the forest's edge last night by these phantom beasts you name Vissl. A sickness spreads among the Eighth Forelegion scouts who braved the enemy-held mountain trails at great disadvantage. The healers call it White Rot, as fingers grow white then black, which spreads with tendrils seeking the heart. Men are found as if struck by arrows with the force of great hammers. The enemy dares our approach with mountains to throw at us. And we wait and idle as the Obantum Carre plays with rocks!"

The darkness of the hood hid Bela's smile. Turan understood little of Axi'arch Tiem's efforts to wrangle this massive host of Genisans and conscripts into a force that would shake the world. And so, too, did Tiem fail to see the intricacies of Turan's masterful plan—each piece exquisitely crafted and set in place.

"Indeed, tell us of the stones," said Turan turning to her.

Bela stiffened; she had not expected to speak so soon. "Accepted Yerrat has accomplished much. He has refined the contraption: three rings driven by three questions move the cut stone along a beam tilted toward the city. Instead of missing mountains, my spies report four landing within the walls for six rocks thrown."

The High Axi'arch snorted. "Four? We had a hundred catapults landing all their stones within the city walls of Novantum for days. It broke their houses, not their spirits. To my ears, some of those same enemies now stand upon the formidable North Wall that will laugh at stones of every size." He searched the faces of his legion commanders for agreement, but only half-hearted nods came in reply. None dared side against the Obantum.

"Does it ring to your ears that I might wish them to laugh?" asked Turan.

Tiem batted the question away and launched again into the ill-fated attacks from Taichleach's Vissl. The ancient guardians were unkillable but only dangerous if provoked. The Obantum had issued countless warnings and instructions to avoid the bait, the horses. Still, soldiers felt invincible through the strength of this host. Or they wished to prove themselves. Either way, not all could be saved, and small losses would continue until the legions were once more gone from this valley. A useless distraction.

"Enough," said Turan with a wave of his hand. Tiem's eyes widened, perhaps wondering if that command contained any Stochal. Bela could not imagine what it must be like not possessing the Sense. "You speak to me of idle soldiers, and I offer you a deadline. By the day's end, we must stand within the walls of Portcullis, or all is lost."

"I expect you have more of a plan than smashing good men into that wall."

"It is as before."

Tiem threw those arms covered in obsidian black wide. Bela found herself dreaming of how that armor might look upon her. Indeed, thinner plate with more joints to flex, accommodations for her womanhood, and of course, the sides would have to be taken in. But it would be sleek, imposing.

"Calm," said Turan. "We reach desperation, as you say, but we are not heartless. Bela has seen to the threat of their rockslides, and much more will come before we ask you to pry open that city with Genisan blood. Mind you, what we bleed here is less we bleed elsewhere. The moment we win at Portcullis is the moment we win this entire war."

Lady Ceal was perched on a knoll overlooking their rest stop. They were well beyond the mountains, now, into flatland forests where the trees still clung to autumn. She stood at the highest point, ostensibly to get a look around, but Dr. Pat knew it was just to be seen. Those blue robes flapping in the cold wind made her a beacon, almost a tragic figure. *Heavy is the crown* and all that shit.

"I think something about her Long Voice call bothered her," said Micky, eager to hump it up that hill like a dog after its master. *Gee, is Lady Ceal replacing me as Micky's favorite?* Dr. Pat dared not dream of such good fortune.

Still, up they went.

Once they reached the top, it was clear the knoll did little to improve the view. Instead of seeing the tops of trees from below, it was from slightly above. What became apparent was that the warm shafts of sunlight pouring through the canopy were a tease. A new front was racing in from the south. Billowing white at the head, dragging night behind.

"Looks like more cover for Portcullis," chirped Micky.

Ceal just stared, silent.

Dr. Pat folded her arms, refusing to be made uncomfortable or play whatever this morning's outrage game might be. "Captain Rath is back from . . . um, that village we spotted."

"Yordel," said Micky.

Oh, right. Yordel. Memorable because it was so much different than the last ten villages. Not. "From what I could see, they didn't get more than a cart of last-pick provisions."

"They totally gave us their garbage truck. Nom nom!" giggled Micky.

Ceal finally moved. "The Anticult's strength in these lands is greater than expected. A trouble."

"It feels like we're the invaders," said Dr. Pat. Just like Hudud and every foreign assignment. Nothing new.

"Mayhap we are," Ceal spun and started in with her princess-cut emerald witch eyes. "We hath but a day before we reach Oxhold. I fear the enemy knows this and mayhap the fullness of our plans despite the many deceptions we hath laid. We must make haste."

Haste? They'd been hauling ass through the snow, sleet, and rain for days. Any faster, and there'd be no one left. Still, they *had* made up for lost time. "Most of our people can't—"

"She's not talking about miles per hour," whispered Micky.

. . . once the walking piles of rags begin to die off.

The five-year-old living inside Dr. Pat's head, preserved and protected for all time, knocked on her art-covered door and asked, *Can I tell her she's stupid?*

Dr. Pat would love nothing more. There was a lot she didn't understand about this world, its people, and magic. But she knew she would never respond well to wizard school, even if Ceal thought she had some sort of aptitude. Put simply, it required a murderous dictator's level of arrogance.

Also, a level of belief that didn't pass the intelligence check.

The whole deal was also too artsy. *Use the flow, feel the flow, know the flow.* It gave Dr. Pat cramps just thinking about it, which was probably something women here could just wish away, too. *Great, but sorry I didn't grow up speaking bullshit. Learning it as a second language will take longer than five days.*

Ceal turned back to the darkening horizon. "We are closer than ye think, *Pat.*"

Dr. Pat didn't let that get to her. Plenty of people called her by her first name. Patients, especially children. Her friends. It's not like she called Ceal *lady*. Totally fine.

"Okay, that one was lame," Micky half-whispered to Ceal. "Pat isn't entitled enough. I could try slapping her ass, but it needs to come from within, right?"

Ceal nodded.

Dammit, we're talking about leaving, and they're still trying to cattle-prod me into reading a letter or some shit. Dr. Pat was tempted to let her mind run wild, and maybe something would happen, but getting people in gear was the priority. This was precisely about miles per hour, and half their walkers were days past dead on their feet.

"Dear, tell me of this storm."

Earth Science, if that even applied here, was not Dr. Pat's strong suit. Even if she wanted to impress Ceal with her advanced scientific knowledge, she wasn't a dictionary of obscure cloud types. Dr. Pat knew the big ones charging north were cumulonimbus, but that was it. The evil wash of swirling black behind it was something else. Something . . . her mind blanked like it was getting ready to steal her from wakefulness.

The Primal.

"Dangerous," she whispered.

Ceal rubbed her forearms. "Interesting. Aye, a Storm of the South hath risen. It is a most . . . unnatural creation. I hath seen only four in mine days."

Dr. Pat shook her head. Yes, it was dangerous; it didn't take a shaman to peg that one. "Then we need to find shelter until it passes."

Ceal glanced down at the sprawling camp. Smoke was rising among the trees bringing the smells of boiling porridge and spitting fats. Considering everyone, even Ceal, and the Watchmen, were only getting about 500 calories per meal, it smelled fucking delicious.

"No," she said. "Our time is nigh. The enemy wields their Powers in desperation to break Portcullis. In doing so, they hath invoked the wrath of this storm to the peril of us all. We must ride."

———

Bela Rastaw, Moderator of the Fist, Direct Adjunct to Master Turan Rilseri, and Commander of the Stretched Guard, stood with her troops. She was not raised high on a wooden platform, but among them. Close enough to touch.

Cohort Captain Ibraham Tolly finished his walk through the ranks. They were assembled by tens into their blocks, over 500 strong in Redstone-crusted dark plate. Helms raised, they were stiff and eager, but many eyes wandered to the distance where trumpets blew, and legions marched.

"Mistrus," regarded Captain Ibraham. "They be ready. Sharp steel and strong backs for all. Be thinkin' we go early or late in the day?"

Bela imagined waiting in these packed blocks for a war that failed to come each day was agonizing. Its own eternity beyond scale. She, however, was the patient predator, every passing minute driving more lust and excitement into the impending pounce. Today was the thrill built upon that of yesterday.

It was almost more than she could bear.

She brushed the plain silver band around her thumb with her fingertips. *Shall I be heard by the farthest of my soldiers?* "Stretched Guard," she began, voice loud as if she were shouting within a cave, "our long march from the sea is ended!"

The ranks shifted, metal clanking and heads nodding.

"For far longer than the simple measure of years, we have fought untold battles across lands and waters fraught with danger. Away from our homes and families, our victories and defeats come at greater costs. But we welcome this burden, for we are the world's shield. And as we stand upon this hallowed ground, know that our once invincible enemy now cowers in the last of their strongholds."

"What of the Corsan Carre?" interrupted a voice spoiling the mood.

Bela calmed her urges. Such disrespect was a weed ready to seed. Oh, how she loved to watch a fine wilting, but it was the wrong occasion for an example. And it was a fair question worthy of the Quotidian's ears. "Hear me! As your brethren march up the mountain pass to face the enemy's place of greatest strength, I tell you . . . the Corsan Carre are revealed!"

As one, the entire cohort nearly sucked the breath out of the valley. This was why Master Turan and the others had decided to keep Isllor's reports a secret. Fear. No matter the might, a fly could still make a horse jump.

"They are men," she continued. "From a world beyond the Voidrock." She might have said *another land*, hinting at one of Scianas' famed landmasses that eluded discovery. But the old tales of Voidrock sweeping people away to fantastic realms had breathed new life around campfires here in the Vigil Valley. And it was the truth. "I know this because the Obantum Carre has been there. Is there! The Three are our vanguard, the strongest of us in defiance of prophecy. In time, they shall destroy the Corsan Carre world, forever protecting ours."

"I 'eard some got 'ere."

Another! She wanted to make this one writhe, tear him from the glory of an ancient prophecy fulfilled.

"Yes," she allowed. "A ten of their kind cowers behind the enemy's great wall." Grumbles rose from the mass of metal now. "Hear me. They are men! Weak to steel and bereft of the Powers." She paused, letting those thoughts settle. Then she screamed, "They are trophies!" And with that, every man's vision of himself became epic. Each was a legend, their hands slaying the storied demons from their childhoods. Each was the Herald—the stopper of the Second Stochasm.

She dared not mention their actual prey was protected by more than mere walls and metal.

Captain Ibraham started a cheer the men fast took to. Song rose as the forward legions marched and boulders whooshed into battle against the barrier of winter peaks in the distance.

Bela stepped back, allowing the soldiers to have their moment. Suddenly, she felt a presence at her side. Her skin tingled, heart throbbed, and body quivered with excitement, fear, lust, admiration, and aching need. It was a hunger for power. His power.

"I would have burned the first insolent and made the second wear his smoldering armor," spoke Master Turan's grave voice.

"They have felt my might, fear to even look upon my eyes. But so do I wish them to know my compassion."

"Bah," he swatted. "For what purpose?"

"It harrows them, never knowing whether the parting of my lips will bring agony or pleasure."

Turan smiled, a rarity. "Walk with me." Nearby, Yerrat's boulder thrower heaved. Whoosh!

"Perhaps it is our fortune that a boulder will strike the Bark," she said as they wormed through the 15th Legion's tents.

"The Tel'racs was sent for more than just charting the city, dear. He opportuned to test the Bark's vault and found it quite sturdy. I think one boulder, no matter the size, will not suffice."

"A pity." She took a quick breath, which he caught with a raised eyebrow, before admitting the next part. "Our time is shorter than the High Axi'arch knows. Do you Sense what lies beyond those mountains?"

"A counterstroke to the Nepitine interference. Indeed, it will matter little."

So, he is *aware of the consequences of disrupting Taichleach's Vigil.* Still, knowing and then seeing were incomparable. This blasted storm was no trifle. "We may have to wait for the legions to . . ."

Turan spun and grabbed her arm. Her skin burned and chilled; her tongue popped at the potent taste of his mastery. He was a living legend striding among the common as—

"You must not fail!"

"As the cut tree strikes the ground, so shall I claim victory," she hissed back. Her arm bristled with a torrent of Power, and approval returned to his aged face.

"Come, I have something for you," he said. They entered his tent, and he led her to a gilded chest. Within were furs of beasts gathered from across the world, whites and blacks, supple leathers, and soft finery that she was surprised to see accommodating such a . . . frugal man. "To defeat the Corsan Carre, you must face Isllor's old enemy."

"Ceal," she whispered, her doubt returning. So too, with the horse and the fly, part of her respected the legends.

"You cannot over-prepare for her. She is the Origin, the first to Retether."

"Isllor beat her, and I am greater than he."

"Isllor won battles; she won the war. He lies dead."

"Then I shall bring Yerrat and Estir and our combined might . . ." she began.

"They cannot help you," he said with *another* smile. Before she could ask, he pressed something into her hand.

Something... Powerful.

She flushed as her being came to life, radiant and searing. The world begged for the whisper of command to melt at her feet. The torrent was endless, limitless. She felt dizzy, wonderous.

"What..." she tried to ask, enraptured.

"One of our most precious artifacts. It is much unlike your rings and conquests from these lands. Adapt to it fast; I fear you will need it to face her."

Face who? Ceal? In that moment, Bela was sure she could reach up and tear Bergreth's Lamp from the skies.

Dr. Pat found Captain Rath with Sergeant Orrugant in a clearing conducting what they called Morning Briefing. It had become a routine for them to review the epic "military strategy" and "security protocols" guiding and securing the convoy. Really, it was a rundown of quartermaster, casualty, and scouting reports.

And loathing.

The evacuation effort was in worse shape than anyone expected. It wasn't orderly or secure. More like a beached whale trying to convulse its way back to the water, hemorrhaging a trail of blood and organs the whole way. If Scianas had any sort of functioning human rights organization, the whole bunch of them would be wanted criminals. Dr. Pat, too, it now seemed.

"Doc," acknowledged Buontempo stifling a yawn. Since Rath went with the Watchmen to beg for supplies from Yordel, Buontempo probably doubled up on the early shift. That, or he was bored from whatever monologue Rath was reciting.

"Milady," said Sergeant Orrugant.

Rath stopped talking and turned, surprised to see her. "Hey, Dr. Pat. No joy from Yordel if that's what you're—"

"We've got problems," she said with a chin thrust up at the dark horizon.

"Oh yeah, the storm. We're on it. Tight formations and making sure people tarp and double lash everything. Same shit, different—"

"Ceal says it'll be bad."

That got Orrugant's attention, and he cut his eyes to the roiling clouds and rustling treetops. Rath just shrugged as most Marines would. Orders were to go through, so that's what would happen. Discussing or thinking about the danger was counterproductive.

"How bad?" asked Buontempo for everyone like he was part of the discussion and not just Captain Rath's attaché. He was one of the good ones, having retained a degree of cerebral wit after Marine Corps' brainwashing into an obedient killing machine. His jokes were also tasteful, which Dr. Pat appreciated.

"Bad. Ceal called it a south storm."

Orrugant swallowed hard. "She . . . she said 'twas Southron? Naught a trick of rendered words to mine ears?"

"Her words," said Dr. Pat.

"This like a lake-effect thing or Nor'easter or whatnot?" asked Rath, squinting into the distance.

"A blizzard?" asked Buontempo.

"Nay, lad," said Orrugant. "A storm of anger, driven by Powers the likes none know for truth."

"Well, it's heading north. Maybe it'll take its anger out on the Genisans," said Rath.

"'Twill go through us, afore," said Orrugant.

Rath brightened like a kid who just found out school was canceled because of snow. "Wait, this is good, right?"

No one answered.

"Hear me out. I can't tell you how many times our squadron got actionable intel on a target only to get grounded on account of bad weather." It made sense to Dr. Pat. Dad, a career naval officer, had bitched about the sky shitting on an otherwise solid operation more than once. More so in recent years when he was on the carriers.

"Insurgents lived and died by the weather report because they knew exactly what conditions would shut us down," Rath continued. "So, screw this bullshit deadline and trying to drive these people through a frozen monsoon. We hunker down, survive the wrath, and bail while they're all getting pounded to hell up north. If it lives up to the hype, this storm buys us days, maybe weeks."

It made sense, but only in a world that made sense. "Ceal thinks the race is on." Dr. Pat said. "Something about the Black Robes not being stopped by weather. She's already ordered her horses hitched up. We've got to go."

"I shall order the camp struck," said Orrugant waving over one of his subordinates.

"No." She held up a hand, feeling the tug of Ceal's puppeteer strings. "Rath's right. Everyone else needs to hunker down to have any chance of surviving." The words hurt, but it was the right decision.

Orrugant stopped, sporting a mix of confusion and anger. "These people no follow me," he said. "Lady Ceal and the Corsan Carre kept their frozen feet trudging through snow and muck these yesterdays. Ye leave, they follow. Many die."

Dr. Pat looked to Captain Rath for that USMC, forward-and-forget attitude, but from the moment she mentioned Ceal's decision, he was on mute. *You on the take too?* she wanted to scream. Maybe if she screamed loud enough, she could touch the skies again. That would at least get the conversation moving.

A warm hand gripped her wrist. It should've startled her, just like the other five thousand times Micky had snuck up on her, but this was different. It was comforting. She turned and found a little girl at her side. Ann.

Oh, come on. Do not fuck with me like this!

"Y . . . ye are leaving?" Ann asked.

Professional and dispassionate; this needs to happen. "Yes."

"To go where?"

She knelt. "To bring back help."

Ann's eyes glistened as she stammered, "But . . . but ye are the help."

If truths stung, those words were a mile of barbed wire pulled through Dr. Pat's beating heart. Pure innocence recognizing everything she ever wanted to be to anyone and everything.

I'll see yer ass in the morning.

Fuck! Dr. Pat stood. *Not now. Get out of my head, Mike!*

"Lass," said Orrugant. "Back to ye's parents. We be keeping everyone safe, Dr. Pat and yeself too."

Ann stared at her for a moment. A faint smile crossed her lips, and she whispered, "Heroes are real." Then that little warm hand was gone.

"Hey. I got an idea," said Buontempo bringing the meeting back into focus and reminding them that time was wasting. "Why don't I hang back?"

"Negative," said Captain Rath.

"Think about it, sir. What value do I add to a carriage race through the back roads?" he nodded to his slung rifle. "I like to think I'm a raging badass who can hold off a thousand purple-headed warriors at the last stand of all light in the universe, but I'm a radio operator with a rifle. If I stay here, though, I'm the figurehead Orrugant needs to keep people in line. Then maybe no one flips cannibal overnight, and there's still something worth saving when you get back. Right?"

Saunders would've devised a Plan C, but Rath just nodded and said, "Okay."

CHAPTER 14

UXO

"Fine morn for a battle," called Sir Rampo from the observation deck. He gave his polished white armor a tug as the early light showered it in peachy cream and the illusion of warmth.

Saunders ignored the display as Lieutenant Maon finished his damage assessment of the Sticks. "Most fires are doused; Wesdip Street is ash to Old Towne Hall. Ten dead, thirty-two taken to Wisewoman Alena."

"Okay, pull the fire control teams and get everyone to the north ward shelters. Boulders are coming in heavy," Saunders said.

Dalmore was technically in charge of the Watch, but Saunders had radios and was getting information faster. With the skies cleared, the enemy had dramatically refined their targeting process. They scored two hits on the ruined Provincial Post somehow sparing the clinic in its depths. Another landed close to Uumhrat's, but the mountainous innkeeper refused to abandon the place. Saunders didn't understand it but respected the decision.

"Sir," said PFC Licht returning from topside observation. "Got white smoke from Francisco's position. Enemy on the move."

Things were happening fast. It was day five for the evacuation convoy, and damn if the enemy didn't somehow sense a deadline.

You're just paranoid. They're moving on the weather window, Saunders told himself. The white-out conditions of the past week ended with a pelting, tropical rain before vanishing overnight. From the haunting darkness swallowing mountains to the south, another storm was on the way. And the enemy was aware.

Distant horn blasts reached NWCC. *Perfect.*

The main streets in Portcullis were de-iced and clear due to raw manpower and that melting downpour, but the mountain road leading to the

Doormat was snowshoes only. Sending columns up was a logistical nightmare that no sane commander would authorize. But there was no underestimating impatience in war, and the enemy had no idea about the second, bigger landslide. Not to mention the surprises he and Examiner Creed had planned. "Who's on the Vault?"

"Gladstone and Fischer just started their watch."

"Great, get me Stone."

"Let them come, says I," said Benton, mailed fists at his side. He was tense. Given the history and campfire stories about some mercenary company he was once part of, he should've been a little more seasoned. Then again, it was Benton. Legend bigger than the man and all that. Except when he got ahold of a sword and a reason.

Then it was fucking unbelievable.

"We just need one more day," Saunders said as Licht passed the mic. "Let's see how they like a couple hundred tons of rock."

The cliffside breeze smelled clean.

Francisco always thought a heavy snow pulling all the crap out of the air was the best part of winter. Although particulate pollution was more applicable back home than here. Second place was the quiet, a world hosed down with R-60 spray insulation that could make a city feel empty as the woods.

Third was a day like this. Clear skies and white floors. It was still cold, below freezing, but the sun felt good on his back. Warm, but not melting everything yet. It was the perfect equilibrium for lying in the snow. Just a nice day.

Except . . .

Horns blasted below as a black ramrod of armored infantry pushed up the Twin Tithes. Out front was what registered to Francisco's brain as mammoths. Brown, furry elephants with about zero point one fucks to give about two feet of snow. Pairs were dragging roller barges compacting everything for follow-on cavalry and banners. Behind that, the heavy-armored troops were basically walking.

The columns stretched into the frosted Del and beyond. It was just a trickle draining from the encampments in the valley, but that much marching metal armor could intimidate a 70-ton Abrams tank. To Francisco, high above on a windswept outcropping, they resembled ants coming for the sugar bowl.

His Barrett XM500 "Bullpup" rested on its bipod beside him. The mean piece of black metal looked great contrasted against the snow versus the Genisan horde below. Sleek with space-age angles and a barrel so short it could fit in a carry-on, it still had the figure of an unfired virgin after all these years. Francisco wasn't sentimental, but his thoughts drifted back to Mina Bazar and the agonizing decision to bring it. A long barrel would've been fine in the fight, and there were plenty of carbines to go around. But something in the zero-dark sea breeze that fateful morning shut down the concept of standard issue.

He glassed the Genisans again through the spotter. Since Captain Saunders had decided to split him and Fischer up, he couldn't scout targets and pin a reticle simultaneously. Likewise, the two Watchmen—Nosb and Earnan from the Watch's Ranging Detachment—covering his six weren't up to speed on the tripoded M151 or how to talk the shot.

Another one-man show.

It didn't matter. Once Francisco made a Black Robe, he could have the gun lined up in seconds. What he really wanted was to catch one in the captain's trap. So far, it was just knuckle-dragging regulars.

And those mammoths. Nickels would love hearing about them. The guy was hell-bent on naming every new plant, animal, and mineral they came across with screwed-up names to mess with future scientists writing textbooks on discovering an alien planet.

The lead element entered the landslide kill box.

"Ssst," Francisco said, sending Nosb to cover. They were high enough to be beyond safe distance, but Francisco had difficulty fully trusting 20-year-old explosives experts.

Earnan pulled out a bow and moved toward the southern face. He nocked an arrow with an M18 "lime" taped to the end. It wouldn't fly straight for shit, but even if it blew up in their faces, the city would see green smoke and hit the button. Faster than Long Voice, and they couldn't talk back.

Francisco waited until all the mammoths and cavalry were in the kill box before motioning for Earnan to yank the pin and loose. There were thousands of eyes waiting for their signal. After a short delay in relaying the signal to Gladstone, it'd be a stone avalanche from hell.

And this time, it would be more than just a blocked road. Bodies. Hundreds of them, by the look of it.

The billowing green arrow launched, and Francisco tucked into the cold rock. He also ensured a bedding of brush was beneath him to dampen the explosive shockwave riding up through the stone.

A full minute passed before he raised his head. No mountain-shaking blast. Daring a peek through the scope, he couldn't help but question his foolproof flaring arrow plan. That or Gladstone fat-fingering the detonator. The mammoths were almost past the kill box. He had Earnan fire another.

This time, Francisco watched it go. No missing that unless the city was asleep.

Another minute of waiting knifed little thrill shivers into the small of his back. Then the third minute passed, a fucking lifetime when the ol' infantry faucet was left open.

"Ye wants I should loose another?" asked Earnan.

Francisco stood. Killing those mammoths wasn't happening now. Burning another precious flare might wake someone up, but he suspected the malfunction was deeper. Part of him wanted to peg that Vault with a .50 caliber bullet as a gentle reminder that everyone had one fucking job to do and that the point of failure was now his personal project.

Instead, he said, "Mission's over. Need to let command know they've got incoming. A fuckload of incoming."

With the sun cresting Portcullis, its crown of proud mountains shined golden. Mighty and towering, the stone city lorded over the expansive Dowdale Valley and barred the way south to Galimay as it always had.

But its time was ending.

A stiff wind kicked up, whisking away the last illusion of warmth. Emptiness occupied its homes, and echoes replaced the liveliness of its streets. Only a thin line of men remained to deter the enemy from occupation. After four days of blizzards, burdens, and boulders, more than a few heads turned toward the South Gate.

Toward escape.

Saunders refused to condone it but wasn't without empathy. All war was terror; be scary or be scared. There was no denying the intimidation factor of their microscopic force facing down an enemy who could befriend dragons and had beaten most of the planet in war. But it wasn't until shit started to go wrong that it all went to hell.

"I'm sorry, sir, it's FUBAR. Remote's battery died," came the reply.

Saunders ground his teeth. Mike would've dropped the mic, marched down to the Vault, and evacuated the stupidity right out of Gladstone's skull. Every second that second rockslide didn't happen meant more troops through the goalposts. The hope of having Leod's cavalry sweep out and scoop up prisoners trapped on this side was going down like a stroke victim on a ladder. A stream of expletives detailing the proper protocol for battery replacement boiled up on the tip of Saunders' tongue, but all that made it out was: "Fucking fix it!"

Gladstone was once a good Marine, part of an invaluable combat demolitions unit on loan from Captain Anderson, CO of Bravo Company. But something happened after Operation *Sea Monster*. Maybe the same thing happened to everyone, but the others, even Cpl Nickels, were still locked on and capable of executing their duties. Gladstone was waffling between skittish and distant to exaggerated in his interests and self-guided.

Self-guided was the worst. A Marine who couldn't follow orders was like an extra arm you couldn't control. One minute it was patting you on the back; the next it was trying to rip your dick off.

Gladstone needs to be benched. Unreliable at best.

Saunders realized the NWCC was silent, eyes on him like he'd just knocked over the glass filled with all their hopes and dreams. Well, except Sir Rampo. He was a dog at the window waiting for his next meal. Still, Plan 4A had failed spectacularly through a timeless and intractable enemy: incompetence.

"Timetable's moved up; we're still nominal," Saunders said. Without further discussion, he joined Sir Rampo on the walk-out portion of the observation deck.

The air was wet with fresh melt as sunlight spilled into the canyon. Sweet woodsmoke hit his nose from the fire baskets on the lower tiers still hidden in shadows. Long icicles were already forming on the mesh drop-awning above, a promise that every drop of water would eventually find a nice quiet place and turn to ice.

Crampons. Hell, ice cleats would be a game-changer, came the idle thought. The walkways were shoveled, but his boots were gripping like fresh-waxed skis.

Immaculate, white-armored Rampo was more intent on the skid mark below—the Doormat—that had somehow melted off its snow without a touch of sunlight. "A shame we shall not meet their host in the muck," he said. "I should like to see a clash among the graves of their fellows. Mayhaps grappling and goring with the bones of their kin, flush with the battle fever."

"Because that would mean we'd be fielding a force capable of a stand-up fight?" Saunders asked.

Rampo turned. "Nay. The fever brings out the truth of a man. Farmers and noblemen alike made wild and vicious. Hands to claws, teeth to snouts."

"Dicks hard. Yeah, it's a breed."

Laughter. Weird coming from Bayliss' deranged knight, but it sounded genuine. "Aye, some find their pleasure," he said. "But oft it follows them home and whispers in the quiet. A memory calling like a hunger growing. In time, it consumes them." He pointed over the edge. "I wish them consumed. If not here, then later.

Traumatize the enemy by mudwrestling in a field of corpses bubbling up from shallow graves?

"Copy."

Saunders turned to go back inside. Maybe Benton had a different perspective.

Before he could take a step, movement caught his eye from the western cliffs above. Binocs up, he saw Francisco's team slinking through the back trails, probably on mission to find out what malfunctioned. Gladstone's failure shot back to the forefront, but before Saunders could act on that rush of rage, Rampo grunted and pointed over the edge.

The enemy.

The first columns of horse and heavyweight infantry were entering the canyon. Oozing was a better word to describe their movement. For some reason, Saunders had envisioned them charging in, grabbing ground and cover. But maybe this was how it was.

As if commanded to *sic* by Rampo's finger, Benton rushed out of the NWCC and jumped onto the crenulations at the deck's edge. In an instant, nothing was stopping a quick breeze from puffing the lord governor into an eight-story swan dive.

"Mayhap the morrow will inspire ye's steps to quicken!" he shouted.

Saunders was a little surprised the Procult hero's voice didn't somehow thunder across the battlefield. No, just a guy yelling. "They're just forming up," he offered, approaching slowly.

"Nay, I hath met these foes oft afore, and their vigor is well known. To dally within our sight is their peril!"

"What else would they do?" The cliffs rang with a familiar crack. Another boulder, but it was old news now. Most of the city was empty, and the wall had taken a few hits without a single fucking scratch. Unless it struck a bullseye on the top, there wasn't much to do but flinch.

Which would be bad for Benton.

"I should expect them," Benton said, taking a breath, "to seize the wall's base and burrow. Build their nests and bores so they might pierce stone and iron in peace."

"Tactics change," Saunders said. It was too early to tell if this was a real delay or Benton blowing a relay, but any delay was good. Right? "Come back inside, and let's figure it out."

Benton looked at his feet as if realizing his precarious perch but spun on his heel as if surrounded by flat, firm sea-level ground. The man was a damned cat but tell that to the anxiety. Saunders didn't have a fear of heights, but watching someone else's carelessness was nerve-wracking. Finally, Benton hopped down.

Horns sounded as the columns fanned out where the terrain widened into those brownish fields. Still, no hurry to advance. They respected the elevated position and wanted numbers before slapping up against this bitch.

Dammit, we need to crimp that hose.

Saunders glanced at PFC Licht back inside for an update on the goddamned battery problem, but all he got was a head shake. It was enough to make him scream, but he needed to stay cooler than Benton.

"For what demon do ye wait?" Benton shouted again.

Crazy, but he did have a point. Troops massing pointed to a green light for direct action; they had the numbers. But this felt hauntingly more like stacking a chessboard.

By the time Francisco got his Watchmen escort reassigned and climbed up to the NWCC, the enemy had done little more than deepen their ranks at the canyon's entrance. There were undoubtedly a few cherry targets in sniper rifle range, but that was a reserve option. Also, Fischer was the only redundancy Saunders had in case Gladstone lost another pack of unbelievably precious batteries or the correct protocol for not pissing on his hands.

Not now; Gladstone gets reamed later.

"Report," said Saunders as Francisco managed to darken the NWCC's already dark mood.

Cold eyes touched on the PFC's radio before meeting his. "No detonation, UXO. Road remains open, enemy movement unmitigated. Glassed scout formations moving in force to secure the trails. Got a few claymores planted up there. Once they go boom, the backstop is Herms' people at the first checkpoint."

Dux Herms turned away from the marshaling battlefield and said, "They will hold."

Saunders rested his hand on the hilt of his sword as he'd seen other medieval heroic figures do and nodded. It seemed to be well received.

"We give up on blowing the road, sir?" asked Francisco.

It was a respectful question from a dangerous man. Francisco was what Saunders would consider a friend, but the emotional connection did not blind the guy to fuckups. *Maybe now is later, after all.* "PFC, get me Gladstone again," Saunders said without breaking eye contact with Francisco. Battery replacement should have taken five minutes with time left over for a ten-minute nap. Something else was up.

"Fish on for you, sir. Stone's busy with the remote."

Saunders wanted to crush the mic in his hand, wishing Mike were down there instead of Fischer. *Now is not the goddamned time to be misinterpreting orders.* "Fischer, put the lance corporal on. Now!"

"Sir," the radio crackled with a voice hesitating like a virgin twerking on Broadway. "He says he just needs a few more minutes. Got the casing all pried off and—"

"I'll go," said Francisco.

"Stand fast," Saunders said. The enemy wasn't hesitating or forming up for a parade out there. They were waiting on something big, a Black Robe or twenty that would only be susceptible to either discrete or continuous rates of fire. There wasn't anyone to spare except . . . He clicked the mic. "I'm sending PFC Licht to relieve him. Gladstone is to report to the NWCC immediately."

Silence for a lot longer than it should've been. "Roger that, sir. Gladstone will wait for—"

"Negative, send him now! Licht's on the move. Out." He turned to the PFC, who almost looked relieved to be heading rearward. "Go."

Sir Rampo laughed, rattling his plate armor, and said, "As mites bicker. Stung, unstung, the Last Army comes. I take mine leave for the east battlements. Summon us if ye find yeselves overwhelmed."

Saunders ignored the ego and looked to the enemy formations for a distraction. They were larger in scale than anything he'd seen so far and different from medieval war movies. Absent were the lumbering siege engines and massing cavalry. The few mounted units were on the flanks as if sidelined. Black and gray banners flew but like one for every few groups instead of fluttering crops. There also weren't any what he'd consider fodder—poorly equipped infantry conscripted to soak defender munitions. It was just solid rows of mean metal.

Their maneuvers were the most impressive part. Like flocks of predators air dancing, every vector was chosen for maximum efficiency and zero entanglements to achieve position. Their deployment was either planned to the *T,* or their command and control were operating at a supernatural level. Bare minimum, it reinforced the fact that they were a disciplined and determined fighting force.

That made Benton's unease at their shift in tactics even more troubling.

Intent was everything in combat. After that, the strategies and executions themselves were generally unsurprising. As XO of the combat instructor battalion during a tactical decision game at The Basic School had put it, "At any given time, there are a finite number of moves in chess. It's easy to play a few moves ahead, but exponentially harder the farther out you go." He raised a finger at that. "Unless you know what your enemy wants. Masters understand the game as a series of goals, which forces opponents into predictable patterns. Let me restate that: your enemy's objectives are opportunity choke points. If I know you'll knock on every door in the neighborhood, I know how to wreck your day with minimal resources." Everyone nodded at that. None of them were seasoned back then, but everyone had a

TV. "Know your enemy; it's a strategy old as time and forgotten just as often. Know what they want. That's the hard part. That's your mission."

In this specific and unique case, the situation was reversed. Saunders knew exactly what the enemy wanted but had no idea what all the pieces on the board could do. It was one of those things Sun Tzu didn't bother covering because understanding battlefield implements was *that* elementary. If Saunders ever got home, he might look up Major Eric Almasy and tell him there were always exceptions. For now, the rest of the advice rang loud.

"Sir, we dug in," came a thick voice as Sergeant Smith entered the fortified command post.

"You mean Nickels didn't drop the batteries?" spat Francisco. Then, remembering himself, he said, "Sorry, sir."

"Somethin' I should know about, sir?" said Smith puffing his chest out.

"It's being handled. Your team packed up, ready to exfil if we go bright?"

Benton raised an eyebrow, maybe wondering if the translation of "bright" was incorrect. *Yeah, buddy, we aren't talking about the oil lamps.*

"One hundred and ten percent online, sir," said Smith. "Hopin' we get to see this place weather a beating first, though."

"Amen," said Francisco thumping a fist against the stone.

Saunders agreed. He wanted to win, he wanted to survive, but he also wanted to see a standup fight. See the wall take the hit it was built for, like when it shook off those fucking boulders. That was amazing.

It wasn't hard to imagine what stratagems the enemy might employ to get around a fixed position considering the Marine Corps doctrine was literally mobility. Still, the engineers, or wizard architects, of Galimay had given treatment to an enemy with vertical leverage and ranged superiority. Portcullis' walls were crenulated to protect against direct fire and honeycombed with interior spaces to allow fighters to take cover as the situation demanded. The towers were all capped with bunker-like shelters for observation and retaliation.

Then there was the NWCC sitting high and reinforced with thicker stone, steelworks, and doors, meaning an invader would need to bring a warrant along with that knock. All in all, it was the ultimate battlefield penthouse.

"Good," said Saunders without turning away from the forces arrayed in the distance. Benton was right; the enemy was exposing themselves for no perceivable advantage. A mad dash at the wall with that many troops would just result in a logjam and a shooting gallery.

"Got any last orders, sir?"

Saunders considered following Smith back to the Marine fireteam handling the retail side and giving them one of his famous—infamous—pep talks. But they'd been through this already over four days of constant readiness and red lights. Squeezing another drop of *oorah* wouldn't happen without high-velocity ammunition going loud.

"Negative; let's keep it professional today. The second we get the all-clear from Captain Rath, Plan 4B goes live. They compromise us before that, it's Plan C."

Plan 4B was inevitable. Evacuation. But Smith nodded solemnly at Plan C before heading back down to Tier Three. Probably because it represented warfare at its finest. Unfiltered and unquestioning. It was business upfront and knowing exactly where and when not to be when things *go bright* in the back.

"Smite this fell disquiet," said Benton pointing to one of the Caranuscan conscripts manning the pulleys. Twenty ropes connected the NWCC to the various ramparts. Simple binary commands authorized fire, movement, and city-wide alert bells. "Remind them of our reach. Loose!"

So much for a delay.

The Genisan army uncorked like it had Taco Bell for breakfast.

Smith got back to his post in time to find Jersey up Bulb's ass. On top of the kid, chewing him out probably because he had jack shit else to do but wait for his goddamned orders. *Fuck is it with people today?*

Before Smith could assert dominance, A horn blew high up on the wall above, and a voice echoed through the canyon. "LOOSE!"

Suddenly, the neat formations downrange were scrambling beneath a pelting of brown rice.

"Whoa," said Garcia coming up from deeper within the wall where the Watch had a whole cafeteria set up for the troops. Hull said this thing was designed to staff thousands. *Unreal.* "Those arrows got some hang time."

"You are lucky I find that shit more interesting than you, *Bulb*," said Jersey admiring the display. Pilots like Captain Rath got to see devastation like this on their screens, but even that was more bang and smoke than blood and writhing. For Smith on the ground, rifle in hand, everything was frantic snapshots—super zoomed in and populated by bodies between takes. Violent, but something to survive, not watch. Not like this.

The enemy blocks looked like black sugar cubes left out in the rain. Half-dissolved with little bits flying off askew, sucked into the mud. Smith pulled his binocs to his eyes. Red mud.

Suddenly, those dissolving sugar cubes were a flood of molasses.

Incoming.

"Dawgs, this is it," Smith shouted, heart pounding. Chainmail jangled as the Watchmen moved through the stone arches and staffed the shutters. Three stories up, arrows were their only real problem and the wall was made to batten down at the drop of a hat.

"Imagine a ma-deuce for each of us," said Nickels grabbing the parallel grips on an invisible M2 .50 caliber machine gun. "Bullets would be doin' dudes three, four at a time."

"Getting me moist, Corp," said Garcia.

"Hey, we done playin'. GIT!" Smith shouted. The jokers snapped to and took their positions. The plan called for them to be spread out in case something big hit. But Smith kept everyone close enough to catch hand signals. Otherwise, it'd be stupid since they didn't have radios.

He patted Bulb—LCpl Light—on the back. "You good, dawg?" *Dawg* always lifted his spirits.

"You think they're scared, Sergeant? Like us, I mean."

Classic Andrew Light. "Naw. Know how I know? 'Cause we ain't scared."

"Oh, okay."

"Keep it cool and watch your ammo," he said. Then, popping the clutch on the Pig, he added, "This is the battle we born to fight."

By the time Smith was set up behind iron sights, topside had launched two more volleys. The charge was halfway through the Doormat, in rifle range, but not for point targets. Captain's orders were 300 meters, minimum.

Smith felt some butterflies flapping their shit under his abs. Bulb was probably right that all those screaming troops, huffing and puffing through the mud toward this colossal stronghold, were scared shitless. They were people too, each once a baby and all with stories and families.

But so was everyone in war.

Truth was, Smith had been dreaming about this ever since they first laid eyes on medieval Portcullis. Finally, a straight-up fight. Steel on steel core. Hack and slash against cyclic firepower. He missed out when the shit hit the fan at the Assembly Hall, and by the time he tagged in to retake the South Wall, the fighting was too mixed to rock out on full auto.

This time we go full, show 'em who we is.

Suddenly, the charge stopped. The molasses sucked back into sugar cubes, and the metal men tucked under long black shields arranged like roof shingles. The next round of arrows bounced off harmlessly. And the field grew quiet.

Smith groaned and relaxed his grip on the Pig.

———

Benton raised the Corsan Carre's two-eyed sight glass and winced. It twisted his eyes in some way.

"You can adjust the . . . no, right th— . . . no. Just push the lenses closer until you see something," said Captain Saunders.

True to his words, the distant mess of the Pandonis Immortalis became as if it laid upon the Ripolis Barbican's very floor.

Whispix Wood arrows were long dominant on the Caranuscan fields of battle. They were light, stiff, and struck with the weight of Blackwood. So too were Caranuscan bows made from a particular timber found deep within the Haquatian Wetwood. It flexed, but so did it snap right with a vigor all its own. Still, Benton had never seen them used in such a deadly manner.

"We call it fire for effect," said Captain Saunders.

Naught of Dux Herms' arrows were alight, but *effect* was apt. All had pelted the strong blocks of pikers, spears, throwers, and shielders at once as rain. Iron rain. Benton had seen such tried before but more to the injury of empty ground than enemy flesh. Captain Saunders had told them: aim not; loose together. Beyond reason, it worked.

"Again, m'lord?" asked the conscript beside the rope leading up to Dux Herms.

"Nay, few of their blocks broke ranks. The rest hold at the Doormat's middling, wisened to our attack and cowering beneath their shields for *effect*."

"Is this a breakdown of command and control?" asked Captain Saunders, pointing at the nearest blocks. "Or a deliberate probing force? A little closer, and they would've triggered Smith's team."

"Mayhap purposeful. They hath used such before."

"What's the holdup?"

"They know naught of Ceal or other Stochists we might employ. They wait until we reveal our strength in the Power."

Saunders looked to his Long Voice box and tightened the grip on the peculiar sword he had acquired. Mayhap his thoughts once more settled upon the one called Gladstone. Benton knew little of how their . . . what he called magic to their laughter, performed. But each of these Marines had an ability.

Gladstone's was to break the ground with eruptive force.

"Is all well with the Vault?" Benton asked.

"Huh? Oh, they're five by five. One of my men was lipping about being pulled off a cake watch for some hazard pay. It's fine."

Benton marveled at how similar the Corsan Carre were to common men. Eager to battle, eager to rest, but never to switch betwixt the two. Ceal oft spoke of the ancient records from the time of Lord Taichleach. Most were lost to time and Stochasm, but those that persisted in dusty shelves, rotten chests, and dank cellars told of a doorway. Within the Vigil Valley, now styled Dowdale, it reached beyond the stars. Also, they spoke of an exodus of peoples from this world to another.

Were the Corsan Carre the lost cousins of Scianas?

Mayhap it is lies, my love, Ceal had once said. *Mayhap the Dowdale is a great pit of death, a way to dispose of the unwanted.* Still, she had spoken those words before the Strangers, now heralded as Corsan Carre, emerged from that pit of death.

Flee, her memory warned. He dismissed it.

"Sergeant Segar," Benton called to a fallen Blue Cloak who awaited purpose.

"M'lord."

"Travel to City Square and bring news of the Corsan Carre within the Vault. Be fast."

"Aye."

"Appreciate it," said Captain Saunders.

"Ho," shouted Chief Dalmore as his gleaming plate brightened the room. "This day languishes, and our enemy rests at the tips of our noses."

Captain Saunders gave a hungry stare and said, "You thinking what I'm thinking, Dalmore?"

"Leod's cavalry remains mounted and fierce. I see naught of pikers, only those burdened with armor and shields."

"Smash and grab?"

"A fine trap to lure us out," Benton said before their plans could deepen. "What might this strike gain us?"

"Prisoners," spoke both men at once.

"Why? There is no hope for their release after battle, and there are none to spare as guards." Of course, capturing was better than killing an army risen from a conquered world. Stripped of their commanders, armors, and weapons, some could one day go home in peace. It was an ideal—a weakness, as Ceal would call it. Still, the just fight.

But to capture in the stead of kill cost thrice the men and effort in routing, surrounding, disarming, and guarding. In the attempt, Leod's strike cavalry would sink as a skiff in false waters.

Captain Saunders peered at his Long Voice box again, then the vanguard holding beyond the range of his relics. His face held a look all too familiar: that of a Red Cloak Questioner.

"To learn of the designs guiding this strange attack," Benton guessed.

"Of great battles and last armies, I know only the tell of scarred veterans and the weavings of tapestries," said Chief Dalmore. "But of men, I know much. Cut them from their block of armor and armsmen, and their pride of nations and lordship withers."

"For some," said Captain Saunders in a low voice. "But he's right. We grab a few and then—"

"Forsaken Mindears," Chief Dalmore swore under his breath.

"The fuck is a—"

"Riders upon the flanks!"

Two charges of horse broke free of the far Genisan lines and raced down the Doormat's edges. Cries for arrows went out, but they were too fast. Both groups turned toward the middle, then back out again. Impossible to hit. Leod's cavalry would have no chance against them.

"Mindears, indeed," said Benton as their prized prisoners began a slow retreat.

Corporal Nickels was a mix of anxious and bored. Not long had passed since Bone sent everyone to their posts, but eternity was officially defined as the moments leading up to a fight.

Agony.

The quiet never used to be a problem. He could sit still and wait for the bus or that fucking guy to finish his ten-part sandwich order cool as a seal on ice. Didn't even need to bust out the phone. Then that call before they left the ship for *Sea Monster* changed everything. Turned his brain into a roller-coaster at night. Raging highs, suicidal lows. Through raw willpower and a little fucking advice from someone deeper in the abyss, he'd since wrestled it down to an occasional distraction instead of a constant presence.

But one thing he still couldn't do was downtime.

Nickels needed someone sponge-like to piss his angst into. LCpl Andrew 'Bulb' Light, set up between him and Smith, was not only a perfect but also a willing victim. *Another couple whacks at him might be enough to break this mood.*

"Come on, Bone. One quick burst," Nickels said, rising and stalking through the square columns and arches toward his prey.

"Negative. We got nothin' but time," called Smith from behind his two-forty.

Bullshit. Darker clouds were pushing in now, dropping flurries and twilight on the canyon. If the past few days were any indication, an inch of snow could shut this whole thing down.

More waiting, more pacing, more thinking about shit a trillion miles away.

Sometimes Nickels wished the others noticed his personal baggage, maybe sensed he was hurting without him having to be a bitch about it. But with everything going on, there wasn't time. Even Bone only skirted the fringe, which came out as tension between them. Nickels would love to spill it all, but Smith wouldn't understand. No one would.

Except Gunny.

Somehow that scar-faced motherfucker had seen right through the jokes and *oorah*. Understood. Knew the right cards to play and things to say. Goddamned guy turned on the lights to that rollercoaster with a twitch of his dick and became the only solid ground in a world of fakeness.

But he was dead now, absorbed into that dark presence fucking up an otherwise perfect moment of peace.

When Nickels got to Bulb, he made sure to squat down nice and close so the kid could feel the heat from his thigh. "You scared, son?"

"Kinda weird," said Bulb ignoring the question. He was admiring the cascading ranks of dark metal just past that arbitrary 300-meter line. "I mean, the way we're looking them right in the eye like this. Don't you think?"

"Seen plenty of motherfuckers downrange, bro," Nickels said. "You've seen one pile of shit; you've seen 'em all."

"Yeah, but they can't shoot back. There's like, no tension. I kinda feel sorry for them."

There it is.

Bulb had the social intelligence of an erection. The littlest things set him off, and there was no shutting him up without a shit-ton of lube. Still, that was Sergeant Bone's job. Nickels' was the sandpaper. "I'm sorry, does our numerically inferior, tactically superior posture offend your sense of right and wrong? Should we be wearing blindfolds, too?"

"Oh no. I . . . I mean, if I were out there, I'd be scared."

"Bitch, this ain't cutting up a village full of women and children. This is David's only chance of ramming a sword up Goliath's ass. If that magic shield goes down while we still got our dicks in our hands, they'll toss this entire fuckin' wall into orbit as a warmup for the real anal shit."

"I know, but we're like ready for that. They're just walking into another fight with no clue what we can do." The fucking tree-hugging, Genisan-loving asshole then actually batted his dick-sucking eyes at them. Like: *aww, poor puppy don't know it's standing on the twain twacks.*

The pump was coming back, brightening Nickels' day despite that new storm surging up from the south. LCpl Light was classic material. Playdough to be fucked down all day long. Before Nickels could do the kind of damage that would wet the stone between the kid's legs, though, motion downrange hit the play button.

"Back to positions!" Smith roared as hordes of black and silver armored knights charged downfield on both sides.

Nickels gave Bulb that gametime slap on the back and jetted. It was feast or famine as far as distractions went, but he wasn't one to turn down a meal.

The incoming was straight out of the movies, glinting jockeys with spears strapped to racing mounts barreling through flurries and mud. The crazy part was the horses were Bone's great great great grandpa black with manes more gorgeous than Leod's hair. Fuckin' grade-A thoroughbreds charging into the shit, not knowing what was about to hit them.

Smith raised a fist signaling a hold.

"Come on!" Nickels yelled.

"Captain said 300 meters," shouted Bulb. "That's right about where the graves end."

Snow was falling steadily now. Everything beyond the gap leading down the mountain road was lost to the swirl. But that long carpet of grave markers and evil shit stretching out from the wall was clear as day. "Thanks for the fucking update!" Nickels pressed the SAW's stock deep into his shoulder.

The thunder of hooves crashed through the breeze and blood rushing in his ears. Ants compared to the wall, but a no-bullshit force, nonetheless.

Horns and baritone barks came from above. From the wall's third tier, the signal banners were out of view, but that's how the Portcullisers communicated. Ropes changed the flags and set the engagement status of different units. The shouts and horns were probably the Caranuscans relaying the message down the line. Once again, they got first dibs.

A dozen arrows, an appetizer, flew, and the cavalry cut hard, driving for the middle. Only one managed to get caught and ate mud. The next volley didn't hit shit, and Nickels couldn't help but laugh. "That's why Earth grew the fuck up and stopped throwing sticks at each other. Can't outrun a bullet, am I right, Bulb?"

"This is so cool," he shouted back.

A third volley went after the group that banked right but flew wide. "Fuckers need to lead 'em left to right, not just front to back!" Nickels shouted. Closest horses approached the 400-meter mark; infantry used the distraction to pull back.

Smith still had his fist raised, but he was one with that machine gun. Primed and jacked like the old days when it was just the two of them sporting a couple stripes and zero fucks. The sweat pouring down his face in the snow and cold wasn't from exertion. No, that was sex sweat, five seconds from cracking the crust.

Horns again as the cavalry swept around the company of cowering block formations and lit a fire under them. They dropped their shields and broke into a mad dash.

"Bone, you seein' this shit?" Nickels called.

Fist raised was the reply, and the cavalry, now in four groups, kept fainting and pulling back to distract the arrows from their foot mobiles.

Worse than being bored, Nickels hated losing. He caught eyes with Watchman Hull, ready to send him up to the command post with a request to clip these zip ties and let the rifleman operate as intended. But horns thundered above and out went a heavy flight.

"There it is," Nickels whispered as arrows rained on the unprotected infantry. Bodies dropped, and pants got shit. Another round or two would make that force completely combat ineffective. Back to winning.

In reaction, the four groups of knights banked and made a hard charge for the wall. Nickels guessed it was like covering fire, except in terms of tonnage instead of pounds of spent brass. Beautiful, and it would've worked.

Except they crossed that 300-meter threshold before breaking off.

Smith didn't waste a second. He dropped that fist and the Pig went live. Glorious, ratcheting gunfire flipped the calendars back to the 21st century.

Nickels' first burst cut the lead elements. They didn't have time to blink, let alone dodge. Armored jockeys flew back, horses fell, and tripped up the ones behind them. It was like the mass of them was stumbling into a big invisible hole.

The next salvo was longer, SAW buzzing in his arm as he ran a line across their shit-eating horror.

The rightmost flock banked left, kept dying.

The two in the center merged and banked right, leaving a trail of writhing bodies.

Leftmost managed to wheel it around but took the turn too wide and crashed into the retreating infantry. It became a fuckfest of tangled horses and waving arms.

The rest of them, no matter where they ran, mostly did it together in tight formation, which made Nickels' job easy.

He was almost a box down when Smith's fist went up again, and he had to summon that coital strength to let up on the trigger. The surviving cavalry was out of momentum and leadership. Horses were backing up, others rearing and throwing their riders. Those in control made for the clusterfuck of metal-swimming infantry for safety. That's when the horns above sounded again.

"Don't let it hit you on the way out!" Nickels shouted as the snowy sky filled with arrows.

Shuffling through city streets thick with flurries, Gladstone wanted to scream.

The weight of all his desires was smashing down on the last remaining shreds of duty and obligation. Mistrus shrieked in his head while drill instructors barked orders to keep fighting.

Ignore pain. Ignore the self. Duty above all.

Death and thunder! she howled as if her voice were a planet-wide address system. ***Death and thunder from the wall that knows no Power! What lies have you fed us?***

The frenzied snowflakes and sharp-roofed buildings blurred. Even in anger, her words were honey, and Gladstone longed to give her an answer gift wrapped with a bow. But nothing he could say would satisfy her. Only what he could do.

And for some reason, distant and confusing to him, his legs were carrying him away from her love and bliss toward the North Wall and duty.

I sabotaged the detonator, he thought, hoping the terminology wouldn't piss her off. *The road is still clear.*

Hundreds of legionaries lie dead! Their commanders scream and howl between retreat and maddened assault where thousands will see their last breaths. Is that how you wish to arrive in our grace?

His boots kept marching as if Captain Saunders controlled them with an implanted Marine Corps override chip, and a new fear took hold. Not of betraying either side but somehow failing both and falling into that place where he wasn't welcome anywhere.

What happened? he asked.

Gladstone forced a nod to a two-man crew of conscripts wearing the yellow tabards of the Korigi Carre firefighters. *Everything's cool; just a stroll through the snow.* One thing that didn't make sense was why Mistrus and her legions couldn't just go a few miles west or east where there was no Bark and use the Power to rip a canyon through the mountains. Totally bypass Portcullis. But to ask would invite the kind of pain or pleasure that would leave him fetal on the street, sucking his thumb for hours. Conspicuous, even here.

His eyeballs burned as the wintry market district turned to a visage of dozens of black horses screeching and kicking as rifle fire popped in the distance. ***The Corund Corps! It must be. Speak their numbers!***

No, it's. . . he wasn't sure how to explain modern weaponry, and she wasn't giving him time.

You take us for fools! More burning. His legs wobbled on the slippery, uneven cobblestones. A small part of him hoped no one was watching. A smaller part hoped someone was.

Suddenly, the pain was gone, and he was wrapped in a warm embrace. Intimate, a heated blanket pressing into his soul, a flow of liquid love over all the places that felt good.

Gladstone stopped marching.

Sweet words drenched his thoughts. ***What reaps the common soldier in trade for his life? Death for the sake of making great men greater. I wish no more of our legions to die, but I would trade them all for you. You are my prize, my treasure. What a life I can give you if this world can be saved. What a life we can give them all.***

Pain was something the primal, proto-human force within could fight. Something the drill instructors knew how to handle. But this was wonderful. Gladstone could die happy right here and now.

It ended like stepping back from a hug. She was still there, staring. Offering.

His thoughts came slow, lazy. An urge to please, a need to know.

Return now and see to your task, she said. ***This day cannot be forfeit.***

Anxiety flared. *Fischer knows. He'll—*

Ambition is no dish to be prepared and served to your liking. It must be seized!

To punctuate her point, a vice gripped Gladstone's head and squeezed. The pressure was unreal, sapping his strength. With a blink, his brain would collapse, and he would cease.

"Gladstone!" called a voice from across the street.

PFC Licht, his replacement.

The vice released, and the sensations of cold toes in his boots and fresh manure in the air returned. Turned out he'd zombie-walked through most of the abandoned Market District. The accumulated inch on the street was littered with fresh hoof tracks from the Watch Cavalry on their way to City Square. Aside from one or two small foot patrols, everyone was in North Ward or on the perimeter. They were alone.

Licht trotted over, huffing like he'd run the whole way. "Hey, I think there's still time to blow that pass. Captain's kinda pissed, but we just gave the enemy something to think about, and they're kinda stalled." He mopped his brow and blew hot breath into cupped hands. "You okay?"

"You gotta help me, man. I need to get back to the Vault," Gladstone said. The brainpower required to generate a reason was absent. But his appeal to Licht was genuine. *Please give me an out.*

"Look, it's cool. I told the captain that the transmitter's just out of range. Maybe not just a battery issue, you know? Like, not your fault. Anyway, he'll try it up top and maybe get Francisco to look at it."

Gladstone offered the broken remote. "Take it to him; I've gotta get back."

The PFC held up his hands. "Whoa, orders are orders. I'm just giving you a heads-up." He moved closer to confide something. "Dude, you *want* to be up there. The wall is awesome. Less wire and more front row, you know? It's gonna rock. Plus, if they ever get a foothold, having that shotty in those narrow corridors will be dope."

Gladstone fingered the Benelli 12-gauge autoloader slung across his chest. David Licht—his friend for a day, buddy for a lifetime—wasn't getting it. He needed to stop inferring, asking, suggesting, figuring, thinking, and standing in the way. "Head back, PFC," Gladstone said. "And take this with you." He shoved the olive-green remote into the Marine's hands.

Licht tossed it back. "Come on man, that's—

Whatever else he said was lost as sweetness thundered in his skull. ***Show me!***

Gladstone did as commanded, trying to remember everything he knew about Licht while giving the guy a solid, head-to-toe terminator scan.

Mistrus was on the verge of tasking the shotgun to Licht's face for a repeat of 2ndLt Weber when suddenly she purred with Power and desire. She forced Gladstone's memories of that strange, green-glowing shrapnel lodged in Licht's abdomen to the surface. Curiosity, craving, then a spark of recognition became an inferno.

Another marvel! Perhaps this delay proves fruitful. I must have him.

Gladstone relaxed, happy he'd found something she wanted, and assessed the situation. The North Wall loomed in the distance, impressive as a sandcastle. All eyes were on it, waiting to see how it would stand against the ocean, hoping that sand would not crumble this time. And as they watched, he was here, unwatched.

"Okay, so how about we both go see the captain?" Licht said. "He'll be pissed about the Vault, but seriously there's an army down there, and Fischer can handle things a little longer."

The gray skies rumbled, electrifying Mistrus within Gladstone's thoughts. Suddenly, the path forward was crystal clear.

"Looks like this storm's gonna be bigger than the last one," said Licht. "Maybe it'll shut things down again; get us to tomorrow. Y'know? Come on, let's go."

Gladstone stepped forward and said, "It's a Southborn Storm."

"Cool story."

"Mistrus says they're most unpleasant."

Licht's eyes went wide. Finally, the kid understood how far apart they were. That he—like Weber, like Fischer—wasn't safe with his buddy and brother Marine. Shaking hands began the arduous journey down to his rifle, which was much too cumbersome against a trained killer this close and determined.

Distantly, Gladstone pitied him.

CHAPTER 15

HARD POWER

"Aye, quite a noise. Go ensure Sir Rampo needs naught of fresh loins," said Dalmore, dismissing a green-armored Caranuscan.

The NWCC was in ovation. Smith's team, plus those *whatever*wood arrows, had synergized beautifully. Enemy fast movers were offline, and the remains of that vanguard were flopping around like bait in the Doormat's middle. If the Watch Cavalry moved quick, they could chop down a sizable portion of the forces remaining in the Doormat. It wouldn't win the war, but it'd win a battle. And that's what Saunders did, win battles. One at a time.

"I don't like it, sir," said Francisco coming off the observation deck. "They can field twenty times that number and not break a sweat. More than enough to soak up every bullet, arrow, and pot of piss we've got to throw at them. Whatever they're waiting on has got to be damned diabolical. Permission to go do my thing?"

Saunders nodded, and the Marine Corps sniper, with a service record that recruiters would pass around like porn if they ever got clearance to see it, left the NWCC with two long guns slung across his back.

Alone.

It was a moment lost to a world struggling to outrun its history, but Saunders gave it the respect it deserved. And with came that pang of . . . guilt, longing, a hole in his soul . . .

Something like that.

Francisco was a reminder of Mike from a time when it was just the three of them. Imprisoned, tortured, and witnesses to the murder of their Marine brethren, they became killers. Inhuman. Every second of those five days it took to escape was savage, brutal, and one away from their last. Every split-up was goodbye forever. But somehow, their number always came back to three.

Saunders thought of the pack resting against the wall in the next room. *Except here. We're two, maybe one.*

And you'll be zero if you don't figure this shit out.

Saunders forced his awareness back into the damp NWCC. The wind was kicking up outside, blowing in some big flakes. The storm looked worse than yesterday's, but the enemy still wanted in. *Good.* "Benton," he said, done with defense. "If this is all they're willing to field right now, maybe we should alter the battle plan."

The lord governor cocked his head toward the NWCC's flanking balcony. It was an outcropping meant for archers and people throwing anvils over the side. Right now, it was empty, and Saunders followed him into the falling snow.

"Ye wish to send Leod's riders?"

"Yes. And more. I want to aggress their false sense of security."

Benton stuffed his white helm onto his head, likely to keep his ears warm against the blowing cold, and stared, thoughtful. "Mayhap their sense is founded in the strength of their numbers."

"No question. But whoever built this city and wall understood the strategic power of choke points. They can only come at us in bite-sized quantities. It'll eventually overwhelm us but at a huge cost. A cost they clearly don't want to pay."

"Aye," Benton monotoned like that helmet was some sensory deprivation job, and he was talking to himself in the middle of a cosmic void. "They hold until their true plan unfolds and can destroy us without loss."

Maybe it was a better discussion to have with Dalmore. Rampo, even. Benton had all the right cards, but when it came to playing them, he was... *Shit, he's just as ditzy as Admiral Bowman was during that last-minute briefing on the VIP.* What did that mean? Emotional distraction, which made sense if Ceal was factored in. But it didn't lend any specifics, just an extra yank on the ol' stomach knot. "Right. And I don't want to wait around for it."

"Flee?" he asked in that dubbed way of speaking but made a face like the word came out half-strangled.

Not even worth dignifying.

Saunders pointed down at the little black corpses slowly turning white throughout the muddy field. "Our weapons are undeniably effective. I've got a team of US Marines capable of asymmetric action against any position we choose. Francisco's out there scouting high-value targets. Officers, Black Robes, anything that looks like command, control, and artillery. We know the Bark reaches the Upper Del. That's now inside their lines, meaning we can gut this masterplan from the inside out."

Benton rested a hand on the longsword strapped to his hip. It was a struck pose for anyone else, but the guy was a dangerous motherfucker, and that sword was lightning in his hands. It almost made Saunders embarrassed for wearing his. Almost, but not quite, because the thing felt pretty good whenever he pulled it out.

"I remain impressed by ye's abilities," said Benton, fully rejoining the conversation. "But I fear that if Ceal is wrong, keeping ye protected is of a greater value than ye's capacity for war."

Saunders raised an eyebrow. "Huh?" Maybe he didn't hear it right, but that sounded like Ceal believed the Corsan Carre were expendable. Was that what Benton was chewing on?

Benton never got to explain as his eyes flicked up like a cat spotting a bird.

Saunders, unthinking, dove for the pile of gilded white armor to flatten him against the deck. But Benton reacted faster. Suddenly, Saunders was caught in a metal vice, legs kicking air. Then they were back inside the dim and smokey NWCC.

A split second later, the wall quaked.

"We are hit!" someone shouted. Dust billowed in, and communication drowned in a sickbay of coughing.

That old familiar adrenaline spike buzzed as Saunders pulled his shirt out of the vest and covered his face. *What are the chances they just dusted us with poison?* There was no way to test the air, but his teeth were grinding grit. So, it was more wait-and-see than anything.

"Left Flanking Tower, m'lord."

Saunders blew out his dust goggles and put them on. It was still difficult to see who was talking.

"Damage?"

"The stonework hath buckled. Methinks men be trapped within."

"Eyes forward!" That sounded like Dalmore with the right idea: get a visual on the enemy. Whether they meant to hit that tower and blind the NWCC or not, it was an obvious opportunity.

Saunders felt his way to the exit and found himself in the USMC armory beside Brines' and Williamson's packs. The air was much better, like in the old non-smoking sections of restaurants.

Resting next to the beige packs was the SINCGARS radio PFC had left behind.

Gladstone.

Saunders grabbed the unit but held off on screaming into the mic. Yes, the enemy scoring a direct hit and their newfound capability for visual confirmation meant good odds of an encore. But as the wind carried away most of the dust outside, Saunders saw what Dalmore was worried about.

The tide was coming in.

So much for us seizing the initiative.

When visibility was restored in the NWCC, sheets of freezing rain were slapping the exposed observation deck like angry sea swells coming over the bow. The unexpected shift in precipitation was rhythmic, almost soothing, as it tried to soak everyone to the bone. Dalmore ordered Portcullis' famed fires lit; huge braziers with water-resistant fuel sent light and heat radiating through the mammoth structure. Warmth for the defenders and a warning to the enemy.

The black metal advance remained undaunted as endless ranks filled in from behind. Without the rockslide, the Twin Tithes road was an open sewer pumping the Doormat full of shit.

Saunders really needed to know where the hell Gladstone was.

An explosion, not thunder, rang out, and the wall shook again. A Deadlie confirmed an impact on the solid face of Tier Four. No damage. Another rock fell short, splashing into the mud. Something sailed right over into the city so high it probably cleared the South Wall.

"The prophecy rises," shouted Dalmore through the wind-whipped command bridge. "The Last Army brings its fury! RESIST DEATH!"

"Resist death!" belted everyone.

"I take to the west flank, be well."

"See you on the other side, Dalmore," said Saunders watching him and the Deadlies file up the stairwell. Unlike Benton and his plans to retrograde through the South Gate, Dalmore was willing to bleed it out here. Neither plan fit with the Marine mission, but one garnered a hair more respect than the other.

Likewise, the wet masses of metal outside continued to shuffle toward their deaths. Regardless of what the enemy had up their sleeves, even if they dialed in those boulders perfectly, those forward units weren't coming back.

What kind of commander sends infantry and biological cavalry against an elevated position?

A historian would give him a thirty-pager replete with examples. Part of it, at least on Earth, came down to tactical stagnation in the face of improving weapons and defensive technologies. The rest was the value of sacrifice—troops were currency to buy wins. Today, the Genisans seemed willing to pay through the nose for expedited service and same-day shipping.

"Is Segar still out there?" asked Benton, suddenly at his side.

Who? It took a moment, but the name connected to the runner they'd sent to check on Gladstone and Licht. Then Saunders' analytical mind sped forward and struck something hard. *The Bark!*

He was at the back wall in a flash, ordering a SITREP from Fischer. Seconds passed as boulders pounded the city. The enemy's sudden urgency presented the real possibility that the Bark was compromised. Saunders felt the blood drain out of his cheeks, his first taste of terror.

"Still five by five here, sir," came the reply from Fischer, finally. "No sign of PFC Licht yet. Want I should send some folks to hunt 'em down?"

Saunders made sure the mic wasn't hot when he breathed that sigh of relief. "Negative. Alert locals to take cover from enemy artillery and hold station." He gave Benton a thumbs up in case something was lost in translation.

"Copy. Will contact y'all in five mikes with update. Out."

As Saunders set the mic down, the sword dug into his hip.

Smallfoot.

The little troll's loyalties were hard to peg, but his presence confirmed that unknowns—insurgents—remained in the city. Segar and, more importantly, PFC Licht should've reported in by now. Was the Anticult ambushing people transiting through North Ward? It was a strong possibility, one Saunders needed to bring force against. But he didn't have the time or the manpower.

Fuck it, he thought. *Marines come first.*

The NWCC shook again. Another hit. Howling from the stairwell drew the eye to stones slick with dark cherry as wounded were carried down below. Still no Gladstone. "Benton," Saunders said, "I've got two Marines missing."

Instead of balking or prioritizing, the lord governor waved over one of the armoires of polished armor standing guard. "Sergeant Aldun, take a man. Find Segar and the two-wayward Corsan Carre. All haste, as we believe them in dire need."

A nod and it was done.

Saunders moved the issue to the back burner and said, "Thanks. Now, what are we doing about those rocks?"

"Me, or is it gettin' colder?" Smith asked. The huge brazier lighting up his position felt like it had stopped throwing heat.

The Genisans were still advancing but slower like they were strutting in for the kill. *Or they pushing back against their whips.* He hoped it was the latter—them woke to the knowledge that they were being driven like cattle toward their deaths.

Toward the Pig.

Horns sounded above, and deep throats cut through the wind, barking orders down the line. Smith had his poncho on, but everything was icing over fast. The Pig would fire wet, iced, or full of sand, but it ruined his fantasy of how this fight would go down. Instead of nice and clean, the mix of snow and whitish rain was killing visibility. It was also thousands stomping through that cold hell. So many that when they charged, some would reach the wall. His team just didn't have enough ammo.

"We go loud at 250," he shouted over another gust.

He shivered, back soaked. The freezing rain was getting through the poncho now. Government-issue waterproof. Never failed. To be fair, though, their original Operation *Sea Monster* loadout was for arid and hot, not the death of winter.

Jersey blew a whistle and pointed. Smith snapped his head around in time to see the first volley of arrows pound the enemy center. They just took it, not even bothering to bring up their shields like they'd done when it was clear out.

Smith covered his eyes as a wet spray of ice shards and snow came in. He considered his dust goggles, but that would just end in a blurry mess. "Think that hurt 'em?" he shouted.

Nickels said something that got lost in the wind but kept pointing.

"I see 'em. Hold fa—" Smith cut himself off as the neat infantry columns broke step and blended into a wave.

No molasses this time. They were coming. Fast.

Garcia thudded down beside him.

"Back to your post. 250 meters!" Smith yelled, heart hitting the hydraulics. This was gonna be a full-on shoulder thudding, metal shredding event. Fuckers were about to scream from a new kind of warfare, the best kind of warfare. The only kind of warfare.

Superiority.

"Sergeant!" cried Garcia into his fucking ear. Smith got ready to repeat himself much louder but saw Garcia pointing at something up high.

The same something as Jersey.

On a bluff near the top of the canyon were two black dots. Smith could barely make them out through the rain slanting down, but there wasn't much guesswork.

Black Robes.

CHAPTER 16

DAGGER

Shall I send a patrol?" shouted Leod through the big iron gate they'd fixed up to replace the Vault's busted doors. "The square is over-guarded. Thousands could not fast wade through this field of steel to reach ye. I can spare a half ten."

Lance Corporal Ted Fischer, M4 carbine slung across his chest while his M40 sniper sat nice and dry by the glowing gem, shrugged. This was Leod's third time asking. Out there in that ice shower, it was no wonder his men were looking for something to do. Moreover, the rattle of gunfire coming over the North Wall was putting ants to pants. "Captain said he'd take care of it, but they got them a ruckus up there. Maybe a few guys lookin' for Licht ain't a bad idea."

"Mayhaps he sought shelter from this wicked storm."

The sky had that angry, born and raised in West Virginia look to it. "This ain't gonna stop no Marine. More like he got lost or hung up when those boulders hit o'er yonder 'cause there ain't enough Korigi Carre to go 'round. Still, we need him here."

Leod nodded, looking ready to wrangle in his silvery chainmail and studded leather. It was cool watching him climb the ranks, starting as just one of the Watch grunts and now in charge of a whole platoon of horsemen that he hand-built stirrups to formations. Lotta guys would've lost that arm and drowned themselves in a cabin somewhere.

Two frosty tabards came over, and Leod gave them the rundown. Fischer half-listened as the crackle of gunfire echoing off the slopes tripled in volume. He cocked an ear back at the radio, hoping it'd come to life with news, orders. Anything. But not a peep.

Everyone was doing something but him.

Francisco was probably off by himself, panning that reticle over some lucky sons of bitches until finding that one unfortunate enough to matter. An officer or a Black Robe. Then, boom: pulped by a high-velocity .50 caliber bullet. Not on the outside, that would just look like a hole. But inside where massive soft tissue trauma came from being exploded from within.

Come on, Cap'n, send me in!

Babysitting the Bark wasn't a bad posting, but it wasn't the war Francisco had prepped him for. Chalk it up to luck of the draw, but this shit seemed deliberate. Fischer had gotten a fuckload more Vault assignments than anyone else except Gladstone, who somehow got paired up with him every damned time. Anyone else would be fine, but the freaking guy was a ping-pong ball between slumber party friendly and unapproachable. That shit with the batteries might've surprised the captain, but it was a par-for-the-course fuckup. He even—

Leod pounded on the gate. "He comes! We hath fulfilled our tasks as the Watch with nary a need for becoming the Search. The Corsan Carre's fears are allayed; I stand mighty and noble in accepting no reward for mine services."

The numb shoulder tension let go with a rush of relief. Bullshit posting or not, the buddy system was still in effect for a reason. The Bark was alive and well when that shapeshifting Black Robe got Williamson. No time soon was anyone forgetting that nothing was what it seemed. The only security was numbers—a brother Marine watching your six.

When that Marine turned out to be Gladstone again, Fischer's shoulders practically rammed into his neck. *What's going on here?*

"The attack's started; they're coming hard," puffed Gladstone, soaked to the bone and red in the face. "Get up on overwatch, and I'll head inside." He patted his shotgun. "I got the door if anyone knocks."

Overwatch?

The Vault was iced over and literally an igloo. Even if Fischer could climb back up there, he'd be a frost-bit hash brown in a cold minute. Better to set up under one of the Watch's tarps and zero the entrance. More importantly, where was PFC Licht?

Fischer kept his concerns quiet, followed Gladstone inside, and headed for the radio.

Gonna make a quick call, just following protocol. Everything's cool.

No one should have ever questioned it.

But Gladstone spun like Fischer was reaching for the last slice of pecan pie and said, "Hey! Whoa. What's wrong?"

"Missed the last check-in jawin' with Leod."

"I can do it."

"So can I. Just want to make sure the PFC got back okay."

"Dude, he's fine. Met up with him near the markets and handed off the remote. You hear that shit out there? Captain's got his hands full, and we got our orders."

It made perfect sense against the backdrop of that battle echoing off the slopes and stone. But it also reeked of cock blocking. "You never saw the captain?" Fischer asked.

Gladstone stiffened, straining to keep that goofy smile on his face. "What? Ah, nah. We figured it out."

"Yeah . . . bud, I gotta check on Licht." Fischer reached down to grab the handset. If it were any other day, he would've let the dude explain himself, but this was war. *Unfucking things comes first.* Plus, If the captain didn't nail him and Nickels to the cross that one time they shot at that horse and nearly got everyone killed, he wouldn't ruin Gladstone's career for fucking up some detonator.

"Please go up on overwatch," Gladstone whispered.

It was the tone, more than anything, that registered. That wasn't a plea from someone on their knees; it was a threat. Something bigger than the business with the detonator had the boy in its grips.

Fischer stood up to his full height, a half head taller, and squared his shoulders, a good thirty pounds heavier. "Okay, maybe you should clue me in."

Gladstone shook his head and shrugged. He glanced at the Bark, swirls of red and blue spiraling up to pour out purple light at the diamond tip. It was beautiful, a definite conversation piece. Fischer didn't take his eyes off the Marine, however.

"You remember Mina Bazar?" Gladstone finally asked.

It was an open sore in Fischer's mind. He remembered what happened, but focusing on the details blew up into a frenzy of terror, exertion, and a need to survive. Stuff was out of sequence and hard to process. Every time he thought about it, events grew more twisted, and he felt less like a Marine and more like a wild animal charging through a thunderstorm. "Ain't somethin' you forget," he said.

There was a pause. Gladstone rubbed his fingers together, fidgeting. Then, he stepped forward as if catapulting something off his chest and said, "Weber?"

That memory was intact and vivid. "Yeah, ate it when we were baitin' those tanks."

Gladstone grimaced, maybe remembering that blown apart face, maybe that 2ndLt Weber had two young kids waiting for him back home. It was all sorts of terrible, but what the hell did it have to do with . . .

Gladstone charged into the swirling dust storm and unexplainable blackout smoke that Fischer was sure the enemy was responsible for. Five-five-six crackled in the distance, maybe Gunny's team. Then, thunder.

A shotgun blast.

Fischer couldn't cover shit from his position and moved up. Collided with Gladstone running from something. Nearly fragged the guy in the process. Stone was frantic, couldn't speak. Eventually, he coughed out, "Weber."

Fischer advanced and found the body. It was fucked, face blown in half, uniform splattered, and drowned in blood. Somehow the light caught that steel wedding band with the etched Xs on his left ring finger.

No question it was 2ndLt Weber. Fischer opened fire in a rage, but against what? There was no one around.

"So, you knew," Gladstone said in that quiet dad voice during a gotcha moment.

"Was Weber friendly fire?"

A nod.

The past two months suddenly made sense.

"Oh god, bud," Fischer gasped. "You been walking around with that this whole time? Shit . . . hell, we all thought you were . . . I mean, look where we are." At best, if they faced the curved wall of stacked stone and ignored that it was bathed in purple light passed through rippling water, they might imagine themselves in some well-preserved ruins. An old medieval tourist site in northern Europe. That's it. Everything else, from the Bark, altimeters, plants, animals, and impossibly high mountains, screamed they were somewhere else. A constant mindfuck.

And Gladstone had been dealing with that plus a mortifying fratricide incident. Fischer wanted to hug him; tell him it was okay.

"You're saying you didn't know?"

"Bud, if I'd known you were carrying this shit around, I'd have fuckin' lent a shoulder. Y'know? Any of us. The C-monster ain't leavin' no Marine behind."

Gladstone trembled, but his face was his namesake. Stone. "Would you have reported it to the captain?"

"I woulda come to you first. You and me woulda gone to Gunny and figured out how to pull your brain outta that shit. If that meant bringing the captain in, then that's what we'd do. The Corps ain't gonna hold you responsible. There's a whole class about Blue on Blue. Error of Identification. Error of Response Inhibition. Hell, you think marksmen don't make mistakes?" He blew out a breath. This was a talk Francisco gave when they first got paired, and Fischer was damned glad for more to say than *aww, sucks bruh*.

"Shit happens," Fischer continued, "and unless you got malicious intent, they're more worried about *you*. Corps protects its own. I mean, fuck, bud, you coulda come to any of us at any time. Even Corporal Nickels would stow his shit for this."

Gladstone licked his lips. "That's . . . that's what I've been waiting to hear. You're right; it's been hard . . ."

Fischer relaxed. He couldn't imagine being hounded by that guilt. Weber wouldn't be easy to get over, but at least Stone wouldn't have to go it alone anymore. The captain would understand and probably be relieved this clusterfuck was something addressable. And that's where it'd stay: between the three of them. That is if any of them survived the next few hours.

". . . not knowing if you reported me. Tiptoeing around Gunny and the captain, guessing the meaning behind their accusing stares. They knew all along, didn't they?"

Shit.

Fischer held up his hands. "Whoa, no. No one knows. And even if I did, I woulda come to you first. Bud, this stays here for now. Alright? Let me get a twenty on the PFC, let the captain know this Vault is manned, and we can get back to winnin' this medieval alien war. Copy?"

A weird smile spread across Stone's face, shadowy dimples surrounded by the Bark's purple light. Fischer took it as acceptance but quickly thought he should tell Leod to park some of his people in here. Psyche problems—dad's stories about Uncle Gary came to mind—had a way of twisting reality. Like typing 2+2 into a broken calculator might spit back 49 because the 2 and + buttons were crossing wires with 7 and X. Gladstone froze up a month ago in that creepy wolf cave, and the risk of something similar here was far from zero. Better to have assurances than liabilities.

Kneeling beside the radio, Fischer clicked the mic. Suddenly his combat senses rushed to life.

A glint in the purple light arced in. Fischer reacted fast, knocking Gladstone's arm away. Then he was on his feet, shoving the Marine back and grabbing for his pistol.

Stone dove behind the Bark's pedestal.

Fischer yanked his M9 free and started to ask what the fuck that was. Instead of words, something wet hawked up out of his mouth and flowed down his chin. His legs started to shake as pain and warmth spread throughout his side. Worse than the pain, he realized as the pistol drooped, was the silence.

That constant background pulse of a beating heart was gone.

He stumbled back, legs turning to rubber, arms burning from exhaustion. Any other day he could run miles, but that five feet to the iron gate where one of Leod's people might see him was forever too far. Head swimming, he saw the gun slip from his fingers just before the floor rushed up to meet his ass.

The pain was gone, and the Vault went on mute as the cold soaked through his uniform. He tried again to call out, but his lungs were empty.

Gladstone crept around from behind the Bark, watching with black eyes.

Fischer could only stare back. There were no questions, no answers. No flashbacks of his life or grand revelations beyond the fact that this fucking guy was standing over his corpse. Before his world shrank into the delirium of crumbling memories exploding from dying brain matter, Fischer bore witness to the worst death.

Indifference.

Gladstone turned away as everlasting darkness set in, intent on the purple gem.

Ice pelted the cobblestones, and a hard pour hammered the slate roofs above. Fog hissed from melting snow and hung in the chill air as if frozen. Where rime sheathed stone in one place, it boiled dry in another. Rain, snow, heat, and wind rushed through the city in maddened argument over the season.

Magnus Smallfoot stepped through it uncaring. To him, Portcullis was as still as a tomb waiting to be filled. The wet and frost were but goosebumps to the galloping steed. The Southborn Storm—a thing of storied legend that would inspire men's tell for ages to come—was ill-timed but paled against the northborn shadow. The great Genisan claw would do far worse than mar the gables.

He sucked a breath. The stench of men and their beasts was fast fading from the streets, but it was not gone. Many lingered in City Square, guarding against that which had already slipped behind their backs.

Smallfoot could not see the happenings within the Vault but felt them through Mistrus.

One Corsan Carre lay dead; the other was gathering his courage. Mayhaps this Gladstone's hesitation was the legacy of the commonfolk's uncertainty, a lifetime of worshiping false idols called nobles or highborns. Always were the low raised to conform, serve, and please in the hopes of reward. They were fed, watered, and boarded but never given enough to feel comfort. That was always a labor away.

Until the new master. Mistrus.

Smallfoot, too, had questioned. Thrown down the sword and left in search of the Watch intending to tell all. He spanned not half of Song Street before remembering the treatment he would receive. Suspicion, mistrust. They would pat him but also at arm's length keep him. When he could provide no more of the enemy's plans, in a cage, they would throw him.

He had returned to the forge and finished his work as he knew Gladstone would. Only one more task lingered in this dying stone husk before Smallfoot could slink back into the shadows.

Through the gray and swirling sheets of ice rain, his eyes could not reach the North Wall where mayhaps the Genisan swarm—the convicts and conscripts of a conquered world driven out before the ranks of pure-hearted homelanders—climbed its face and battled for its tiers. But he could see that Uumhrat's inn alone still glowed with warmth. A shame he would not pass it on his way to the common homes in North Ward.

Thunder boomed as clouds crashed together, and Smallfoot cut through an alley behind Master Walram's. The Market District was cluttered with tents and mules. The free Caranuscans had camped here, but all were gone. Still, he knew not if their stewards or camp followers lingered, so he turned left down a nameless street and entered North Ward's block residences. The houses stood empty of their families who, in the like of animals, had fled but could never outrun the slaughter.

The sword.

The cold voice swept aside stray throughts, and his purpose sharpened. The North Wall now loomed ethereal in the misting fog.

"Ho, what d'we hath here?" barked a voice.

Dull mail took the stage as two Deadlies stepped into Smallfoot's path. Sergeant Aldun and his man Evrat. When they had been Blue Cloaks, they were regulars on Song Street. Recognition flickered across Aldun's broad face. "Smallfoot! Did none warn ye to leave the city?"

Smallfoot gave no answer.

"Gone daft. Mayhaps the drink washed out his ears," said Evrat.

"Aye now, aid us Smallfoot," said Aldun. Within, Mistrus vibrated. "Enemy's pressing the wall. Hath ye seen Sergeant Segar or a wayward Corsan Carre?"

Smallfoot stayed in his place. Words he could speak to pass, but Mistrus misliked their inquest into the Corsan Carre. Her fury thrilled him, but the men were tall, armed, and mailed. Smallfoot concealed a tap-forged dagger within his sleeves, but it was blunt beneath the Bark. He could not hope to overcome them without aid.

Trust your blade.

"See, naught of his tongue moves. Vermin from the filth he loves must'o ate it out," said Evrat stepping forward.

"Ye hurt?" asked Aldun, confused and closer still.

"Are ye?" Smallfoot said, launching two swift strikes. The blade, marked by a single ribbon of silvery Renderstone along its length, slipped through solid plate like threadbare cloth. It touched the warmth of Aldun's life and drove it from his body. Evrat watched stupidly, mayhap wondering why Aldun staggered so. And then his heat, too, did flee.

Smallfoot released a breath and smiled at the bodies beneath his bloodied dagger. *Gladstone.* Above, one of the street's Q-lights began to brighten.

Great horns rose in the distance. The sword and Mistrus' anger flashed again, kicking his short legs into a run. Death was too fine a fate for the Corsan Carre.

To Micky's delight, Lady Ceal was, for once, not seated at her writing desk dreaming up dispatches for all the world's minions to follow. She was back-of-the-bus with the Earth aliens, clutching the wooden bench with both hands as the coach rocketed over the worst-maintained road in all Galimay.

The interior flashed white, and Micky's ears popped.

"Too close!" Dr. Pat shouted. Then the bench heaved, knifing her bony ass into Micky's thigh. It would surely leave a bruise, but Pat squirmed like it would also leave her gay.

So tempting.

But riling her up for another test was multi-point futile. First, there was the situation with this storm and the haunting absence of Oxhold's patrols. The two made sense when balanced in an equation—storm keeping people off the roads—but Ceal stressing over it was prescient.

Sometimes local reactions are the only take home, spoke a friend's voice from happier times.

Second, setting off dynamite repeatedly was not constructive. Exactly the opposite. They needed to move Ceal's plan forward, and pissing Pat off only made it harder. Of course, Ceal wasn't helping either by keeping all the details close to the chest.

Micky pushed Pat back into her seat and offered one of her famous giggles. "Gee, normally, there's a three-hour wait to get on a ride like this!"

Ceal scoffed. "This is but a rough—" Boom! The coach pitched.

Micky's shoulder exploded in pain, and her butt landed on something soft and bony but not warm like Pat.

Ceal.

It was Micky's turn to scramble off like she might get contact-turned into a toad. Fortunately, the strongest magician in Galimay's arsenal hardly noticed and finished her sentence, "—a rough span lingering from last Greth's Spring when the Birtchriff overflowed its banks."

Still following the river. Good to know. Micky had stolen a look at Ceal's maps, but distances were relative, not absolute. They did have some sort of time grid, but the measurements assumed a standard rate of travel. The horse-drawn coach at full gallop was anything but. "With this storm, it might flood again," Micky said. "Don't you think?"

"We shall—"

The ride smoothed out.

"Ah, better." Ceal stood, pausing to steady herself because the new road was still a fire road on a good day, and made for the desk.

"Is it still snowing?" asked Dr. Pat, watching rain pelt the window. "Looks like a monsoon punched through the blizzard."

"A Storm of the South abides naught of the wilds and weather," said Ceal. "In moments, the air may bake the waters to steam or etch the lands in Everice. So may come winds with might to push stone keeps aside and flash so terrible it takes the sight from our eyes."

Fuck that. "Any chance we're far enough away from the front lines and those black robe disruptors so you can fly us the rest of the way?" Micky asked. Her knowledge of the different Powers had grown considerably over the past few days as they tried to unlock Dr. Pat's strange abilities. The Stochal—Ceal's only conduit despite the universality of the Quotidian—was wielded through a combination of innate talent and a fuckload of knowledge.

At least, according to Ceal.

Knowledge and ability got fire shooting from your fingertips, but there was another underappreciated layer after that. Creativity. For example, Ceal had never seen an episode of Superman. *Or was he just in the movies?* Point was that it explained the perplexed look on her face.

She couldn't fathom people flying.

Ceal, of course, recovered quickly and gave a snarky glance out the window.

"Okay, fine, no flying in stormy weather," Micky conceded. "But command that shit to be calm! Can't you?"

The comment earned her a limp-wristed jab from Pat and a rare smile—half-smile, smirk, maybe a facial tick—from the magic lady herself.

"In strength," Ceal said, "the Quotidian and Stochal are close matches. Before . . ." it sounded like she was going to reference some point in time, but let it hang ". . . masters of each craft would try their earnest to best each other in sport. It was . . . *is* a game called Cintup. A sphere of oiled iron is risen between two contenders—one red and one blue. It is released, and through their force of *ask* or *command* . . ." she glanced at Pat, who was probably thinking about all the possible sports injuries from using an iron basketball ". . . the sphere is moved. First to push it past their opponent wins."

"Kinda game that's over before it starts, huh?" Micky said, imagining a ball-shoving match trying to gain traction back in the states. Sportscasters becoming aeronautical experts spending hours of pregame time analyzing the environmental variables that might affect that stupid iron ball.

The players' sob stories about how much they sacrificed to come this far. *I always asked so many questions in school, now I only need to ask one: Ball, will you fly away from me?* Then the announcers: *in this corner, weighing in at 65 pounds—because this sport still has weight classes for some reason—the undefeated champion of the worlllllllldddd . . .*

Five seconds later, everyone goes home.

"Mayhap as students play it," Ceal said. "The sphere may not move for half days when locked between the wills of two masters. Oft victory comes from fatigue than skill."

"Sounds stupid," muttered Pat.

Micky slid across the bench, nice and close. "Oh dear, does it piss you off?" Then to Ceal, she said, "Back up; she might read something locked in one of your drawers this time!"

Micky, shorter but certainly a few pounds and important sizes larger than Pat, got airtime as she was shoved back to her side. The chick was strong when she wanted to be. No yellow glow like Ceal had told her to look for, though. That was raw bitch strength.

"The Base outmatches both," continued Ceal like nothing happened. "In a game of Cintup, if one could wield the Base, then not ten opponents could stand against her." She sliced her hand through the air for effect while casting the weirdest expression. Like, laser eyes.

Reactions.

Micky kept the silly smile plastered on her face, but thoughts came fast. That look was hard to place because it came from Ceal—someone who moved the game pieces, not waited to be moved. But it was a momentary lapse. Hunger for something Ceal wanted more than anything.

The Base.

It was the third Power, some sort of Mother Nature vegan energy that people could not control. But up to this point, they hadn't discussed its relative strength. And that much power wasn't an impossibility to people like Ceal.

It was motivation.

Oh wow.

"So, the storm is a Base storm and therefore unstoppable?" Dr. Pat asked, pouty. She kept looking out the windows, probably trying to see if the other carriages were keeping pace. The evacuees were long gone, hunkered down near Yordel with the Deadlies, Buontempo, and Sergeant Orrugant. The "strike force"—as no one called it but Pat—amounted to a convoy of passenger vans. Watchmen and a few tens of able-bodied men at arms with Captain Rath were packed into four heavy carriages. Bulky, bloated, but their best shot at reaching Oxhold. Then, ostensibly, Durador in time to save Portcullis, but . . .

We're not racing toward; we're running from.

Ceal started to explain the very unusual cause-and-effect relationships of planet Scianas. Storms rising because some magical butterfly in the Dowdale Valley turned back into a caterpillar instead of flapping its wings. Micky kinda understood, but applied sciences and engineering were never her thing. They were too sterile and clinical, which meant shit when they touched human hands.

Motivations.

They were her domain, and Ceal just gave her the proper prescription lenses to see how this would play out. The whole war had nothing to do with saving the planet, conquest, revenge, or even money. It boiled down to one singular element: that impossible, incredible Power.

The next piece of the puzzle clicked into place faster than Micky's brain could process it. Like, her mind ran a query for everything falling into the category of impossible and then filtered by credible, Scianas-based sources: Defeating Isllor Mortund's immense power, restoring Ceal to health, blocking a blade strike from Benton, prophetic dreams, and blowing past the world's greatest Stochist to read a damned letter . . .

Dr. Pat could wield the Base.

Micky's training prevented her from wearing that eureka moment on her face, but everything suddenly made sense. It was Christmas Day, and all the presents were open. But before she could feast, Ceal grimaced and slammed a hand down on the desk for support.

"What is it?" asked Dr. Pat.

Features tight, Ceal stared past them to some distant horror. If it was anyone else, Micky would be five seconds from slapping her drama-queen ass across the face. But it wasn't, and the calm, Caribbean waters of Ceal's eyes went bloodshot, rogue Sahara.

When it passed, Ceal rose, clutching her head. "Cintup indeed," she whispered, then snapped to life and called for the driver to go faster. Behind closed eyes, she whispered for tireless horses and strength to their legs. The coach surged forward, almost sending Micky ass over teakettle.

"What happened?" cried Pat, scrambling to hang onto something.

Micky looked at Ceal, and they shared a moment of understanding. What happened was nothing compared to what was coming. And, worse, Dr. Pat was nowhere near ready.

"Well?"

"The Bark hath fallen," answered Ceal.

CHAPTER 17

STROKE

In spite of the Ripolis Barbican's might and roaring fires, Ajid's fury pressed inward. White, dry frost gripped the flanking machicolations and the forewall. A pond of ice crept from the observation deck in defiance of wood's heat. Benton could now see his breath, and his armor sounded of *coldcreak*.

Strange how rain still falls in this dire chill, he thought, wishing for Ceal's council. The weather was familiar, reminiscent of his and Lord Dain's disastrous journey to the White. It held meaning, but always his thoughts were returned to the horrors unfolding upon the Doormat below.

Great sheets of white and wet lashed down upon the oily legions of the Pandonis Immortalis, yet still they surged. Benton knew Dux Herm's arrows loosed at will into the mess but could see naught of it. Only the leavings of bodies in the wakes of their blocks spoke of the effect. Closer, where ranks took to their shields then scattered as broken troops were wont, was the work of the Corsan Carre. Thus far, none had touched the wall's base.

"Benton, this is ridiculous," called Captain Saunders from the doorway to the left machicolation. Unarmored in those flaxen garments, his resistance to the elements was impressive. "They're just taking it, sacking men to deplete our ammo. How long can we keep this up?"

It was the vast question of all battles that summed the many smaller ones. Captain Saunders mayhap knew this and overspoke in wishing to know of their arms stockpiles.

Two yesterdays ago, Dux Herms inventoried their loosed, thrown, and tossed weapons. The wooden arrows now in use were but kindling for the inferno to come. Iron arrows, Wraithstone, even Erus Fire—clay bulbs with a reddish oil that would burn through the freeze and soak—sat in deadly reserve.

The mightier question was found in the will and stamina of men. Mayhap Captain Saunders wished to know of Sir Rampo, sworn knight of Artur Bayliss, who had yet to turn treacherous.

"Long," Benton answered, confident. To bolster chilled spirits, he waved to a bannerman. "Fireline."

The lad, a Caranuscan whose bronzed face marked him of Hastadonia's salted warmth, grabbed the red rope and yanked. Above, a horn blew thrice. Benton beckoned Saunders inward as Dalmore ordered the mesh awning lowered to protect from counterstriking arrows.

The Corsan Carre wore a hard look, mayhap to conceal his confusion. Through the mesh, they watched Dux Herms' next volley streak bright through the storm. It slashed a swath of sparks across the Doormat, and then the very mud and snow burst bright into flames.

Great flames.

Impassible flames.

The Genisan blocks recoiled as oil to water. Those behind tried to turn but were pushed into the pyre by the crush of their advancing companions. Those forward broke into a frantic run to face judgment upon the wall. Dux Herms' arrows and the thunder of the Corsan Carre proved a merciless gavel.

"Heat's off," said Captain Saunders studying the Genisan masses penned behind the flaming fence. Then he turned upon his heels. "Goddamn, Benton, we need to work on our communication. Why didn't you tell me that was a capability?"

"Hath ye explained the many ways of ye's relics?"

The faded bronze of his jaw that likewise spoke of a birthplace touched by warm seas tightened. "Point taken." He returned his gaze to the Doormat. "Look, we've got a minute here. I will let you rattle off a full mag on auto like a total redneck asshole if you bring me up to speed on what they've got up top."

Benton smiled, unsure that he wished for such a gift. Still, he relayed the inventory as he remembered. As he reached the red oil and its strange origins from the piss of a beast found in the wetwoods north of Lumberland, he was halted by strange sensations.

Warmth.

A weight lifted.

Captain Saunders gave no notice nor any other in the room. As Benton's nose still nipped of cold, the air had not changed.

Nay, the warmth was coming from his armor—the Everwinter Steel bequeathed from Lord Dain afore their disaster in the White. After so long dormant, it somehow breathed life. Rendercrafted metals held extraordinary properties, even beneath the Bark. The armor could turn blades and tap-forged spears alike. But the Quotidian effects of warmth, featherweight, and mar-less were supposed to be . . .

The great barbican grew bright. The gathered men-at-arms, awash in pale light, gasped, and heads tilted to the thick-beam ceiling.

The Q-lights.

Benton reacted first as a soldier, pulling Captain Saunders back from the chain mesh, and second as a commander ordering the bells rung to warn the city.

"What is this?" shouted Dalmore stumbling down the stairs as a commotion rose among the Watchmen, Deadlies, and bannermen. Little did they know of the Powers, but with certainty, the Bark kept the Q-lights dark.

"Power's back on," spat the Corsan Carre, relic in hand, as he rushed past. Benton thought the words made sense and considered drawing his sword, Dawn of Mourn, which surely glowed blue within its sheath. But there was no tell of how the Obantum Carre would strike. Treacherous as poison or with such fury that a sword would stand as straw before a twelve-horsed battle carriage.

"Vault Team, report!" screamed Captain Saunders into his Long Voice.

Outside, black-armored infantry throughout the Doormat raised their jagged swords and unleashed a roar. It shook the canyon, and the air cracked with lightning. The rear bulk stood in reserve no longer, and dark riders rushed from the deeper roads to fill out the flanks. The fireline snuffed to smoke, and they charged once more.

All of them.

"Vault, respond!" Saunders yelled into the mic. He pressed the headset against his ear to muffle the panic in the NWCC.

Nothing.

"Fischer, Gladstone, Licht. Report, over." The NWCC shook, grout and sand poured down as the superstructure groaned in protest. There was no telling how much force the Black Robes could project on this place, but Mendo—Isllor—all but tore down the Assembly Hall with a few whispers and took out the Blue Cloak keep with a fucking meteor.

This is the goddamned wrong side of asymmetric warfare.

Around him, questions shouted over orders, crackling gunfire, and a new type of thunder.

"What of the Bark?"

"Hath the city fallen behind us?"

"What of the South Gate?"

Saunders didn't engage. The Bark's failure was bad but baked into the plan. Losing contact with Vault Team, however, was not. Between Fischer on overwatch, a platoon of Watchmen stationed outside, the Bark active, and fucking radios, he had expected at least a heads up.

"Soldier," called Benton over the chaos, "Go atop and look upon the city. Hath the South Wall fallen? Do we hold City Square?"

"At once!" replied a sopping wet, shivering Deadlie.

"Ring the bells; we must prepare for withdrawal," ordered Dalmore, following his subordinate up the stairs.

"Aye," said Benton. "The wall will hold, but not long. We must begin our flight."

Saunders grimaced. The Benton Plan called for retrograde at the first of either Ceal reaching Oxhold or Portcullis losing the tactical advantage. But the last report from Captain Rath put them six to seven hours out if this storm didn't intensify. Win or lose, the mission was still to keep the Genisans penned in the city.

The detonator. It was everything now.

Clanging broke through the clamor as the silver bells up top went loud.

Good, that'll get Smith's team on the move.

Saunders just hoped it wasn't too late.

Turning back to the nightmare unfolding in the canyon, his bile duct seized as a wave of fire rose and swallowed their eastern flank. The wall held, but anyone exposed was char. More flashes pulsed from deep within the enemy ranks, and explosions rattled teeth. Saunders spat, spun around, and met Benton's wild eyes. "Options?"

The lord governor managed to unclench his jaw to form words. "They must claim this wall with soldiers. It gives us time."

"What does that mean? Looks like they can split this place in half by waving their dicks at it."

"The North Wall is wrought with Renderstone; it can resist the Obantum."

"I need numbers. How long can we hold against shit like that blowtorch?" He pointed to the blackened flank in case the translation was insufficient.

"For what span?"

Saunders let it slide. There wasn't enough emotional capital to rage at the half-assed, unquantifiable way these people accounted time. "Tomorrow."

The stone snapped at his boots as a concussive wave rode through the wall. Everyone staggered, but the room held its shape. Still, it was enough to pluck a particular fear about reliving the last moments of the World Trade Center, a sturdy steel building suddenly imploding. Waiting around for that was not how he wanted to earn Sarah's tax-free bereavement payout.

"Widths, not days," said Benton.

"Dusk?"

"Lords of Galimay, they have reached the base!" cried a green-armored archer coming in from the western balcony.

"Swords and spears! Resist death!" boomed Dalmore storming out of the stairwell, his polished plate streaked with soot.

"Resist death!" came more shouts as Deadlie sergeants poured in after him.

"What news?" asked Benton.

"Sir Rampo is driven from the battlements by fire and unspeakable elements," said Dalmore. "Dux Herms holds and tasks teams to the lower tiers. The dump of pots and rocks strikes few below as an evil wind whisks it all away. The battle draws close; be ready." He grabbed his men into a huddle.

"Dalmore, hold fast," said Saunders. The Portcullis' Chief of the Watch turned, pulling off his armored helmet to dry his head with a small, blue towel. "You get eyes on the Vault?"

"Nay, the storm veils much of the city. It is a boon, I say. The enemy oft misses."

"Okay, let's pull it. Phased withdrawal. We need a rearguard to hold here while we set defensive positions in North Ward. Then that line will cover the rear. After that, it'll be running and gunning, avoiding contact with those Black Robes."

Both medieval commanders stared. "Was not the agreement to marshal at the South Gate?" asked Benton. Dalmore didn't bother with questions; he folded his arms to watch the train wreck unfold.

"Fight's here." Saunders pulled the city map out of his pack. It was hand-drawn with disproportionate sizing for everything, but it worked in a pinch. He pointed to North Ward with its packed middle-class neighborhoods. "Once the wall falls, we draw their ground in to negate their big strike capabilities. Then we push back. It won't be pretty, but every alley and corner is a choke point in our favor. We do it right; we stall their advance."

Dalmore nodded; Benton frowned.

"I want evacuation corridors secured along these side streets." He traced the pre-drawn line snaking toward Westside Dip. "Logistical elements and the clinic go first. When we're out of options, half our forces there, and the other half go with Rampo up Eastside. Under no circumstances does anyone withdraw through the South Gate."

"But I thought . . ." began Benton.

Saunders gave him a hard look before dropping the hammer. "I rigged a rockslide on the south pass. Exit closed."

Dalmore's eyes flared like a puffed stogie in the dark. "Ruthless!"

Benton was unreadable. In his white plate mail with that blue glow seeping from his sword's sheath and documented ability to move like lightning, some men might've considered him intimidating. But contests of wills operated outside the physical, and whatever Benton had cut his teeth on was nothing compared to dealing with Brines daily.

"My team's already on the move," Saunders continued. "We'll assess and take charge of the situation in City Square. If Leod's cavalry is operational, they'll work hit and run on the streets to keep our lines open and cover the withdrawal. After that, it's every man for himself. Rah?"

The response came in the form of a skull-shattering explosion as the NWCC was rocked by another blast. Dust and smoke billowed in, reraising the question of aerosolized agents. Coughing and an annoying ringing in the ears were all it amounted to.

"The Deadlies shall give ye this time," vowed Dalmore marching his men back to the stairs.

"Where you going to be?" Saunders asked Benton.

That jaw worked overtime to form words while swallowing a bowling ball of need-to-know motherfuckery. "I shall aid Sir Rampo and Dux Herms, then stand with ye after the wall is overcome."

"Benton, I know it looks like a buddy fuck. But this shitfest is crawling with spies. *Mindears,* as you said. Someone on the inside hit the Bark, probably killed three of my men. The enemy needed to think we were going to cut and run. By holding, we fuck their timeline. Read? That's a win. For us, for Ceal."

He didn't like it, wanted to spit it out, but chewed until his esophagus could handle it. That last part about Ceal got a weird reaction, but old married couples had landmines attached to every word in the dictionary. "Aye," Benton said.

"Right, let's get it done." Saunders grabbed his gear from the armory next door. Brines' and Williamson's packs were covered in dust and debris as if already lost to the ages. Fucked up, but there was no time to say goodbye.

Back in the NWCC, most of the staff were evacuated, and Benton was starting to get over the shock of finding out he was riding in the passenger seat this whole time. That blueish sword was in hand as he prepared to take charge of the rearguard and do what he did best. Saunders realized now was probably his last opportunity to mention the surprise he and Examiner Creed had prepared.

He snagged Benton by the stairs. "One more thing. You might notice some of the lights behaving erratically . . ."

"Ho, let them breathe, Estir," said Yerrat Rutvor to his brother in service. "The rats will hold faster to a ship they do not think will sink."

As the winds and wet slashed and slapped beyond their weather bubble, Estir Denormild smiled most wicked and said, "I wish to break a piece of this legendary wall. Make my mark upon it."

"You will, but Moderator Bela's call for a hold has a greater purpose than to torment your desires. Listen, already the Quotidian builds."

Estir swiped at the whine growing in his ears. "Bah, let me toss some rock."

Yerrat looked around. The high cliff was barren of free boulders, and the few protruding from the wet snow would take much effort to release with no certainty about their composition. "No, flame and flash will do. See that group of spring leaves scurrying across the top? They will rain more fire upon the ladders. A waste of life. Sate your ire there."

The air cracked, and those little green leaves upon Portcullis' wall withered to a winter brown. Some rose again only to wander aimless. Fire claimed another as he tugged on the crisp meat of his friend. The rest vanished as vermin were wont.

"This is the work of novices," cried Estir. "We stand closest now, beyond even her Stretched Guard! Their belly lies bare; what harm comes from the strike? Legions suffer below as we delay."

Yerrat nodded, conceding the loss of life was terrible. Honestly, he cared more for his own and Estir's, but only a monster would argue such. Instead, he spoke simple in the way it had been explained. "By holding, we keep the enemy upon the wall instead of fleeing into the city."

"Let me strike the city, then. We are high enough; the wall will not interfere. I shall make it a place of fear."

"More that we shall have to rebuild."

"Such sudden concern! What of the damage you wrought with your rocks, Yerrat?"

A good question. The great catapult was a mad idea born of urgency. Master Turan and the much-feared Bela had demanded a way to strike the enemy. When these powerful commanders of the Eyes and Fist had chanced to ask Yerrat, he sputtered out something akin to a child throwing stones. It stuck. Worse, after many trials, it worked. Where the rock landed, only devastation remained. The prospects for future battles were limitless, especially considering the enemy's famed Corund Corps had yet to be faced.

"A test. One now ended," Yerrat answered as his ears tingled from the piercing noise. "Can you hear it? It is almost time. We are privileged to have the finest vantage."

"Hear? Yerrat, I have sworn myself to the Eyes. I watch with shivers and tension needing release. Still, is it so terrible to tell me what Bela of the Fist has planned? Are we safe here?" Estir whispered into the blue ring upon his left thumb, and their wardings strengthened. Neither the Quotidian nor the Stochal would fast harm them here. And arrows had no chance of flying this high.

"Quite, dear friend." Indeed, Yerrat was sure both Moderators and Masters could read lips and hear thoughts. "Be joyous and watch the finish of many labors. Who else among the lowly Accepted could wriggle to such a tremendous position? Of all the Obantum, we struck first against the enemy and now shall watch his end. Thousands will whisper our names in glory and terror."

Impatient Estir shook his head and stepped closer to the ledge, leaving no footprints in the snow. Red tendrils of Slowlight crept from the folds of his Pan'jid Mantel as he prepared to defy Bela. Bold but not wild. The Fist would condemn him, but the Eyes would laud him and offer rewards unknown to any Accepted.

Estir settled on his prize, the piece he would tear asunder to make his mark. Yerrat needed not hear the whole of his questioning whispers to know the massive outcropping where the enemy's commanders stood would soon fly free. He could have intervened; the whole war was useless if it meant trading a destroyed world for a lawless one. But here, Yerrat knew he could and would cover for his friend.

"Have at it, brother."

Estir raised his arms, a meaningless gesture but elegant in the ways of the Obantum. Master Dushon oft taught that the dance was just if not more important than the Power.

An odd sound—a soft pop like a wet fruit falling from a tree—slipped through the ringing and otherwise quiet weather bubble.

Yerrat saw neither trees nor disturbed snow where something might have fallen. *An echo from elsewhere?* Yerrat's senses sharpened. A ten of liners from the Seventh Legion guarded the approach to this bluff, and a quick ask told him they still lived.

Suddenly, Estir fell back and plunged deep into the snow.

Red snow.

Yerrat searched his friend's face for playfulness, wondering if his defiance was a rouse. But only a mask draped upon slaughter stared back.

Thoughts came fast. No enemies drew near, and the wards held firm. No shaft nor feathers poked from Estir's head, and Yerrat Sensed nothing of the Power. Still, a strike.

Breath quickening, Yerrat tried to watch every direction at once. Estir's head was devastated.

Like the city struck by my boulders.

At once he understood and dropped low. The air above popped not a moment later.

———

"A-goddamn-men, Pete," Sergeant Smith whispered as the Black Robes on the cliff dropped. It was only 50 meters to the stairwell with intermittent cover from the battlements. But those fuckin' wizards had pinned them down like eagle-eyed sharpshooters with howitzers.

"Heavies offline, Marines. We on the move!"

Nickels took point, and Garcia skirted the edge, grabbing a read on the situation below. "Sergeant, they're up to the first tier."

He meant the first level with interior access, Tier Two, one down from them. "We ram through; stack up on the door!" Smith said.

The blood was pumping now. This was Smith's element, and the Pig still had plenty to give. Not enough to hold the entire wall, but anyone coming down those tight corridors would squeal like a stuck . . .

Never mind.

"Two by two, Bone," said Jersey with LCpl Light latched to his ass. The formation made sense since Nickels was carrying a SAW, the Pig's little brother. Bulb and Garcia were better off letting the machine guns lead and giving point cover with their M4s.

"Aight, we go hard. Watch for friendlies!"

"Oorah!"

The door was solid, banded 2x4s with iron hinges anchored deep into the stone. Smith didn't bother kicking it because the latch worked just fine. He pushed it open, half expecting to meet resistance. It swung free, and Nickels swept in with Bulb on his six, weapons and heads swiveling. Inside was bright, like someone had turned on the lights. The pair disappeared down the spiral stairs. Situational awareness sucked, so Smith followed a few meters back with Garcia in case some crazy magic shit spooked them. There was enough to worry about without friendly fire.

Smooth and quiet until Tier Two, when something exploded below.

"Fuck, go go go. This is our floor!" screamed Nickels, SAW blazing as he dragged Bulb back up the stairs.

The racket blew through the active ear plugs that were on their last legs anyway, and Smith felt a tap on the back. Garcia was pointing to this level's door. There was no latch or knob on this one, just flat planks and nowhere to grab. Garcia slammed it with his shoulder, but it held firm. Nickels pulled a grenade and tossed it below before Smith could think.

They had four seconds to clear that door.

Heart pounding, Smith knocked Garcia aside and launched the heel of his boot. The hinges blew dust and pebbles back at him, but it didn't open.

"Up, up, up," he barked.

Suddenly the door swung open, and a black metal arm with a jagged sword emerged.

Smith didn't wait for an invitation and let the Pig jackhammer that arm and the attached motherfucker to pieces. Then he was throwing beige Marines through the hole.

Leaping after them, the grenade's detonation beat Smith on the back of the skull, and he went face-first onto cold stone. He based up seeing stars and bodies and breathing the ass of a busy subway station before soap was invented. *Out of the blast radius and into the bull's horns.*

Gunfire.

Smith joined in, forgetting about friendlies, and chewed through anything that got too close. He was dizzy, gagging on cordite, but managed to control his burn rate. The narrow, arched stone hallway was sardine-packed with a platoon of dark plate warriors. There wasn't enough space to swing those jagged swords, so they charged in with knives and fists.

Only a bloody mist and bad breath made it through the Marine fire line.

The survivors retreated behind the growing corpse defilade, tangling with reinforcements pouring in from the outer walkway. Smith let up on the trigger once they learned their respect. Garcia and Light continued to drill single shots into anything needing a reminder.

"That grenade clear the stairs?" Smith asked Nickels.

"No way. Fuckers got some big metal shields. We ain't punching through that."

Another blast from the SAW dropped two trying to skirt along the walls. The main horde had sorted itself out and was edging closer.

"Someone crackin' whips out there; gotta move!" Smith roared before the heavy gun dug into his shoulder and ripped across a trio of badasses who decided to charge. The hallway was getting humid, nasty, and gut-wrenching with the moans of the dying. His boots were sopped in blood, and the floor writhing with bodies. Problem was that every way forward had enemy infil.

Gotta back out and head up.

Suddenly, LCpl Light stumbled forward as a dark-plated soldier slammed into the stairwell door behind him. Garcia jumped in and helped Bulb force it closed and secure the latch, but there went their exit.

"Fuck we doin', Bone?" shouted Nickels.

The options weren't good. Holding meant dealing with a swarm scenario that ended with them out of ammo and buried. Driving hard and taking a left down the hallway put them deeper into the wall and exposed them to more angles of aggress. To the right was that nasty pile of bodies with a crop of sharps waiting on the other side.

"Gotta risk the stairs," he said, wheeling the Pig around and locking eyes with Nickels. "Bang and boom!"

"Negative, we . . . Fuck!" The SAW went loud.

Smith wheeled—a tiny part of his brain praising what was left of the active hearing protection plugs preventing him from going deaf by 30—in time to see a solid two-by-two column of metal storming in from the left. They were moving fast, hard. Zero fucks for their lives.

The Pig dug in.

Metal sparked and ripped, bodies crumbled and peeled off, but the ones behind just trampled their buddies. It was a mad dash to get in close.

Nickels' SAW clicked empty; Smith didn't hear it so much as felt it. Garcia and Light were firing but in the opposite direction. Smith didn't dare look, just kept hammering as the column split, trying to dodge the blazing stream of steel core.

Thunk.

The Pig was dry, and with it, the thunder and strobing fire that earned the USMC their respect.

Swords and screaming filled the void.

Smith fell back, wrenching his pistol out of its holster. He wanted to panic big time, but the training kept it by the numbers.

Safety off.

Aim.

Squeeze trigger until empty.

The 9 mm rounds did exactly shit to those breastplates but were punching through on the legs. There wasn't time to analyze it, just to reload and keep going.

The pistol went dead in his hands as two fuckheads scrambled over the pile of their dead and dying friends. Black boots found solid ground and sped to close the gap. There was plenty of space this time to get those swords whipping around and test the ESAPI plates in Smith's body armor.

Seconds from pain, gunfire ripped from beyond the corpse pile.

That ain't a carbine.

Smith never closed his eyes but definitely opened them to see the two dudes splash down inches from his feet. Sweeping in behind was something beautiful.

Beige and a full combat loadout.

"Move, Marines!" boomed Captain Saunders, pulling the exterior door closed behind him and barring it. Leak plugged; the way right was clear.

Smith obeyed with extreme prejudice, using skulls like steppingstones and swapping ammo boxes mid-stride. Jersey brought the others on his six, yelling about the enemy massing left for another attack.

"Far stairs," the captain shouted. "Covering." He dropped to a knee and lined up his MP5.

"Jersey, the cap'n."

Nickels took cover behind a stone column and zeroed their former tomb. Garcia and Light moved ahead and secured entry to the stairwell.

"Clear," said Garcia.

"Go!" said Smith as Jersey's SAW, freshly reloaded, drew a curtain. The enemy fell back, but some of those two-meter, heavy shields Jersey was talking about were making their way forward.

Next charge won't stop.

Garcia and Light made entry. Smith slapped the captain. "You up, sir."

The captain shook his head like Gunny always said he would. "Pull out; I'll cover."

Smith wasn't going to argue when seconds were hemorrhaging bullets and heartbeats. Orders were orders. He pulled Nickels off the line and shoved him into the stairwell. Before Smith followed, his eyes caught the black scabbard of that creepy sword strapped to the captain's side. He'd seen it before, but now, it seemed important somehow.

He shook it off and shouted, "Clear, sir!" but it was lost as the MP5 went loud again.

Nickels had an adrenal hardon.

This was the gut check that minted motherfuckers like Gunny. It was bloodlust in the truest sense, a killing spree with each wave harder to beat back.

Chest heaving, Nickels' lungs were barely keeping pace with his heart and never enough to meet the burning in his arms and legs. The SAW was sizzling, smoking like tits at a barbecue. When the captain and his swinging bag of brass cantaloupes cut an exit, Nickels was almost afraid to slap on another ammo box before the barrel could cool down.

Almost.

The stairs emptied into the dark tunnel of the wall's hollow bottom—a deathtrap for hostiles thinking they could exit at the ground level. Technically they could, but to reach the central gate meant running the gauntlet—a single-file path through a maze of sharps and chokepoints where soldiers with spears were posted.

The subway-station-damp floor was littered with bodies.

"Goggles on," snapped a voice following them out of the stairwell. The captain.

Goddamn, how the fuck did he get out? Nickels wondered. But now wasn't time for questions, just respect.

The gauntlet's torches were doused or never lit, and there were none of those fancy, fluorescent crystal lights either. Nickels lowered his NVGs, bringing it all back to daylight while shrinking his visual field to a coke bottle circle. The corpses at the stair base were mostly fuckheads, but a few white-tabarded Watchmen were in the mix. Nickels avoided looking at their faces.

"Scared me, sir," said Smith locking eyes with the captain. Whatever happened up there stayed up there, and Smith let it drop with, "Okay, we online." Then he took point and waved the team forward.

Nickels grabbed the rear, not because it was remotely on his mind that it would have any sexual connotation, but because he wanted first blood on anyone with the balls to come after them.

Rifle fire popped forward.

RUSH.

It turned out to be LCpl Light earning his nickname Bulb with the bright idea of wasting a bullet in a straggler who hadn't yet figured out how to die. Otherwise, it was clean moving until they hit the maze. The jagged shit everywhere made it like wading through barbed wire in high winds. Nickels took more than a few cuts on his shoulders and thighs. *Bone's big ass must be loving this.*

"Where's the Watch?" he called forward, seeing the empty ambush positions behind the metal grating.

"Couldn't hold, fell back to the gate," answered the captain kicking a pole on the ground. It was a spear with a retractable set of wicked blades at the end. Sorta thing that could fit through the slats and slice up the Watchmen on the other side.

"Fuckers came prepared," huffed Smith.

"Keep moving," said the captain. "Last report said the main gate was secure. Enemy couldn't crack it. They pivoted vertical to hit the exit on Tier Five, which is where you should've fucking gone." The bus-sized foundation stones around them groaned as if to emphasize his point.

"Sorry, Cap'n," said Smith.

Nickels began replaying the decision to go down instead of up when rifles spat, and the walls flashed.

"Fuck, we're cut off!" came the shout; it could've been anyone. Bulb's skinny—but still too big—frame was blocking the view forward. Gunfire snapped.

Movement from behind.

Nickels spun to find a SWAT team of medieval infantry coming in hard. And in that heavy armor, they didn't give a fuck about all the spikes and barbs.

Nickels' cooled-down SAW went live, pounding them full of America. Sparks flared in his image-enhanced vision as metal armor shattered and crumpled to the deck. Unlike the guys upstairs, these learned fast and pulled their macho shit back.

An epic one-liner that only Smith would get was about to jump off Nickels' tongue when something pinged the wrought iron cage beside him.

A quarrel.

Crossbows!

That adrenal hardon saw red, and Nickels dove straight in, SAW blazing. No one was getting drilled in the back on his watch. Godawful gurgles and screams passed through his active earplugs, drowning out the muted thunder of exploding cartridges. Rivers ran down his face, no time to check if it was blood or sweat.

More armor dumped out of the stairwell carrying those big shields. *Not this time, fuckers!* Nickels dropped to single-shot fire, aiming for exposed feet.

Marine voices barked from behind, but tracking targets was hard enough through the NVG peepholes. Turning to see what was up would burn seconds he didn't have.

The stone walls flickered lightning, and hot air blew past.

The SAW was running low. He called for covering fire, but no one came. The second it went empty, he'd be on the pistol. That might buy just enough time to fish out his last grenade. His only regret would be that he never bothered to write *Toblerone* on it.

The smokey tunnel exploded.

Nickels kept his footing, but the shock slapped him like a bare-assed child taking daddy's hand.

Thoughts oozed as he tried to reacquire his targets. *Was that us or them?* All he knew was that his ears were ringing.

Cold.

Someone was pissing ice water on his neck, and the whole place became one big wind tunnel.

He knocked the over-saturated NVGs off his face. Daylight.

A meaty palm landed on his shoulder. Then Bone's big lips were right in his ringing ear. "This way, bro!"

Nickels forgot about the enemy and followed. Someone had blown a hole in the gigantic, impenetrable wall. Just wide enough for Smith. Legs turning to rubber, Nickels let a pair, or trio, of strong arms pull him through.

Sleet whipped at his face as he slapped down onto iced-over cobblestones. Despite his ears ringing louder than ever, the fresh air felt amazing, and he gulped lungfuls. Once his head stopped spinning, he crawled through the writhing bodies and gear of Marines. Finally oriented enough to get up on all fours, he lifted his head.

Not twenty feet away was another wall of pure motherfuckery.

Rows and rows of armored infantry.

"Relax, dawg, they friendly," shouted Smith, but it was barely audible. That crazy ringing had turned into a high-pitched whine. Strange part was that it was familiar. Not the aftereffect of the blast but something more recent and unnatural.

By the time Nickels remembered it as the noise they heard in the wolf cave before the Black Robe dropped in, it was too late.

———

It was a meteorologist's cold day in hell.

Right now, the sky was spitting sleet, while five minutes ago was a steaming, sideways downpour. Before that, hail. The shooting mat (half a horse blanket) beneath Francisco was soaked like he'd laid it in a creek instead of a snowbank. His poncho might as well have been made of tissue paper.

The wind was the real problem. Whipping in all directions, it was impossible to correct shots. That one Black Robe was a one in a million. Like sinking a putt from fucking orbit. The follow-up, of course, missed, but Francisco kept the weapon's reticle trained on the little bluff below. The other was still there, somewhere.

Francisco decided against poking the nest. If a wizard got an inkling he was up here, his lifespan would be measurable in parts per billion.

The M151 Spotting Scope was aimed at the city. The storm-ravaged scene was like watching those old, blocked-out porno channels on cable—heavy static, but enough to hold that immediate interest. The wall was inundated, smoke billowing through the tiers and gusting off the top. Nothing was moving. Behind that, familiar groups of greens and whites were massing in North Ward. No indication of where his brother Marines were.

The Doormat was a different story: full retreat.

Francisco had several different words for it: regrouping, reforming ranks, tactical withdrawal, retrograde, coffee break, etc. Point was that the offensive had stalled. The Genisans maintained a solid foothold on the wall's third tier but weren't moving higher from what he could see. Likely, battles were ongoing within, especially in the bowels that Sir Rampo had declared would "grind men's bones and shred their metal."

Pulling back left that foothold unsupported, which didn't make sense. Maybe the Genisans figured they could hold and bring up engineers. Meanwhile, everyone else got out of arrow range and rotated out of this insane weather.

Whatever was going on, it was the break Portcullis needed. Saunders had some wild plan to burn bridges. The details were hazy, but it called for Cork Team to live up to its name and a lateral evacuation for the locals. Deeper in the city, friendly troops were already moving to establish secure evacuation routes. Soon thousands of soldiers would flood the back trails leading into the mountain range, a place of choke points where numerical superiority became a liability.

Francisco panned the Doormat again. No Black Robes and the infantry squares were dug in at the canyon's entrance like they were preparing to lay siege. Portcullis still stood strong.

Like a burger with its bun about to slide off.

Wall clouds were sweeping in from the south as if a tornado were about to drop. The stone city with its spider web of streets—now lit with those magical lights—would probably handle high winds just fine. Another plus for the sheltered defenders versus the mostly exposed OpFor.

A pan right brought a reminder that the Sticks would see the worst of it. Even now, smoke blew between the houses as flames crept beneath rooftops. The city was compartmentalized by stone walls that once formed its earlier boundaries, so the fire wouldn't threaten the evacuation corridors or North Ward. Plus, the abnormal mix of snow, sleet, hail, and spring rain was better than any type of fire suppression they had on hand.

Movement below got him behind the Bullpup. It was a plated soldier inspecting the corpse of the dead Black Robe. Classic bait to draw out a sniper.

Something pricked the edge of Francisco's hearing, a whine that sent shivers to his core and his hand to his pistol. It was faint, though, not like before in the Assembly Hall. He rolled back to his spotter and scanned Sir Rampo's defensive line forming up in North Ward.

It took a minute, but he finally got eyes on a cluster of beige. The Marines were out of the wall and panning their rifles in all directions. All of them were pawing at their ears.

Firing off a warning flare came to mind, but it looked like they knew what kind of hell was about to drop on them.

The whine rose to its dreaded peak, and Francisco was back behind his rifle. The reticle moved to North Ward, and he slowed his breathing. One shot, that's all he'd get before the one hiding on the cliff below had a chance to react.

"Strike first," he whispered.

A flash and the gray clouds above became suns. Francisco jerked away from the scope, but it was too late. In the darkness behind his right eyelid stood a city of white magnesium. The pain drove deep through his optic nerve, and the back of his head pounded. Still, he did have another eye.

He shifted the Bullpup to his left shoulder. Long ago, he'd made a point to train once with the right and twice with the left. His non-dominant side never really caught up, but it served as a useful backup.

His left pupil was constricting like a snake on a mouse, but it worked. The gloomy clouds were back, and the city was still standing. He panned North Ward. Wet, dark stone pocketed with snowdrifts and icicles glistening off the little streetlights. Not torched, not blown to bits.

The enemy didn't want to destroy their prize. Capture. Focusing on the streets, Francisco discovered they were now covered in little dark figures that sparkled like they were encrusted with rubies.

The ultimate landing force.

Gunfire echoed up through the mountains as he panned right, panned everywhere. The whole city was infested.

CHAPTER 18

NEARER, MY GOD, TO THEE

The grand fireplace of fitted stones laid by Uumhrat's own hands crackled and popped as roaring flames ate through last season's parched wood. It bathed the great room in comfortable warmth, but so too the inn's upper two floors. The heat gusted up and through spaces behind the wallboards to the rooms, flowing as if the air were blood and the hearth a beating heart.

Today was a fine day for a fire, with the terrible storm forcing cold and damp into the city's many crevices. Uumhrat turned his ears to the pelt of ice upon the windows and envisioned a wayward group ducking in with their collars turned and cloaks frosted. Shivers fading to cheer as they took their meals in the plush chairs gathered around. 'Twas a longing Uumhrat knew well.

No matter the storm or wear of the road, these walls will keep ye safe.

His words. His promise to himself more than others.

The meal tables were set, he made sure of that, and the dishes clean. Naught a width prior saw the last of the night's soiled mugs wiped with a damp rag and tucked away in the cupboard lest any judge him a poor host.

Much, small and large, went to running an inn. Oft, it was more than his help could tend, but always were the pots, pans, and dishes ready for the next guest. Days of hungry Caranuscans had tested him, but to song and ruckus, Uumhrat cooked, cleaned, served, and bedded those in need. Naught for a single coin, stamped or otherwise.

It was his joy to share with a city that had given its love.

Love, but so too ire in equal heaping. A year of jeers and taunts, empty tables, and spitting folk knocked from the overlarge darkness in his mind.

The Blue Cloaks under Lord Bayliss had taken, not given, at each turn. Stripped his friends of their earned places, poisoned their deeds, and quieted the inns of their praise. And Uumhrat had sat idle, safe within his dream of welcoming those in need. His selfish and remorseful hope was that he was working to encourage fellowship over spite. But truly, he was hiding.

Until the Corsan Carre.

Uumhrat knew much of the world's men, but never before such arrogance from strangers who would call themselves friends. Brines—the enduring warrior heart of old and new and all—was the first, striding forth and seeing through the smile and apron to the man within. His presence so inspired Uumhrat that he nigh broke his oaths. Those cutting eyes in the like of an Everwinter sky left a wound that no dressing could mend. Then the lass, Micky, with questions that would humble their Reverence's red spies. Eyes only for the truth.

Truth that freed Palefang, Benton, and Ceal. Three of Uumhrat's finest companions, restored and envigored as in the days of old.

He glanced at the Q-lights, now shining throughout the rooms. In this last moment, the inn was restored to its full glory. It was heartening.

Alas, he knew it false, as Brines had known him false. The lights were brighter than before, glowing ever brighter still. Uumhrat tried to remember what Examiner Creed had said in his stupor. That the return of the Quotidian would herald the end for Portcullis.

More loss. It was enough to know without needing the deep sorrow of how and why. Uumhrat closed his ears to what might come so he might enjoy the last bits of his waking dream. A deep-cushioned chair before the fire beckoned. A fine tome from the Inn's small collection could spark his wit as he waited for his next customer. Alas, it would have to wait.

The rooms were where he most wanted to go. The Corsan Carre forbade him from entering during their stay, and surely they held the musts and leavings of old guests and happier days. There was no time to fold the linens—a wild desire akin to dressing the dead before feeding them to the worms—but his last request was to feel this place lived in once more.

To his surprise, the beds were made, sheets crisply stretched over the mattresses, and not a speck of dust could be found that was not there before. He beamed. Dressed to its best, the inn would meet its fate regal as a king. He did not know if this was their gift to him, but he savored the moment until he could ignore the call no longer.

Uumhrat opened his ears to the steady thudding from below. What began as a knock, and taps against the windows, had become a ram driven against the front door. The banging echoed through the empty halls until giving way to the cracking of wood.

He walked down the stairs for the last time, soaking himself in the warmth and welcome he had come to love. It was difficult to believe that in a few short moments, this place would be closed to him forever. Nevermore would he set out the mugs or tap a fresh keg of Almon's finest. No more meals, mirth, or fireside drinks with Benton.

The main door bowed upon its hinges, yielding to the shouts and batter of men. Uumhrat stepped up to the bar and set his thick hands upon the long counter in the fashion of a customer. With a sigh, he said, "I'll be needin' to settle up with ye barkeep."

None answered, of course, so he spoke in their stead. "Ye be leavin' us now, Uumhrat?"

"Aye."

"When will ye be back?"

Bits of dust puffed out of the door's seams where the frame met the masonry walls. Suddenly, it crashed inward. Armor-laden soldiers tracked muck and street slosh across the fine plank floors. The stampede of steel crashed through the smooth wooden tables where his friends of old and new had eaten and shared in the good times.

Uumhrat closed his fingers around the handle of his ax—Dusk of Sorrow, down from its forever place above the mantel—and felt an old, familiar tingle.

"Never," he growled.

Pride, mayhap the bloodlust, drove the warriors in their dark, reddish armor forward. An easy kill, they saw. So young were they, mayhaps younger than the Corsan Carre, that they did not recognize him as he turned. A simple man in an apron.

But they stumbled at the ax.

The beautiful haft was engraved with the language of demons, warning other demons to beware. The metal, thick at the base and thinning into a seductive and deadly curve at the edge, glowed blue in his hands.

Bluer still as that old tingle in Uumhrat's heart simmered to a roil.

Wire, walls, towers, 500-mile tactical zones, no man's lands, oceans, moats, and stratospheric bombing campaigns.

All bullshit.

This was war. On the ground, in the now of people beating each other to death. Ugly, carnal, desperate. It was the final test: impossible to study for and the only one that counted.

Kill to survive.

Saunders' Marines were a combat starfish—back-to-back, firing in all directions. Red-glittered soldiers were falling, bumbling around, disoriented from translocating. The green Caranuscans were surprised, too, but organized in battle formation thanks to Dux Herms. For the moment, they were moving as cohesive units, tanks through a stampede of red sheep.

It wouldn't last.

The same thing, albeit at a smaller scale, happened when Mendo/Isllor blew up at Benton's trial. The reds flashed in and took time to form ranks. When they did, the city barely survived.

A voice boomed above the clash. "Protect the gate!" Dux Herms, in his blood-splattered armor, was pointing a sword back at the North Wall. Between bursts of his running dry MP5, Saunders had trouble imagining the gate complex's strategic value now that thousands of troops had dropped behind it. True, it could still slow reinforcements, but for all practical concerns, the city had fallen.

Fallen, but didn't know it was dead yet.

"Back to the greens; cover fire!" Saunders ordered.

Smith roared something, slammed a fresh box on his M240, and the Marine starfish made for the bulk of the Caranuscans protecting Dux Herms. It was like one of those football drills with the team running through a course of tires, trying not to trip. Except here it was bodies. Some were alive, writhing. Others, gargling up crimson gobs, swiped at ankles, desperate for one last opportunity to make a difference.

The rifles took a breather when the starfish got behind the shield wall. Saunders considered keeping Nickels and Garcia out there, but killing grunts was a poor use of bullets. Black Robes were coming.

A boom followed by a long rumble shook the city from the south. A few heads turned, but it didn't stop the fighting. Saunders recognized it as Marine ordnance, not some Black Robe bullshit, and could've cried for joy.

Someone had figured out the battery situation on one of the detonators and followed orders for a change.

The only road south was now buried under a few thousand tons of rock.

And someone from Vault Team is still alive.

"Herms!" Saunders called, wiping his face with numb hands and dimly realizing they were in an open downpour. "The gate's lost; the plan's fucked. We need to move on the evacuation corridors."

The Caranuscan commander both shook his head and nodded, adding to the confusion. "The Deadlies and Lord Benton are within the wall," he said. "Sir Rampo works to free them."

Last count put almost 500 men up there. Enough to make a difference, but not if they couldn't get out. "Place is probably crawling with reds." He aimed a finger at the enemy ranks driving into the shield wall in case the color coding wasn't clear. "We don't have the manpower to extract them."

A head shake, no nod. "Reds only outside. They struck same in Drethanum. Obantum Carre sent birds over the walls to scout the streets. But they could not see in our towers or homes." Herms snapped to his left. "Pull them back!" Two wounded greens were dragged behind lines, hot life spilling onto the ice at their feet. "The wall is free, I swear it. We must give them time."

That didn't exactly align with Saunders' recent experience. However, the Doormat was in retrograde for some reason. Maybe it was a classic case of ignoring a formidable defensive position by finding a way around it. Regardless, no one on any world needed to sell Saunders on giving warfighters time to get themselves unfucked. "We hold," he said.

True to the timeline, the red lines stiffened and surged south to cut off exfil. The Caranuscans responded by splitting their forces: half in ranks to crash and bash, the rest behind with the ranged gear—crossbows and bows. They drove hard into the main body. It worked, and the enemy lost thrust. But the burn rate was high, and more reinforcements were flashing into North Ward.

The second we lose momentum, our defense is dead.

Suddenly, Dux Herms' gamble paid off. Silver plate mail, bright against the dark stone, appeared at the North Gate and scaffolding on Tier Five. Before Saunders could think to get their attention, they became columns. Not an orderly evacuation, but hardened soldiers charging into battle three abreast.

The fresh—well, fresher—troops pumped into the front lines. Bolstered, the Caranuscan mass redoubled their push, forcing the reds into a defensive shield wall.

Sir Rampo was the first familiar face to appear from the exodus. He strode up, white plate gleaming in defiance of the dark day and icing rain. His helmet stayed, but he lifted the face shield to show that he was loving every minute. "Hail! The North Wall fast became a boring post, so we hath come hither. What tell of North Ward?"

"Where's Dalmore? Benton?" Saunders asked.

"Last to leave or some foolery. Hath the Corsan Carre encumbered us with a plan, or shall I compose mine own?"

"We can't hold; need to keep our exits open." Saunders almost wanted to touch on the fact that Sir Rampo had gone back into the wall at enormous personal risk to help the Deadlies, but time was tight, and the guy would just spin out some psychotic rationale anyway.

"When the eyes say nay, we turn to the heart," said the knight, raising his sword like a beacon in storming seas. When he dropped it, literal waves rippled through the tight Caranuscan formations. The men surged. Each rank threw its weight into the next, building momentum until smashing into the enemy shield wall. By the fifth wave, they had cracked the stalemate.

Former Blue Cloaks stormed into the brief rout, reclaiming several streets to the east and west. It was enough space that Saunders could almost breathe again. He directed Smith's team to help haul wounded.

Dalmore and Benton were the last to emerge from the tunnel. Two Deadlies dropped the gate and jammed the gears. "Those able hath left," said Dalmore. The wall is now our foe."

"Roger that," said Saunders waving Sir Rampo and Dux Herms over. "Okay, listen up. Plan's shot to shit; we need to leave. The Watch has established east and western evacuation corridors. Dalmore, I want the Deadlies to secure the western evac site and facilitate CASEVAC from the clinic. Then you pull it. Rampo and Herms, push toward Eastside Rise."

"What of the lord governor?" asked Rampo.

"Benton's commanding the rearguard here in North Ward with us. We'll hold until people start moving into the mountain trails."

Dalmore panned the clash and snorted. "For widths."

"Heartbeats, mine man," said Sir Rampo smiling at some private thought. Benton's stare was ice.

"What of the Obantum?" asked Herms, staring up at the wall. The top was lost in a cloud of snow chasing the rain down.

"They will show themselves no matter our place. Let them, too, find themselves in this dark trap ye hath created, *Captain Saunders,*" spat Benton.

Formal. It appeared that Benton wasn't the same blind-faith, dick-sucking believer in the *Corsan Carre* he'd been ten seconds before hearing about the plan to nuke this place to shit.

Tough luck, buddy. You wanted unicorns to sweep in and make the flowers blossom, but you got Marines. We go big.

Ignoring the attitude, Saunders said, "The moment the evacuation rallies are on the move, you blow your horns, and we'll fall back east in collapsing echelons. We don't get cut off. Understood?"

Nickels' SAW ripped, shattering the moment. Part of the Caranuscan shield wall had buckled under the sheer human mass pressing into it. The breakthrough reds ate iced-over cobblestone, and the hole was plugged fast, but it was just a matter of time.

"Tell them," growled Benton through teeth and wet snow sticking to his face.

Suddenly, the flashing, frothing, frozen hellscape of war went on mute as Dalmore, Herms, and even Rampo leaned in to hear what managed to upset the lord governor.

Saunders licked his lips; the rain tasted freezer burned. "Creed and I rigged the Q-stone to overcharge the city lattice." He mimed an explosion with his hands. By their expressions, they understood.

Except maybe Rampo; he just laughed.

"Lord Benton," said Dalmore after a few seconds. "'Tis the Last Army. All are promised to the fight." He panned the sturdy homes and battlements. "Mayhaps even the stone and sticks."

"It has no precedent," said Dux Herms.

"I shall enjoy the sight from the high slopes," said Sir Rampo.

"May that we draw more to the trap?" said Dalmore, a damned fine attritionist if anyone ever was. "Take the fight to South Ward. Let the legions lingering in the Doormat rush forth into a hungry North Gate. Fill this great pyre. What say ye?"

"Nay," said Benton, stepping up. "If the builds and toils of men are to fight in their stead, then those men shall live to carry it forth. Through spies and mayhap the Tel'racs, we are bare to the Obantum in these streets. But along the back trails, covered and hidden, the enemy can only follow and not swarm." He looked at Saunders. "Thence, the battle shall rekindle."

It was unclear whether that was a threat, a promise, or a pact, but Saunders sealed it with a nod and said, "Right, let's get it done."

"Ho, mine men in the square," said Dalmore. "If any live, they must be warned. Can we speak to them with Long Voice or else now possible by the Bark's fall?"

Benton shook his head, and Rampo dropped his face shield in anticipation of more gore. Saunders pulled the SINCGARS mic off his back. "Vault Team, come in."

Sergeant Smith was by his side now, waiting for the reply like there was absolutely nothing else interesting happening. The crackle of an American voice out of that speaker would make everything easier.

No dice.

Questions crowded into whatever part of the brain was responsible for processing stuff. Someone had blown the south pass, and the people in this medieval, sci-fi-fantasy world were not natural button pushers. Saunders had to believe his Marines were alive in some form.

But if they were, why no radio, smoke, or gunfire?

Only dark answers came back. Insubordination had reared its head long before the Bark blew up. And now, thanks to what Benton said about the Tel'racs running recon for them, Saunders wondered if the Black Robes could get into peoples' heads. Make them do shit.

He flashed back to Mina Bazar.

Gunfire all around. The MG3 nest Saunders' team was using for cover was almost overrun. Suddenly, he was yanked from the fight to a dark, quiet place. Tied down and weak, a voice from the shadows enticed him, taunted him, threatened him. **Surrender.**

Saunders resisted, clawed his way back to the world, and told himself it was a near-death delusion.

Was it?

Or was the Black Robe trying to get into my head? Did that happen to anyone else? Who can I trust?

"Benton, you hear back from that patrol you sent after PFC Licht?" he asked.

"Nay." The lord governor had his glowing sword out and was already eye-fucking the screaming, dark-armored reds.

Time to go.

"I'll handle it," said Saunders slapping the mag on his MP5. He had a full load and more in the vest. Then it was the pistol, the knife, and the sword on his hip. *Can't trust anyone else.* "Rest of you stick with the plan. Sergeant Smith, I want you to exfil east with Benton. Consider him a priority VIP; make sure he gets out." They were less his words and, strangely, those of Captain Rath's impassioned plea to ensure Benton's safety. It wasn't ideal since it tethered Marines to Benton's fate rather than carving their own, but Ceal was vital to them getting back to Earth. *Gotta keep keeping her happy.* Plus, Rampo was going that way, safety in numbers.

"What about you, sir?"

"I'll make contact with Vault Team and—"

"Request permission to ride shotgun, sir," interrupted raw American vocal cords.

Nickels.

Of all fucking people. The corporal's shit-stained resume included almost executing a bunch of civvies at Mina Bazar, nearly fragging the whole team trying to shoot a fucking horse, and then brushing with a bullet to the head after trying to tuck tail in the wolf cave. But the thing was, for all his chicken, bull, horse, and straight fat-dude-on-the-pot shit, he never actually let anyone down. *Almost* was his operating tempo, cut-to-shit edging that line, yet never falling. No way was a Black Robe in his head.

"Agreed."

"Sir, let me," protested Smith.

"Your job is the men, Sergeant. We'll toss a red flare when we're ready to exfil."

The meeting broke there, participants wishing each other well and storming headlong into violence.

Dread.

It clung to Dalmore like a maimed companion desperate for aid. It was a manifest of his desires, a torment upon hisself from which he ran but could not bear to be free. Always sicker and worse did it become until, in the direst moment, did it sound its harrowing rattle.

"Chief Dalmore," came the voice of Sir Rampo, dread incarnate. The knight stepped out of the piss ice into the foreroom of the stout house where Dalmore conferred with his sergeants.

Naught of time could be bought by gold stamped and bitten by the First Corsan Carre themselves, but this fell discussion was fated. "Resist death!" Dalmore roared, dismissing the Deadlies to their tasks. Soon only Sir Rampo remained.

"Quite the storm this day," he said.

Dalmore's heart quickened, but not so fast as the day's pace. "Speak naught of storms but with haste. I hath upheld our fell bargain; ye's armor unscuffed, mine men enduring the worst of ye's battles. Pray tell, what mind hath ye for the Corsan Carre? What shall Lord Bayliss hear of Portcullis' last stand?"

Sir Rampo smiled with mirthless eyes. Dalmore considered his sword, but it would be naught against the Reverent Armor now that the Bark had waned. So, he waited evermore frantic to hear the destinies of all.

And Lord Bayliss' sworn man fed as once the Hungries did upon human misery.

"Come now," Rampo said, ending it at last. "Do ye still think me a mud-caked cutthroat? A dagger in the night as legions, the Obantum, the Procult, and the Corsan Carre themselves battle?"

"Then ye believe them to be Corsan Carre?" Dalmore asked without revealing his desire for such.

"Aye."

"What swayed ye?"

Sir Rampo's face wore its joy this time. "'Twas their man Brines, truly. But all doubt fled when Captain Saunders said he had buried the way south. Such men are treasure, naught to be discarded."

Dalmore's shoulders lightened despite the heavy plate adorning them. "Then Lord Bayliss will rally?"

"Indeed," Sir Rampo said, drawing closer. "Alas, he cannot hear mine praise for Portcullis and its discovery of the Corsan Carre if I am trapped here."

Dalmore began to suggest the Long Voice but quick saw what Sir Rampo desired. "All are needed to fight until the rearguard can withdraw. Once they—"

"Nay, I must retire, and so too, mine men."

Dalmore could not help but gasp. In a single breath, Sir Rampo had sealed Benton's fate in North Ward. Recovering, he spoke quick; the knight's mind could yet be swayed. "Come to Westside Dip; I shall send ye with 100 of mine best Deadlies."

Rampo rested a hand upon Dalmore's shoulder. "Why travel with 100 when it could be 1,000? All oathed and beholden to their beloved Princeps, who now takes both knees before my Lord Bayliss. Come now, think it a courtesy that I bring ye into mine confidence." Then, by some trick, the Reverent white plate grew darker, and he said, "Benton was always the price."

The lordly cost of allies twisted and soured Dalmore's stomach, but to turn away from Bayliss—indeed, His Reverence hisself—would find the Corsan Carre slaughtered, the Last Army victorious, the world in ruins, and a promise to his brother unfulfilled.

In the end, Dalmore had no words, only the truth of Sir Rampo. And a forthcoming dead friend hung about his neck forevermore.

The view was that of a bird's: all the world little and trivial.

A firm hand pulled Bela Rastaw back from the great wall's edge. "The Corsan Carre still lurk among the fighting," cautioned Master Turan.

She wished to shrug him off. The two of them stood dry and warm within an impenetrable dome high above the biting, chopping soldiers and had little to fear elsewise. Still, the death of Estir Denormild of the Eyes was fresh. Accepted Yerrat said their wards failed against an impossible strike. It bore semblance to tell of Isllor's demise at the hands of the Corsan Carre.

"The Guard stands ready," said Turan.

A veiled question. Of course, the Stretched Guard, ever eager to battle, were ready. Was she?

Bela marveled at her delicate hands, glowing bright to her eyes. The pale flesh was ripe and alive. They were pincers, untouchable by the heat of coals or the bite of steel. That same strength, that pent Power coursing through her veins, also screamed to release a torrent upon the city. It was only through a lifetime of discipline, much of that imparted by Master Turan, that she did not light the heavens red with Quotidian.

"I could end the fighting with a whisper between the flash and thunder that curse this place," she breathed. Her words came loud in this bubble of bliss, but Turan did not flinch.

"More than a waste," he said. "To deprive the low of their victories is to sew your fields with weeds."

She bowed. "Indeed, we are joined to a battle greater than any of the legions could fathom." She stepped forward but stopped a span from the edge and cast her sight beyond the city that had resisted longer than all before it. Through the raging skies, clouds, and ice, she searched for her prey: the sole reason the might of the Obantum Carre and High Axi'arch Cemeho had delivered her to this wall on this day.

She gasped.

Nothing.

The storm—born of the south and unknown elements—denied her through some impossible means.

An eternity passed before she turned to face Turan's disappointment. Instead of rage, he was placid. Even . . . she dared think it . . . sympathetic.

"I shall aid you," he said. "Much of war will change and challenge as we draw closer to the Origins and the Stochasm. We would do well to remember these are not the fodder who fell on the slopes of Val'Narden."

The enemy's poor counter to the Obantum Carre was the Corund Corps. *Violets*, as many a tortured prisoner called them, were a mass of flesh hastily trained to work Renderstone by asking small questions prepared by limited military minds. Indeed, fireballs looked mighty when trained against piles of hay that could not ask back.

The few Violets sent to Val'Narden had fallen in their sleep without raising a single voice.

"Will *she* not block you?" Bela wondered with true concern. Turan surely meant to use the Stochal. If Ceal discovered his command, she could harm him from afar. Worse, she might wait until his Power enveloped others. A vision of the Stretched Guard and herself stepping through the *Quick* only to never appear on the other side gave her a shudder. She was not ready to die.

"The storm clouds all."

His words were strong, confident. She found herself wanting only to hear more. That was part of his power, she knew, but it only held sway when she wanted it to. Their bond was their conjoining desires. *Ceal and the Corsan Carre must die.*

"Even I cannot see Oxhold from here, but close enough. Ceal is lost among the raging winds and driving snows, but Oxhold remains her only refuge."

"It is already besieged, my master," Bela whispered. "My spies gathered days ago and drove its patrols from the lands around. She will have no warning."

Turan smiled and gripped her shoulders, aged fingers showing their strength. "You are ready."

"I am."

The smile faded, and his eyes softened. He was slow to release her as if . . .

Her heart raced.

. . . as if letting go of something precious.

In the span of eye blinks, Bela's thoughts spun a myriad. Turan was a hard Master, risen through the force of his determination and single-minded desire for success. He had no time for the distractions of mortal men. But that did not mean he was without them.

Was it a carnal need he now cast upon her? A lifetime of discipline yearning for the vibrance of young flesh.

No, he could have his pick of the ripest. Or the unripe as Isllor oft sought.

Was it respect? She dared believe. Her accomplishments towered above many of her peers, but not all. Turan regarded few, even his fellow Masters on the High Council, with what she might call respect. No, that could not be . . .

A rush rippled to her knees, and she gazed into those pale eyes in awe.

Affection.

Their stare, their mutual admission, held forever and ended far too soon. He stepped back, composed himself, and planted his feet. The bubble of their private world fell, unleashing the southern might upon their senses. "It will take much. Do not fail!" he shouted above the roar of the storm.

Cold and wetness sopped through her robe, carrying the wind's chill deep. But Bela glowed with an inner warmth. Something not of the Quotidian or the Stochal. Something...

Human.

"Down," whispered the captain ducking behind a wooden horse trough. Taking cover in a world without gunpowder would never not be ridiculous to Nickels. Sure, there were arrows and feces the enemy might sling, but it seemed like a bad idea to get cornered when everyone else was stomping around with swords and axes.

Fuck it. If kneeling before a horse's feed bowl makes us invisible, then praise fuckin' Horsezeus.

An enemy patrol clanked by, ignoring the brutal stabfest a few blocks up. *Bitches.* Suddenly, the trough lit up like they were caught in someone's headlights. The captain spun to engage while Nickels, through sheer discipline, kept his SAW trained forward.

A quiet *fuck* and a tap on the shoulder gave their six priority. Nickels put his back to the frozen trough and got ready to pound shit into more of the Cockhelms—close cousins to the Snouthelms who learned the meaning of *Toblerone* last week—swarming the city.

The wintry street was empty except for a blinding white ribbon cutting its way through the air. Same deal as when Ceal teleported them all to the Assembly Hall that one badass time. "Enemy reinforcing, sir," he said.

Captain Saunders' MP5 dropped beside the sword on his belt, and an M67 baseball appeared in his hand. When the sliver began to widen, exposing another place of snow-dusted green grass and endless ranks of fresh infantry, he tossed the grenade through.

"Go!"

Nickels didn't think, just hit the gas and followed him up the street. At the intersection, they found that patrol waiting for them. Fuckers had caught their scent and pivoted into a nasty brick of pikes and shields.

The explosion from the bright portal turned some heads. Hesitation.

The captain's MP5 rattled, an explicit authorization to engage.

The SAW quaked and tore a line through half the Cockhelms before the captain shouted, "Alley!" and cut a hard right.

Breathing hard, they burned it through the tight squeeze between the up-each-others-asses houses of this weird neighborhood. There was no shortage of tightly packed homes in Portcullis, but ants could walk across the roofs here. Scooting sideways where the stone walls sagged narrower toward the midpoint, it was clear the enemy couldn't follow. Marine body armor was bulky, but not plate-mail-over-hoodies bulky.

Next street was clear, but a total blizzard as if a one-block difference put them in a whole different weather pattern. The nearby buildings had their doors and windows smashed in. Hard to know if that happened from looting or the enemy occupying with the intent to ambush two asshole Marines.

If the captain cared, it was not evident by the pace he set through the ankle-deep snow. The street below was solid ice, forcing Nickels into quick, short steps to keep his footing. His lungs were burning in no time as he tried to pull air from the billion ice shards coming in at every angle.

Something crashed through a window, and laughter whipped by.

"Go. Go. Go."

They ducked down another, wider alley. Back home in Newark, it'd have thirty dudes living in it and twenty parked cars. Here, there wasn't even a horse hitch.

"Hold!"

Nickels instinctively grabbed cover and set security. To his mild disappointment, the clowns who'd smashed that window weren't in pursuit. But the moment they came around that corner, some dicks were getting blown off.

A quick check on the captain reprioritized Nickels' concerns. The guy was fully exposed, bent over like an old woman trying to pluck a penny off the street in the middle of a crosswalk. *Not the time!*

"Shit," the captain muttered, head snapping around like maybe there were more golden pennies.

Shouting back the way they came juiced Nickels' get-the-hell-out-of-here nerves. *Are we hesitating?* Was the captain—the most decisive fucking guy on the planet—suddenly weighing his options and pondering the right path?

"One of the people Benton sent searching for PFC Licht," the captain said, digging through the snow. Beneath was an iced-over helm and red.

"No way, sir. Fucker looks like he was left out overnight."

"Yeah, doesn't add up. But he's a dead ringer for that Deadlie with the flat face. Segar." He stuffed whatever that golden penny was into his pocket. "Keep your eyes peeled."

Nickels' adrenaline-fried brain wondered if it meant a Black Robe was involved. Wizards could probably turn people to ice. Before he could bring it up, they were on the move.

The next street was a downpour with crunchy ice at their feet. Traction.

Portcullis had no concept of a grid system, so the roads and houses were a maze of shit. But a glimpse through the foggy side yards to the right put them within striking distance of Middleton Avenue—the city's big west-east bisect. It still had bare cobblestones, but crossing it would leave them uncomfortably exposed. An alley with some crates at the end offered a good vantage point.

But the captain made for one of the houses instead.

Without glancing through the windows or checking the latch, Charlie Company's commanding officer slammed his damned boot into that meaty front door. Nickels just about crapped himself when it cracked off its hinges; the guy's stamina was unreal.

Inside was a mess, but less shithouse and more *slave's day off.* Wooden figurines—carvings of animals and little soldiers—were stashed in one room with couches that no longer had their cushions. The carpets were all tousled, and piles of clothing were everywhere. It wasn't from looting; this was people with kids leaving for church.

Or a refugee camp.

Saunders led him to the back kitchen and drew the cloth across its one window. Smart. After scanning the avenue, he lowered his rifle and licked his lips. "We've got a problem."

"Thanksgiving Day Parade out there, sir?"

"Curb to curb, probably massing against the evacuation corridors. We can't get through." He sighed, but not like a man who just ran into a wall that needed a bigger bomb; no, it was the golden penny moment again. "There's something else," he said.

Nickels' mind raced. After all this, what the fuck couldn't they handle? *Please don't tell me you're hit and launch into one of those last-minute confessionals. If you tell me I'm a good Marine or some fake shit, I will piss on those toys in the other room.*

"We need to get observation on the Vault before we approach." The captain reached into his pocket and dropped a beige American flag patch on the wooden counter. They both stared at it.

The golden penny.

"Whose?" Nickels asked. Everyone had one stuck to each shoulder of their uniform. They were fixed with hook and loop, easy enough to remove. But no Marine was gonna give it up easily.

"I think someone is comp—"

The ceiling creaked.

Not alone.

Nickels swept into the hallway, pistol drawn. The front door was still closed, but they hadn't checked the stairs.

No fear.

With the captain on his six, he switched to the SAW and found a set of swinging doors in the cluttered living room, exactly where the stairs in a normal house would be.

The captain opened, and Nickels made entry.

At the top of a long stairway, a silhouette registered. Evil and short, just like in all those horror movies. Nickels' brain signaled his trigger finger to light the bitch up.

"Hold, friendly," said the captain cutting him off at the balls.

The SAW stayed cool, but no fucking way was that midget friendly.

CHAPTER 19

THE GIFT

"You alone?" Saunders shouted up the stairs.

Holdouts weren't surprising; the same thing happened during hurricane evacuations. A few crackpots always figured their trailer was made of *American* aluminum and not that Chinese crap.

"Nay, milord," sniveled Smallfoot.

THAT was the kick in the dick. Of all the people to find, the half-midget, half-ginger blacksmith was the bottom. Just putting him in their sights was wasting time they didn't have. The enemy deployment on Middleton Avenue was a significant threat to the evacuation corridors, not to mention reaching the Vault.

"No one will know, sir . . ." whispered Nickels.

Saunders considered the corporal's meaning.

Leave him? Sure, besides a dagger stuffed down his tattered pants, the guy was unarmed and less-than-able. Deadweight at best. Then again, if Brines were here, the only decision would be whether to piss on the corpse. Nickels was like him in many ways. Hard to see at chow, but it came out under pressure. That stubborn desire to win devalued elements that did not lead to victory.

"Negative, Corporal. Smallfoot, I thought I told you to get the fuck out of here a few days ago?"

He slunk down the stairs, wringing his hands like he'd just swallowed six cups of coffee and bet everything on red. "Where wouldst I go, milord? This is mine home, and," those gnarled fingers raked through the reddish nest on his head, "much business was left unfinished."

"You up there sniffing panties, bro?" asked Nickels, not lowering his SAW. "Ten says he's a looter, sir. Waste of time and that road is only getting busier. Suggest we move east and hope Rampo's people are holding."

"Can't afford a 30-minute detour. And we have no way—"

"Milord, if it pleases ye," said Smallfoot, little yellow eyes blinking in earnest. "The slippery stone is not the only path across Middleton."

There it is. The most frustrating thing about bottom-feeding assholes was they survived by pulling a mission-critical need out of their asses at the last second. The sword was another prime example. Not critical, but it helped ease the pressure off Saunders' trigger finger at the time.

"Where?"

"Take me with ye."

"Sir, we can do that thirty in a hot ten if we book," said Nickels.

"Milord, there is little time. As the proud Blue Cloaks walked these streets now taken by the Genisans, a secret city thrived below. Come, I shall show ye, and we can be free of this cage."

Saunders' instincts said no, but minutes mattered. They were at ground zero for a blast that would probably be measured in kilotons. He had missing Marines and clear evidence of a double-cross. There were no friends, only assets now.

"Okay."

"You get tunnels like this in places where police don't need warrants, sir," said Cpl Nickels as they crept through the city's bedrock.

Much to Saunders' chagrin, and unlike Brines, the corporal was one of those people who dealt with stress by running their mouths. Childhood memories, inane observations, and now an off-mission analysis of criminal activity. The strangest part was the anxiety had nothing to do with being wet, tired, and stuffed into this cramped tunnel. It was Smallfoot.

"Back home," Nickels continued, "your house and garage are safe. You can just pull the blinds and leave your shit out. Load up in the garage and drive to another garage. Unload. Profit. But where the pigs can come in whenever they want, you get secret doors and tunnels."

"Plenty of that in Afghanistan," Saunders said. The problem with having an over-analytical mind was it latched onto oddities like this secret tunnel network connecting residential homes. A literal underground crime element in Portcullis wasn't surprising, but damn if Benton or Dalmore even hinted at it. Either the black market was invisible to the Watch or tolerated. Since guys like Sergeant Orrugant weren't morons, the latter seemed to apply.

"Much passes through these passages, milord," said Smallfoot on point. Nickels was right behind him, SAW practically jammed up his ass. "Each city in Galimay is home to mayhaps five council lords. All lords want what other lords possess. So, they hide, and steal, and sneak."

"They ever feed you the Toblerone?" asked Nickels.

"Enough discussion," Saunders said, not wanting a pissed-off midget to sandbag and leave them lost in this maze.

The tunnel emptied into a room much like the one they found in the subbasement of the first house. It was unfinished, more dug than built. Four wooden posts supported the plank ceiling. It was also super dry. The fine brown dirt filling in around the cracked stones had never gotten a breath of humidity.

Nickels eyed the ladder. "I'll go, sir."

"Negative. Sit tight, and don't hesitate if it hits the fan up there."

Nickels slung his SAW and aimed his pistol at Smallfoot's head. "Won't, sir."

The MP5 snapped to Saunders' shoulder, ready to pelt the able into corpses. The cellar above was dank and wet from the storm oozing through the retaining stones. It wasn't a flood yet, more like a weird reminder of Sarah's parents' house in New York and the adage: basements suck.

A set of narrow stairs led topside, and the steps creaked like an old dorm room bedframe. God willing, the tempest outside was louder.

The MP5 took point through the access hatch as Saunders tried not to flinch back against someone getting ready to piss lead into his face. It was a sensible fear; weapons stayed trained on entryways. A few bad experiences meant every door had the power to raise his blood pressure. Coming up through a hatch was doors on steroids.

Empty.

Saunders threw it back and hoisted himself up. Not a house, but a store. A big one. Basically, a medieval Home Depot, complete with a materials yard outside.

Walram's place.

According to Uumhrat, "magic" negated the need for a scaled construction and manufacturing industry. But, when Benton's Bark shut it all down, Walram went from boutique handyman supply to regional provider. The guy got rich as fuck, place up on Eastside Rise and everything.

Never too rich for crime, though.

Whistling an *all-clear* down below, Saunders moved to the window. They were well beyond Middleton and deep within the Market District. Red-glinting soldiers were everywhere, tearing into the shops. Some were boarded up, but that only proved a short delay. Walram, however, had bars on the windows and an iron gate with rods driven into the stone behind his front door. Clearly, he intended to return for his stuff.

The backdoor only had a crude deadbolt. The perimeter fence around the materials yard was formidable enough to keep the rampaging hordes out for now. Across the far street were the admin buildings bordering City Square. Tall lumber stacks throughout the yard meant a good chance of a vantage point on the Vault. *Couldn't ask for a better spot.*

"Climb, motherfucker," shouted Nickels. Smallfoot popped out of the hatch like a cartoon character that just got the horns. Maybe they were being a little too harsh on the guy; he did deliver, after all.

"Ease up, Corporal."

"Fucker busted ass in my face, sir."

Kids. They always find a way to play. "Eyes forward, objective on our twelve. Establish observation for risk assessment. Copy?"

Nickels put his game face back on and scanned the yard. Stacked stones of assorted sizes and textures were arranged in a grid. Toward the far part, lumber piles were higher and more haphazard, maybe because they sold faster. From an infantryman's point of view, it was a cover-move-cover fantasy come true. "No problem, sir. I'll keep this bi—"

"Negative," Saunder said, grabbing the hilt of his sword. It felt right for the moment. "Smallfoot's mine. Move out."

Eye of the storm.

Walram's materials yard was a bubble of dark tranquility enwebbed by lighting and total blackout horror. Cold, muddy, and quiet. No telling how long it would last.

"Keep up or stay behind," Saunders hissed, quick stepping to a pile of quarried rock. It had the same texture and scatter pattern of granite but could've been a type of wood for all he knew. If he came under fire, it was substantial enough to take a few hits.

And while fire could mean anything from arrows to elemental death rays, cover was still cover.

"Naught of the enemy here, milord."

Meanwhile, Smallfoot—strolling across the yard without a care—was a constant reminder that tactics often lagged capabilities.

"They don't need to be here to hit you with a crossbow. Move!"

Nickels was three rows up, advancing diagonally to a three-meter stack of ten-by-tens. Icicles hung off the ebony wood like tinsel, but it looked climbable.

Smallfoot stopped by a snow mound and cocked his head. "But ye hath the sword, milord. If the legends speak true, it shall parry any bolt, fell any foe, and blind all who would do ye harm."

Sure, toss a rifle in someone's hands, and they're Rambo. Not without training, kid. "I said move!"

Nickels was on his way up the icy wood stack, practically scampering despite the added weight of his pack. His holds were good, skillful use of the arms to secure and legs to drive. If it came to bets, Saunders would not have guessed the kid from New Jersey knew anything about climbing.

"The sword," whispered Smallfoot, now beside him.

Saunders reached for his Ka-bar fighting knife, seconds away from demonstrating what American steel could do when a metallic crash rang out. Shouts followed.

Pressing Smallfoot to the ground with one arm, Saunders popped his head up. Reds were pouring in from a breach in the fence along Gates Street.

Something cracked into the stone beside his helmet, and the MP5 responded by punching two of their point men in the faces with 9x19 mm FMJ. Twanging crossbows drove him back behind cover.

The reds fanned out, teams breaking off and moving into the flanking material stacks. Two columns behind rectangular breach shields advanced down the center. It all came down to time. Enough bullets might score enough lucky hits to drop those shields, but not before they got within chopping range.

Suddenly, one of the shield bearers pitched face-first into the slush, comically tripping up the rest of his column. The second followed a split-second later. Then came the unmistakable reports of a .50 caliber rifle. Francisco!

With a clear shot, it was go time.

From ten o'clock, a stream of heat from Nickels' SAW tore out the center of both columns. The lead elements kept charging. Driven, desperate, or just dumb, the MP5's payload gave them the closure they deserved. The rear pulled back to the fence.

Flanking units scattered into the stacks. No target.

More booms in the distance said Francisco was sparing no expense.

Mobility and initiative.

Saunders released the blacksmith, got his feet under him, and zigzagged toward Nickels. The SAW was spitting small bursts over a wide arc, probably tracking movement all over the yard.

Gotta grab a good angle to cover him.

A cut west brought Saunders back into contact. The narrow path between the towering lumber went to the yard's edge. Right at the end was an enemy squad, dark and menacing, blending into the mists and shadows. Too bad they couldn't shake that red glint.

The MP5 shuddered, knocking down two. Shouts, shuffling, and then two crossbowers appeared over their fallen buddies. Saunders ducked behind a stone footer. But he didn't hide. He set his profile minimal as bolts pelted the wood and mud. Knees anchored, he tipped his torso back and squeezed the trigger.

The bolts stopped.

The SAW ripped above. Instead of driving the remaining soldiers to cover, it had the paradoxical effect of sending them in a wild charge toward Saunders. The reds didn't bother with defilades or leapfrogging between the stacks because they didn't understand the nature of their adversary. In their world, getting in close and doing damage was the drill. Move fast and get there. A straight line was their best friend.

It was also a rifleman's.

Trusting Nickels to watch east, Saunders broke cover and advanced while unleashing controlled bursts of gunfire. When he arrived at the yard's edge, he was stepping over corpses. They trailed along the fence where they'd been exposed to Nickels' SAW.

Movement.

He felt it before he heard it, heightened combat senses pulling a puff of hot breath out of a downpour. He wheeled the machine pistol around in time to catch a jet, jagged blade arcing around the corner to take his head.

Splat.

The sword flew wide, and a body dropped to his feet as a .50 caliber report echoed through the yard. Two more reds tore around the corner, but Saunders was ready for them. One shot to the chest each, sledgehammers forever stopping them in place.

Blowing out a breath, his ears strained against the hammering rain and wind. The storm had reintensified, and battles still raged throughout the city. There was no way to tell if stragglers were skulking among the endless rows of supplies that would never go on to complete someone's dream home.

"Sound off," he shouted.

"Negative contacts," called Nickels. The Marine wasn't confident enough to declare it clear, but at least nothing was out in the open.

Weapon trained on the bodies because bullets sometimes knocked people out with non-critical injuries that left them combat effective, Saunders fell back to the corporal's position. "Give me a read on City Square."

"Snowing over there. Zero vis, need to get closer," Nickels called down.

Christ. Before he could figure out how they were scaling that eight-foot iron fence on full display in an occupied city, frozen mud crunched behind him.

"Friendly," spoke the calm voice of the only guy on the planet not having blood pressure issues right now. Francisco.

"Fuck," Saunders huffed. Part of him wanted to ask the sniper where he'd been, but that was like asking his best friend Kyle (before he met Jane) where he was the previous night. *Getting laid.* The details were either legendary or mundane, but always on mission. "Bark's down. You get eyes on the Vault?"

"Yeah, figured that's what you two were after."

"Fuck you, Francis. All those kills are mine," Nickels shouted from above.

"Vault's open; Watch holding the square," Francisco continued, ignoring the corporal. "No sign of our people."

"Think you can cover us from here?" Saunders stopped short of bringing up his suspicions of a Blue Falcon in their midst. They needed less, not more paranoia right now. Then again, if someone—Gladstone kept coming to mind—was waiting in ambush, Francisco would have to make a tough judgment call since he did not have comms.

Gotta hope he's seeing straight.

"Yard's compromised, sir. Prefer another location." He pointed through the sheets of rain and cold fog to one of the administration buildings bordering the square.

"Roger that." Saunders noticed the bolt to his MP5 was open. His vest was cleaned out, but he found two mags in his left leg cargo pocket. Sixty more rounds, and he'd be out of ammo. Just another guy walking around with a sword, except he didn't grow up swinging the thing.

Hell with it; I can't do this alone.

"Be on alert; possibility Vault Team got buddy fucked."

Francisco lost that perpetual trace of a smile. "Local or one of ours?"

"Unclear." Saunders showed him the patch. "Found it on the Deadlie we sent to find the PFC and Gladstone. Both Marines are MIA."

Storm clouds built behind cold eyes. "Fischer?"

"Praying to God he's still alive."

Walram's perimeter fence was a proper antipersonnel barrier. Taller with thicker gauge bars than the vehicle deterrent surrounding Camp Lejeune, it would take something like an MRAP with well over 300 horsepower to bring down. Here, that probably meant 300 actual horses.

"How the fuck did the Cockhelms get through back there?" asked Nickels pulling on the crossbeam bars drilled down into what looked to be poured concrete.

"I'll give you a leg up," said Saunders dropping his pack.

Francisco tossed a stick up at the spiked top. It clattered against the iron and fell back. "Making sure there isn't some magical, electrified crap going on," he explained.

"Good thinking," said Saunders. With the city's Q-lattice nearing overload, any and all unexpected effects could be expected. He wove his fingers together and braced them against his knee. Nickels planted his muddy heel and grabbed the fence to hoist himself up.

The dim day flashed bright and crashed down on them.

. . .

Saunders came back to life with a jerk. Wet. Cold. Ozone.

His mind laid down the memory of an explosion, but missing was the head ringing and deep bone ache. Instead, he was six cups of coffee jittery.

Was that the fucking fence?

Shaking hard, the MP5 stuck to his shoulder, and he squinted through a haze that had appeared. It wasn't damp like fog or smell like smoke. Something else entirely. A call for his Marines to sound off got stuck in his throat like he needed a drink of water. Then he saw the reddish outline of a dark figure.

A Black Robe.

The hammer came down, and his weapon spat out a single round. Boom, Saunders was flat on his back again, shaking hard like he'd just jumped naked into a frozen lake.

Gunfire to the left.

The unmistakable purr of a SAW going full auto in desperation mode was cut short. More cracks and flashes beat against the raging storm above. Then everything was wet. Rain was coming down so hard that it was difficult to grab air. Saunders managed to turn his head to the side and pull a protected lungful. Sweet oxygen quenched the flames in his frozen chest.

Thunder rumbled, but not from above. It rolled through the yard and appeared as a tidal wave of mud.

Drowning.

Something snared his vest as his arms fought a losing battle through a viscous hell. It pulled him with the force of a tow truck out of the muddy grave. Air hit his face, and he huffed, not caring how much grime, blood, and rain got in with it.

"Can you move?" Francisco shouted right into his ear.

Slurred sputtering fell from Saunders' lips in response; the damned brain was issuing orders to a quivering pile of raw poultry. He tried to roll over, but his legs kicked out instead. Francisco dragged him behind something that blocked the wind.

"It's a Black Robe, sir, quick on the draw too. Nickels is down, but I think he got a hit in. Lost my weapon; you aren't using this are you?" He cut the strap to the MP5 and checked the magazine. "Stay down. If he sees you, it's done."

The desire to respond burned, but not hot enough to get an infantry captain's jaw working or move his 210 pounds of mass. Francisco darted into the rain and wind, MP5 shouldered. It took all of ten seconds before the fireworks started again, but none of it sounded anything like Marine hardware.

Saunders' limbs were starting to flop in the directions he wanted them to. His hand found purchase on his M9 pistol but didn't yet have the coordination to pull it out. His molars mashed grit that tasted like manure smelled as his mouth worked itself up to forming human words. A hoarse, "Sound off," was his reward for what felt like hours of work.

"Pinned, don—" cut short the only reply.

It was an all-too-familiar scene. The fight at the Assembly Hall had gone similarly, with everyone getting magically immobilized and disarmed by one fucking guy. Hundreds, thousands of people couldn't overcome that without magic support from Ceal.

What chance do the three of us have?

Feet, not boots, splashed in the slush next to his head. A reflex jerked him upright, his body finally shaking off whatever had hit him, and he got the pistol out. The target was decidedly smaller and much less black and red than expected.

Smallfoot.

"Milord, ye live!"

So many questions and infinitely dwindling time. "Where are my men?" he gasped.

"They lie as the spider's prey, milord." The short blacksmith glanced at the gun. "The sword, milord, it is the only way."

"Can't . . . can't get near him. Need a rifle," Saunders stammered. He might've been moving again, but goddamn he was in a world of hurt. Probably how Mike Brines used to feel every morning of his life.

"The sword can protect ye, milord. Ward away their Powers."

Say what? These fucking people and their communication issues. "This sword is like a mini-Bark?"

"Aye, milord."

"What makes you think that?"

"Ye live. I saw the might of the Southborn Storm slam down upon ye. Look upon the hole that remains of ye's stead." Saunders kept his weapon trained on the midget and confirmed the presence of an impact crater, filling fast into a muddy pool. "How else if not the sword?" Smallfoot whispered. "Wield it, and it shall block the full fury of the Obantum Carre's might, milord."

It was the sort of thing that could only be tested in action, which came down to relying on trust.

A big red flag.

However, Smallfoot was right about the tunnels and always seemed decent enough despite a raw deal with life. Also, it was *do or die,* and the three of them hadn't done shit with their rifles. "Okay, what do I do?"

The little guy's eyes glowed, probably an illusion of reflected lightning from the background, and he said, "Draw it and strike true."

"Capta—" croaked a voice, probably Nickels being tortured as bait.

You want it? I got it.

Standing up put Saunders on steady legs and solid balance, so he drew the black blade and stepped out like a badass.

The Black Robe was in a circle of little fires burning where the metal of Walram's fence had wilted away. He wore the same robes as Isllor during the Assembly Hall fight, but these were leaking red tendrils instead of purple.

He also didn't waste time with conversation.

Saunders raised the sword to crossguard in an instinctive defensive pose. He planned to rush in and start hacking away. Instead, a bomb went off inches from his chest. The world turned bright white, and the blast echoed off the lumber and stone stacks.

But nothing touched him; even the flash registered as if it were just a picture of something bright. The sword's pommel warmed as if sucking the energy from the Black Robe's attack.

Holy shit! Smallfoot had somehow ponied up a simple sword that could've instantly ended the Assembly Hall fight. Something like those Vissl hides that Bayliss' people had stolen. Magic-proof gear that conveyed invulnerability to the enemy's superpowers.

But why me?

"The Corsan Carre." The Black Robe's words came to his ears clear as if spoken in a church.

Right.

"I have wondered what tricks you possessed to defeat such as Isllor Mortund," he continued. That dark hood turned left to a beige pile. Francisco. "Relics. Powerful indeed, but there is else." The Black Robe stepped closer, leaving no ripples in the puddles at his feet. "You are but an ember to flame yet stand in defiance."

"Semper fi," Saunders growled back. This wasn't a conversation; it was positioning. Another foot closer, and that thing was within striking distance.

Unintelligible whispers floated into the air, and the din of battle beyond the yard changed flavors. Shouting—the kind that issued new orders from the throats of sergeants—cut through the storm.

Positioning. The wizard just called for reinforcements.

A sudden gasp put the posturing on pause. The Black Robe stepped back. "How do you resist? The other was told to possess such strength, not you." Another gasp.

Saunders wanted to whip in and finish the fight, seize the initiative before it fizzled, but he held back. "What other?" Probably a case of Brines' reputation preceding him, but he had to be sure.

Somehow the void beneath the hood smiled. "The Corsan Carre who fled. The one with the Power to stop us. Did you think she would be safe at Oxhold?"

She.

The chill of the raging storm suddenly soaked through, and Saunders shivered. *They've been one step ahead of us the whole time.* Nothing anyone had done here mattered. The wall, the delaying actions, blowing the pass. None of it! All those little victories zeroed out the second the Bark fell.

It was their game the whole time.

Mission failure!

Saunders saw red. Not from the ethereal glow from the Black Robe, Marine Corps red. He two-handed that fucking sword like the bat he needed it to be and charged. The Black Robe raised his hands, evil voice whispering shit, but something cut him short. Suddenly, that face under the hood was clear as day. Those dark eyes latched onto the weapon, wild with recognition.

"She forsakes me?" he cried as the blade bit into meat. The only other noise was the sound of steel wicking through buttered bologna and the two halves of a formidable creature splashing into the mud.

"That part of your plan?" Saunders spat at the corpse.

Elation.

Fucking Smallfoot had saved the damned day and given him a shot and killing more of these invincible fuckers. It was the edge they needed, but too soon to tell if it was sharp enough.

Saunders spun to do a status check on his men. Next order was to grab that SINCGARS from his pack and warn Captain Rath to avoid Oxhold. Before he could do any of it, an immense voice pounded through his skull.

Mine.

Darkness followed.

CHAPTER 20

OXHOLD

Captain Rath was soaked. Fire-hosed for eight hours, pulling the sort of duty he specifically tried to avoid by becoming an aviator. Up ahead was the Command Coach, where Micky, Dr. Pat, and Lady Ceal were nestled all comfortable and dry. Meanwhile, he was in an open-air cart riding shotgun with a carbine as seven Watchmen and some men-at-arms clung to the bed. It had to be the most miserable excuse for a security escort in recorded history.

Rath's skin was soggy like rotten peaches. The stiff bench was starting to hurt too. The medievals in the back had it worse, but they were raised in the rain and cold. Rath wanted to ask the driver how much longer, but the guy would just make some vague reference to mealtime or something. It wasn't like this busted-up highway had mile markers and signs.

37 Miles to Oxhold *and we're doing 12 mph . . .*

Instead, it was an ass-jarring hayride into endless, whipping rain. A check of his watch, which he tried to reset to sunrise every day, said dusk was approaching. But it was already dark, lightning giving glimpses of a leafless, spiderweb canopy above. About once a minute, a loud crack would precede a thump in the distance; trees going down in the wind. It was a wonder one wasn't laid across the road yet.

Nothing magic can't handle!

Rath sighed. The storm was shit, but the tree-lined road was probably gorgeous on a normal day. From what little he'd heard of Oxhold, it was the dream country residence. *If fortified castles are your thing.* Right now, a roaring fire and chow were enough; artsy stuff could take a seat by the cold parts of his ass.

He considered the DCS-10B crash kit survival radio. Comms had been quiet since the fiasco with the detonator. There were several possible explanations, but he chose to believe that no news was good news. The enemy was *corked* as planned, and the Marines were bored. The only concern was whether Saunders was keeping tabs on Benton.

Benton must stay safe.

He couldn't order the infantry commander to put all his capabilities and eyes on the lord governor, but he had planted the right seeds: Strategic partner, proximity to Ceal, and critical land navigation asset. The last one was probably what got the biggest grunt of agreement. *Not that it will make any difference.*

Captain Rath recalled those blue robes flowing over the ice seconds before Gunny Brines was buried beneath a hundred tons of snow.

She'll do what needs to be done.

A face-numbing gust blasted the carriage. In seconds, the temperature felt like it dropped 30 degrees. Somehow, it was refreshing and pulled Rath back into the situation. *Fuck is the point of all this?*

Storm-crazy.

That's what he called this mad dash to safety. Like cats running back and forth out of their minds after that first clap of thunder. Same shit happened to people, and no amount of reasoning could calm the hen house.

Worse, with Buontempo and Orrugant hanging back in Yordel with the main body of refugees, Rath had no one to talk with.

At least Oxhold would be worth the trip. First step, after something to chew and forget about ever needing to drink again with the amount of water his body must've absorbed, he was getting some dry clothes. No more uniform; there was no one around to give a fuck.

And, if Ceal's right about the Gra'nuul, that's how it will stay . . .

"Still naught," said Stebbin, the driver.

The single-skillset Watchman still hoped to run into Oxhold's outer patrols that should've intercepted them hours ago. Poor guy was reading off a duty schedule recovered from a smoldering crater. "Pretty sure they're hunkered down and out of this storm," Rath said.

"This be a Southron Storm, milord." *Oh, so* now *I'm a lord.* "Sir Thode knows the danger t' us; should be out in thrice strength."

Rath snorted. South or southern born storms had this whole mystique about them. Probably just a cold version of what the meteorologists back home would call a hurricane. The strange element here was these people believed the storms were magical. It had merit because magic was a real force on this planet, but it couldn't and didn't account for every unexplained occurrence. Physics and scientific principles still held firm in the absence of the Powers.

"If it gets any worse, we'll have to shelter too," Rath said as ice somehow whipped under his skull-tight helmet. It was a half-hearted sentiment; the only acceptable rest stop now had thick stone walls and roaring fires.

And more troops. *Fuck this storm's evil vibe.*

"Stone's Ferry just ahead, milord. Methinks two widths t' the castellum."

Music to Rath's ears, but he couldn't see anything. After a minute the bucking carriage smoothed out, and he could hear rushing water below. A bridge, he guessed, sitting up a little straighter as that last-leg excitement started to build. Soon he'd be able to put the fucking day to bed. Other people could handle security and end-of-the-world shit.

Durador.

The word shot out of his memory like a forgotten appointment.

The plan wasn't to hunker down for the night. It was to double-time it through Oxhold's magical gateway and land in Galimay's capital city. According to the locals, Durador's splendor put Oxhold and Portcullis to shame by orders of magnitude. Plus, the place was a fortress.

The biggest and baddest ever built on this world.

Not much perspective there. Nicer and drier than Portcullis would work. Still, Durador didn't sound welcoming, more like they'd have to hit the ground running. Ceal and Benton had pissed off Galimay's leadership to the point where they ignored Portcullis' requests for reinforcements. Left their key frontier city to fend for itself.

We'll be greeted as motherfuckers.

Fortunately, there were some hurdles to reaching the capital. The mounting liabilities of leaving the refugees behind and burning it to Oxhold would catch up with them. And if Portcullis was holding, there was zero urgency.

There'd be discussions and decisions. The plan would be rethought and hopefully shelved for tomorrow. *Yeah.* The deciders might not get that into their heads by themselves, but the pressure was there, and Rath just needed to get his voice heard. *Screw the redeye; do the layover.*

Rath settled back into his wooden board bench to enjoy the rest of the ride. Most of his body, including his ass, had gone numb, which felt nice for the moment.

A little while later, shouting from the coach ahead suggested they were close. He straightened and started working his quads to get the blood back into his legs. The last thing he needed was to get up and start hobbling around like one of those astronauts returning from the old orbital missions.

The DCS-10B suddenly squawked to life. It was hard to make out, but definitely a Marine transmission. Something about—

As he was seating his earpiece, the shouting ahead turned to screams, and the carriage banked hard right. What looked like a flare shot into the sky, bright orange cutting through the hellish storm. Before Rath could right himself, it slammed into the road where they'd just been.

A moment of silence was all Rath had to ponder the implications. His mind raced, connecting the possibilities, but it was instinctive memory that nailed it on the first try. The orange orb moved like a JDAM, a guided munition used to destroy airfield tarmacs back home. The bombs were designed to drive down real hard, burrow, and then . . .

The ground heaved before he was able to complete the thought.

———

Numb, dumb, and angry.

Cpl Nickels was back in that fugue when Smith went down at Mina Bazar, standing over a fallen Marine during a fight, unable to process it.

"I say again to anyone who can read: report status," shouted Francisco into the captain's SINCGARS receiver.

"Fuck happened? Who the fuck got him?" Nickels demanded from no one who would answer. Francis didn't know, and from the look on the half of that Bath Robe that still had a face, he died confused as fuck too. The captain had walked up and chopped him down like a raging badass but then dropped like he got hit. No blood, no wound. Just out cold.

"Pulse?" Francisco asked.

Nickels shook the shock and tore off his glove. The captain's carotids were still thumping strong and fast. "He's alive. Captain, we need to move." The red-glittered Cockhelms were swarming into the yard behind.

"No one's answering," said Francisco, slinging the radio.

"Fuck! Fuck happened?" Nickels pawed over the captain's uniform, searching for blood for anything that might indicate an injury. Nothing. Nobody.

Not nobody.

Cowering right where the captain got laid out in the first blast was that fucking midget Smallfoot. Probably nicked the captain with poison or some shit, same as what happened to Gunny at Mina Bazar.

Nickels didn't need a single fucking reason. "Shoot him!"

Apparently, neither did Francisco, who grabbed the captain's MP5 and lit that motherfucker up. Bullets hit air as the midget sucked behind cover. "Fuck, missed."

Of all the goddamned times . . .

A chase through the lumber stacks would probably net them a kill, but then they'd be tangling with Cockhelms. "Forget him; we gotta move."

"You cover; I'll carry."

As if. "You ain't gettin' those wet noodles under this guy. Grab his pack, keep your ear on the radio." Francisco didn't protest, and Nickels soon had an extra 230 pounds on his shoulders in a classic fireman's carry. The captain still had body tension and laid a lot better than dead weight across his shoulders. "The square," he huffed, lunging forward into the snow rain.

Francisco stuck the captain's Black Robe-killing sword in his belt. Then he advanced all gangsta special forces style. Dude's head was locked down on the MP5's iron sights and sweeping. The second he got through the hole left in the fence by the Black Robe, the gun started spitting fire to the right. With his free hand, he waved left.

Nickels concentrated on keeping his lungs pumping oxygen down to his legs, which were already talking like they wouldn't make the distance. Francisco was out in front again, signaling.

Hold. Flank right.

Gunfire.

Nickels sucked wind, air, ice, mud, and cordite. Everything he could to blow off the fire in his legs and lower back. *Fuck it'd be nice if you woke up right about now, sir.*

Whoosh.

Something flew by, and it wasn't a bat or bullet. An arrow, maybe. Way too close.

Nickels tried to add some zigzagging into the mix, but it was all he could do not to trip over the puddles, ice, snow, and bodies. Worse, he could barely see where he was going. It was just dark shapes of buildings and Francisco running course correction.

Right.

Left.

Alley.

"Cover!" shouted Francisco suddenly beside him. Nickels got his back against a stone wall and slid the captain off his shoulders. The relief of that burden was what heroin addicts talked about when they shot that boiling spoon of tar into their veins. Fucking goddamned amazing. "Looks like we gotta fight through."

Nickels' arms and legs were rubber, but he swung his SAW around and took stock. They were in an alley running between the admin buildings. Clear except for that platoon of Cockhelms at the exit into City Square.

"My mag's light. You?" asked Francisco.

"Last box, maybe 90 rounds." The building beside them was two stories high with a flat rooftop like Uumhrat's. No fire escapes or anything that would make scaling it easy, but there were footholds. Francisco could get up there and get an area assessment. If he wasn't a bitch, that was. "I'll cover, you climb."

He glanced at the captain.

"Bro, up high, you're a god with that Bullpup, and we'll need something to pray to. Go!"

Francisco, again, didn't question it and started grabbing the holds in the stacked stone exterior. The Cocks were treating this like a bank robbery or something. They had the area cordoned and were standing behind those shields but not moving in.

That was bad.

Stupid people charged and swung their dicks first. Smart, tactically minded people who won battles held back and let the prey wriggle in the trap. *Goddamn it.* The worst part was those shields were too thick for his 5.56 mm bullets to penetrate reliably. Getting Francisco's .50 cal operational was the right call.

The captain still hadn't so much as twitched.

"It fears us!" cried some fucking guy. The Cockhelms roared and cheered, banging their shields.

Not good. The SAW was a badass piece of gear, but it wouldn't stop a steel stampede. If Francisco could drop those shields like before, maybe 5.56 mm ammunition could drive them back. But the moment this puppy thunked empty, it was game over.

"I know you ain't keen on getting captured, Captain," Nickels said with surprising calmness. His pistol was full; he could do them both in the head. It'd be murder, but fuck it, what was the alternative? To the bad guys, *Corsan Carre* meant Nazis or something. So, zero-fucks torture was probably just the beginning.

He searched the captain's blank face. "Kinda hoping you'd give me a sign, sir."

Nickels did get a sign as clanking noises filled the alley behind him, cutting off any hope of retreat, but the only question it answered was how long he had left.

"We cannot hold," panted Dux Herms, his hands braced against his knees.

Smith was feeling it, too; the more they fought, the harder it got. The green formations were buckling, and the reds were getting better organized every minute. Every block they lost meant more houses with archers and crossbowers in the windows. "How's our link west?"

"Collapsed."

Just when Smith thought he was too tired and aching to feel anything else, in went another nail. They were now cut off from Captain Saunders. "What's Benton wanna do?"

"He thinks to gather a hundred and rally a charge through Middleton Avenue, but to what good? That we might shake hands and exchange pleasantries once more? Look how the lights burn bright. Your captain's murderous plan draws near to harming our health. We must withdraw."

Frustrating, but the orders were clear: Benton and safe exfil were the priorities. If Leod and Vault Team were still operating, the captain and Jersey would have no trouble getting to Dalmore and the western exfil. There was no reason to fuck the entire plan to rescue someone who didn't need saving.

Still, Smith had a terrible feeling it wasn't so peachy over there.

"Wish I had comms," he muttered. Rifles cracked above. Garcia and

Light were up in some kid's bedroom taking out targets of opportunity from the window. Everyone was bone dry on ammo and minutes away from being useless in this fight.

"I need Benton to hear the wisdom of the Corsan Carre," said Herms. "North Ward is lost, and so will we be if we do not rejoin Sir Rampo." Originally, Rampo was going to leave more troops behind when securing Eastside Rise, but some sort of shuffle happened, and he tried to pull everyone. Fortunately, Herms planted his feet, and about half the greens stayed.

Wouldn't be no west or east routes without him. And it was no joke about those streetlights glowing like little suns about to burst. Herms was right; they needed to link up with Rampo in Eastside and use what gas they had left to cover the evacuation.

"Yo, Benton!" Smith called into the crashing, clashing metal. Snow was dumping again, making it a white Christmas with all the red and green troops hacking each other up. Right in the middle was a bluish whirlwind weaving in and out of the red lines with superhero impunity. "Benton!"

The Tasmanian Devil slipped behind green lines, and the white-armored lord governor emerged.

"Gotta pull it, dawg."

"I hath seen naught of red smoke."

Full stop. Sledge to the chest. With all the shit going on, Smith forgot about the captain's exit signal. That meant they hadn't reached Vault Team yet. *If we pull out, that's gonna send all these fuckers we got tied up racing after the captain.*

"C'mon. With all the magic shit bein' active again, ain't there a way to figure out their status?" Smith asked.

Benton lifted his helmet's white metal visor. Face was red and wet from freezer burn and exertion, but his expression was placid, thoughtful. "Nay, the city draws too much of the Quotidian to make safe use of its tools. To reach the Vault, we must abandon the east passage and push through the city core. The enemy host is strongest there."

Smith wasn't ready to back down from that challenge, but he had to think about the others. The mission. That's how the captain made his decisions. Sometimes it hurt, but that's what it took to win. "Then we gotta trust 'em to get it done just like they trustin' us to get these people safe."

Benton's jaw tightened, but then he looked over that red sea he'd have to Moses through. "Aye."

Smith glanced at their exit, but Eastside Rise was lost in the blizzard. From memory, Westside Dip had cover and clear trails snaking up to Almon's Peak. Over here, the slopes up were gradual and baren. Completely exposed for the first half-mile, making their troops easy targets for a Black Robe. Worse, they'd have no cover if the city exploded ala Nagasaki.

"What's gonna stop those reds from pelting us with arrows and fireballs as we try to climb out of here?"

Benton pressed his lips together like he had an answer but didn't want to say it. Seconds were burning, men dying, brass raining down as his Marines tried to plug another breach in the lines, and Benton just stood there. Not thinking, but like resisting interrogation or something.

"Hey, look. My Marines can work miracles here, but only if we movin'. You got another way that gives us some cover, and we'll save some fuckin' lives."

Those pale lips stayed pressed as some kind of battle got fought inside his head. Meanwhile, the situation shit-ragged from desperate to gasping. There were just too many, a monster weight pressing in, and Herms didn't have enough people to push back.

Just as Smith was about to take charge, as he imagined Gunny would, Benton came to life and made airwaves. "Withdraw!"

In an instant, the fight went from linebackers grappling over yards to a free-for-all.

The front lines became rear lines, and the north ward AO popped like a balloon. Friendlies crashed into each other, desperate to outrun the enemy pincer. Smith barely had time to pull his Marines out of that house before he was screaming for them to triple-time it.

The run toward Rampo's position was a stampede, one step ahead of the rear guard almost surfing the enemy's initiative down the evacuation corridor.

More than a few got trampled.

The Marines did not stand a chance against all that metal, so Smith kept his team along the edges. The reds redoubled their efforts to cut the corridor, especially at Middleton Avenue, but by some damned magic—probably real magic—the lines held just long enough.

The final sprint up the slush and ice to Eastside Rise had Smith conjuring fantasies of collapsing behind an impenetrable wall of fresh troops and giving thanks to his lungs. Then, he'd piston-up and take charge of the evacuation.

No more splitting up.

When he crested the hill to those fine estates and rich-people homes expecting locked shields and mean green, he found only a confused Dux Herms.

Sir Rampo's men were nowhere to be seen.

Bronchioles seizing, ears ringing, and eyes stinging, Dr. Pat had the strangest sense of *déjà vu*. She was back in Hudud moments before her life turned upside down. Explosions, gunfire, bodies. War as seen on TV but with all five senses and the certainty of death. It was the stuff of nightmares until the next act—that otherworldly pulse of light—blew it right out of the water. She suspected the same would happen here.

The coach was on fire, smokey, and cold. She wrenched her left eye open long enough to determine they'd flipped over. The forward area containing Ceal's desk was a pile of cracked boards hissing smoke. Dr. Pat dared to hope.

Really? Because if she's dead, you're next.

It was her voice in her head, but Micky's words.

Crazy!

The scattered thoughts were a probable indicator of cranial trauma. Dizziness, disorientation, and difficulty maintaining consciousness were all stuff she didn't need right now.

People are hurt.

Dr. Pat gave her head a shake, a counter-indicated move. A bruised brain did not need more rattling, which could trigger and amplify a more devastating secondary wave a few hours later. But she needed clarity, and a little pain-induced adrenaline pump was just the ticket.

The world solidified, filling out with toxic fumes and indistinct noise. There was a disturbing lack of gunfire, but Captain Rath and the Watchmen could take care of themselves. Dr. Pat needed to get outside and start the triage. Even if they lost the battle, there was a chance the enemy would bring healers, wisewomen, or better.

Frigid air blew across her knees where her skirt was torn. She gulped a few fresh breaths and followed it to the source. One of the windows was smashed out.

Wait, Micky!

Dr. Pat turned back. The flames spreading through the remains of the front provided just enough light as she dug through the mess. Every cushion and cute decoration, all the books on the shelves, the papers—letters as Ceal called them in a world without post offices—were now trash covering potential bodies. She kept going until the smoke was overwhelming.

Nothing.

Not even an ounce of blood to say anyone had been with her when the coach turned into a giant blender. *They were here, though. Right?*

Dr. Pat found the window again and pulled herself through, caring nothing about broken glass or anything but escape. Then it was all about breathing and hoping she hadn't overdosed on carbon monoxide.

Outside was a pitch-black blizzard. Wind carried shouts and thick gobs of snow into her face. In seconds, the fear of being snap-frozen like a bag of peas overrode her disorientation and pain.

Keep moving; follow the voices. You can help them.

Dr. Pat pushed into the gusts like she was wading out to sea on a red flag day. Two steps, and she was lost. Hands going numb, she groped for the coach. Panic swelled, but then a merciful flash of lightning gave her a look at the wreck. It was like they had a head-on collision with the ground.

How the hell am I alive?

Grabbing the side for support, she turned to her other senses. The wind was howling, but if she cupped her ear just right, she could pick out the sounds of fighting or maybe just dying.

A beam cut through the storm.

Remembering Hudud, her heart jumped. *A Black Robe!* It had to be. In a world where everything was natural, that pure, white light was anything but.

"Ma'am!" came a shout in beautiful, unadulterated American English.

"Captain Rath?" she called back, scolding herself for losing her shit over a flashlight.

The beam clicked off, and he was by her side. "Can you walk?" His words fought the rudder, sails, and gods themselves to reach her ears. "Where's Micky?"

"What hit us?" she shouted back. The cold was pressing through the wool of her blouse. They needed to move. "Who are they?"

"Came from Oxhold. Sergeant Abhan took his men forward to support Ceal." To mark that point, the snow flashed red, and what sounded like mountains tore. "It's a hell of a fight, but you and Micky are the priority."

"Why would Oxhold attack us?"

"They're compromised. Gotta find Micky and book it outta here." The flashlight mounted to his rifle came back on, and he started calling into the smoking coach.

That rifle needed to get into the fight.

"Micky's not here. Go see if you can help the Watchmen. I'll find her," Dr. Pat said. Division of labor made sense. If he was worried about the enemy sneaking around and getting the drop on them, visibility was so low that nothing he did would change that. Plus . . . magic. Ceal was the only reason they weren't all dead. "Go help Ceal," she repeated when he didn't budge.

"Negative; Ceal and them are covering our six so we can evac."

That made zero point zero sense. Dr. Pat grabbed his shoulders. "Ceal is the priority. Without her, everyone dies. That's why we left the city, left thousands of refugees at Yordel."

His eyes went wild. "No, YOU and Micky are the mission! Ceal needs you alive at all costs. And Saunders . . . he told . . . told me the whole fucking reason we dropped into Mina Bazar was bec—"

The sky lit up with a million suns, forcing Dr. Pat's eyes closed. Splashes in the slush rode up through the wind, and she stepped back, swiping at the air that felt like it would reach out and grab her throat.

Rath's rifle crackled. Once, twice. A grunt silenced the affair.

Blackness.

Oxhold was a functional military space. Less palace and more stone for the sake of holding up more stone.

The outer wall was tiny by Portcullis standards but high enough that four people stacked on each other's shoulders couldn't dunk on it. The top was lined with that wooden scaffolding they put over sidewalks when skyscrapers were under construction. Cheap, wooden, just enough to make pedestrians feel safe from falling debris. Lit up with flaming braziers, it was somehow holding against the high winds.

Inside the courtyard was a mix of stone and stick buildings. The cobble walkways were plowed, but everything off the beaten path was buried under snow. The keep loomed large—at four stories high, it was still smaller than most Comfort Inns—as part of the rear wall. It came complete with two flanking towers and all the medieval frills and décor.

Then there were the bodies.

I can literally see how that guy died, Micky realized, studying the remains of a husky man in small clothes. Beside him, just past a door cracked off its hinges, rested a familiar, white helmet.

A knight's helmet.

A red imprint about the same size as the pulped remains of the man's face was on the stone wall behind him. The rest of the body was dented and twisted at inhuman angles, the work of hard-toed boots and heels. Still, he fit the description of Sir Thode, the castellum steward.

Why wasn't he in the keep? she wondered, imagining several compromising possibilities. It reeked of an inside job, but there were more pressing needs for her brainpower.

At least Oxhold was shielding the storm's crosswinds, which allowed the occupiers—the same elite Stretched Guard that had attacked the Assembly Hall—to set a bonfire in the courtyard. That didn't make it warm, but it attracted the soldiers, making them easier to count and observe.

A body thudded down in the snow. Micky didn't bother turning her head; it could only be Dr. Pat.

And here we are again.

Somehow the Obantum Carre knew; they always knew. Didn't matter where or how, they were always coming, always fixated on that one prize. Next would come the beatings.

The torture.

The worst kind of torture where the act itself was the ends, not the means.

Micky shuddered. Dealing with Ra'num at Mina Bazar had been par for the course. He was especially nasty, but interrogators generally came in two types: the ones working a job and those in it for the rush. The varying degrees of sadism and, yes, even masochism fell into those two containers.

For the record, the number two container was already overflowing by the time she met Ra'num.

When Gallor Creetdel—a Black Robe on Earth, one of the so-called Three—walked in, she learned there was a third kind. They wanted more than just intellectual or emotional gratification, which could be satisfied by a masterful performer. A good lie mixed with old truths scratched Type One right in the logic spot, while Type Two just needed to feel like they hurt someone. Easy enough without losing too much blood.

Type Three, however, was after something more profound than consciousness, something that couldn't be given freely or falsely. It had to be extracted through careful dissection. The process itself was what they craved, like an artist with her brush. Each scream was a fancy stroke across a naked canvas, leaving a bright, never-before-seen color.

Hearing that Mike Brines killed Creetdel before they were yanked off Earth was probably the only justice Micky would ever feel.

The sky clapped with thunder, but the lightning flashed blue. Ceal was still fighting, somehow, somewhere. But it didn't look good. It was like that stupid game Cintup she mentioned. Over in five seconds unless two badasses were playing. Micky shuddered at the memory of what attacked them on the road to Oxhold.

The coach landed upside down. Micky too, but amazingly, without a scratch on her. Ceal, still standing, lowered her hands, breathless. "Oxhold is besieged, mayhaps fallen. I must go."

"Let's get Rath. He can— "

"No," she said, eyes glowing green. "A force more terrible than I feared possible hath come. I know not what it is, but to battle, I must. See her safe!"

Micky wasn't one to argue. If Ceal said she couldn't handle something, it was fucked. Dr. Pat had smacked her head and was sporting some honey-glazed donut eyes. She would be okay for a few minutes.

Captain Rath.

The door was stuck, so Micky smashed out a window. Expecting to find the Watch carriage nearby, she was swallowed by a blinding blizzard.

The relatively flat road at her feet was the only guide, but ankle-deep slush and snow soon led her astray. The shivers started sooner than expected. Before she could translate them into a death-from-exposure countdown, a pack of clanking soldiers from the Stretched Guard was on her. Defenseless and fucking drained from days of futility, Micky put her hands up and prepared for death's warm embrace.

But they denied her that too.

After a frigid wait, she met Ceal's newest foe. A Black Robe—as the Marines called them—walked through the storm untouched and surrounded by purple brilliance. That meant full command over both the Stochal (blue) and Quotidian (red), which was the same as Isllor Mortund, who'd beaten Ceal numerous times. Ceal's aura was blue because, for some reason, she refused to adorn herself with Quotidian gear.

The encircling dark armored soldiers tensed—puckered—as the almost ethereal being approached. Micky imagined herself seconds away from becoming a soot stain on the snow, but the Black Robe stopped. "Not her," spoke a feminine but ice-cold bitch voice. Then she shot up in the air like a superwoman and collided with an orb of blue. The explosion dropped the atmosphere on them, driving Micky to her knees. Everything after was a jumble until regaining consciousness in this frozen courtyard.

"Pat, wake up," Micky said.

No response.

Not her, the female Black Robe had said. She might've been talking about Ceal, but that would imply she gave her soldiers zero intel or preamble on a dangerous, high-value target. Mistaking Micky for Ceal would be like mistaking a cairn for Portcullis' North Wall. No, the Stretched Guard had been hunting with nets, not spears, for a weapon that hadn't armed itself yet.

Dr. Pat: the critical Corsan Carre.

In the flickering light of the bonfire, Pat's medical status was unclear. Given the nature of most warrior grunts—which was conserved between Earth and Scianas—their captors probably clubbed her over the head. Same time, the Anticulties who attacked them in Portcullis used drugs. Good old knife in the back for everyone's favorite Micky, but Dr. Pat got jabbed with something potent.

"Girl, your eleventh toe is telling me a story." That usually got a rise out of her. Nothing.

Another boom and the ocean of raging clouds flashed purple. Within was a trace of blue, but Micky was sure Ceal was losing. This wasn't an opportunistic grab; Oxhold was always the Obantum's target. They knew that Ceal, or better yet, Pat, would be here.

Do ye not see her importance? Ceal's words to Captain Saunders, selling him on the Oxhold plan. At least, that's what Watchman Mos said he overheard. Micky was inclined to believe it, considering the kid had been too busy drooling over her cleavage to come up with a solid lie.

"What was the last thing Brines said to you again?" Micky asked. Not so much as a shudder. Pat's blonde hair was messy but didn't have dark spots sopping with blood. The head injury idea jumped into the backseat. Drugs, or some magical shit.

"Pat, Ceal was getting close to figuring you out. Remember when you read that letter? You've got something in you, something that can help us." That last part was a whisper as a guard stalked by. He thudded his worn, unlaced boot into Pat's thigh. Once again, nothing. Micky wanted to nick a couple of his arteries and see how long it took before the snow started collecting on his cooling corpse.

Nope! Play the long game in case Pat doesn't work out.

But work out to what? Pat's access to the overpowered Base appeared random and only when she completely lost her shit. Unreliable and unsustainable as a weapon. No way would she stand a chance against the female Black Robe who could strike fifty times in a million different ways before Pat could sport a frown.

Rare and unpredictable.

"Is that why Ceal waited? Are you dangerous?" Pat's abilities were probably evident when she shattered Isllor Mortund's hold over Ceal and Benton, along with her lack of control. That would explain why Ceal spent two months watching instead of dragging her to Durador.

What changed?

Urgency? Between the Tel'racs and the Bark fracturing, the Procult was up against a deadline. But that wasn't a significant upset to what they already knew: winter was a predictable adversary, and the Pandonis Immortalis had too many forward troops in Val'Narden to wait for spring.

The Anticult? Another wake-up to danger. But it wasn't like Ceal showed up at the clinic with their bags packed and a carriage waiting. Pat and Micky had gone to her and only then did sh—

The dream.

It hit like Einstein or whoever when they figured out the first atomic bomb. That *Vision* of a future Portcullis changed Ceal's entire outlook. Sure, she denied it because no one could have Visions of anything but the past or near present, but something in Pat's description registered. Probably that doomsday shit about Primal, whatever that was.

Then came the weird tests and revelation that Pat only responded when pushed to the extreme. Any progress there was stymied as Pat tucked her triggers behind mental walls. So, that put them back to square one: unpredictable and random. Unless . . .

Oh hell.

Micky suddenly understood what the whole Corsan Carre thing was about. And Dr. Pat was the worst possible choice for what needed to happen.

CHAPTER 21

LAST STAND

Corporal Ryan 'Jersey' Nickels of Charlie Company First Battalion, Second Marines was going to die in a third-world, shithole alley. Just like Uncle Harry always said he would. The details of how and where might surprise the fat fuck, but he'd still claim credit.

Two targets and one decision: pick one or die like playground Play-Doh.

You'd like that wouldn't you, Harry?

The troops in City Square were planted to catch whatever flushed out of the alley and less of an immediate threat.

Flushers on my six it is!

The Cockhelm ramrod was charging in with those bullet-resistant shields out front and over top. Too bad for them that tight quarters and point-blank range meant landing steel core on target. Small targets.

The SAW went to work, sparks tracing a line just beneath their shields and into their little booties. Another thing Uncle Harry liked to say was: "Can't work if you don't take care of those feet." Goddamned guy with his half-amputated trotters up on the coffee table pulling disability knew what was up. And the Cockhelms learned it fucking nasty just as he had. Their front men dropped, and the rest became enfiladed bullet sponges.

Something bit into Nickels' left armpit.

I'm hit!

He rolled across the alley, bringing the SAW up to kill whoever was behind him, but it was clear. He pawed the place where it hurt and pulled back a crossbow bolt. No idea if he just ripped that shit out of himself or what. The pain wasn't enough to stop him from finishing what he started.

The SAW jackhammered into his right shoulder, driving hot irons into the wound on his left. Nickels let up before the agony summoned his spirit animal or something worse. With the weird way the captain was still out cold, that shit was no joke.

The flushers learned their place and pulled back. Made a point to leave their steaming pile of wounded behind like not giving a damn was a badge of pride. *Assholes.*

Shuffling at six o'clock.

Nickels tried to pivot, but his exhausted body was too slow. His knees were on fire, hips about to pop off like those little GI-Joe action figures he had growing up. The cheap plastic ones, not the fully articulable badasses kids had nowadays. Two catchers coming from City Square were feet away by the time he even got eyes on them.

Boom.

The slush jumped once from Francisco's Bullpup, but both Cockhelms got knocked off their feet. One stayed down, but the other was making moves like he didn't know he was dead yet. He got his hands under him before the SAW delivered a gentle reminder.

Time slowed as the armpit pain raised its voice. Wound was deep; bleeder like that would take its toll in short order.

Gotta move.

The catchers in the square were reconfiguring to offense, while the flushers on the other end of the alley became defense. Nickels could punch through if he had a full load of ammo. Another ass-saving option was climbing up to Francisco, but that would mean tossing the captain to the wolves.

Ain't no one gettin' left behind.

They weren't his words. That ratfuck Gunny Brines was rasping his broke-fuck voice in his ear, setting an unmeetable standard just so he could be there when Nickels failed. It was fucked, but that's what the guy did. Even in death, he was still barking.

A thrill tore through Nickels, the last of his adrenaline hitching a ride on a dwindling blood supply to plug 220 volts into his brain. *You don't have to win, but you* do *have to not die like a bitch.*

Nickels tossed a grenade into City Square and hip-fired a burst to keep the alley suppressed. When the frag blew, he charged. That's how Brines would've gone out if he hadn't bitten it in an avalanche. Not waiting for the gauge to read empty and a sword to slide by, but out there. In their faces, taking it to them.

The SAW popped once, and the bolt locked forward. Empty.

Fuck!

Seeing red, mind frothing, Nickels' pistol replaced the rifle as he entered the lingering smoke from the grenade. Usually, it would suck for cover, but combined with the storm, dickheads with crossbows would have to check themselves.

A gagging lungful of nitroglycerin later, he burst out into the open ready to fight hand-to-hand with the pistol delivering his haymakers. Except, there was no one around. Just a few bodies and endless snow.

His weapon snapped right; his head went left.

There! Massing at the end of the street. No, wait, running away?

He had another grenade. *If this party popper scares them that much it—*

A roar beat back the clanking of metal, the storm, and every memory of sound that Nickels ever had.

The grenade was not their fear.

The city square Cockhelms were back on defense, pulling together a shield line and scrambling to reload their crossbows against something out of view. Nickels fired into the mass to make it easier for his wood-be rescuers. Leod came to mind. Maybe Smith talked Benton into crossing the city. He even dared hope Vault Team might be operational.

Then something big slammed into that shield wall.

Bodies and jagged swords flew. Those still standing went into an uncontrolled, double-shit pants retrograde. Nickels got a taste of their command structure as one dude with fins on his bullet helmet tried to turn panic into a regroup.

All the shouting, stomping, and waving of *Lieutenant Cockfin's* more-normal looking silver sword got negative results. Then there were two of Cockfin, two halves falling away from each other to reveal a massive figure behind.

Nickels' jaw tried to drop and smile at the same time.

The new champion of City Square was decked out in silvery plate armor that shimmered with color. Against the drab backdrop of a soaked city being pelted by snow the consistency of wet bird shit, it was gorgeous. Even more impressive was the ax, which was easily two meters long, double-gripped, and glowing blue. Nickels racked his redlining brain for where he'd seen it before.

Oh shit.

It was that skull splitter in the inn's lobby he walked past every day.

Fuck, is that Uumhrat?

White tabards descended on the Cockhelm's disorganized flanks. As shields turned to brace against the pincer, Uumhrat was left completely unsuppressed. That big ax moved like a windshield wiper.

Goddamn, the hotel clerk cleans up good.

Suddenly, someone yelled *cut* and the fight was over. Nickels could hear himself breathing again along with gobs of snow splashing down on piles of slush. Pressure was off and the Watchmen were advancing. Nickels ran back to the alley and found the captain covered in a half-inch of watery snow. Lungs still working; still out cold. No sign of enemy presence at the other end.

"You gonna tell Uumhrat all those kills were yours?" called Francisco from the rooftop.

"Fucking beautiful son of a bitch can have 'em. You too, fucker," Nickels managed. He was alive and still on mission. No telling how long before he bled out, but that was secondary while Marines were in danger. He rolled the captain onto his shoulders and hoisted him on shaky legs.

"Help 'em, lads," boomed Uumhrat in a voice that could stop a stampede. The subdued innkeeper with his *may ye* and *please* was gone, murdered in some side street and reborn as silverback apeshit.

When Watchmen Hull and Mel grabbed the captain, Nickels didn't protest. He was on the verge of asking for a human crutch himself. Panting hard, he took a second to swallow the saliva in his mouth and reformat his hard drive for human speech. Uumhrat loomed large at the mouth of the narrow alley.

On closer inspection, the thick metal beneath his tattered apron wasn't just polished like what the Deadlies wore, but painstakingly etched and dyed to depict various images over every available square inch of space. It was like those guys who got their life's story tattooed all over their bodies. Beautiful, haunting. It was also nearly immaculate, save for a few scratches.

"Well met," Nickels said. *Fuck it, you saved my ass, I'll speak the damned language.*

Uumhrat lifted his helmet grill and said, "The city be lost; we head west."

"I've got Marines trapped in the Vault. We need to secure the square.

Can you assist?" He posed it as a question because no one was giving orders to the guy who'd just wasted two dozen armored infantry during the apocalypse.

Sure enough, Uumhrat roared, "I do be the fury of Portcullis!" Then he took a step forward. Brines wouldn't have moved back, but Nickels did. "They came to face me and none other. If the Corsan Carre do be wishing the Sorrow of Dusk to drink its fill here in the square, then I do be living to serve, milord."

Every Marine a rifleman; every clerk a cracked-out ax murderer.

Exactly what the Marine Corps needed. "Let's move."

———

The banging and pleading became the screams and crash of melee once more. Gladstone pulled his hands away from his ears. The active hearing protection was designed to muffle anything above 80 decibels—gunshots, explosions, clanging swords. But not voices.

Gladstone, Fischer, are ye within? We are here to ye's aid!

The city is taken!

Mistrus had promised their sudden silence, but no matter the battling, the Watchmen always came back. Knocking. Asking. Poking their torches through the gate. Searching.

What should I do? he asked the lonely space in his head. There would be no hiding from the captain this time. Even if what happened here in the Vault could be covered up, Gladstone had disobeyed direct orders in a combat situation. That was grounds for a no-questions-asked bullet to the head, especially here where Saunders had absolute authority.

The only way out was for the Genisans to deliver that sweeping victory they promised.

"Did I pick the wrong side?" he whispered, not daring to think it.

Suddenly, warmth and sureness filled the cold, damp Vault. Mistrus had not forgotten him.

Instead of words, she gave him incredible visions of an epic battle ripping through the dark tempest above. She was an A-10 Warthog, blowing up bandits and raining death with absolute impunity. Then in what felt like a near future, she was a colossus stomping all the world flat to begin construction of their paradise.

Nothing can hurt me, he realized. She was like having a personal fleet of battleships just over the horizon. If Saunders so much as twitched his upper cheek muscle in a displeasing way, his day would turn cloudy with a 100% chance of sixteen-inch crater makers.

The clash outside faded. They would be coming again.

Gladstone considered turning the radio back on to eavesdrop on the chatter but hesitated. It was beside Fischer's cooling corpse, which was a representation of relief and elation. The freedom only a guilty man could know. Still, part of him was coded to believe that beige sack of decay was his friend. His brother Marine.

His heart fluttered as if rebelling at his newfound understanding.

Banging.

Barking, demanding voices in unfiltered English.

"Stone, Fish, report. You in there? Open the fuck up!"

Gladstone blew out a breath and smiled. Alone in the dying purplish embers of the shattered Bark, he could just wait until their shouts turned to screams turned to silence. Between the eight-foot-thick walls and drop-down iron gate that wasn't budging for anything smaller than a dragon, it was inevitable.

"They can't get us," he whispered to Fish. No answer, obviously, but it seemed part of him didn't appreciate the idea of being alone.

Suddenly, the Vault rang like a bell, and Gladstone's hands were back over his ears. Then it happened again.

Heart pounding, he scrambled to his feet. His brother Marines weren't a bunch of medieval assholes. They had C4 and other explosive ordnance. If they wanted in, it would happen. The only question was whether these idiots killed him by overpacking the charge. Before he could get to the gate, it crashed in with a freezing blast of wet snow.

Gladstone stared, dumbfounded, as a silvery mountain of human stepped through. *Not C4.*

Around the armored figure swept beige and LED beams, Cpl Nickels and Francisco with their side arms drawn.

Gladstone could only stare as their mouths moved and words echoed off distant places in his mind. With his sanctuary gone, he lived now only to face the captain. Part of him, the tiny piece of hard drive irreparably damaged by boot camp and his time in the Marines, welcomed it. Welcomed death for the disgrace of treason.

Bright white brought him back to the cold Vault floor and he squinted.

"Fucker's in shock or something. No sign of injury," said Cpl Nickels shining a flashlight in his face. "Fuck happened in here?"

Gladstone turned his head. Francisco was kneeling over Fischer like a kid who just found his dog in the middle of the road. Mistrus and all her battleships couldn't help now.

"I . . . I," Gladstone stammered, searching for elements to compose a good lie. The Bark was shattered, his Ka-bar had Fischer's blood on it, and there were no enemy bodies. *Deflection.* "Where's the captain?"

"We be needin' to move," came a recognizable voice from the armored figure. *Uumbrat?* The little broken part of his hard drive was delighted.

"Captain got put out tangling with a Black Robe." Cpl Nickels looked at Francisco. "Jesus Christ. Is Fish . . . ?"

A metallic click and Francisco pocketing a dog tag was the answer. He then started rummaging through the body.

Cpl Nickels' lower jaw quivered for a second before snapping shut. With a hard stare, he asked again, "Fuck happened here? Where's the PFC?"

The captain's offline? Mistrus had delivered on all her impossible promises. Gladstone let a little moisture into his eyes and said, "I . . . I met up with Licht in North Ward. He said he'd take the detonator back to the captain. I . . . came back and . . . and . . ." Francisco was unreadable. Dangerous. Gladstone's frantic mind almost blurted out the truth, but then a stroke of brilliance seized him. "Then it's like the world froze." He sat up, letting bewilderment pull his strings. It was easy because these men and their petty concerns felt foreign and unreal. He let that little broken part play its audio file. "Oh god, Fish!"

"Hey, fuck, easy man," said Nickels grabbing his shoulders. "He's gone, Bark's torched and we got a world coming down on us." He turned away. "Francisco . . ."

"We're done here," snapped the sniper tucking something into his pack. Gladstone wished he'd paid more attention to what he'd lifted off the corpse, probably weapons or other essential gear. There weren't too many Marine Corps Supply Depots here on Scianas. "Semper Fi, brother."

Francisco grabbed Fischer's M40 sniper rifle and stomped out, whispering something to Cpl Nickels. Gladstone strained to hear it, but it was too quiet and short. A vow of revenge or something, but no names. No names meant no blame. Yet.

Gladstone kept his eyes and mouth wide, forcing the blood from his face to simulate pale shock. It wasn't easy because he was on the verge of scoring an opportunity to re-embed with the Marines as another war swept through and wiped out the evidence of his crimes.

Not crimes. Victories.

Nickels caught Francisco by the arm. "If Licht was in North Ward, then Smith's his best chance for exfil. Agreed?"

"Not like there's a decision to make here," Francisco said through his teeth.

"Fucking hell." Nickels turned to Gladstone. "Can you move?"

"Yeah, I'm shaky, but I think I'm okay." *I'm your friend, a survivor.*

"Okay, we're in a bad place and bone dry on ammo. Gotta kill our way out; need you on that shotty. Oorah?"

Gladstone hid a dark smile. "Oorah, Corporal."

Nickels' head was spinning from having to leave Fischer, PFC Licht's MIA status, and probably blood loss. Still, he forced his back straight and stride confident. Brines never let on that he was injured until he was three-past dead. Not because he was a badass, but like right now, a hundred fucking pairs of eyes were on him.

And this wasn't a stage where a stumble led to a poor review; it was a battlefield.

Leod—*thank god*—trotted over on a chestnut stallion. "Our high eyes send tell that Lord Benton withdraws. The enemy tide shifts to us."

Somehow Leod and his Watchmen cavalry unit had avoided getting hemmed in by the Cockhelms closing off streets. Through hit and run, they managed to keep City Square accessible. According to Uumhrat, they didn't even realize the Vault was offline until they found the gate shut tight during one of their passes.

"Dalmore's people are holding Westside Dip," Nickels panted. Everything was becoming tiring. But he was still standing. *Fuck it; drive on.*

"We are nearer to South Gate," said Leod. "Benton's banners still fly. Its might will hold the enemy within and the road beyond gives our horse a field to fight."

It made some goddamned sense if ever he'd heard any.

"Negative," said Francisco, but not to Leod. This was Marine talk.

"The hell? We don't leave people behind."

Those marksman's eyes were ice, but not throwing shade. Hard like he was holding back actual human emotion. "Captain closed the south road."

Leod went whiter than his blood-stained tabard and reared off to find out what happened. Nickels didn't need to guess. It was another rockslide, maybe the South Gate itself. Saunders' dead man's switch: no easy way out. *That's what Benton and the others were pissing about back in North Ward.* "The fuck kind of evil shit is that? They have men in South Ward!"

"We can't help them."

Nickels' insides boiled. "Screw that. We push south, get those guys out of there, and hit Westside Dip. That's the plan."

"All roads are one way now." Francisco grabbed his good shoulder. "I don't like it, but those are the orders. The mission was never to save lives; it was to stop the enemy from moving south. It's done. So, we can all die fighting to save a few or push west and try to get clear before we're overrun. It's every team for themselves now, read?"

Nickels didn't want half, he wanted all. The more time they stood around jawing about it, the farther away any of it got. He could lash out, snarl at people, maybe give Francisco a shot to the chin. Or he could eat it and ask for more. Brines made these sorts of calls like he was begging for a seat on the vac-tube to hell. It ate him up, but he spat it out and kept letting good men die to win. Because . . . and Nickels hated to admit it . . . that's what it took.

Leod's horse whinnied as its back hooves skidded to a stop on the ice. "A great slide blocks the Palings Pass! Lieutenant Maon is missing. In his stead, I hath flagged South Gate. Sergeant Batoth's men are given leave to flee as they can. To aid them is folly; our hand is forced." He glared at them both with loathing. But the Corsan Carre were a shit sandwich he couldn't turn down.

Nickels took a last look at the square, men fighting against surging columns and walls of shield-bearing metal motherfuckers. Bodies falling, horses driving in with spears and rearing back against an unstoppable flow. And riding above all that were the streetlights burning so bright they looked ready to pop.

It was now or never.

"We push for the dip."

Bows twanged as teams of ten covered teams of ten leapfrogging up the slick slope. Iron-forged quads burning and lungs heaving, Sergeant Smith was barely keeping pace. *Goddamned mountain goats.* It was the same story back in Afghanistan. Wiry locals who looked sick from hunger made insane time across terrain choppers wouldn't even fly over.

An arrow clattered against a boulder inches away. "Fuckers are getting' closer, Benton," Smith said, managing to turn the thinning air into words. The rearguard, dragging shields and chucking spears to keep that reddish tide from rising too high, was now only 50 meters behind them.

"Can't keep this up," he added. His Marines were winded, and even Dux Herm's Caranuscans were losing their footing on the icy patches hidden beneath deepening snow.

It was worse upslope.

Not only was it getting steeper, but the ground was all broken. That fuckhead Rampo and the bulk of the Caranuscan ground forces had gotten through, but they weren't under fire. And everyone knew it. So, morale was dead; discipline and organization were toast. Any tactical advantage the high ground gave them was air kicks from a dude with two broken legs.

None of that mattered, though, because they still had no freaking cover and no telling how big a bang Portcullis would make. Smith tried to put it in terms he understood: A Mark 84, 2,000-pound bomb was ground-burst lethal up to half a klick. The fuck-you-up range was double, which put minimum safe distance well past that damned rock field.

The city lights below were blazing, high beams at night cutting through all the snow slopping down. It could blow at any second.

Would it be like a heavy bomb smacking soil a mile away, or a thousand little hand grenades going off? Smith had too little info and no way to know how much time to figure it all out.

We need to put some rock between us and the blast.

Instead of responding, Benton just stared at the reds, shifting his weight between attack dog wanting to leap and cat knowing the best place to hide.

"Dawg..." Smith began knowing the word wouldn't translate but he wanted Benton to hear it real. "Whatever you chewin' on, I can tell you it ain't worse than what's about to happen.

Before the white-armored hero could update the shitty options deck, the world went gray.

Slap-stunned.

That's what came to mind as every inch of Smith's body exploded in pain and went numb.

Time passed like a dropped call; no telling how much he missed.

Distant shouting was the first sign of a mental reboot. Somehow, Smith was still standing, still armed. Wheeling the Pig around brought a wave of gut-gutting vertigo and disorientation. Jersey's stupid concussion obsession popped onto radar. *How would I know if my brain got rocked? Maybe just keep fighting and figure it out later.*

"Black Robe!" someone shouted. Garcia. But no one was shooting yet.

Smith got himself moving like he was in the sniper's crosshairs. A forward roll landed him with a weird stress headache and bout of motion sickness. But he came out of the maneuver with the Pig mounted up and his vision back to normal.

Fuck.

The wizard was 100 meters out and glowing purple, not red like those two on the bluff above the North Wall. Smith didn't understand the different colors, but everyone said the one at the Assembly Hall had glowed purple. And he was, by all accounts, a bad mofo.

The Pig shook his shoulder sending a full spread of 7.62 mm in the off chance that rifle fire might kill one of these things.

The Black Robe jerked and disappeared.

"Oh shit, you see that?" Smith breathed, expecting Garcia to drop some badass one-liner. But there was no one around. The spot where he and Benton had stopped to discuss the plan was twenty meters away on the edge of a brand-new crater. Green-armored corpses—the guys breathing hard, fighting for every step just moments ago—littered the snowy slope.

"Sound off!" he boomed. Below, the rear guard was collapsing, green lines scattering before the rush. Rage brought the Pig online and Smith lit into the neat wall of advancing reds like a goddamned revolutionary war hero. His ammo was low; it was a waste, but it made a difference. Dudes in heavy plate pitched back tripping up others.

"Sergeant," came a gasp. A Caranuscan archer's corpse rolled to the side revealing a beige Marine beneath. A human shield saved Garcia's life, it seemed.

Smith ran to his side. "Where's it hurt?"

"Think I . . . fuck . . . my back again." Garcia tried to laugh but pain tightened his face into a silent scream.

His uniform was clean, soaked from the climate change falling from the sky but none of it blotched red. Legs were still kicking meaning it might just be another torn muscle like what happened during that crazy animal attack when they first arrived.

Downslope, horns blew and the red ranks regrouped. The green rearguard used the respite to fully break contact and haul ass up the slope. But their lead sucked. It was like when mice tried to climb out of the tank before the snake got 'em. Never turned out well.

"Smith," said Benton skidding across the ice with his bluish sword drawn. "I shall go to their aid. Carry forward with Dux Herms. If ye can pass the rough rock, mayhap there is a chance to reach—"

Liquid fire poured through the air turning the blizzard into a July barbecue. All that froze-ass snow and ice harrying their retreat was suddenly Smith's best friend as the mountainside broiled. Benton didn't hit the deck but stood up tall, defiant against something at nine o'clock. Smith didn't need to guess.

The Black Robe was back.

Smith rolled onto his back, and the Pig snapped to, but the target had abandoned the floating duck approach and was zipping through the air like a fly.

No shot.

Fire missiles streaked down toward the scattering rearguard and for a moment the fight looked like it would end real quick. But then Smith noticed a pattern.

"Yo, he's . . . ack . . . he's penning us in," said Garcia pushing himself to a sitting position.

"Aye, mayhap they wish prisoners," said Benton, snapping like a dog on a way-too-short leash every time the Black Robe flew by.

Smith stood and grabbed the mythical fucking hero by his white chest-plate. "Ain't nobody becomin' a prisoner. Fuck climbing this shit. We NEED an out."

Benton stared, eyes darting between the Black Robe and that big crater where they'd been standing a few minutes ago. But all he said was, "Ye know not what ye ask."

Fine. Lead, follow, but get out of the way.

"Garcia, can you walk?"

Like he was deadlifting four times his bodyweight, the Marine grunted his way to a standing position. Waves of heat and steam buffeted them, screaming from upslope and down. "Online, Sergeant."

"Move to crater at three o'clock. Pop red and bring our boys in," he ordered. Garcia hobbled off, and Smith readied the Pig. The Black Robe's passes *were* predictable: big circle cut twice like an X. Smith set his iron sights on a spot in the grey, raging sky and let his peripheral vision track the violet fairy.

The Pig fired.

The Black Robe flew right into the stream of white-hot metal.

Vanished.

Either Smith just bought some time or zeroed a huge fuckin' target on his back. "On me! Follow me!" he shouted to the greens trying to hide among the pebbles and hissing steam. Benton was transfixed on the crater. Smith had questions but all that came out was, "We gonna make a stand. Do what you gotta do."

The lord governor of the city about to explode stayed behind, pained like he was having trouble deciding which type of acid to pour on his dick. Smith couldn't waste any more time with it. Either there was some cover in that crater, or the rally would give them enough troops massed for one last epic charge.

By the time Smith arrived, the greens had figured out the plan for themselves. Dux Herms had them planting shields and fortifying a perimeter. Knowing the Caranuscan sergeant was still going strong was a relief. The dude was action and leadership, a refreshing break from Benton.

The crater was narrower than a bomb would make. It was more like a flaming ax had chopped into the slope, leaving the rock blackened and hot to the touch. The angle was too shallow to shield them from Portcullis, though. A good position to take on the way up the mountain, but bullshit otherwise.

Dig became the operative word and anyone not fortifying the perimeter attacked the charred ground like it was all buried treasure. Smith prayed that he read Benton right and there was something special about this spot. Whatever happened, it would be a hell of a fight. Well, until a Black Robe came by and iced them. *Maybe we should spread out?* He dismissed the notion. This wasn't about hunkering down or finding a hill to die on; it was surviving the blast.

"We got a plan?" asked Garcia panning the blasted rock for answers. The remains of Cork Team looked like spent shit with rifles slung and pistols drawn.

"Yeah, you shoot that fucking Black Robe if he comes back," Smith said. He stomped his leg into the ground. Solid. No way they were digging this out in time.

"Last one, Sergeant," said LCpl Bulb, checking his M4 behind one of the Caranuscan shields.

"Got you," said Garcia, tossing a thirty-round rifle magazine.

"Oh wow, was this your rainy-day fund?" asked Bulb.

"Dividend from the Make It Rain Foundation, friend," said Garcia.

Smith also had some spares, but there'd be time to dole them out later. He needed an exit from this stupid crater like a ghost pepper casserole. Dux Herms approached, flanked by two guys with a ton of dark red smeared across their beat-up green armor. Smith wasn't sure what to tell the guy and started to mumble something about holding.

"Lord Benton!" said Dux Herms said suddenly.

Smith turned. Low and behold it was the white knight himself, face still scrunched up like he was about to stick his hand in a bag of worms. Smith stepped in front of Herms and said, "We fucked. Diggin' our graves out here. If you got another option, by all means, brother."

Benton faced the thin line of shields and soldiers bracing for the Genisans and scanned the storming clouds. The word *fucked* was written on his face in every language known and unknown to man since before the history of all time. Then something clicked, and those plated-stacked shoulders slumped in resignation. "I need only moments."

It looked like he needed some room, too. "Marines, perimeter. Move!" Smith boomed.

Bulb helped Garcia set up on the two o'clock position and grabbed ten o'clock for himself. Rifles aimed downrange, but they didn't have enough to do more than piss into the wind. A quick scan of the skies showed more driving snow coming in and the shields outside of the crater were starting to frost over. Fortunately, there was still no sign of a high-flying Black Robe.

The reddish infantry stampeding upslope with unnatural endurance killed the buzz quickly.

Smith didn't want to expend the last of their ammo on a bunch of medieval kids who got sold the big lie about adventure and glory, but there wasn't much choice. He popped out the Pig's bipod and set it on the crater's edge. He didn't know how many rounds were left but knew this was goodbye to the M240.

Dux Herms saved the day.

To the cry of "loose," a wall of arrows whipped over Smith's head and crashed into the front chargers. Another three volleys pounded down, collapsing their center. That left the flanks still coming hard but at different rates.

"Baby, we still gots some time!" Smith sang to the Pig as the greens reconfigured to meet the more bite-sized threats. He wouldn't put his lips on an oily machine gun, but it crossed his mind.

The ground lurched, and Smith's skull rang.

When the ringing stopped, everything hurt, but not like he'd been hit. It was his joints. *No, my bones.* Pounding headache and deep limb pain that nothing could make better.

Smith's senses rebooted slowly, concussion number ten for the day, and everyone around him was spitting out snow and dirt. The enemy was in a halt. Lead elements hunkering behind shields, uncertain. Whatever just happened had come from behind.

From within the crater.

Smith looked back, expecting to find a Black Robe seconds away from laser-eying them all to death like Bizarro Superman. Instead, Benton was brushing black gravel off his armor with his free hand while his bluish badass sword pointed into the mouth of a newly formed cave.

All my fucking prayers! Smith muscled up and let the orders fly. "Herms. Start pullin' your dudes into the cave. Bulb, grab Garcia. Give it a sweep, report back a read. Depth, size, exits. And figure out if it's gonna fuckin' collapse on us."

"Oorah," came the winded reply as Bulb picked himself up and re-learned how to walk. It was like that for all the greens, too. People were in shock, but getting it done.

Benton held position at the mouth like something might come out as the first Caranuscans made entry. "Dawg, I got rearguard," Smith shouted as the enemy charge regained momentum downslope. "Get your ass in there and make sure no one gets lost." He didn't have a count on how many greens they had left, but it was enough to require a phased withdrawal. He sent a spread of 7.62 mm across enemy lines, and Dux Herms ordered up another two salvos of arrows.

It helped, maybe bought them a few minutes, but the reds eventually reached the crater's edge, and it went to spears and swords.

As the smarter red columns flanked the crater to come down on it from the rear, Dux Herms emerged from the stream of archers heading into the cave. "We have pulled all we can," he shouted. "The Corsan Carre must not be spent on this dire slope." He pointed his sword at the entrance. Amazingly, Benton was still fucking standing there.

Smith shook his head and said, "I'll hold 'em, you git—"

"Men die so YOU may live. Go!"

Being polite was done. Someone had swiped the card, and the meter was running. "Coming in, Marines!" Smith boomed. His bones protested rising from a kneel like he had a 500-pound barbell across his back. LCpl Bulb met him at the entrance.

"Sergeant, plenty of space. Deep tunnels; all rock. Like, stuff you'd find the Taliban hiding in from our bombers."

"Aight, let's hope them Taliban smart enough to stay out the way," Smith said. A memory scratched at the back of his mind, something about everyone being really lucky when Gunny Brines led them into the caves the first time. Not because they found the Black Robe down there, but because they didn't find something else. He put it aside and tagged Benton, "You good?"

A column of blood-soaked Caranuscans blew past them. The rear-guard. Before Smith could ask how they broke contact, Herms hollered that the enemy was pulling back. Smith had to see for himself and ran back to the perimeter. Sure enough, the reds were conducting an orderly disengagement. It made zero sense and gave that scratching in the back of his head some nails, but Smith accepted the reprieve at face value.

The rearguard's wounded came last, hauled by pairs of Caranuscans. Then it was done. There was nothing to stop the enemy from advancing again, but they held outside of spear-chucking range, maybe respecting the Pig or the legendary swordsman guarding the maw. Maybe they were counting on the Black Robe to bring down the mountain.

"It is time, gentlemen," huffed Herms.

Benton stared off, past the enemy encirclement to the glowing city below, and sighed. "The horrors we hath faced do not compare with what may yet come. Alas, mine eyes tell me the dark designs of Saunders and Examiner Creed come to completion. We can wait no longer. *Flee.*" That last word came out soft and sad like it was more a memory than an order. But that shit made sense, too.

There was still no telling how big an explosion would come from Portcullis, but LCpl Light was right; the rock here was bunker-solid. The sorta shit they buried NORAD in. "Hey Benton, you think they'll come after us?" Smith asked after the brooding knight.

The answer came from a shadow crossing the entrance. Flying high above, far away, was the Black Robe. Not attacking or approaching. Just watching. An evil, spine-tingling sendoff.

"Copy that. Outta the pisser and into the puddle." Smith muttered as he joined the rest in the cluttered and noisy dark.

The Southborn Storm lashed at Turan Rilseri's protective wards with ice, flash, and wind. *Impressive*, he thought as chill air seeped through. The streaks of Quotidian and Stochal ripping apart the skies were neither granted nor compelled by rendercraft or voice. It was a horror born of the three Powers, driven by a raging heart of Base.

Not the combined glow of the Obantum Carre could dare hope to turn such.

He grasped the amulet, the Scry once give to Isllor. It was thought lost to the enemy after his disastrous defeat, but Bela's spies had proved their worth once more. Recovered and smuggled from the might of Durador itself, it was returned. Without it, the tempest would have swallowed him long ago.

Chancing Scianas' ancient ire, Turan asked the air clear itself to his eyes. The Scry became a live coal in his hand as it surged against the infinite Base. He knew little about the cosmic struggle that unfolded in the span of two heartbeats, but through some Power, conscious or not, his request was granted.

This time.

The wash of white and gray faded to crisp mountain slopes littered with metal and corpses.

A dozen green ants—free Caranuscans—scurried through the high rockslide. They were inconsequential deserters who would find neither lord nor cause for comfort awaiting them behind the enemy's lines. Others, cut off from the main host, had surrendered. Their thin ranks shuffled down the slick slopes with screams caught in their throats. For now.

Benton was wise to bar the south road and scale the mountain. The dangers lurking within the rock had tempered Turan's fury and forced High Axi'arch Cremeho's men to pursue. When ineptitude allowed Benton near that cursed rockslide, Turan's patience withered and he struck with the Power in defiance of the Gra'nuul. It worked, herding and pinning the survivors to a fight without awakening one of the world's oldest evils. Victory was within reach.

Then the fool Benton unsealed the caverns himself!

The threat of Gra'nuul returning to the surface was no small worry but assuaged by the hundreds Benton had led below. The creatures would be sated until long after this outpost—so critical to claim and folly to hold—was deserted.

Is it worth an ask in this horror storm so I might hear the feasting of ice upon warmth?

Master Turan's elation turned his thoughts to Bela and her impending victory.

Her . . . magnificence.

Together they had smashed the greatest obstacle of the war and would soon claim the heads of two Origins and the Procult itself.

Together.

The word rang foreign in his mind. Never in his life of solitude had another so tempted reason. Beyond lust, Bela's presence and mind set alight a thrill that he could no longer live without. It was no Power she wielded, for he knew her snared by the same need. They were two halves of a tome that could only tell its tale . . .

Together.

Turan forced his idle musings back to the battlefield and what he had seen of the Corsan Carre. Indeed, as Bela had said, they were men. They employed nothing of the Powers, but their weapons were astounding.

He regarded the two holes in his flowing robes where the mess of his flesh still stained. Such shock and sting he had not felt since boyhood when the world was new. Still, a taste of Thorn Water and a trick he learned from a Caranuscan cripple—who used the Powers to mend wounds in all but himself—healed them.

What most disturbed Turan was that the prophecies spoke of the Corsan Carre—all of them—using the Power. But these fought as simple liners in molten forged plate. Pithy against what Bela expected to find at Oxhold.

The prophesies were wrong elsewhere too. The Corsan Carre were to be unlike the people of Scianas, yet of those he saw, their faces could place them from around this world.

Movement below.

The legion was advancing on the cavern entrance. *Fools.* "Will their commander not heed my warnings?" he asked with a firm touch upon his amulet. At once, a retreat was sounded, and the two-legged began their amble back to the shelter of stone and slate.

The city.

Once dim, it glowed as the high moon on Ajid's Long Night. Not from fire but the webbing of Renderstone lights. They were bright, too bright. A sure oddity that now commanded his attention.

He moved through the biting and howling air.

The streets were calmed. Those cutoff from Benton had fled west and were climbing through the narrow paths and cracks that ran up that obscene mountain. But they unknowingly traveled with the one given to Him and would find no safe hiding place.

Accepted of the Eyes stalked the city, collecting those too feeble to fight and sending them to the camp where they might rise again in a new life with the strength to hold a sword.

The South Wall was the last bastion of defiance where a single, tattered banner flew. It bore Benton's colors, barely clinging to a cracking mast.

The city was taken in presence and spirit.

So, what drove the lights to such brightness? For what purpose? Did the enemy believe the Obantum to be demons of shadow so easily dispelled? What madness could . . .

The streets flared as fire fed with dry wood and heaving bellows. Turan at once understood. The Southborn Storm could not hurt him, but it could blind him to his enemy's designs.

Bela . . .

The city disappeared in a silent rush of light. By the time the roar of the explosion hit, there was no one left to hear it.

CHAPTER 22

THE BEGOTTEN

Frozen.

At last, as endless husks of green and brown whitened and stilled, a place once teaming and writhing was now quiet and soft to his ears and paws.

Hunger.

Pounding ice and the great breath had taken the heat from much of the prey. Their meat called to his teeth, stiff and crunching as he liked, while the rest cowered in burrows and quivered beneath dead furs. Above it all, he ran free. The cold bore old strength into his legs, driving high leaps through the dusted and silent forest.

Far from his domain, this was his dominion.

He left the place of chopped trees for howling fields. Above the endless drifts, the sky was dark, wroth, and smelled of his birth and roam. The great storm had come.

But so too did another scent fill the air, that of burning rock deep and far from the sky. It brought memories of cloaked blackness and treachery.

A cage of stone and metal that would not yield to his bite. Hunger gnawed at his insides until it ate through all hope of running free through grass and snow. Broken, he laid down and waited for the great storm to take him.

Then the others came. They filled the dark with new, but old scents. Those of predators. They broke his cage and rid the land of the burning rock stench.

After was a time of freedom and joy, the wilds reveling in his frolic. As the days cooled, the places of man were once more welcoming and without fear.

But the evil returned.

It came slow: a taste upon the breath, a slither through dry leaves. Then it burned the skies and filled the green dip beyond the stone city.

Strength rose to face it, but others left.

The man—his friend—bade him follow and protect the woman who led the others. It was a long stalk through wet rock and dry leaves. Then the great storm came. And with it, the evil.

Thudding turned his ears to the raging skies and the plight within. The man's woman—her scent of trees and berries—struggled against burnt rock. They were as birds, pecking and pecking, flying and pecking high above the drifts. Trees and berries fading with each peck.

He whimpered, wishing he could leap to such heights.

Distant man sounds drew his ears, and he bounded through the snow. Beyond the fields was home to his friends. It smelled not of horse and sweat but soiled stone and char.

And succulence.

He let his tongue ride along long rows of teeth. The man's home was cold, filled with unwelcome warmbloods. They reeked of the burnt rock that bristled his fur. They thought themselves strong, safe from the storm and other men who might come.

But they knew naught of Palefang. Born in the great storm and nursed by its cold heart, here he was what predators called predator.

Micky's body went from fetal tensing to full-on, involuntary shivering. Everything was numb and just . . . jiggling.

It would be a lot cuter if that whole hypothermia thing wasn't kicking in.

"Jesus, Pat," she said, voice weaker than expected. "If I'm cold, your chicken legs must be c-coccyx deep in an epidural right now." Silence except for the wind whipping over the wall behind them and the creaking of frozen armor on the guards. "Oh, come on! G-goddamned medical joke like that deserves at least a twitch. Fucking m-move, girl, or it'll fall off!"

Snow was starting to stick on Pat's face, meaning her body temperature was plummeting. Micky wished she could squirm over there, but she was still seeing teams of dancing unicorns from the last time. Real nice shiner on her face too, she was sure. At least all that was numb now.

"W-what about Rath? He's still out there, you know. W-with guns. Never thought that would make your day, huh? Well, he's not going to deal with you sandbagging, so limber up. G-get that blood into your cheeks."

The skies flashed from Ceal's blue light again, but it was quickly countered by three purple strikes. It meant Ceal was on the defensive. Magical duels were outside of Micky's repertoire, but all battles small and large had a point where the scales tipped. Like in Cintup when the ball got moving and the only thing that would stop it was the loser's face. Or so she imagined.

"Fuck." It came out as a squeak, a verbal white flag. Embarrassing, but between the shaking, impossible number of guards, zero support anywhere in all the world, Micky was about done. "Pat, I'm hurt; I . . . c-can't get us out of this." Her eyes felt wetter than usual, making her wish she had the strength to scream.

Shuffling.

Probably one of the guards coming to shut her up again. Micky closed her eyes, not because she didn't want to see it coming, but the appearance of tears might invite something worse than passing peacefully in her sleep from hypothermia. She just didn't have the heart right now to go through another Mina Bazar.

"Micky," floated a whisper.

Maybe adrenaline, maybe a death throe, but Micky surged back to life. Her arms and legs unfroze, and mind cleared. Sure enough, the good doctor had righted herself against the stacked stone foundation. "Pat!" Micky croaked. "That's what gets your attention? Not impending death, rescue, or even all the sex stuff. 'I'm hurt?' God you one-dimensional cluster fuck."

"I . . . I'm sorry. I could hear you the whole time, couldn't move or speak. You scared me when you got quiet. That did something."

"Sure, got you hot, made you just want to flop over here and cuddle for warmth so we can die into each other's eyes. Wait, don't do that. The guards will hit us."

"They got Captain Rath," Dr. Pat muttered.

The cold started to sink in again, but not like before. Micky flexed her fingers. They moved freely, pulsing with hot blood. Her whole body was limber like stepping out of a steaming shower. Yes, the chill was still there, but she wasn't a couple of hours numb to it. Something more than a she-woman hero surge of adrenaline just happened.

Second chance girl; figure Dr. Pat out. Now!

"Dead?" Micky asked, racking her brain for something fresh that could provoke Pat into more than just a little antifreeze in the veins.

"I don't know. Micky, I'm not cold anymore. I . . . got that rush like with the letter. But it's gone."

Micky had theories, maybe answers, but now wasn't the time for philosophy. Dr. Pat's unconscious ability to manipulate the world was connected to her emotional state. Since she had that on lockdown, her powers only manifested under two conditions: duress and drugs.

The drugs thing probably worked by lowering her inhibitions. But a quart of vodka and a Cherry Coke chaser weren't an option. They needed to figure out what she was suppressing or avoiding.

"Pat, I need you to think about how you just warmed us up. Was it words? An image in your head? Get scientific and isolate what you did differently."

The problem with Pat was that it was all scientific. Her narrow jaw tightened as she put on that logic cap and went into academic mode.

Wrong direction.

At first, Pat's abilities appeared related to sexual frustration. Whenever Micky pushed the limits—teasing, flirting, touching, and straight palm on ass—extraordinary shit seemed to follow. Turned out it was just the pot boiling over because she was an uptight prude. Until Brines came along, anyway. And the world didn't shake when he slept over.

Well, maybe a little.

"I don't remember," Pat said. "No images, just you edging into Severe Hypothermia."

The skies exploded purple, and the storm calmed for a second. Exactly one second. Then the blizzard became a snowblower to the face. "Hon, we do not need a medical workup right now," Micky shouted through numbing cheeks. "Not what you were thinking. What were you *feeling*?"

Through the harrowing, white-out tidal gusts, Pat dared to click her tongue and double down on that rational disposition. "Helpless. Worried about you. Especially since you're not thinking clearly."

Micky could've exploded. If their roles were reversed, Micky would have enough of every prerequisite emotion in the bank to throw the planet into the sun. Instead, she was out in the middle of a blizzard trying to thaw the ice queen while freezing to death. *Is there no task I shall be spared?* Guiding Pat to a state where she could release her lifetime of pent-up frustrations and baggage wasn't going to happen any more than someone could be commanded to laugh. If they didn't get powerful emotions bucking from this chick in the next five minutes, everything everywhere was fucked.

No more carrots; it's stick time.

A howl pierced the courtyard, stopping the patrols of darkened soldiers in their tracks.

Men on the wall cried out as a white shadow moved among them.

"Is that . . . ?" Pat began.

Yes, it was Palefang. Maybe Ceal had summoned him, maybe it was just how this world worked. But if Micky had any magic whatsoever, she would've banished him to the far side of the planet's moon.

Hope was the exact opposite of what they needed right now. Strong emotions: anger, lust . . . loss.

That's it.

Micky snapped her head to Dr. Pat as the guards sounded the alarm. "You want thinking clearly? How about you stop with the band-aids."

Pat was scanning the darkness, head turning toward each scream as Palefang swept through the raging snow pour. She didn't care about introspection right now, just that white blur of hope.

"You hear me? Fuck this stoic shit." Shouts ordered troops to ranks and formations. *Fall back to the yard. Guard the gate. Up on the wall.* Metal banged; blood gurgled in throats. Time was running out.

"You know what happens when we die, Pat?" Micky continued. "Nothing. We build our lives to create a world that we will leave. But that's the point. When we die, it is up to others to carry us forward."

"What are you—"

"His last words to you: I'll see you in the morning. That wasn't a promise from him, it was a promise from both of you. And you're throwing all that away if you won't carry *him* forward."

Like that, she had Pat's attention; her drop-jawed, ball-fisted, red-eyed attention.

Just in time for a violet comet to slam down in the middle of the yard.

"Enough," said the Black Robe. The woman. The no-nonsense sort, like Pat.

The white wolf lunged for the Black Robe's throat. The action was distant to Dr. Pat, a TV show playing in the background.

Stop with the band-aids.

Micky's words burrowed deep and knocked on the pink bedroom. Since childhood, the little girl within had sung sweet songs about healing hurts and keeping people alive at all costs. Not just persons, but populations. As many as possible. *Gotta save them all.*

But death was also a process, a preprogrammed eventuality for all organisms. Individual human beings were designed to die after 80-100 years of optimal operating conditions. At a population level, a lot of death was front-loaded at conception to preserve genetic integrity, and some during childhood and early adulthood to eliminate viable but compromised phenotypes. Those sacrifices ensured an optimal population reached reproductive age. The 80-year lifespan was secondary to all that, a reward for not eating the wrong plant.

Only what carries on, what we carry on, matters.

Palefang's hulking form never reached the Black Robe. He collided with something in midair and was sucked to the ground. A single yelp escaped as he was squished flat like a bug under a microscope.

Micky was quiet for once. Maybe succumbing to the cold again, but more likely resigned to their fate.

Whether the Black Robe snapped her fingers or let hypothermia do its insidious work, Micky would be dead soon. Would Pat wall it off as a population statistic and ignore their friendship? Did she deny people their place in her memory because that's how she dealt with grief?

Or was it the shame of failure? Failure to keep them alive forever.

"Return to your posts," commanded the Black Robe. The remaining guards lowered their weapons and returned to their firepits. "Up."

The air squeezed, and Dr. Pat found herself standing if not consciously supporting her weight.

The Black Robe slid the dark hood of her robe back. In the place of some twisted hag or witch was a girl in her twenties. Not made-up, but beautiful in that natural way. Hazel eyes harbored intelligence. She could've been a college student, a young resident. Quick lips and a pointed nose made her the quiet nurse who spent way too much time on Pinterest or searching for cat toys online. Anything but the fucking monster she was.

"I expected more but am pleased to discover less." Her voice held the maturity of Wisewoman Alena. An old soul.

"Where's Ceal?" Dr. Pat asked.

The Black Robe gazed at the sky and gave a light laugh. "Elsewhere, in the snow battling phantoms as her body fails to this Southborn Storm. It is quite cold."

Her musings were flat and disconnected. Ceal was powerful, but this woman was off the scale. Everyone and everything, maybe even the storm, were ants to her.

And she could flick them all away to be forgotten in an instant.

Saunders, Benton, and Ceal—people who made a difference—were about to be wiped out by history's eraser. Portcullis would fade to just another battle in a footnote war; its lifeblood and people distilled to promote whatever regime had control of the narrative. The Marines, Dr. Pat, and Micky, despite all their struggles, would end as a deep-state file somewhere stamped with an MIA along with a thousand other stories never told.

Still, only what they did might be forgotten, not who they were.

Friends and relatives would share them in their prayers and gossip. Chuckle at the memories of things they found funny. Mom and Dad would forgive Pat for leaving, her brothers would forget all the times *Aunt* Pat wasn't around. Saunders had a family, same deal. His wife would sit his kid down and tell stories about his brave dad and the ultimate sacrifice.

Mike Brines.

But not everyone had that, did they? Mike started as an infatuation—a summer fling in late fall on a distant world. Maybe she felt sorry for him living among so much respect and camaraderie but also completely alone. Maybe it was how he gave it all; gave more than he had and never took any for himself.

And like everyone else, she took and gave nothing.

I'll see yer ass in the morning.

His last words to her, a stupid man thing to say. She told herself that's all she meant to him—some side action while he lived the boyish dream of swords, knights, and dragons. But Micky was right. Mike wasn't telling her.

He was asking.

"Unassuming, but potent," noted the Black Robe like this was part of a laboratory experiment. "All the ill-begotten charms of a conquered world added to mine, and still your thoughts are silent. Were the danger not so great, I might spend my many lifetimes in careful dissection of the Corsan Carre. Those prophesized demons who eat, fight, weep, and bleed as common people, yet are favored by the Base."

Micky stiffened and tried to rise.

"Sleep, useless one," she said, her purplish glow shifting blue for an instant.

"Veris Loar has a message for you!" Micky managed before she was gagged by a yawn and slumped back into the snow.

The Black Robe's hazel eyes cracked a millimeter wider, and the glow turned red as her lips moved in a whisper. "What do you know of the Three?"

Micky bolted upright, awake.

What's the point, Micky? Buying time only worked when there was something to hope for. Maybe Ceal was about to step out of thin air and rescue them, but even Dr. Pat could sense the immense Power at work here. Wizardry couldn't win this any more than guns and the will to use them.

"Would you believe," began Micky in her singsong voice, "that he's the reason we're here? I mean, it was exciting enough to be visited by three of the Obantum Carre but then sent to the famed Scianas. Hello, is that not amazing?"

"Speak quick, or I shall turn your bones to water and watch you drown beneath your soft weight."

The imagery killed any desire to eat ever again.

"Okay, I'll tell you everything. The Three came to our world and took over a whole country. Other nations tried to fight them but got totally outclassed. I mean, we've got no idea about magic back home. It was a wicked fight, too; you would've loved it. The skies on fire, stuff blowing up on the ground, huge armies beating the crap out of each other from as far apart as we are to Portcullis. We tend to wear entire houses as armor instead of suits like your people, but I mean, we never learned to access the Powers. Right? Makes sense."

The Black Robe hung on every word. Somehow, Micky knew this was hot gossip. Kindergarten teacher Micky had also guessed the name of one of those Black Robes. It didn't make sense, but what did?

"So right, Veris Loar. Last report had him in a place called Rawalpindi, Pakistan. Meanwhile, Gallor Creetdel, you know him, right? Third of the

Three: short hair, kinda doesn't shave, but also it doesn't grow in right. He's more academic than the other two. Anyway, he was assigned to a place called Mina Bazar to see a real fight up close."

The Black Robe's brow furrowed. "A *real* fight?" Dr. Pat cut her eyes to Palefang. He looked like roadkill, but little white puffs still came from his snout.

"Oh gosh, there are so many ways to kill each other back home! Before Mina Bazar, most of the skirmishes Creetdel saw were between trailer-trash armies. But when the rich nations got notice, they sent in all the best. Cree. Can I call him Cree? Must've been like a whittler in a woodshop. Right, Pat?"

Pakistani wounded pouring into the infirmary. The fear in the guards' eyes as the thudding outside the bunker got closer . . .

"Ugh, ignore her. So, it was a done deal. Cree let the two sides fight it out until he got bored. Then, with a wave of his hand, shut it all down. Savage! I mean, the BEST soldiers on Earth . . ."

"Marines," Dr. Pat whispered. It was stupid, but something was building within her. An understanding.

"Dammit, I always do that! Marines. They got sent packing. An army of advanced weaponry stretched across an entire country, wiped out in the blink of an eye. Totally emasculated. You know that word, right?"

The Black Robe's eyes blazed. She was loving it.

"It was all hunky-dory except for one small element. What do they call it, Pat? We probably hear it a hundred times a day."

"The Ground Combat Element," she answered with an odd sense of pride.

"The goddamned C-monster," Micky chirped. "They stayed in the fight when it all went to hell, kept driving in because that's what they do."

"What of Loar's message?" demanded the Black Robe.

"There was one Marine in particular," said Micky, ignoring her. "This guy does NOT like to lose. You know? He charged when he shoulda hunkered. Blew up when he shoulda tucked. They cut him, burned him, but couldn't stop him. That's when he met Gallor Creetdel."

"Was this man your world's champion?" the Black Robe asked breathlessly.

"Nope, just a guy trying to redeem himself for all the corpses in his wake." Micky wasn't looking at their purple-glowing executioner anymore.

"And he didn't ask for a dime or ounce of credit when he rammed his knife into Cree. Just looked him in the eyes and said, 'Fuck you.'"

"Impossible," the Black Robe snorted, producing a scintillating crystal sphere in her hand. Back home, it would be a plastic princess toy filled with red LEDs and powered by a tiny, three-volt battery. Here it was hot as a plutonium core and infinitely more deadly.

Micky spoke quickly. "His name was Mike T. Brines, but everyone called him Gunny. He was a loner, a living apology to the horrors of war. And whatever anyone might think they know about the Corsan Carre, he was a good man."

Dr. Pat's throat tightened as the macho asshole she built him up to be disappeared. In its place sat the man's worth. Not a rap sheet of accomplishments or CV of skills, but someone who cared.

Tears.

"You speak of the past," said the Black Robe with a wicked smile. "A painful past," she added, staring at those tears.

Pat let her eyes run. Her heart was pounding, but she held the Black Robe's stare. Above, the dark clouds gathered for another round of blistering snow and ice.

The Black Robe delighted in the contest. "I shall glean the truth from your minds as your bodies writhe."

"I . . ." Pat began. Her chin was quivering, but not from the impending death. It was loss, all loss. The worst loss. Mike's loss. Indifference.

I'll see yer ass in the morning?

"Yes," she whispered, finally hearing him.

As the words left her lips, she flushed with unbelievable relief. She couldn't heal or help Mike but could carry him forward in her heart. A lifetime of guilt released, and the lock on that pink bedroom cracked. The five-year-old version of herself—guarded and protected for all time—stepped out ready to heal hurts and, apparently, take names.

Suddenly the storm, the castle of Oxhold, the snow, the ground, and the purple-glowing bitch were tiny and insignificant.

Time slowed.

Everywhere. Even the damned atomic clocks in Earth's orbit got dropped in cryogenic honey, each second drawn out for what used to be an hour.

Purple tendrils, a careful twining of red and blue light conduit, oozed from the Black Robe to herself, Micky, and Palefang. Those got clipped first.

Next, Pat's eyes became an x-ray microscope with impossible zoom to peer deep into the Black Robe's tissues, searching for weaknesses. Her name was Bela Rastaw, and she was human, complete with red and white cells creeping through her veins. Her mind was electric, prismatic. She was a rock star. A young, hungry force ready to take the world by storm.

She was also in love.

I can't, Pat realized, pulling back. Killing was the easy path. Instead, she became a telescope, laying all the world and cosmos bare.

Portcullis was destroyed; most of her Marines were alive but scattered. The planet spun in an odd, wobbly orbit around a sun that gave her a sense of hope. But what caused that wobble drew her interest more. It was an incredible darkness that she had seen before. A pure evil she had named Primal.

Overwhelming Power.

She recoiled as if the blackness were blinding light. Before retreating to the snowy courtyard of Oxhold, she glimpsed a red tendril wrapped in black, slithering down from Primal to the small sphere in Bela's hand.

Back in her body, Pat realized reality was a canvas. She could touch all of it, change any of it. Bela, the cold, the reddish metal soldiers, Micky, and the Marines were all penciled in. But she also understood the ephemeral nature of this state. It was a lucid dream where reality was hers to command, but she was on the verge of waking up.

She struck fast, summoning a yellow beam from the sun itself. Arcing through the night and dark clouds, it slammed into Bela's scintillating orb pumping it with the heat of a fusing star. The color shifted from red to orange, and finally, the powerful artifact exploded.

Time resumed.

Bela flew back into a pile of snow. She cried out for her guards, but words became muffled screams as a hulking white form landed on her, jaws snapping for her neck.

"Did I miss someth—" Micky began.

The yard became a fury of snow and wind.

Something knocked Pat flat on her ass. Apparently, she was no longer in control of the universe. When the snow stopped blasting into her face—*so fucking cold*—Palefang was gone.

Bela, the Black Robe, rose from a blackened crater, sputtering and screaming nonsense.

"All you did was break her geode?" Micky gasped beside her. "Why the fuck didn't you smoke her?"

Pat's chest tightened. She probably chose wrong, but also knew that killing Bela would kill the little girl within.

Suddenly, a high-pitched ringing replaced every sound ever made. Dr. Pat didn't need to see to know. The flash of blue was nuclear-bright, followed by a roar of wind that threw Micky back into her arms. The light intensified, and the soldiers ran, trying to shield themselves as they burst into flames.

When it was over, a quiet night lingered. The snow was gone, fires extinguished, and piles of ash rested in the places of their captors. And in the center of that crater where Bela had been stood a figure in blue.

"The Corsan Carre," breathed Ceal with a deep bow. Beside her, Palefang howled at the twilight glow on the dark sky's horizon like a rooster welcoming the coming dawn.

EPILOGUE

Corporal Ryan Nickels of Newark, New Jersey, studied the three medieval soldiers at his feet. Two of Sergeant Teague's men, Tuathal and Aodhan, and a Deadlie. Not airmen, Marines, sailors, or "ain't readys," but the same breed—the hard.

They caught a piece of that . . . that fucking snow monster's swipe before Uumhrat buried his ax in it. The hushed circle of his shit-pantsed point men around the corpse were whispering the word *Sclerti*.

Nickels was too tired to come up with a better name right now. "Will they recover?"

"By dawn, they be standing on shaking legs with aid," Uumhrat said, muscling through the gawkers. He picked up the furry white body with one arm and looked it over.

If there were any doubts left about Uumhrat's freakish strength, that settled them. The humanoid beast weighed half a ton easily. "Can we eat it?" Nickels almost regretted asking. Last week, Uumhrat might've been flipping mancakes for a living, but since then, he was a fucking battle tank charging into the mountains with everyone else clinging on. He was the reason they'd gotten clear before the city exploded. He was the reason shit like this Sclerti weren't dropping them by the dozens. Still, food was one of the top priorities right now, even higher than the motherfuckery.

"Nay, a morsel would fog the head. More is a long sleep. A bellyful might . . ." he trailed off.

No question who he was about to reference. The captain hadn't moved a muscle other than to breathe since that episode with Smallfoot. And so far, everyone agreed that little shithead was the culprit. Poison, maybe some ass-eel magic. Nothing anyone here had seen before.

Francisco, up on a frost-bitten rock panning his scope down the mountainside, tapped his wrist. *Clock's running.* Behind them, a couple hundred Deadlies, Watchmen, and Caranuscan armsmen were crouched among the snow, rocks, and shrubs, waiting on a decision. Further rear were the casualties, camp followers, and civvies depending on them.

Nickels bit down on his teeth. "Teague, get some stretchers up here. Half-width piss break, then we move."

"Milord," answered the Watch sergeant with a fist-to-chest bump before humping it downslope.

"Corporal," came the pure tongue of an American who grew up in no-leak diapers eating motherfucking Gerber. Same guy who could not seem to get with the program. Ranks were paygrades, not ball sack boilerplates. If Nickels was going to be a leader, it wasn't coming from a label.

"I told you before, *Stone*; Jersey is fine," Nickels said in his nicest and most patient tone. Losing the city, Fischer, Licht, and not knowing about Smith and the others had messed with Gladstone in weird ways. It made him ultra-formal, like an Asperger's grandmaster or some shit. So bad it made Bulb look like the cool kid on the block.

"Nickels," Gladstone sort of corrected, "we could use the tower shields as sleds and strap the wounded down. It might be easier."

Finally, some adaptive, initialized utility.

"Good thinking, Stone." He snapped his fingers, and some of the up-armored Deadlies got on it. Speaking of which, the piss break was probably a good time to snag Dalmore for a chat. "Yo, Leod." The one-armed badass still had his horse somehow. Literally, *somehow* because the trail was all nail-biting cliff edges and sheets of ice. Even with twenty dudes stomping it down upfront, the snow was up to their knees if they stepped on a soft spot.

The horse spun like it was in one of those fancy dance-offs on ESPN-8 and trotted over. "Highnoon huddle?" Leod asked.

"You read my balls, my dude. Grab the chief, and let's take a knee over in that clearing." It was less a clearing and more a windswept crop of sharp rocks. Places to sit without getting their asses wet.

Decisions.

Until now, the ragtag, mixed-unit company had stayed tight through a mutual need to survive. Portcullis was gone, winter was a bitch, and these mountains were savage five feet from the trailhead. The survivors were following Marine authority—which Francisco had flippantly passed down to *Corporal* Nickels—because no one had the sack to look a Corsan Carre in the eye and call bullshit. But they were coming to an impasse: the easy or hard path.

Both meant losing people.

Francisco was the last to arrive in the clearing sporting the three-wolf overcoat he'd stitched together from nasty, wet hides. Likewise, Dalmore was keeping warm with the black fur cape of some bear-thing they speared a few days ago. Beneath was his grey plate mail in need of bodywork. Leod's standard-issue Watchman outfit had an actual insulation layer under the chainmail and whitish tabard. The bloodstains made the orange eye hardly noticeable now. Uumhrat had a few threads of shit-stained apron over that prismatic, cold-conducting armor, which was apparently sufficient. Nickels was the only one man enough to still be in desert combat beige but had a thermal wrap underneath to stay warm.

Standard-issue boots crunched in the snow beside him from the guy who wouldn't take a seat.

Okay, Gladstone is still technically in uniform, but fuck that section-eight shit.

"Right, we're all here," Nickels began, unsure how he wanted this to go. Most officers and NCOs would at least try some small talk. But it never translated well, except with Leod. Cutting to the chase made sense, so he tagged Francisco. "Bro, report."

"Main force is still a half-day behind. But a splinter group is scaling that cliff we had to bypass. That'll put them in front of us." Asses shifted as those dry rocks suddenly became a lot less comfortable.

Dalmore nodded. "Mine scouts tell the same."

"Methinks they hath seen naught of us, else the Obantum we would face," said Uumhrat.

"Splinter group is small, aye?" asked Leod.

"It is, but they might be spotters for a Black Robe," said Francisco.

"Their mages probably already know where we are," flat-toned Gladstone. At least he didn't start rank-dropping.

"Yeah, maybe," Nickels said.

"What stays their fury?" asked Dalmore.

Nickels shrugged. "We can't pretend to understand the Black Robes." *I don't have to plan for every contingency because I plan for outcomes.* The captain's words from what seemed like ages ago. "Plenty of times back home, we knew where the bad guys were, but the plan held us back. Maybe these high king klan wizards are trying to hem us in. Maybe they think we'll lead them to more of our people. Or . . ." He patted the sword hanging off his ruck. Whatever Smallfoot did to the captain, this melon splitter had delivered against that Black Robe. Total immunity to magic, like those Vissl Robes that the Sapphire Branch ganked. "They respect the hardware."

"'Tis a dark binding that wraps this sword," cautioned Uumhrat.

"Yeah, 'swhy you don't see me tucking it into my waistband. Anyway, whatever the case, we gotta assume we're blown."

Silence. It was weird because usually, this was when the captain or Gunny would keep the conversation moving.

"Options?" he asked.

Everyone spoke at once.

Dalmore and Leod wanted to charge in and own their shit. Wipe 'em out before they could call in support. Francisco needed two archers to watch his six while he popped some heads and set an ambush for any Black Robes. Uumhrat wanted to double back and climb until they reached this fucking brewery on Almon's Peak. Crazy, but not something they could kick out of bed right away—man rules and whatnot. But Stone came up with the embarrassing stuff someone's kids would say at a funeral.

"Let's go underground like Benton and Smith did."

The tunnels.

The Paling Mountains—the chain they were now balls deep into—were sitting on top of a giant anthill. It was all dug by an evil cave-dwelling species that shouldn't still be around, but everyone agreed was. Francisco spotted Bone and them ducking in right before Portcullis blew its flashbulb. No contact since.

No thanks.

"This ain't Afghanistan, bro," Nickels said. "We stride on the surface, and skull fuck anyone who wants it." It's what Brines would've said, or so he hoped. The next part was more Saunders. "That said, we decide how and when they want it. We got elevation right now, but we're spread out, dragging baggage, and mosta you are used to formations and flat ground. Not sure we can handle a stand-up fight."

Uumhrat bristled, but Leod spoke. "To fight as an army takes much learning. I think our company would make a poor army. But. To battle with brothers is in the blood of all."

Gladstone perked up, maybe prodded by some memory of what it was like to be a Marine, and held out his shotgun. "We've still got some advantages."

"He's right," said Nickels, trying to push back the doom and gloom. "They may know our capabilities after that shitfest in the city, but they ain't experienced with them. Hack this shotty down, and it'll be a standard-issue sawed-off. Every shit-eating motherfucker in this crazy world will be linin' up to brush his teeth with it."

Leod smiled. "Mayhaps they would unbutton their trousers with mine dagger."

"Scratch their backs with Sorrow of Dusk," rumbled Uumhrat with that eight volunteer tours in Vietnam look in his eyes.

"You guys get it. Close-in, hard-hitting."

Francisco tapped Fischer's M40 and said, "Marines were meant to outlive their weapons." He carried the rifle everywhere like it was the only friend he had left.

Dalmore roared with laughter. "'Tis why every boy carries his father's sword to war!"

Francisco stared at him for a moment. It was that dangerous side that Nickels always got near but never wanted to cross because, at the end of the day, Peter Francisco was razor blades.

"But where shall we channel our ferocity?" asked Dalmore, side-stepping the crazy. Francisco was also in full brood mode after Fish. It was a rotgut gut punch for everyone, but the company sniper uncorked that pain randomly and in weird directions. To him, everyone was a suspect.

"This would be easier if we could contact Captain Rath, but it's been radio silence since we left the city," Nickels said. "If Licht or Buontempo were here, maybe we'd figure out if it's a tech problem, but they ain't. Still, fighting our way out and joining the women at Oxhold is an option." Regardless of Captain Rath's status, Oxhold made sense because there was probably someone who could help the captain, not to mention the evacuees. But it meant an influx of lords, ladies, wizards, witches, and red tape that would delay finding Smith and the others. It sucked, but it was math—the easy path. "Or we head back in. Take it to them and find our fucking friends."

Gladstone made some kind of bitch face. Active bitch face.

"Arms and wit are our allies," said Dalmore, throwing heat on the ice. "Strike and flee, raid; let the land provision us. We can seek our brethren, harry the enemy from his true purpose."

"To what end is mayhaps what the men will ask," said Leod.

"Glory," said Dalmore.

"Vengeance," said Uumhrat.

Francisco was impossible to read. He knew it meant shelving the captain, but Smith was also his friend, and there wasn't time for both.

The decision sat like an entire habanero pepper in Nickels' stomach because the safer road was so goddamned tempting. Hell, not too long ago, there would've been no question. Fuck the motarded *above and beyond* crap. But that was before his friends, even Gunny, had died fighting a war for everyone but themselves. To run away now was to piss on their graves.

"We're done leaving people behind," he said. Francisco forced the nod.

Nickels didn't try to shore it up with a fist bump or anything. That nod was reserved for the likes of Gunny and meant worlds. There were a lot of temptations and paths, but only one mission. And it was clear as ever.

To Leod's question, he answered, "We fight to win, same as it's always been."

"They don't have a teatime here in Durador, but only because we're not mainstream socialites yet," said Micky, setting two steaming cups down on the rickety table.

Dr. Pat grabbed hers and brought it under her nose. The liquid was brewed from a red leaf that contained a mild stimulant. Not caffeine, because it lacked the body buzz and jitters no matter how much you drank. Taste hinted at berries, but the smell was what mattered. Citrus and a nip of cocoa pushed back the mildew and black mold permeating their bottom barrel accommodations.

For a moment she felt normal, back at Mom and Dad's talking on the porch before cocktail hour.

"I thought Ceal said they had some posh version of Teatime over in Hilltop Rose," Dr. Pat said, trying to make conversation. Waiting on Ceal—always on Ceal—to finish her underground politicking in the city was worse than their mad dash from Portcullis and Oxhold. Less dangerous, perhaps, but par with their moth—*please be moths*—eaten beds next to the Shitchair™.

"That's just their water break from all-day Happy Hour. God, people with money, am I right?" Micky took a sip of her drink. "Fuck yeah, I steeped this shit into gold."

It *was* better than usual. A hint of something like cinnamon accentuated the heat. Still, it didn't smooth over the lump in Dr. Pat's stomach. Durador, the fortified capital of Galimay, wasn't the safety and salvation she expected. They'd been here for two weeks, and after the hurried entrance with hooded guards and torches through a maze of stone streets, all they'd done was sit here reliving the same day. Ceal left early, Captain Rath and the Watchmen took turns on guard, and she and Micky played house. Then Ceal returned to sulk about Benton, and it was Micky's turn to prowl the nightlife. Dr. Pat, of course, was too valuable to go out.

"It's not forever," said Micky, reading her face. They'd gotten good at knowing what each other was thinking. Micky, behind those chestnut saucers, was scheming about her nightly trawl. Planning which taverns, how much to drink, and whether to even come home. She'd never admit it, but she was having the time of her life.

Meanwhile, the world was going to hell.

Portcullis was destroyed like in that dream, and the Genisans were moving unopposed. Lord Dain, one of Ceal's allies, confirmed that the Sapphire Branch had withdrawn to the major cities, leaving the countryside lawless. Worse, with Captain Rath's radio lost in the fighting at Oxhold, there had been zero contact with Saunders, his men, Benton, or any of the refugees they'd left back at Yordel. Even finding out what happened to Wisewoman Alena would be *something.*

"I just want to be a part of this. You know?'

"Totally, and it'll happen soon," Micky reached across the table and put a warm hand on hers. "You're like an A-list celeb, girl. Most of your time is spent locked away from the public, but when you do come out, you unroll the peacock, and everyone goes wild. All worth it."

"Yeah? So, what about you? Someone figures out who you are and . . ."

Micky pulled back, hands raised. "Hon, I am a walking vagina. That's all you and anyone need to know."

Yes? No? Not every man was hell-bent on his next lay, especially regarding security matters. Hearing Micky and Ceal talk, these people they were befriending weren't shoveling manure for a living. It was high stakes all around. "Someone might ask about someone's new consort," Dr. Pat said, taking another swallow of tea.

Micky went serious. "You're right. Look, I'm careful, but sex isn't the only tool in the kit, far from it. And you've got to understand that I'm a minor player here. That Black Robe, Bela, didn't care about me, nor do the people publicly denouncing the Corsan Carre. They only care about one person. You. What you did at Oxhold sent ripples through the regime here. It's gossip on the streets and terror in the towers. Savior shit, Pat. And that means finding you is political priority number one."

Dr. Pat sighed. She was arguing with a wall. "You're literally an alien, Micky. And Ceal's high up on the most-wanted list, too. In the long run, the house always wins."

Micky cut her eyes to the door, maybe considering the argument's truth for a minute. But then she had an answer for that, too. "And we're in a race against time. Idle is not an option."

Pat took a long, calming sip of her tea. The same tea that seemed to have the opposite effect on Micky. "Yet low and slow is the current plan. I mean, what if I went out there and showed—"

"Let me explain it like this: Pat, you're a nuke."

A nuke? She felt she should be more outraged by the comparison, but curiosity won out. "How so?"

Micky studied her face, maybe trying to gauge her words. "In the beginning, nuclear weapons were the holy grail of men at war. Right? A fantasy. In the '30s, a scientist dreamt them up, prophesized them, if you will. After that, the race was on, and the world tore itself apart trying to get them. Then, boom, endgame weapons were a reality, a paradigm shift in human history. And what did they do when they had them?"

"We used them," said Pat. Micky's knowledge of military history almost made her sound like Saunders.

Micky nodded. "No one would've believed us if we didn't."

The connection to what happened at Oxhold, that unlimited Power, was easy to make. Until that demonstration, the power of the Corsan Carre was all prophecy, a fantasy.

Micky sighed. "But then what happened? The arsenal got shelved because nukes are fucking horrible."

"Yes." An image of a mushroom cloud rising over a helpless city appeared in Dr. Pat's thoughts. She remained oddly disconnected from the burning populace below. Its use came down to numbers, whether the nuke would save more lives than sending in troops. Same with sending Saunders to Mina Bazar. Lives to save lives. She set down her empty cup. "But the world still built thousands. Came close to erasing the gains more than once."

"No doubt, but by then, the purpose of the nuke had changed. It wasn't a goal or a weapon anymore. It became a chess piece."

"A diplomatic tool," Pat reasoned. Eighty years of history backed it up, but that was no guarantee going forward.

"Do you want to see my tits, Pat?"

An absurd question that had no bearing on the discussion. "No."

"Right," Micky said, confirming something in her head. "So that's the deal. You were something both sides needed to find. Then you showed the world what you can do." She glanced at the door again. "Now, and hon, I say this with love . . ."

Micky drummed her nails on the tabletop, usually super annoying, but everything was nice and tolerable right now.

". . . you're a chess piece."

Shouting from outside followed. Dr. Pat started to rise, but Micky grabbed her arm with surprising strength and shook her head. The door crashed in, and gruff men wearing burgundy tabards over red armor surrounded the table, swords drawn.

Dr. Pat watched with detached interest.

"She's safe! She's safe. Stay back!" Micky yelled, getting up. "Touch her and answer to His Reverence."

"Huh?" Dr. Pat asked, confused as to why Micky would have any sway here. Then it occurred that she should be horrified, upset. Something was calming her, keeping the limbic centers of her brain disconnected. She looked at the teacup.

That cinnamon spice.

"We can't have you going off," whispered Micky, sliding around the table. "I made tea for Rath and the others, too. They're fine; I'm sorry."

Part of Dr. Pat was screaming, struggling to reach out and grab the Power she'd embraced at Oxhold. But it was too far away, and the screams were lost in the calm waters of her mind. She could fight, scratch Micky's eyes out for betraying her, but the logical conclusion was to let it play out. Live to fight another day.

Another set of boots stomped across the uneven floorboards. They brought a familiar blue cape and shining armor that should've inspired terror but only registered as cogently unfortunate.

"Welcome to Durador," said Lord Bayliss.

ACKNOWLEDGMENTS

Let me get *you* out of the way first. Thanks, You. *Realms' Anchor* may be near and dear to me, but it's a super niche, self/indie publication that doesn't get found by accident. You hunted it down and held the horns through the third book. That humbles me. In thanks and lieu of a card, I'll write book IV and deliver on all those narrative promises.

Second, phew. Coming off the 700-page monster *Semper Gumby*, I wanted to cut weight and run a leaner story. I aimed for 110,000 words, but then the buffet got the best of book III. Rather, the story evolved into something needing the extra pages. Where I started and where I ended were two separate places and mindsets. The series has a defined ending, but how and if the characters get there is a living process. I am thankful for the opportunity to explore the gold hiding between the narrative puzzle pieces.

Yes, back to acknowledging. My team has remained consistent. Ronald Volpicella has maintained his sense of humor and interest even though we aren't teenagers screaming at each other about how cool it'd be to see a modern infantry squad light up a dark elf phalanx anymore. For the record, most people had that same itch but scratched it with the zombie apocalypse craze. So we're in touch with the world, just differently guided.

Ron was instrumental in narrative feedback. Likewise, Nicholas Pullen—same deal with the screaming in each other's faces—contributed his careful eye to the manuscript. I am again grateful for Sean Murphy's vast understanding of storytelling and effective writing. His feedback improved flow and immersion.

I also thank Julie, Ryan, and Mike at Mayfly Design for the typesetting and wonderful cover designs. Mayfly also prepared the second edition of *Contact* and *Semper Gumby* for publication, giving this trilogy its professional and consistent look.

For every person in the hole, on the wire, and operating forward, there are a dozen in the rear. I want to thank all those who supported and continue to support the writing in tangible and intangible ways. I don't need much to keep the fire lit, and every little smile or spark of interest counts.

Finally, thanks to my wife, kids aged 4-11, Dad, and siblings. They can pick their friends, but my family is stuck with me. There is no finer group.

ABOUT THE AUTHOR

William H. Nugent is a biomedical researcher and author of the *Realms' Anchor* fantasy series. As a research physiologist, he works in the fields of reproductive physiology, combat trauma, sickle cell anemia, blood substitutes, and sepsis. Fictional literary influences are best represented by (but not limited to) Tom Clancy, Stephen Ambrose, J.R.R. Tolkien, Brandon Sanderson, John Scalzi, G.R.R. Martin, R.A. Salvatore, and many more in the genres of military fiction and fantasy.

When Will is not writing, editing, reading, begging for readers, or the science stuff, he enjoys the fruits of rural Virginia with his wife and three children. There is a purported enjoyment of video games as well. And two cats. He has two cats, too. They eat food.

Twitter-is-now-X handle: @Vagus001.

www.ingramcontent.com/pod-product-compliance
Lightning Source LLC
Chambersburg PA
CBHW030349310726
48979CB00001B/240

9781732795082